CARVED GENES

CARVED GENES

KAGAN TUMER

LUMINARE PRESS
WWW.LUMINAREPRESS.COM

Carved Genes
Copyright © 2021 by Kagan Tumer

All rights reserved. This book or any portion thereof may not be reproduced or used in any manner whatsoever without the express written permission of the publisher, except for the use of brief quotations in a book review.

Printed in the United States of America

Copy editing by Catherine Rourke and Julia Houston
Cover art by Colas Gauthier
Author photograph by Kara Cooper Photography
Cover design by Claire Flint Last

Luminare Press
442 Charnelton St.
Eugene, OR 97401
www.luminarepress.com

LCCN: 2021910983
ISBN: 978-1-64388-585-8

PART I
DRIZZLE

CHAPTER 1

CRASH LANDING

"The truth is everyone is going to hurt you. You just have to find the ones worth suffering for."

—BOB MARLEY

Metal grinding on metal screeched inside his cockpit. Mika tapped the control screen, overriding the safeguards on the forces his damaged aircraft was sanctioned to apply. Speech mode still set to mute, the autopilot admonished him for his questionable decision in a range of hues, crackles, and tremors.

Released from its directive not to pulp its human pilot, the transport banked hard then dove harder. The strap bit into his shoulder, pressing him into his chair. The dry, rough leather sanded his cheek as the craft accelerated and vibrated.

A little more of this, and half his bones would break without colliding with anything. Still, it was better than colliding with something. A chorus of wailing alarms joined the autopilot's complaints, warning him that his descent angle and velocity ranged far outside safe landing bounds.

Like he didn't know.

He had too little thrust and even less lift—not surprising since his port wing was nothing but a stump. The only figure trending upward was the stress on the hull, ready to tear his craft apart at twenty thousand feet and a thousand miles an hour. The reptilian portion of his brain insisted he bail. His mammalian brain urged him to go through his options again for any solution he had overlooked. His rational brain counseled him to trust the autopilot's infinitely faster reactions and take in the scenery.

The craft brought the roll under control by diving more. The ground hurtled toward him at bullet speed, and it was bigger. As the autopilot pulled out of the dive, the stern warning from the comms reached its third repetition: "Unidentified aircraft." A two-second pause. "You are in restricted airspace." Another pause. "If you do not alter course, you will be shot down."

Target Lock flashed red on the screen. He pointed forward with his hands flat, thumbs up, and pitched his wrists back as though he were bringing a barrel to his lips. The autopilot considered his input, and the nose pointed up ever so slightly.

His descent slowed, but the shaking intensified. He eased back down, and the craft plunged again. The shaking did not let up.

"This is your last warning. Identify yourself and alter course."

They still hadn't shot him down, but he was pushing his luck. He swiped the panel to enable his commlink. "Not in control of aircraft. All systems critical. I need assistance."

"Identify yourself."

"This is Scout Delta-One-Six." He tapped the screen and lifted the hold that had prevented his autopilot from sending its identification codes.

The silence extended long enough for them to run a mission check that wouldn't bring anything up. He tapped again to transmit an encoded message that would appear like gibberish.

"Alter course. Now."

"Can't do that."

"You have five seconds to alter course, or you will be shot down."

He kept his craft pointed southwest. He had sustained most of the damage in his first crash landing and burned his engines in the ensuing takeoff. "That'd be redundant."

The five seconds passed without shots being fired. "Explain."

He stretched the story to buy another minute, reaching the status update. "Port winglet and engine are gone. Main starboard at sixty percent. Aft at thirty. The compensators fade in and out, so I'm pitching and rolling all over the place. I'm not flying; I'm in a controlled fall."

There was no response.

"And I use the word 'controlled' loosely. My hull is minutes from tearing itself apart. I can't bank or do much of anything other than go straight and down."

"Proceed to these coordinates."

A spot east of Lake Tahoe popped up on his screen. Were they kidding? That was two hundred and fifty miles southeast with the high peaks of the Sierras between them.

"Not a chance. I don't have enough power or lift to get there. Have you heard a thing I said? I have, at most, eighty miles on a tight, downward cone."

"There are no places you can land within eighty miles." She was firm as though by speaking forcefully she could rescind the laws of physics.

Sweat dripped into his eyes and burned as he rolled. "I'm not going to land."

"What?" Her voice rose in genuine surprise.

"I won't have enough lift if I cut thrust, so I can't slow down. I'm going to crash." He felt detached as though it were some other pilot falling out of the sky.

"Your flight profile does not match Delta-One-Six."

The lack of urgency in her voice implied she did not believe him. If they were going by flight profile, he did not blame them. He suspected he had the elegance of a wounded bat and the maneuverability of a flowerpot.

If he hadn't known how dire his situation was, the extended silences would have clued him in. "Delta-One-Six." It wasn't a question but came from a new, more authoritative voice.

"Still here."

"Major Tomlin was in command of Scout Delta-One-Six. You are not Major Tomlin."

He had hoped to avoid this conversation until he was on the ground. "Correct."

"Major Tomlin has been missing in action for two weeks."

Yeah, that.

"How did you obtain the authorization codes for this craft?"

"She gave them to me."

"There was no, er, no one with your profile on her crew."

The official crew profile had contained three Marin soldiers, all women. So, they didn't need to identify him to conclude he shouldn't be in the pilot's seat.

"You either stole this aircraft or are responsible for Major Tomlin's disappearance. Is there a reason I should not shoot you down?"

None came to mind. "Major Tomlin is not missing in action." He took a deep breath and exhaled. "She's dead."

An audible gasp came across the link. Several voices talked at the same time. The confident voice cut through the chatter. "Have you witnessed that firsthand?"

He wished he hadn't, but the moment was etched in his memory. "Yes."

"How did she die?"

Lin's serenity filled his mind, urging him to grasp his predicament and choose every word he uttered with care. And then Lin's face fought the pain to flash a contorted smile and winked. It wasn't a playful wink but one that forced him to face the ugly truth.

"I shot her."

"Are you trying to provoke me into blowing you out of the sky?" The shout became a hiss before the sentence ended.

"Just setting the record straight in case this crash-landing turns into more crash and less landing." His encoded file revealed all that, but he wanted to say it out loud anyway. He owed Lin that much.

"You have ten seconds to explain."

That was a laugh. His screen flashed and displayed new projections. His path had not improved. "I can use some assistance in picking a place to touch down."

"Assistance?" The intonation went up though it wasn't a real question. "You are in restricted airspace with forged identification codes and a stolen craft. You admitted killing a Marin officer." She hesitated as though she contemplated adding to the list of his offenses. The list must have been damning enough. "I have my finger on the missiles targeting you. I'm debating whether to shoot you down or watch you crash."

"So, no assistance?"

After fifteen seconds of silence, the red *Target Lock* disappeared from his screen, and a new voice came on the line.

"I need access to your system health diagnostics and engine data."

His speed had dropped to six hundred miles an hour with the starboard engines about to burn. He tapped the screen and flicked his index finger to send the requested information.

"Not receiving anything. Untap the autopilot and tilt main starboard engine forward by three degrees."

He did so.

"Any change in heading?"

He waited for two seconds, but nothing happened. "No."

"The change in drag differential should give you maneuverability. That's strange." She hesitated, umming and ahhing. She must have decided he needed the truth more than he needed hope, as her words cut through the cacophony of displays. "Based on the little data I'm receiving, you shouldn't even be in the air."

"Good to know."

Five more seconds passed. "Can't link to your autopilot. The damage is with the data feed. Can't land you from here."

Of course not. Why should that have worked when nothing else did?

The thrust had dropped to 24 percent. The descent angle was three shades in the red. The path he was tracing wasn't promising.

"I'm also getting an error from the landing gear. There are no diagnostics, though, so something might be wrong with the sensors," she said.

"That's because there are no sensors. Or landing gear. I lost them at my last crash."

The six-second silence unnerved him more than a shriek would have.

"Let's find you someplace soft then and see if we can get you to land this thing manually." She shot instructions as fast as he processed and implemented them.

He followed her mechanically. His mind let go of every conscious thought and focused on the one verb she had uttered that had resonated.

Land. It was a good verb. He visualized that outcome, but the rate of the dropping altimeter didn't let him believe it.

MIKA TOOK HIS HELMET OFF AND BLINKED. THE ACRID STINK OF FOAM greeted him. The fire-suppression system had squirted the cabin with a preemptive burst but not covered it with a full dose. He blinked again. The nose of the transport was buried under four feet of dirt, and the windshield had a crack running from the bottom left to the top center.

The aircraft listed twenty degrees to his right, and the door to his left was smeared with blood. He wiggled his fingers and rotated his wrists. He moved his shoulders back and down. A sharp pain stabbed at him from his left as the motion stretched his ribcage. Great, an L-bar protruded about three inches from his belly.

He tried to slide forward but was pinned. He traced the bar as far as his reach allowed. The bar came out of his lower back and disappeared somewhere around where his seat met the frame. He stretched back, grabbed the bar behind the seat, and gave it a tug.

A jolt of pain shot through his body like he had touched a live wire. He gritted his teeth and tugged again, but the bar didn't budge. Blood from his gut dripped and pooled by his right foot.

As he contemplated his options, his comms came back to life. "Status?"

It wasn't the one who had helped him land, but the unfriendly one who had elected not to shoot him down. He let the bar go. "Still here."

"Do not move. The extraction team will reach you in fifteen minutes."

"I'm not going anywhere." He chuckled though the irony was lost on his audience.

"What's your condition?"

"Minor injuries. I'll be fine. The frame of the transport is crushed, blocking the door. You're gonna need cutters. Big ones."

"Noted."

Nothing else came through, so he returned to checking for damage. He rotated his ankles and flexed his feet up and down. His left foot moved well, but his right barely twitched, causing a new explosion of pain, as though his right leg were on fire. When the pain subsided, he put his right hand on his upper thigh and squeezed. All good. He then moved down a few inches, squeezed, and released. He kept going, and it was all fine until he hit the knee, but not after.

He had broken his tibia right below the knee, but with no bones misplaced or protruding, he'd be able to run on that in fifteen minutes. All in all, he was in better shape than he had expected.

He leaned back in his chair, closed his eyes, and took a deep breath. He pictured the air mixing with his blood and flowing through him: lungs, belly, pelvis, thighs, calves, and to his toes. He counted to five and pushed the air out through his nose, retracing the steps back up. He repeated the process, calming his mind. He reached fifty-four breaths before gloved knuckles knocked on his windshield.

He tapped the window on his left. The hand wiped the dirt. "Can you hear me?"

He tapped back and gave her a thumbs-up. "Yeah."

"I'm going to cut this window."

The suction grapple stuck to the window, and the saw buzzed. He turned away but didn't need to. She cut the window clean, removing the shatter-proof polycarbonate in one piece. A square face, framed in shoulder-length black hair, stared in.

"Are you hurt?" she asked, eyes on the blood.

You have no idea. The pain in his chest wasn't caused by the puncture wound. "No."

Her eyes lingered on the blood for a few more seconds before moving to the door frame. She ran her hand on the now windowless door.

"This door seems operational."

Before he spoke, she extended her left arm inside the cockpit, palming the windshield. She rotated her arm and tapped the windshield with her knuckles, exposing a faded tattoo on her forearm. A tree trunk came out of the underside of her wrist, branches running up as though trying to capture her elbow. The outside branches were barely visible, the black ink faded with time. A few blues remained on the periphery. Yellow and red branches in the core were still clear.

Someone had paid attention to his encoded message. He raised his left arm, but the pain on his side made him pause. He rested his elbow on the frame of the missing window.

"May I?" she asked at his discomfort.

He nodded. She rotated his arm so his palm faced up. She pulled his jacket sleeve back, exposing his forearm. There was no tattoo to be found.

A tattoo was the result of cells in the dermis reacting to the thousands of needles puncturing the outer skin layer. The immune system sent white cells to repair the skin damage but also unleashed macrophages to absorb the invading ink. But those cells became gorged in ink they couldn't process, creating a permanent blot in the dermis. The Purge virus' repair mechanism gave the immune system a leg up by breaking the ink into smaller and smaller globs, allowing the macrophages to carry it away.

Some inks were easier to break down, so the blacks and blues faded first. Reds and oranges came next, and the yellows and whites were last to go. Each Sentinel got a multicolored tattoo as a marker on their first training day. Watching it fade was a rite of passage, with old-timers sporting the most faded tattoos.

Her eyes drilled into his arm, as though she wanted to convince herself there was a faint outline. There wasn't. She frowned because either he was an impostor or one of the first Sentinels. The blood splattered on the windshield, and the sorry state of his transport must have convinced her. She let go of his arm and greeted him with a single wave.

"Major Judy Wells."

He forced a smile, and recognition dawned on her. Her eyes moved from his arm to his face. "You're Mika Bayley."

"That's me."

His name might have triggered half a dozen different concerns, depending on her security clearance. He was the one who had started the Sentinels with Sierra. The one with a strange connection to General Rose. The one who should be dead. The one who had uncovered the Purge's secrets with Phillips. The one responsible for Chancellor Lester's death.

Then again, since she was on cleanup duty in the Uregs, it was unlikely she was privy to anything incriminating.

"Mr. Sentinel himself." She shook her head. "No one told me it was you."

"Yeah," he mumbled, irritated by the ebullience he couldn't reciprocate.

She fingered the door. "What's the deal with the door?"

"Nothing. It doesn't need cutters." He pulled his jacket back. "But I do."

She leaned in to get a better look. She reached in and put her left hand on the bar. Her right hand found his back, and he suspected she traced the bar to its origin. Wherever it was.

"Not a problem," she declared.

She stepped back and talked to her headset. "Contusions and signs of concussion. No ID. Keep the perimeter but don't advance. He might be contaminated." She listened for a few seconds. "Yes, we need a medical airlift."

His questions must have been plastered on his face.

"We don't want anyone getting too close until we get you out of this mess, and we have to take you into custody. Not carrying an ID, entering and crashing in a restricted airspace, and all." She sounded almost embarrassed. "Will be a lot easier if you disappear from a hospital."

It was good dealing with a Sentinel. Whether they came from Marin, Kern, or New Cal, they all treated the rules of their titular states like an experienced driver treated traffic signs: aware of their presence as potential sources of information but ready to ignore them the moment they became an inconvenience.

She disappeared for thirty seconds then reappeared holding a cutter with a smaller saw wheel. She cut the door in two places, bending and prying it to ensure it was consistent with what he had described after the crash. It took her fifteen seconds to cut the bar free of the chair.

Then the trouble began. Mika's hyperactive repair mechanism had healed the tissue, locking the bar into his flesh. It took her over four minutes to pull the bar out of him, tugging about an inch, stopping for thirty seconds, and tugging again. He stilled his mind and fought the urge to grab her arm.

When he was finally clear of the frame, he collapsed back, putting his head on the solid floor behind him. "Let's not do this again."

"Medical transport is eight minutes out." She hesitated. "What are they going to find?"

"Not much."

"How do we explain all the blood then?"

That was not his problem, so he looked at the transport's ceiling.

"Colonel Rendon is eager to see you," she said.

"I need some time."

"She was adamant—"

"I said I need time."

Judy's expression grew serious. "I have orders to take you to the hospital."

Orders had gotten them into this mess, orders that hailed from hundreds of miles away and forced them into actions that weren't connected to the reality in front of their eyes.

"That's your problem. Me, I'm going to borrow a parachute after we take off."

"What am I supposed to tell the crew here who witnessed your landing?"

He waved at the mess inside the cockpit. It was as good a reminder as any that he hadn't exactly *landed*. "You need a body in much worse shape than I am. The Uregs are full of them. Find one."

"And Colonel Rendon?"

Sierra Rendon was in a bind, trying to fill shoes that were impossible to fill. Her tactics were for a different enemy, her ambitions limited to gaining the approval of a long-lost mentor. But none of that absolved her, not when her pig-headed risk analysis had pushed them to grapple with threats they did not understand.

"Sierra can go fuck herself."

Judy took a step back. Sierra had a loyal following. Some followed her because she was likable and acted like one of the gang. Others followed her because she was their last link to Lori Rose, the general who had redefined Marin's ambition, the general who could have told them they could fly, and they would have jumped off a roof. Was Judy in that camp? He didn't care.

She leaned in again, softening her tone. "You're about to be arrested for murder and board a military medical transport under guard. That transport is landing in Marin."

Mika wiped the foam from the screen with his hand, then rubbed his hand on his pants. "You can land wherever you want. If you need an alibi, I can knock you out or shoot you in the transport." He frowned. "It'll probably be more convenient for you if you resisted a bit."

Her lips tightened and her eyes grew cold. "Is that what happened with Major Tomlin? Was it convenient to shoot her too?"

He grabbed the hand she had rested on the cut door, twisted her thumb, and pulled her in. She stumbled, hitting her forehead on the top of the doorframe. "Do not bring Lin into this."

He let go of her thumb, and she regained her balance. She squinted as though he were an alien. She massaged her thumb. "Just how long have you been gone?"

"Three weeks."

She tilted her head back. "Jeezus."

"What?"

"You don't know, do you? Marin is under martial law. Chancellor Yim is under house arrest. Bodies with Purge-like symptoms are piling up. A convoy came out of the Uregs two days ago. They've dealt with this virus, so they offered to help."

"From the Uregs, you say?"

"That part is sketchy. But General Kuipers is convinced they're not hostile. I'm guessing we're not getting the full story."

"Kuipers?"

"She is the acting chancellor now."

"How about we skip the hospital and go straight to the Shed?"

When Judy didn't reply, he pointed to a two-foot-long, toolbox-like metal case strapped into the cargo hold. "Sierra really needs this."

Judy put her hand on her earpiece but kept her eyes on him. "Transport is almost here."

He shuffled to the cargo hold on shaky legs and unclipped the case.

She tapped the door frame with her index finger. "So, what happened with Tomlin?"

"Did you know her?"

She shook her head. "Not well. But our paths crossed a few times. She was one of the calmest people I've come across. Contagious, you know?"

"I know."

"So, what happened out there?"

His chest tightened again. "I couldn't leave her behind."

He didn't even need to close his eyes to see the moment over and over as though one more look would yield the winning move he had failed to spot the first time, as though one more look through the crosshairs could alter the past.

It wouldn't. There was no way for him to bring back Lin or forgive Sierra. To unmoor his thoughts from the last time he had seen Lin, he nudged them to the time he met her six months ago in a world in which their ignorance allowed them to pretend they lived in a simpler time. If not a safer one, at least one with fewer enemies.

CHAPTER 2

HOSTILE

"We may not have chosen the time, but the time has chosen us."

—JOHN LEWIS

Mika plunged the bowie knife into his left forearm and cut to the elbow. The cold blade moved across his flesh with little resistance, as though splitting a green tomato. He put the knife on the towel and drained his glass. The bourbon lit up his chest, burning down the way it was meant to.

He put down the glass and poured another generous shot. He rested his left arm on the towel but didn't glance at the closing wound.

Drinking alone wasn't a choice but a concession to biology. Unaided, he barely tasted the liquor, much less felt its effects. A tart liquid moved down his throat like burnt, tepid tea. The whiff of oak and smoke hinted at something more but didn't deliver unless he distracted his overgrown repair mechanism for a few seconds. He didn't miss the pointless chatter or the fake intimacy of Macky's bar, but he missed losing himself in the crowd. Even if he had been willing to share his secret, Macky would never have allowed him. Self-immolation tended to chase away customers.

He gripped the knife again, cutting along the new scar running across his forearm. His blood had warmed the blade. It became less an intruder and more an extension of his arm, a deadly weapon in search of a cause, just like he was.

Another shot, another cut. Six cuts away from the bottom of the bottle, his tida chimed to remind him of a promise he mostly intended to keep. He tapped it off, but ten seconds later, the reminder was back, brighter. That his finger-sized glass digital assistant showed the loyalty he lacked jolted him out of his chair. He downed the bottle and headed to the bathroom.

He splashed water on his arm and face. He wiped himself dry, put on his least dirty shirt, and headed out. Five months in, he still viewed the new order with suspicion. He wasn't supposed to gash himself just to enjoy a drink. He wasn't supposed to drive to Marin.

He wasn't supposed to be alive.

He reached Sierra's office late. But showing up was a concession to his history with Sierra, to an understanding they had once shared, an understanding that had descended into a haze of half-promises and full-on disappointments because of his unwillingness to honor simple requests.

He figured Sierra would launch into another one of her tirades about the futility of his quest, how hiding at home or hunting down Kern soldiers didn't advance their cause, and how she needed him here. He knocked on the inside of the open door and walked in.

Sierra sat across a round table to his left with her back to the window, talking to a soldier Mika didn't recognize.

"Mika!" Sierra got up and hugged him, wrapping her arms around his shoulders with a sincerity that shamed him into civility. Sierra had been a competent executive officer to Lori. But now, Special Forces were hers, prodding her to manage up as well as down. Replacing a legend was hard. Replacing a legend while warding off threats to their existence no one even knew existed was impossible.

Sierra pointed to the soldier. "Major Tomlin." Then she pointed to him. "Mika Bayley."

Tomlin gave him half a nod. Sierra sat down and gestured toward the lone empty chair around the table. He stood between Sierra and the large desk to his right. This had been Lori's office. He had been here only once, but that was enough for him to distrust the place. His eyes moved to the leather chair behind the desk, to the screen on the desk, and to the two empty bookshelves connected by a low cabinet. He spun the chair Sierra had pointed to ninety degrees to put the desk behind him and sat down.

"I called you here because we have a serious problem at the border," Sierra said.

It had been weeks since he had been to the Shed, the large metal warehouse that housed Sentinel headquarters and which no one had anything good to say about. He had passed on Sierra's assignments for months because he had no interest in training Sentinels. Border patrol wasn't going to tip the scales either.

He had become an outsider, spying on the petty struggles of those around him, but not letting those struggles touch him or drag him down. It must have been a side effect of coming back from the dead. He had woken up in a world that bore little resemblance to the one he had known. One that held new politics, new biology. Finding purpose in that new world had proven impossible.

At first, Amy had been understanding, helping him put the pieces of his life back together. But she had given up at some point, his one-step-forward-one-back path meandering the wrong way too often for her. As the governor of New Cal and the vice-chancellor of Marin-New Cal, she had bigger fish to fry than mending a damaged soul.

No, that wasn't fair. Amy was still trying. He was the one who had given up on her, on them, on the world.

Sierra clicked on her tida, and the small glass cylinder projected a map between them. Marin-New Cal stretched from Monterey Bay to Mendocino, highlighted in blue. Only five months ago, Marin and the city-states of New Cal had been neighbors who barely tolerated each other. Now, they stood as a single entity with a hyphenated name as though no one expected the union to last. Still, it had become real, at least on maps, if not in citizens' minds.

Kern stood out in shades of red to the south, each shade the domain of a different general. After years of posturing and attempted invasions, Kern's indifference toward them was a distinct improvement in relations. But it wasn't policy. Kern had embarked on an introspection that had the makings of a civil war unfolding in fits and starts: a few days of extreme violence followed by months of inactivity. Mika treated them like he would treat a bloated python, as a momentarily content but dangerous predator he kept his eyes on and gave a wide berth in case it needed another snack.

A dull gray covered the Uregs, the areas stretching between them and Kern and extending to the eastern edges of California. The word "border" didn't make sense. Kern and Marin didn't touch at any point; they didn't come within hundreds of miles of touching. But that wasn't the border they would be discussing.

As if on cue, Sierra moved her finger down, and dark lines appeared to the east and north. "Here are the areas the Sentinels patrolled last month," she said. "All reports are the same: nothing. In fact, in the five months, we've been monitoring these areas, not a single person, vehicle, or transport has been spotted. Then last week we lost four Sentinels."

The Sentinels were Sierra's brainchild, an organization that operated outside the Marin military structure, with members from Marin, New Cal, and even a few from Kern. She had stumbled her way into the process that triggered the Purge's repair mechanism. Mika was an existence proof, not a roadmap, but that had been enough. They now had three dozen hard-to-kill soldiers at various stages of the process.

All to say the Sentinels weren't the sort to die by accident.

"How did it happen?"

"Short on detail. Two disappeared without warning. The next two converged to the area and reported coded transmissions and a convoy. And then nothing."

"Coded transmissions?"

"Working on it, but we have little to go on."

"So, the chancellor is finally ready to investigate?"

Sierra shook her head. "No change in official policy. We are not authorized beyond the Uregs unless provoked."

"I'd say you've just been provoked."

Sierra frowned. "Marin isn't going to sanction an official mission."

Sierra dropped the hyphen for expediency, but he was still glad Amy wasn't here to take offense. He had been chewed out for saying "Marin" enough times to know that for Amy, the name of an entity shaped its essence. As an authority figure caught between two states, Amy fought decades of entrenched preconceptions every day. To her, Marin-New Cal was a federation. Marin was an occupying force.

He brought his attention back to the map. Sierra's words, Tomlin, his presence—all pointed to a simple conclusion. "That's where we come in."

"Major Tomlin can't move across the border. But I need her to."

Tomlin wasn't wearing a Marin uniform. "So, she'll take her jacket off and take a long walk?"

"Sentinel Tomlin can do just that." Sierra missed that he hadn't been serious.

Mika had always operated at the edges of legality. He didn't so much break the law as he poked the empty spaces where conflicting laws met but didn't fit. He had lived mostly alone in that space. But Sierra had now carved it wider, shoving an entire organization into that gap. That Tomlin was here meant she had checked her well-drilled Marin soldier hat at the door.

"Okay, then. How, exactly, do you want us to do this?" he asked.

"I want you to be cautious, systematic. And you do not separate under any circumstance. The Jeep will give you eight hundred miles. Four hundred out, four hundred in."

That put them at the edge of explored space, past the gangs and warlords, past the poisoned streams and mountains. But still, it was nowhere near where they had to be.

"You can cover forty-to-fifty miles a day on foot," she said. "So, head out fifteen days. Observe, return, report. Then repeat from a new spot."

"What exactly are we looking for? Compounds? Military installations? Power plants?"

"Here's all we know." A map centered on Northern California, Nevada, and Oregon floated up.

"That's what, three hundred miles by five hundred? You want us to walk around and see what we can find?" He chuckled. "I get it. We're long-lived now, but I'm guessing you need an answer this century."

Sierra stood and picked up a three-foot cylinder. She removed the top and slid out a bird-shaped drone with rotors where the wings would connect to the body.

"Latest generation flybot. Recharges by solar power in an hour and stays in the air for up to eight hours." She pointed to the flybot's belly. "Acoustic, visual, and infrared sensors. You'll cut a twenty-mile-wide swath over the land." She picked a feathery cover and stretched it over the composite wing. "Stealthy enough to pass for a buzzard unless actively scanned."

She pointed to two spots about eight hundred miles away as the crow flew, but well over nine hundred overland with the mountains between them. "The two settlements we know of are here and here."

At a month per trip, he was signing up for a mission that might last years, but it would get him out of New Cal and Marin. "What do we know about those settlements?"

"Population of a thousand or two, diesel-power plant, mostly agrarian." She flicked a file to the screen, and more details covered the map. "This intel is over six months old."

Which meant it was useless. "Why not send dozens of us? It'll be a lot faster."

"Faster? Sure. Discreet? Not even close. I need stealth, and I need people I trust."

He had given her no reason to trust him in months. His activities questioned everything: trust, existence, life, death, and why the transitions were so hard. "Do you?"

Sierra's glance at Tomlin spoke volumes.

He snorted. "So, we're disposable?"

The left corner of Sierra's lip tightened and drooped. "You're both as indisposable as they come. That's why I need you."

Flattery was not in Sierra's arsenal, so he nodded.

"Get to know each other first and train together. You'll go out when you're ready."

He was trained, body and virus. One look at Tomlin's confident posture and it was clear: so was she. "What are we training for?"

"You're going to be on your own out there for extended periods. You're only going out when I'm convinced you can handle it."

He picked up the flybot. The body's fuselage was rigid with mild flex and lighter than he had expected. He ran his hand over the wing cover. "Teamwork is not my strong suit."

Sierra smiled in her disagreement. "I need to run. Marin business never stops."

Tomlin got up, as did he, but Sierra gestured them down. "Sit, sit. Talk." She pointed to the cabinet that split the bookshelves. "Help yourselves to some wine."

Tomlin sat back down. He put the flybot on the table and followed Sierra out the door. As they turned into the hallway, he reached for her forearm, but she spoke first.

"I need all of you, Mika." She took his silence as a protest. "I need to know you're up for this."

"Does she know?"

Sierra furrowed her brow—more inquiry than displeasure.

"Purge."

Sierra shook her head.

Great, he was dealing with someone who thought their bodies were indestructible because of a miracle drug that didn't exist. "Lester?" he whispered.

Two people had seen and helped him enter ex-Chancellor Lester's compound. No one had seen him leave, at least not through the only door to Lester's office. Lester's death had been announced hours after two bodies had been rushed to a military hospital. No one had identified the bodies after a fifty-foot drop to solid concrete, but simple arithmetic implied a cover-up.

The official line stated that a guard had shielded Chancellor Lester from a bomb and both guard and chancellor had fallen to their deaths. It was true enough to match the scant evidence. But Sierra had cultivated enough conflicting accounts that the truth was nothing more than one more rumor and not even the juiciest one.

She shook her head again. "You were never there," she said and walked away.

Tomlin leaned back on her chair, eyes on him as he strolled back in. She did not speak. In fact, she hadn't said a word since he had walked in.

He sat down and reassessed her: sharp jaw, jet-black hair pulled into a loose ponytail, a collarless brown leather jacket half a size too large framing her broad shoulders, enough pockets to hide weapons for three different battles. She held her shoulders back and neck straight, the posture of a well-trained but bored soldier. It all screamed efficient, unconcerned with appearance, and good at disappearing in plain sight.

If this weren't a front, she had the makings of a solid partner. He waited for her to say something and acknowledge his presence beyond the initial nod she had tossed in his direction. But she didn't. Okay, then. "Any conclusions yet?" he asked.

"You talk a lot but don't say anything."

He took it as a compliment. "So, how long have you known Sierra?"

"I've never met Sierra."

He kept his eyes on her.

"But I've known Colonel Rendon for six years," she added.

"I've met both. And I like Sierra a lot better."

She stood expressionless for a moment. Then she smiled, and he noticed her crow's feet. She was older than he had first guessed. His mind wandered to Phillips, who had looked decades younger than he had been. But Tomlin hadn't had twenty years of repair.

In her, like in Mika, the virus still focused on fixing short-term damage—broken bones and bullet wounds and falls from fifth-floor windows. It wasn't likely to address long-term repair like wrinkles.

"I'm not trying to be difficult, but I'm not good at chit-chat, and I don't know what to talk about without context," she said.

"How do we get context?"

She opened her hands, both palms up.

"How about a personal question each?" he asked.

"I don't do well with sincerity."

"That's kinda the point."

"Okay, then. You start. Why does Colonel Rendon trust you?"

That question launched an investigation, not a conversation. The answer wouldn't tell her much about him, but it would tell her why they stood here. So, she was practical.

"I met her right after the Ross assassination. I was on the witness list, and she was on the investigation team. We didn't see eye-to-eye on much, and her attitude didn't make things any easier."

"We were all a little on edge."

Having two heads of state blown up would do that. He had left that version of Sierra so far behind that it was hard for him to assign motives to her actions.

"I ran into her in the Uregs a week later. A different type of investigation. Considering I was in the wrong place at the wrong time, it was a miracle neither of us got shot. We went on a strange mission a little later. We still didn't agree on most things, but the hostility was toned down. Everything went to shit in a hurry, and that's where I met Sierra. After that, I'd let her watch my back any day."

"I thought the point of this exercise was to tell the truth."

There was nothing he could say to that because the truth was too simple to be believable.

"What you said is you met, took a dislike to each other, almost killed each other, and then decided to trust each other with your lives. Seems you skipped a step or three."

"I didn't see her between those events."

She shut her eyes for fifteen seconds. "Okay, let's say I buy that." She opened her eyes. "Why did you go on a dangerous mission with someone you barely tolerated?"

"It's my turn to ask a question."

"Not till you answer mine to some level of satisfaction. I still have no idea why the colonel trusted you, and all your answers lead to more questions."

"I wasn't crazy about the idea, but saying no wasn't an option."

She chuckled. "I'm guessing she wasn't all warm and fuzzy about you either. So, she was asked. Ordered, more likely."

He waited for her to go through the options. Someone high enough in Marin to give orders to Sierra. Someone connected enough to New Cal to do the same to him.

"Chancellor Lester?"

He shook his head. The cover-up that had erased his involvement in Lester's death had also erased Lester's duplicity. But it had been the only way to keep the secret that the virus that had killed most of the human race had left the survivors at a fork in the road, that some were on a path to immortality, healing from injuries and disease, and that others weren't. Each passing day the deception became heavier, crushing the truth a little more.

"Who, then?"

He pointed to the floor.

Lori Rose was not a name anyone felt ambivalent about. She was the pluck Marin had never possessed before or since. She had beaten Kern twice, saving Marin each time. But she had also unleashed a biological weapon on Marin soil. To defang her enemies? To prevent civil war? Or to save him? It was for the best that only a handful knew about the third possibility. Neither her image nor his existence could have handled the resulting public scrutiny.

"Lori Rose?" She didn't blink. "No offense, but isn't that like the lightning asking the flashlight to lead the way?" She chuckled again. "You might be more interesting than you look."

Lin's respect for Lori moved her up two notches in his rating. Lori had become a polarizing figure since her transport had been shot down over the Pacific. There was a campaign to discredit her and paint her as a power-hungry general. The lack of gratitude had angered him at first. But now, he relished the smears because no one would bother bad-mouthing a dead general. This meant someone believed Lori was still alive. And as long as they uttered her name, even in disdain, it meant they feared her return.

"Did she know it would work or was her teaming you two just expedient?"

"Since every decision was made at the edge of the cliff, I'd say expedient."

"Still, she had to suspect it'd work out," she said.

"Kinda like now."

Tomlin laughed. "This isn't expedient. Rendon predicted this will work because she knows both of us. So why did General Rose predict—"

"Now," he interrupted. "It's my turn."

This time she didn't protest.

"Why did Sierra pick you?"

"I don't mind working with men."

That might have set her apart in the old Marin military but not today. Though integration in Marin was slow, they had mixed a lot in five months and far longer in New Cal and the Uregs.

"Not good enough."

"It's closer than you think. You think things are different now? Most Sentinels still view themselves as a branch of the Marin army. A special branch, to be sure, but still within the structure. Very few of us know what we are."

They were not bound by Marin. They had bigger concerns than petty turf wars. They were the eyes and ears of Marin, New Cal, and Kern against a potential enemy no one had seen. The name was meant to emphasize their charter, to stand watch, not to engage in armed conflict. But even then, secrets were stacked three-deep.

"Besides, the colonel is going against Marin policy by sending us out there. So, she's picking someone whose loyalty to Marin brass is frayed."

Marin-New Cal was a testament to someone's folly. Rigid, matriarchal Marin and open, free-wheeling New Cal were two states with fundamentally different worldviews. They were still years away from comprehending each other, much less living together. But "frayed" was a good word to describe a lot of relationships: Tomlin's to Marin, his to New Cal, his to Amy.

"I take it you don't think much of the chancellor?"

"Our policies are idiotic." She frowned. "As are most of our policymakers."

"Not a fan of the executive council?"

She snorted. "I never thought much of the council. They were always insulated, out of touch with Marin's realities, preferring philosophy to practicality. Somehow, they manage to get worse at every incarnation. We went from isolationist to appeaser to chicken-shit in a hurry."

He didn't disagree with her. Amy would have probably agreed as well. "Because you let New Cal into the council?"

"It's a popular call. But it's the easy way out to blame New Cal for everything. Four of five executives are old Marin. So, arithmetic alone absolves New Cal."

Yes, the federation was a shotgun marriage.

"Still, I'd expected more from New Cal. Governor Chipps was promising. I thought she'd shake up the ostriches on the council, but she turned out to be a politician, just like the rest."

"You know about Amy and me, right?"

It took three seconds for Tomlin to connect "Amy" to "Governor Amy Chipps."

"You're bloody serious?"

She was too amused for it to be an act. So, this meeting was as much a surprise to her as it was to him because had she done even a cursory background search on him, she would have known. He stayed in the background and didn't accompany Amy to official functions, but they lived together. There was no way to erase that footprint or any reason to try.

He nodded.

"Interesting," she said. "She made sense now and then, which is more than I can say for the others. But I liked her better as governor of New Cal. She was fresh. Sounded like she wanted to actually get shit done before she got contaminated by Marin politics."

It was his turn to snort. She didn't backtrack now that she had become aware of their connection. She was straight and not willing to bend to demands of circumstance. He suspected they would get along just fine.

He moved toward the wine cabinet. "How about we break into this and see what the good colonel left for us?"

He opened the cabinet. Lori's ports lay on their sides on the bottom shelf, undisturbed by time or Sierra. They brought too many memories for him to even consider touching one. He picked a bottle of merlot from the middle shelf, uncorked it, and poured two glasses. Tomlin took the glass he handed her, smelled it, and took a small sip.

He hadn't expected Tomlin's filters to come down after two glasses of wine. But they weren't filters; she was naturally closed off. It was hard to not like her, even when she was telling you that you were being an idiot, which she did often.

They weren't friends. They weren't even allies yet. But by the second bottle, they had provided enough insight into what made them tick to erase some mistrust. Whether that artificial bond would turn into a real one, he didn't know. The wine offered no help there. He put his glass down and leaned forward, resting his elbows on the table. "One more question."

"Yeah?"

"Major. Sentinel. Tomlin. Do you happen to have a first name?"

She put her glass down, and her jawline tightened. "I go by Lin."

"Short for Tomlin?"

"My parents must have had a peachy outlook on life and a strange sense of humor, neither of which I share." Her eyes lost focus, most likely caught by a stray memory. She blinked back to the present. "I dropped the name they gave me long ago. Even before the Purge, there were enough ways to get into trouble. I didn't need to invite more."

She waved. "I'm Lin."

"Lin." He waved back with one single swipe of his hand, a formal gesture that belied the two bottles of merlot they had burned. "If this partnership is going to work, we're going to have to be honest with each other."

She straightened up. "Yeah?"

"We don't need training of any kind. So, what is Sierra really after?"

"We did fine for a first date. How about we call it a day before we finish the good colonel's wine."

The bemused smile that accompanied her non-answer told him all he wanted to know. Lin was in on Sierra's plan.

And he wasn't.

CHAPTER 3

SENTINEL

*"If you want change, you have to make it.
If you want progress, you have to drive it."*

—SUSAN RICE

Amy Chipps sat in the passenger seat as Nando Cavana drove through the Uregs. The first rain after the cool, dry winter had brought a super bloom with wildflowers exploding into islands of crimson and purple on the green hills. The poppies rustled in the spring breeze traveling along the road in waves. She rolled her window down and extended her hand out. The warm air moved through her fingers, whisking away beads of sweat and infusing the car with a syrupy citrus scent.

She relished the freedom of escaping New California and Marin even if for a few hours, just to remember how tenacious and stunning nature was. Her life was now confined to brick shells, doling decrees while trapped in meeting after meeting, hour after hour, day after day. Somehow, today Cavana had convinced her assistant Ferg to clear her schedule. So even Ferg wasn't immune to Cavana's charm. Too bad Cavana hadn't shared his tricks with Amy. She would have loved to find out how to free an entire afternoon.

The cylindrical chimneys of a biomass power plant poked through the hillside as they came around the bend. The green-coned roofs followed with the rectangular refuse storage appearing last. Four-foot-diameter connectors linked the biofuel to the burners like scaled-up hoses around a motorcycle engine. It was an old, inefficient model that required tons of biofuel, but trash was one thing the old world had left them in abundance. The landfill of a long-gone small town would feed many monsters like this one for decades.

She rolled her window up as the chlorine and sulfur stench assaulted them. "I wish they'd stop using these crappy power plants."

Cavana kept his eyes on the road. He spoke long after the plant disappeared from their rearview mirror.

"Our compound had a power plant just like that one before we joined New Cal. It cost a year's harvest to install and half a year's harvest to maintain. On a good week, we got twenty-percent efficiency, and I would not have bet a worn-out boot that we would get more than five years out of it before the impurities in the steam gummed up the turbine's blades for good. A self-contained fuel-cell turbine hybrid got above forty-percent efficiency and lasted twenty years, maintenance-free. But it cost six times as much to acquire and install."

She tallied the costs but did not reply.

He drummed the wheel with his thumb. "I did not invest in a shitty power plant because I am bad at math. I simply did not have the capital to buy the hybrid. So, we inhaled the sulfur and bled away half our harvest every year to keep the lights on and the water pumps running. Not to mention, we perpetually postponed ventures that would have given us a leg up in trade."

"I didn't know."

"That is one of the reasons I never warmed up to Governor Fontaine. He was not interested in finding out why the Uregs work the way they do. He assumed he was more intelligent than the rest of us and confirmed it to himself every time he visited these compounds."

Eric Fontaine had always been about creating an enviable and believable picture of the future. To him, reality was an inconvenient collection of facts to steamroll with a heavy dose of hope.

Amy had accepted the deal; he spread hope and people like her fixed the plumbing. With Fontaine five months dead, she was no longer the plumber. "What do we do about it?"

"We can give them eight-to-ten-year loans. Since no one out here expects anything or anyone to last that long, that business model is dead. But we can do it. Imagine the expanded industrial base and the growth and specialization in manufacturing capability. It would be a win-win-win. The compounds win because they have a better quality of life. Marin wins because they sell power plants and buy goodwill. We win because we not only quadruple New Cal but also shave a decade off our recovery plan."

"And we'd have to buy the plants from Marin. What resources do we use?"

He smiled. "That is your job, Governor."

She rolled her window back down. He wasn't wrong, though she couldn't fathom the intricacies of the deals she'd have to cut. Her job required the skills of a banker, counselor, motivational speaker, and magician. She was only qualified for one-and-a-half of those, on a good day. "So where exactly are we going again?"

Cavana kept his right hand on the wheel and ran his left hand through his curly hair, his fingers dissolving into his thick mane. "If I had told you, you would not have come."

That simple sentence sat atop a pyramid of trust. Nando Cavana had been an outsider in New Cal, his motives questioned at every turn. He was acerbic but straight and reliable. When Amy had been thrust into power, bringing Cavana to her inner circle had been a no-brainer, providing guns and advice as needed. They now had a comfort level that one would expect of a long history, though they had only known each other seven months.

"You're not getting me in trouble with Yim, are you?"

Cavana shrugged with half a smile, sharing the jab. Chancellor Yim ran Marin-New Cal as a curator ran a museum, as though every law and every edict were delicate pieces that needed to be conserved and as though the world around them was frozen.

"It is Halsan you should worry about," he said.

In the aftermath of Fontaine's assassination, Halsan, the Mayor of Cal City, had challenged her for the governorship. The militia and other mayors had rallied around her, so he had backed down, for now. As vice governor, Cavana was her conduit to the mayors. His job was to worry about what motivated the mayors and how that threatened order. Hers was to heed the warnings but to not overreact.

"He's an agitator, nothing more. Why would I worry about him?" Amy asked.

"He is still fighting you at every turn. He stirs up trouble in the mayoral council every week, with a smile. And he will still sport that fake smile when he knifes you in the back."

"Halsan doesn't sway the council. In Santa Cruz and Mountain View, they barely tolerate him. Even if Halsan's policies occasionally align with San Jose's, you're there to cast the tie-breaking vote. He has no path to policy and no path to even block my initiatives." She waved her hand into the wind. "He's an irritation, but a rival? Not so much."

Cavana chuckled. "You should have seen him last week, going after Sumit when Sumit mentioned every Santa Cruz residence now had running water."

She raised an eyebrow. "What was there to argue about?"

"Nothing, so he went into his labor policies and how he protected his workers. He said, and I quote, 'You may have run your workers to the ground in Mumbai, but in Cal City, we make sure they return home safe after a full day's work.'"

Amy rolled her eyes. Sumit Joy had become Mayor of Santa Cruz when Andrea Wender had perished in the attack at Ross. He was a pragmatic, soft-spoken man, only a few years younger than Cavana. She shared a unique bond with him; they both had to step in and follow well-liked leaders and keep their constituents together. He had kept his end of the bargain. Amy liked and respected Joy, for both his energy and straight talk.

"He really said that?"

Cavana nodded.

"For Pete's sake. Sumit is a third-generation Californian."

"Not to Halsan, he is not."

It was hilarious and sad at the same time. Halsan was an East-Coaster who had moved to California in his twenties. Joy was born and raised in Sunnyvale, having spent his weekends surfing in Santa Cruz throughout his school years. But for Halsan, that wasn't enough. Then again, for people like Halsan, nothing Joy or she did would ever be enough, since they were not the correct race or gender.

"Halsan isn't going to be reelected, much less unseat me."

"I know." Cavana frowned. "And so does he, which is why I worry about what he might do."

"You got two of your best following me around the clock. I feel safer than I ever have."

"You should not—not unless I vet everyone you see."

She smiled, though she did not want to rehash this topic. "You already do, Nando."

Cavana gripped the wheel tighter. "What about Eva Asher?"

Her smile faded. Eva was a mystery to most but not to her. Anyone who had her body mutilated and tested to limits for inhuman experiments had a right to be angry, bitter, and even vengeful. Yet Eva had embraced the outcome while tossing away the process. Her pragmatism bordered on optimism, but then again, if one was nearly immortal, was there any difference?

Even finding the orphanage she had called home destroyed and most of her friends scattered or killed hadn't pushed her to lash out. She had grieved in her way, honoring those she had loved. Along the way, she had become a fixture in her house to the point where Mika set three plates at the dinner table by default.

Amy had first thought it had been because Eva felt a kinship to Mika. They were two of a kind, indestructible biological machines. But as Mika's funk turned into gloom and he disappeared for days at a time, Eva kept coming. It finally dawned on Amy that Eva might have liked, or even needed, her company as well. Eva was now the friend Amy needed as much as Eva needed her. Eva was the one person who wanted to spend time with Amy, not Governor Chipps.

She evened her tone. "What about Eva?"

Cavana tapped the wheel again. "She is Marin Special Forces, and she is in your house."

"Nando." Her voice rose to carry a dash of warning. "Don't worry about her."

"I cannot not worry when a trained Marin assassin shares your supper."

"Assassin?" No lens made the figure curled up on her sofa a threat.

"I have seen her fight. I have seen her throw knives. I have seen her disappear for weeks. There is no special mission that covers what she does or where she goes."

She laughed but had to admit Eva's missions or daily whereabouts were a mystery to her. But by that logic, Mika was also a suspected assassin. That stopped her cold because that was not too far wrong. But at some point, she had to stop looking for shadows behind every tree. She only saw the Eva who stacked her carrots to the side of her plate because orange food bothered her.

"Seriously, why am I here?"

He took a deep breath. "Those leads you asked me to chase off the record?"

She had tasked him with digging into the New Cal factions who had collaborated with Marin and Kern operatives to carry out the Ross assassinations. Other than a few business leaders and minor bureaucrats who had been slow reporting disappearing supplies, he had found nothing. "Please tell me the two of us aren't walking into premises linked to Ross."

He narrowed his eyes in disappointment. "Of course not. But I did notice that another organization is asking the same questions. They are also recruiting in New Cal and Marin."

"Recruiting?"

"Some in the militia switched to odd schedules, and more resigned in the last month than in the four before. They were not the kind to quit, so I looked into it. They all come here."

This was not Marin territory. It was well past even the Rim, the sliver of land that pretended to be Marin but wasn't. "What is this place?"

"Colonel Rendon is here every Friday afternoon. So perhaps you can ask her."

It was Friday. Cavana eased to a stop as they reached the gray-and-white-striped lift barrier gate. A Humvee was parked to the gate's right. To the left, a steel-framed canopy provided shade for two guards. The folding chairs and makeshift table with screens implied they rarely received visitors. The guard with mirrored sunglasses stepped around the gate and approached Cavana who rolled down his window.

"Restricted territory, turn around," she said. With her narrow chin, a small mouth, and strands of hair coming around her tight cap, she could have been eighteen or twenty-eight.

The second guard moved twenty feet behind the gate, assault rifle ready but pointing to the ground.

"We are here to see Colonel Rendon," Cavana said.

"Turn around."

Amy did not recognize the uniform. But the multiple chevrons on the shoulder had the same meaning in every organization. She leaned forward, coming into the guard's view.

"Sergeant, I'm going to assume you've been too distracted to recognize your vice-chancellor."

The sergeant's face dropped as recognition hit her. "I'm sorry, Madam Vice-Chancellor." She hesitated. "We're under orders to not let anyone through."

"Correct. But I need to speak to Colonel Rendon urgently. Please, escort me to her."

The guards exchanged looks before the sergeant relented. "I will call for instructions."

"Sergeant, I don't have time for this. I'm late as it is, and I have to be back in San Rafael in two hours."

She must have concluded that the concrete threat of upsetting the vice-chancellor outweighed the abstract threat of disobeying a generic order. She lifted the gate and stepped into the Humvee.

"Follow me, Madam Vice-Chancellor."

They drove to the flat-roofed warehouse sprawled a quarter mile away. It was about thirty feet tall and two hundred feet long. A dozen windows specked the second floor from the middle of the structure to the far corner. The rest consisted of rusted corrugated metal sheets attempting to cover the crumbling brick.

At a right angle to its right, metal girders framed a rectangular, warehouse-sized cage that looked ready to jail a twenty-foot monster. The nearest long side had a three-foot cinderblock wall outside of the shell, making the structure appear half-dressed. An A-shaped roof covered a third of the structure. Another piece dangled from forty feet, suspended from a boom lift, waiting to be welded, while the twang of metal banging on metal rang out as the crew assembled the next roof piece inside the shell.

A hundred yards straight across the old warehouse and parallel to it, eight poles stuck from trenches delineating the first walls of a third building, creating a U-shaped compound. Whatever Sierra was up to, she was expanding fast.

They parked by a metal door below the first window of the old warehouse and walked into a narrow stairwell with metal railings. Sierra appeared across from them, blocking the opening to a wide corridor. Her lips were curled into a sour frown.

"Excuse me, Vice-Chancellor," she said as they made eye contact and grabbed the sergeant's elbow to whisk her three steps away. After a few whispers, she hissed, "What were you thinking?"

"She is the vice-chancellor," the sergeant said in a calm voice.

"I said no one is allowed in, did I not?"

"I'm here, you know," Amy said.

Sierra turned around and crossed her arms. "I apologize, Vice-Chancellor. I did not mean to be rude. This is not a good time or a good place."

"What exactly is this place?"

Sierra's eyes moved to Cavana, then back to her, but she didn't reply.

"Can we get off this stairwell before one of us says something she'll regret?" Amy said.

"Only you," Sierra said.

"No. I am here as the vice-chancellor's security—"

"Mr. Cavana," Sierra said. "I know who you are, and the well-being of the vice-chancellor when you're providing security concerns me far more than her being alone with me."

Amy intervened as Cavana's eyebrows started to merge. "It'll be fine, Nando." She turned to the sergeant. "Vice Governor Cavana likes his coffee with two shots of sugar."

Complete silence reigned for five seconds. Then the sergeant stepped into the corridor and pointed to the left. "This way, Mr. Cavana." Cavana gave Amy one more glance and followed the sergeant.

"What possessed you to come here?" Sierra had more edge than hostility in her voice.

"So, what is this place?"

"A response to revelations we had five months ago and their ramifications. I wasn't expecting visitors or complications."

Five months put them right at Mika's stunt, followed by Lori's stunt.

"Are you, by any chance, referring to the revelation that the virus that killed nine billion people made some of the survivors nearly immortal?" She didn't give Sierra a chance to so much as blink. "Or the ramifications of Mika's walking and talking after being exposed to the nastiest bioweapon ever conceived? Right after breaking his neck in two places flying out of a fifth-floor window?"

Sierra's face turned to stone, eyes darting up and down for eavesdroppers, but they were alone. She stepped into the corridor and gestured for Amy to follow.

The wide corridor ran the length of the building and stank of fresh paint. Uneven, glossy spots on the walls amplified by the harsh artificial light tried to hide decades of neglect but did not succeed. Amy caught up to Sierra.

"Glad we sorted that out. Perhaps we can now move on to complications. Is my presence here, as the vice-chancellor of Marin-New Cal, one of them? Particularly since you've not reported any of these findings or the existence of this facility up the chain of command? Or did you have others in mind?"

Sierra climbed up a set of stairs and darted into an office. It was spartan, with a desk at the center and two chairs covered in jackets as the guards had worn. They gave off a chemical cedar smell. A rectangular hard plastic tray with a glass pitcher of water and two glasses sat at the edge of the side table between the chairs. Two open boxes to her left contained more uniforms, blocking half the window.

Amy put her coat on the desk to avoid it from touching the uniforms. She couldn't think of a joke or a shared memory to defuse the tension. "Since you're uncomfortable that I'm here, why don't I go first? That way, you don't have to divulge anything you don't think I know."

Sierra closed the door and sank into the chair behind her desk. "Please."

Amy picked up the five jackets on the chair closest to her, dumped them on the next chair, and sat down. "The Purge did more than kill billions." Sierra didn't raise an eyebrow. "In some survivors, once triggered by disease and injury, it learned to repair the host. They are nearly immortal but mostly sterile." She locked her eyes on Sierra. "Some survivors just beat the virus. They don't carry the Purge and don't have its healing powers. You scornfully call them Puries, as in 'pure humans.'"

"It's not a term I coined," Sierra said.

"Doesn't matter. A slur is a slur. Anyway, a group of non-Purge carriers infiltrated Marin with Lester as their top agent and attacked the negotiations between New Cal and Marin. They killed the New California governor and the Marin chancellor. In the ensuing chaos, Lester took over Marin and came within inches of destroying both

Kern and Marin. Lori Rose prevented that outcome by foiling the Kern invasion. And Mika nipped it in the bud when he killed Lester."

Sierra winced. "Officially, Mika wasn't there."

"Lori attacked a stronghold of this group in the Uregs, forcing them to fire their last AHtX missile at Marin. On some level, it was brilliant. She neutralized a serious biological weapon, only costing Marin a handful of casualties. The bio-agent also healed Mika by putting his Purge into overdrive. It also infected thousands at background levels. We don't know the full impact of that yet."

Amy had gone over those weeks in her mind a hundred times. Speaking of them calmly made it sound like a well-thought-out plan. In fact, it was a miracle they were all still here.

"I wasn't aware of General Rose's plan with AHtX."

"And if you'd been? Would you have stopped her?"

Sierra looked away because she would have eaten a bag of AHtX if Lori had asked. "How is it all working out for you?"

"What do you mean?"

"Where are these people without the Purge? I'm guessing Lester wasn't alone. How deep was the infiltration? Are they coming back? Are they already here?"

Sierra took a jacket from her desk and tossed it on the pile on the floor. "The Puries had a cell-based structure. Very few of the operatives knew about other Puries' identities because most only interacted with two to three others. For example, Tran, the Special Forces op, was linked to Lester and two others under her command. That's it. She relied on Marin's chain of command for everything else. That structure was repeated in many organizations."

That confirmed Cavana's findings and why all their efforts dead-ended with a handful of suspects. "What's the situation now?"

"Better. We used good old-fashioned spying for a month when I took over Special Forces after Ross. We spotted some suspects but nothing conclusive, particularly since they'd burrowed underground. That's why we performed massive, unannounced blood tests to flush them out."

Amy cringed at the audacity but recalled the drills. Sierra had used the ruse of testing the residual effects of the bio-agent released in Marin five months earlier. "The AHtX tests?"

Sierra nodded. "The tests allowed us to focus on the likely suspects, but that wasn't their main benefit. They forced the Puries to act out in fear or seek instructions, and they gave themselves away. We cleaned up cells in the military and judiciary, as well as in hospitals. If there are any left, they're pretty far down the food chain and keeping silent."

"If they didn't have a chain of command, where did they seek instructions?"

"They didn't link to each other, but they linked to Kern."

"Kern?"

Sierra nodded. "The Puries are entrenched there. They control half their military, including the battalion to our north." She gave a half-snort, half-chuckle. "We excised the cancer in Marin. Unfortunately, it metastasized in Kern."

"How about we use a less denigrating analogy?"

Sierra furrowed her brow as though trying to solve a complex puzzle.

"One-third of Marin-New Cal is Purge-free. You just called them a cancer."

"No." Sierra hesitated. "They don't know. They're not part of the problem."

"That's exactly my point. I don't have to remind you we lost our governor as well. Let's make sure we refer to the organization that attacked us rather than to a section of the population because they carry or do not carry a virus. Once you do that, things get out of hand quickly."

Sierra's jaw pulsated, but she didn't reply.

"How many people know about the Purge in the military?"

Sierra took a deep breath and exhaled slowly. "We're the Phillips tree—those who learned about the Purge from or through Phillips. Eva Asher and I were in the room when Phillips explained the process."

"Chancellor Yim?"

Sierra shook her head.

"General Kuipers?"

Sierra shook her head again. "I wanted to tell her. She's my commanding officer. But those first days, I didn't know how. And every day I didn't, it became harder."

"Kuipers knows something. She's more aggressive, more in charge in the council. Does she know what you're doing here?"

Sierra shook her head. "I'm training Special Forces. She doesn't ask too many questions to maintain plausible deniability."

Amy reached for the pitcher on Sierra's desk and poured herself a glass of water. She drank half the glass and put the glass back down on the tray. She wiped her upper lip with the back of her hand. "Is Mika in on this?"

Sierra's lips distorted one side up, one down. "Part-time. Not as much as I'd like."

That summed him up: part-time data hound, part-time conspirator with Sierra, and part-time partner. "Just how many more branches does this tree have?"

"General Rose and Kevin Jezek, a hound," Sierra said. "Rose told Colonel Ranford, right after your rescue. Beyond that, I don't know, though that's probably it."

Ranford had been the commander of the Kern base where Amy had been held captive for five days. She wasn't eager to relive those memories, but Ranford had been civil. Then again, having eight people in on a secret meant it wasn't a secret at all. And yet it had made it this far.

"Well, Mika isn't the information sharing type. Neither am I."

"He told you."

Was that an accusation? Was Amy not supposed to be part of their inner circle? For a potential ally, Sierra came with a lot of baggage.

"Have you seen Mika cook? It's like a tornado rips through your kitchen. The first two weeks he was home, he burned his hand in three places and cut more fingers than onions. And the wounds were gone before they hit the water. Do you have any idea how disturbing it is to see blood but no cut? Smell charred flesh and see no burn?"

Amy reached for her water glass, took a gulp, and clutched it with both hands. "But I knew before then. I'd been to the hospital every day. Broken necks don't heal, much less in two weeks. Our chat was more confirmation than revelation.

"Anyway, let's get back to what this place is. 'Cause I'm guessing you didn't put all this together for me to stop by and tell you what you already know."

Sierra's voice carried more resignation than agreement. "This is a training facility. An extension of the Special Forces."

"And why are you training New Cal militia?"

Sierra did not reply.

"Come now. You didn't think we'd miss militia resigning and coming here, did you?"

"Yes, we train them too. Our organization spans Marin, New Cal, and even Kern. We guard against Purie threats in Marin but also beyond the Uregs. It's a program called Sentinels."

Amy crossed her legs and leaned back. "What are you not telling me?"

A knock on the door interrupted them.

"Yes," Sierra called.

Eva's head popped in, but she stopped. Her gaze moved from Amy to Sierra, and then back to Amy.

"Eva," Amy said, half-surprised, half-relieved to see a familiar face. Eva had made herself scarce lately, and Amy had assumed it had been because Mika wasn't pleasant company. Just by being here, Eva was now tainted by whatever game Sierra was playing.

"Sorry," Eva muttered and disappeared.

"Vice-Chancellor, was there anything else?"

"Else?" Amy smiled. "We haven't talked about anything yet. How about we start with what's really going on here?"

Sierra launched into logistics, costs, and training schedules, providing enough detail to bore even the most avid bureaucrat. But Sierra wasn't comfortable with deception. She blinked too often; her voice fluctuated too much, betraying her effort to pretend to be boring.

"That's all nice, but does it tell me what's going on here? Not so much."

"Vice-Chancellor, I'm already behind schedule. I really need to go."

"No." It came out more forcefully than she had intended, and Sierra's head shot back a few inches. "I want to know what you're doing because this is not a proper Marin installation."

"You have it wrong. Everything here is by the book."

"Just so we're clear, I'll dig unofficially through Cavana. I'll dig officially through my office, audit every requisition, and scrutinize every assignment. I have a nose for this shit."

"You have no idea how much damage you can do."

"Or you can tell me right now."

"You'll put a lot of people in danger, including Mika."

Mika managed to get in her way even when he wasn't here. Over the last few weeks, he was waking up at a normal hour and going somewhere. He hadn't shared his new project with her, but he had stopped coming home splattered in blood. Early on, she took solace assuming it wasn't his blood, but that no longer comforted her because his wounds might be healing fast enough to disappear before he came home. Also, no matter whose blood was caked on him, his activities were not those of a man of sound mind. He was supposed to be her link to this type of world. Instead, he was becoming her weakness.

She wagged a finger at Sierra, her voice icy. "Don't ever use that line with me."

"As I said, this is a training facility."

Sierra, repeating the trite description, almost pushed Amy over the edge. But she let the words sink in. It dawned on her that Sierra had stepped down a dark, slippery slope, feeling her way around. "Like Mika. Like Eva."

Sierra nodded.

"Are you insane?"

Sierra shook her head, dismissing Amy's concerns.

"Subjecting anyone to what those two have gone through is appalling."

"What happened to Eva was an extreme case. They weren't trying to make her hard to kill. They were trying to extract antibodies from her blood that could heal the Puries. But the Purge didn't cooperate, so they kept pushing and pushing. You don't need to do that."

"Do you even understand the process?"

"If a soldier has been injured a few times, and if they've had a bad illness, they're on the way. We help them along with some poison and some minor injuries."

The definition of "minor" shifted even as they spoke. She had seen the struggle that had broken Mika. And he was one of the strong ones. "And the mind?"

"We've devised a test to make sure they're whole before we release them. If they don't pass, we shuffle them to a desk job in one of the militaries."

Which only worked if they didn't tell the soldiers what they were doing to them. Of course, they didn't. Sierra had said they were all that was left of the Phillips tree. She certainly hadn't forgotten a campful of soldiers.

"You don't even tell them."

"They think they're receiving a new drug."

"Unbelievable." Amy shook her head. "I'm not going to lecture you on ethics. Lying to your soldiers is wrong on so many levels, it doesn't matter how you justify it. All your enemy has to do is tell them the truth, and all that loyalty you think you built will evaporate. Forget ethics. You should tell them out of self-preservation. And tell the world."

"Not the right time. Maybe we had a window, five months ago to lift the lid on this. But we didn't. Now, there's too much pressure."

Those were the most sincere words Sierra had said all afternoon.

"What happens to pressure when you keep the lid on?"

"Nothing good," Sierra said. "But I can't blurt this out. Especially not now."

"What do you mean 'especially now'?" Amy stood, put her fists on Sierra's desk, and leaned forward. "What are you not telling me?"

When Sierra spoke, she didn't sound like a military leader but like a tired shopkeeper, one who dreaded looking at the balance sheet at the end of a long day because she knew she had fallen further in the red.

"We discovered a body in Marin last week. The cause of death is still not confirmed." She swiped her tida and a floating face appeared between them. Blistered lips, open sores, bruises. "Flu-like," Sierra said, though the floating corpse screamed from her blue lips that she'd not died from the flu.

"Flu-like?"

"Lungs full of puss and blood. Kidney and liver failure. Internal bleeding."

Sierra was downplaying the revelation to an absurd degree. Because that was not a flu victim. It was a Purge victim. Amy was transported in time, imagining what they may have thought decades ago when the first Purge victims had appeared. Had they also pretended it was all a bad dream? That they would wake up a few deaths later and get on with their lives?

The human mind didn't process disaster. It grasped pain. It grasped personal tragedy. It did not comprehend pandemic and global-level extinction. The Purge, though, had stopped killing twenty years ago. Why would it be back now?

The image monopolized her attention, preventing her from asking an intelligent question.

"We don't know how she was infected," Sierra said. "We don't know where; there is no way to trace her last few days. She was a loner, so we don't know who she came in contact with. No one reported her missing till the smell alerted the neighbors."

It infuriated Amy that she heard this from Sierra. She had expected resistance to acceptance from Marin hardliners. Amy was from New Cal. And she was young. Those were two strikes against her. She had expected to fight her way through it, but she had been subjected to something far more damaging than hostility: indifference. "Why haven't I heard about this?"

"Kuipers took over the investigation. She's keeping it under wraps, and she's not letting anyone in on what she knows or what she's up to."

As Yim shrank away from power, Lisa Kuipers rushed to fill the void. She flaunted her military credentials at every turn, jostling to replace Yim when her accidental term ended. It would have been entertaining, were it not so transparent.

"Is it contagious?"

"I honestly don't know. But Kuipers isn't acting like it is."

"Okay, let's take that premise for now. How did she get infected?"

"Don't know that either."

"Was there foul play?"

Sierra remained silent because the answer was going to be "I don't know," again.

"I want to be briefed about this every morning, officially, in my Marin office."

"That is not my job."

Amy narrowed her eyes. "It is now."

"In this room, we are not Marin officials," Sierra said in full defiance. "We are civilians."

"Fine. Then I'll request this officially tomorrow morning from Kuipers' office."

Sierra's glare emanated more helplessness than anger. "They'll be short reports."

Amy stood up. "I look forward to them."

She headed to find Cavana. The existence of this facility, coupled with the revelation about the corpse, pointed to dangerous gears clanking their way into position. And Sierra didn't grasp that hiding the truth only ever led to a bigger bang when it finally came out.

Cal City's mayor had his eyes on the short game, jockeying for position in the next election. The situation was no different in Marin. With Yim hoping her way forward, machinations had sprung at every turn. It dawned on Amy that they had lost more than a governor and a chancellor in the Ross attacks. They had lost leaders who had kept them pointed to the future. They no longer had leaders; they had managers. Yim, Kuipers, and even Sierra were all working furiously to keep the trains running on time.

No one bothered checking where the trains were headed.

But now Amy knew.

The trains were picking up speed and heading straight for one another.

CHAPTER 4
BUZZARDS

"Don't play dead with a vulture. That's exactly what they want."

—KEVIN NEALON

They met daily. At the shooting range, on the mat, in the study room. Mika could hit a melon from a mile out with the right rifle. Lin was faster and more precise with a pistol. He grew to appreciate Lin's laconic replies and deadpan humor, a perfect tonic to the noisy hostility all around them. But the walls she had displayed on the first day were real, so he hoped Sierra expected functioning chemistry. If she was after true friendship, they needed a lot more than three weeks—more like three years.

When Lin lost her soothing calm in their last session, he pretended not to notice but followed her. She went straight to Sierra's office and set off again in twenty minutes. He conjured up many reasons why Sierra may have needed to consult with Lin. And he might even have believed some of them had Sierra not informed them they would ship out the next morning.

That Sierra had not asked him for a similar assessment told him all he needed to know. On this team, Sierra deemed him the weak link. He would have barged into Sierra's office and demanded an explanation, but for one thing.

Sierra was right.

Fieldwork was simple, liberating. He focused on what he did, or he didn't come back. Mika let go of Marin, New Cal, and even Amy. Here, his actions didn't need explaining.

They drove northeast and veered due north at Tahoe. The little snow the dry winter had deposited had long been blown from treetops, but it still clung to the dirt and bushes. It covered the hills like an old, decaying beige blanket occasionally poked by boulders and random tree branches. They crossed into Oregon before hiding their truck in a mine near where the Sentinels had disappeared. They proceeded on foot toward the settlements based on Sierra's old data. They hiked from mid-morning to late afternoon and then set up camp. After an hour's rest, they hunted and talked.

A week in and Lin's stories and silences had not bored him. Still, they had achieved nothing. The settlement had been abandoned. About a thousand people could have lived there, but all signs of life were long gone. Farm-like rows of dead ten-foot pine trees adorned the eastern border of the town. Further out, deciduous trees with their branches removed stuck out like scarecrows, packed densely enough to evoke farming but containing nothing edible. Giant wood chippers, empty and rusted, stood guard between the trees and the settlements.

They spent another week spiraling out in a pattern to uncover neighboring activity. They found nothing and their flybot didn't spot anything to suggest the abandoned settlement had trading partners.

Their second excursion was less anticlimactic but only because they had ratcheted down their expectation. The empty jungle gyms and rusted swing-set frames drew a dejected picture at the center of the second settlement. They found no signs of tree farming, and after two months, they had learned little, other than both settlements had been emptied long ago.

As he sat in Sierra's office staring out the window, Lin summarized their fruitless attempts at finding activity around the settlements to Sierra. Their footprint was but a speck on the map floating over Sierra's desk and a reminder that even with a flybot doing the scouting, two people hiking the gap between the Cascades and the Rockies was not a strategy.

"This isn't working." He jumped in when Lin finished the report. Lin had managed to reach a myriad of conclusions based on what they hadn't found, but it didn't get them closer to deciphering what or who moved across their northern border. "We can't go on like this. Even if there's a town to find, it'll take us years."

"I can't send any more teams just yet," Sierra said.

"Then let us do this our way."

"You have leads you haven't told me?"

"That's not the point." He glanced at Lin, who nodded. "We're wasting three-quarters of our time getting in and out. We're not rookies. Let us do what we're good at."

Sierra scowled. "What happens when you poke the bear? 'Cause you're good at that too."

"How about we find the bear and don't poke it?" Lin asked.

Sierra turned to Lin. "You think you can do that?"

Lin stood up and walked to the window. "Mika is right. We know next to nothing. But it can't be a coincidence a body appeared in Marin right after four Sentinels went missing. If those two events are connected, being overcautious may be more dangerous than being reckless."

"What do you suggest?"

He opened his mouth but didn't speak.

"We keep going till we find something," Lin said.

Sierra's eyes moved between them. They had backed each other up, like a team. "Okay," she said. "But if you spot anything, you head straight back. You do not engage. Clear?"

Lin nodded, and he did too.

They topped off their tank at the last Marin outpost and headed north after Lake Tahoe.

"We passed the halfway range of the truck," Lin said when they were well into Oregon. He didn't answer, and she didn't push. He stopped halfway through the Fremont Forest. They would run out of fuel before Tahoe on the way back but hiding the truck there for future retrieval was a manageable problem.

Midday temperatures had risen in the two months since their first excursion. They now hiked in the early morning, rested while the sun was high, and hiked another four hours until sunset. Nine days of this routine brought them more emptiness.

At sundown on the tenth day, the flybot picked up a wreck beyond the next hill. The scale of the V-shaped mangle of metal and composites protruding from the plateau hit them as they cleared the hill. The right side of the wreck was almost two hundred feet long, extending at a twenty-degree angle. The left side was half that but rose at a sharper angle.

Engines encased in conical shells lined the outside edges of the shape, with some dangling at angles that indicated severe damage. Additional engines were half-buried in the hard, dry soil of the high desert. Supporting trusses crisscrossed the structure with bumps the size of bungalows spread over the top of the metal mesh.

"What the fuck is that?"

Lin's lips were pressed together. "A dotri."

"A what?"

"Dotriaconta Turbofan. Like a quadrotor, except it's not a quad and they're not rotors."

"You're going to have to unpack that for me."

She picked up the pace toward the half-buried device. "It's a floating battleship, powered by thirty-two turbofan engines. You park one of these in your enemy's sky, and you've pretty much won. They're pinned, and you've got eyes and guns on every part of their space."

The behemoth grew in size and stature as they approached but still didn't make sense. "Can't you just shoot it down with surface-to-air missiles? How nimble can that thing be?"

"Nimble enough, but that's not the point. It's a floating munitions factory, powered by a pocket nuclear plant. You really want to shoot it down over your city?"

"Good thing this wasn't over a city then."

Her eyes moved to green shrubs poking through the wreckage. "Radiation doesn't appear to be high here, but we shouldn't linger."

"What was it doing here?" he asked.

Lin frowned. "This isn't an exploration vessel. This thing is for occupation or heavy lifting. There is nothing here to occupy or lift."

It took great effort for Mika to peel his eyes from the monstrous turbofans and focus on the ground. He pointed to the tire marks on the far side of the dotri. "These are new."

Lin crouched and put her hands on the dirt. "Now we know which way to go," she said.

Half a walking day later, they spotted a single building in the high plateau with a double-wide carport on its far side. It was pre-Purge construction, 3D-printed panels welded together and capped by a slanted, composite roof, more field station than farmhouse.

A flatbed truck was parked next to the carport with a tarp partially covering digging equipment. Rubble mounds, a mix of plastic and metal that seemed to belong to the dotri, stretched around the building in a line of dots fifteen-to-twenty yards apart to create a checkerboard a hundred yards by fifty.

They pitched their tents on an overlook that towered over the field. With sensors that would alert them if anything larger than a hummingbird moved within fifty yards of their camp, they watched the field station through their scopes.

Lin poured herself a cup of coffee from the pot on the battery pack and sat in her folding chair. "Didn't think I'd see a dotri again. They were majestic, but the power it took to keep those in the air?" She blew air out of her pursed lips. "You could run a small city with it."

"Just thinking about that sucker floating above me gives me the shivers. How do you keep that shit a secret?"

"They were controversial. The Air Force commissioned a handful, not long before…" She shrugged.

Three hours of speculation brought them no closer to why a dotri was in these parts or why anyone would dig decades-old metal to create junk piles. Mika refreshed his coffee and leaned back in his chair. "When did you decide to become a soldier?"

She set her chair next to his and held her coffee in both hands. "I tried very hard not to be one." Her eyes glazed slightly. "My dad was a Marine. Naturally, I wanted nothing to do with Marines or the armed forces. I'd never even touched a gun till I was staying with a friend in San Rafael, hoping to avoid the worst of the Purge when Marin became, well, Marin. Two days into the siege, one of the officers passed out guns to anyone old enough to hold one. The training took minutes, consisting of how to reload and which way to point."

"You were in the battle for Marin?"

"Accidentally. I just happened to be there when the raiders attacked. Anyway, I fired into the distance, imitating those around." She shook her head, "What I was doing was wasting bullets. A few magazines later, this solemn soldier called me out, asking to know what I thought I was doing. 'I'm shooting at the raiders,' I said, trying to sound tough. She put her hand on my gun-holding wrist and lifted it. My knuckles were white from how hard I was squeezing the handle. She nudged my fingertips to loosen my grip, tapped my elbow to straighten it without locking it. 'I don't need you to shoot at them. I need you to kill them,' she said. 'Pick a target and don't lose them till they drop.' She let go of my arm and took a step away and then stopped. 'And breathe,' she called before disappearing into the smoke, no doubt to have the same conversation with another rookie."

She poured herself more coffee, reached over and refilled his cup, put the pot back, and settled in her chair. "It's not like I became a good shot at that moment, but I did get a little better. I had my first kill later that day. I know because I kept my eye on the raider for minutes, hoping he'd get up, then chastising myself for hoping that, then hoping again. But he never got up."

She sipped her coffee. "We were on short shifts, cycling in and out of cots to keep as many alert guns as possible on the perimeter. When it was my turn, I couldn't even shut my eyes I was so wired. I wanted to sleep and wake up with an answer to why I was alive, and he wasn't. And then it dawned on me. This wasn't a nightmare we'd wake up from. This was the new normal. Every day was going to be a battle, and almost everyone out there was better at killing than I was."

She sipped again, then balanced the cup on the soft arm of her chair. It sat ready to topple at the slightest motion. She kept her hand on the handle with her eyes on the steam rising from the cup. She brought the cup to her lips for another sip, then put it back down on her thigh.

"So, when they sought volunteers to start the Marin army, I was one of the first ones to enlist. The old-timer who gave me advice turned out to be a former Marine gunnery sergeant. She trained hundreds of us. She was tough, and some days I hated her for what she put us through. But that toughness in the Marin army? That didn't come from the chancellor or the generals. No, that came straight from Sergeant Tiana Brody."

"I'm sure she's proud of how you turned out."

"I doubt it. This isn't exactly a Marin mission, is it? Brody is still at it, training the next generation. She does less of the day-to-day shit now, but she still has her fingerprints on the entire army." She chuckled. "Everything is so black and white to her, but I guess you need that clarity to keep doing the same thing for decades."

She drained her coffee and grabbed the high-powered binoculars to scan the horizon.

As the last light of day disappeared, two headlights poked over the distant ridge. They grew brighter, flickering and disappearing for seconds at a time when the vehicle went over the rolling hills. The first sign of human life they had spotted in over a thousand miles rolled to a stop behind the bungalow, disappearing into the carport by the flatbed truck. Fifteen minutes later, a man walked out of the building. He wore an outback hat, one brim rolled up. His high cheekbones accentuated his hollow cheeks. He squinted and scanned the field with a hand device, ambled to four mounds, then walked back to the building.

They settled into a watch schedule of three hours on, three off. He took the first watch. Other than mild boredom, he had nothing to report when Lin relieved him. He settled into his sleeping bag, zipping away the frosty high desert night.

Though they were in danger just being there, over the last week he had slept better than he had in months. Politically, they were in limbo. Biologically, they had learned little after the initial revelation about the virus. Personally, he had become a stranger in his skin, having received a new lease on life on terms he might not have accepted had he been asked.

That was three dead ends too many. But here, the only thing that mattered was the mission. He would have never described happiness in such a superficial manner, but perhaps he should have. He closed his eyes and forced his mind to slow down.

He woke to Lin touching his shoulder. "Mika."

His fingers tightened around the gun inside his sleeping bag before he opened his eyes. He was certain he hadn't slept three hours. "What is it?"

"We're fine," Lin reassured him. "But there is activity. Thought you'd want to see."

He blinked three times and let go of his gun. He sat up and stretched his shoulders back, getting his elbows to touch behind his back. He stood and brought his night vision binoculars to his eyes. A dozen workers shuffled around the rubble mounds with wheelbarrows, and more were coming out of a bus parked next to the flatbed.

"They got here ten minutes ago. Twenty of them went into the lab. The rest unpacked excavation equipment from the flatbed and proceeded to dig around those mounds."

"Twenty?" he asked, eyes on the small building.

"Must be an underground installation."

He poured himself a cup of coffee. Their instruments provided no help on the content of the wheelbarrows. They took turns looking through the high-powered binoculars. They each had a pair, but Lin didn't believe in focusing all their eyeballs on the same spot. For the next six hours, thirty workers spread out over the area. They cleared some spots, moved material around, and dug trenches to dig out objects that might have been rebar or tubing.

After the first hour, he stopped obsessing over their activity and focused on how they dragged their feet and jerked their arms in short swings as though moving took conscious effort. Occasionally they crouched but then kept tottering about. Over half of them were hunched over.

Daylight didn't illuminate the mystery. The workers appeared sick but labored for over ten hours in the cold desert night. Their exposed skin glowed red, as though they had spent too long in the sun, but the hue was wrong, grayer than a sunburn. The few who didn't sport bandanas showed bald scalps.

By mid-morning, the man in the hat came out of the building. He stood straight, and though his gait was ordinary, he moved like a dancer compared to the workers. He spoke, and the workers loaded their tools and equipment on the truck and disappeared into the bus, one by one. More workers spilled out of the building and shuffled onto the bus.

Two workers dropped to the ground. Hatman spoke to them. One worker crawled toward the bus, stumbled, and stopped moving. The other stood and hurried with an attempt at running that would have been comical had it not been tragic. He climbed aboard seconds before the doors shut off, and the bus took off.

Hatman walked to the collapsed worker and took blood samples before disappearing inside the building.

Mika put a hand on their flybot, but Lin shook her head. "Don't even think about it."

Before Mika could offer an argument, Hatman reappeared and crouched next to the worker. He checked the worker's pulse, and, after thirty seconds, took a tida out, most likely to record the man's vitals. He put the tida away and dragged the worker by his ankles to a shallow ditch thirty feet from the building.

"Time to go," Lin said after Hatman stepped into the building.

He was itching to send the flybot but remained silent.

"You know they'll have active sensors. Even if he leaves, they'll know if that flybot gets within a hundred feet of that ditch." She took his silence as an argument. "Let's not poke the bear."

The body lay frustratingly out of reach. "Okay. How about we stay a little longer?"

Half her upper lip shot up, radiating surprise. "You're not going to talk me into sending the flybot?

"Not a chance," he said with a straight face.

She shook her head but didn't argue. The buzzards appeared an hour later. They circled first, but as nothing moved, two landed near the ditch. A few minutes later, there were five on the ground, picking at the corpse, flapping away angrily at each other and coming back for more.

"That's bloody disgusting," Lin said.

It was. But it was also useful.

He cataloged the buzzards, focusing on their beaks and markings. Hatman stepped out to chase away the buzzards and spread a blue-white substance over the body in the ditch. He hopped in his Jeep and drove away in a cloud of dust.

Two buzzards flew east. Two stayed high up, circling. One flew over them, headed west. "Time to go," Mika said and shoved the last pieces of equipment into his backpack. He kept his scope on the buzzard that flew past them.

Three miles out, they caught up with it perched on a jutting rock halfway up on a hundred-foot outcrop. They were still too close to Hatman to use a rifle. He attached the suppressor to his pistol, which wasn't suited for buzzard hunting. He aimed for the wing but missed. Instead, he hit the chest. The bird didn't even spread its wings as it fell. It landed hard and splattered.

"I'm not touching that," Lin said over his shoulder, eyes on the mess on the ground.

The buzzard reeked as though it had rolled in a dozen rotten onions. He nearly gagged as he cut the stomach, rinsed it in water to reduce the acidity, and stuffed it into a bag. He triple-sealed it and let it dangle from his backpack as they started on their long hike back.

They were halfway back to the truck when he blurted out, "At what point did you decide I was up for the job?"

Lin slowed down, letting him pull up next to her. "Who says I did?"

"You, to Sierra. You talk to Sierra. The next day we ship out. It's not rocket science."

"Something about you still doesn't add up."

"Can you be more specific?"

She picked up the pace. "It's all about as clear as piss the morning after binge drinking. But I'll let you know when I figure it out."

He let it go, letting the rhythm of their hike clear his mind. It had been a good month. After two false starts, they finally had samples of something. He had to take the little victories as they came. He would have preferred to discover what the underground installation held or what ailed those workers. But Sierra had made it clear they weren't allowed to poke bears.

Good thing she had said nothing about poking buzzards.

CHAPTER 5

DUSK

"Compromise makes a good umbrella, but a poor roof."

—JAMES RUSSELL LOWELL

The imposing mahogany conference table filled half the rectangular council room. Designed to sit a dozen, these days it rarely held half that. Amy sat on the long end facing Lisa Kuipers and Nancy Yim. To her right, the room ended on a window overlooking Declaration Square, separating them from Marin military headquarters. From the third floor, the monuments to Marin's independence only came into view by the window, so she sat close to the door, letting the symbolic boulders hide behind the wall.

It was a cool June morning, and the heaters purred at full blast. Amy still hadn't learned to dress light to account for Marin's high thermostats because Governor Fontaine had always kept the Cal City offices a tick away from a meat locker. With institutional memory and the ancient building dials wreaking havoc when touched, Amy had learned to put on an extra layer in Cal City, even in the summer.

This was typical of Marin: find a problem and overshoot the solution so badly that you created a new problem. Sadly, most Marin-created problems didn't offer a solution as simple as setting the thermostat properly.

She extended her lower lip and blew up toward her nose—not that her breath could help cool anything. She wiped her forehead on the back of her hand, but as the only apparent one sweating in discomfort, she suffered in silence.

A deep, four-inch gouge ran along the side of the tabletop where Amy sat. The dark, shiny polish was interrupted by the rough and splintery core. She ran her finger through the blemish that probably offended the senior Marin officials as much as Amy's presence did.

Chancellor Yim droned on. Amy kept her finger on the gouge and tried to see the world through Yim's eyes. But it was impossible to grasp how Yim got excited about redrawing district boundaries but became withdrawn when confronted with four bizarre deaths in Marin-New Cal.

Four.

The bad news was that the body count had quadrupled while they ignored the problem.

The worse news was that Kuipers had fabricated the timeline, claiming they had discovered the first corpse much later than Sierra had stated.

And the worst news was that the deaths stemmed from Purge-like symptoms. What should have been the most consequential council meeting in years, if not decades, had turned into a catalog of irrelevant details. Yim had allowed Kuipers to scare them for an hour, then bore them for two more by jumping from one irrelevant tangent to another and meandering around points without ever making one.

Kuipers was taking over the council one debate at a time. Yim was either oblivious to the transfer of power or welcomed it as it absolved her from responsibility. Amy felt sorry for the seasoned bureaucrat whose illusion of a safe and peaceful Marin was disintegrating with every word and every new fact.

Amy had never shared Yim's illusion.

Yim believed they had survived a biological attack from militant factions of the Kern army soon after they had pushed back the main Kern offensive. So, she had repaired Marin's fragile psyche in her first year in office based on that false assumption. She had created imaginary demons and shielded her populace from unsavory facts—ironic since her grasp of the facts was tenuous. She had also given everyone on the council what they wanted. The double mistake had created the myth that her council was united and focused on Marin's safety.

But her council now pulled Marin in different directions, ready to be quartered by invisible forces. Ignoring reality worked for a short time, particularly with constituents willing to participate in the deception, but it didn't offer a long-term strategy.

Amy did not bother voicing her concerns because there was no point. When the meeting ended, she walked across Declaration Square to find Sierra. She avoided the circular stacks of monuments and picked up the pace. Symbolic or not, three-to-four-foot boulders were never meant to represent fallen heroes. Some days she saw lifeless rocks. On other days, she saw bodies that had melted like candles and frozen into stone. She doubted the artist had intended either. But whatever the intent had been, the place churned her stomach.

The cool air reset her mood, whisking away the beads of sweat from her face along with the letdown of the meeting. Safely navigating the rocks, she reached the military wing across the square. Sierra was alone in her office. The orderly emptiness struck her, a stark contrast to Sierra's Sentinels office. Three chairs were neatly tucked around the round table to her left. Two wingback chairs faced Sierra's desk where two screens, cups, and a pistol in a holster remained the only signs that someone used this office.

"A word, Colonel," Amy said as she closed the door behind her and sat down. Before Sierra managed a greeting, she added, "Seems your reports missed four new bodies."

Sierra winced and swiped off her screen. "I found out last night."

"And you were going to tell me today, weren't you, Colonel?"

Sierra did not respond.

"See, this is the problem with secrets. Once you accept that it's okay to keep some, there is no way to know what hides behind every conversation."

Sierra activated a privacy sniffer, which superimposed thousands of conversation fragments to their words.

"Kuipers thinks Kern is behind this and that the open border with New Cal is their way in. She is pushing for a quarantine and checkpoints all over Marin."

Amy pushed her hair behind her ear. "Which leads me to believe she knows more than she's letting on."

"Will the council approve the quarantine?" Sierra asked.

"It's only a matter of time before Yim relents. She's scared, and unless someone offers a real solution, she'll grasp at Kuipers' straws. Any chance it can be true?"

Sierra shook her head.

Amy crossed her legs. "So why is Kuipers trying to connect this to Kern?"

"Who is to blame for the rogue Kern force in the Uregs?"

There were half a dozen leaders across three states who shared the blame. But to the current Marin leadership, the answer was always the same. "Lori Rose."

"By shifting her attention to the Purie base with the biological weapons, General Rose gave the Kern contingent in the Uregs time to disappear and regroup. Blaming Kern, even indirectly, puts this on General Rose, which strengthens Kuipers' hold on power."

"I buy that, but Kuipers is more dogmatic, more determined than before. She doesn't just want to blame Kern; she wants to go after the Kern army hiding in the Uregs. That battalion is so quiet we forgot that two thousand Kern soldiers with heavy weapons sit a few hundred miles north. So why does Kuipers want to provoke them?"

Sierra's eyes narrowed, then she shook her head as her eyes relaxed again. "I honestly don't know."

"Okay. Let's forget Lori and the Kern army. Could the virus have mutated?"

"It didn't mutate in the four years it killed nearly everyone. And it didn't mutate in the twenty years since it stopped killing. Why would it suddenly mutate to a new deadly form, afflict a handful of people, and conveniently pick loners?"

"What's our next move?"

Sierra straightened up. "What are you asking, Governor?"

"Must we be this formal?"

Sierra did not reply, implying that they did.

Amy cocked her head. "Can this be related to the Sentinels?"

"Related how?"

"Someone else playing with the virus—like you are, to create indestructible soldiers. Someone failing at it and producing corpses instead of hard-to-kill soldiers."

"Doesn't track. If they'd failed, they'd have poisoned dead soldiers. They wouldn't show symptoms of the Purge."

Amy took a deep breath. "We should have told them, at least the chancellor, about Lester, about the virus, about the conspiracy run by those without the Purge. All of it."

Sierra frowned. "It was not the right time."

Repeating something didn't make it true. "It'll never be the right time." But Sierra's frown attempted to hide as much guilt as a concern. "What do you know, Sierra?"

Sierra didn't reply.

"Whatever you have Mika working on, it is related to this, isn't it?"

Sierra answered in a barely perceptible voice. "We all have agendas."

Soldiers did not. They followed orders. That short sentence spoke volumes. But then, Sierra was now part soldier, part rebel. Still, Sentinel or not, Sierra played a game well above her political skill set.

"Just whose side are you on?"

"Marin's." Sierra took five seconds to add, "And mine."

Amy chuckled, but there was no humor in Sierra's words. Sierra got points for honesty, but not for much else. "Doesn't work that way."

"Lester's network is gone; I saw to that. But if that conspiracy can take root, so can another. Governor, I have one piece of advice. Don't trust anyone. Not your mayors, not Yim, and definitely not Kuipers." She scratched her thumb with her index fingernail. "Not even me."

"That's no way to live."

"It's all I got."

Amy stood. "What exactly is Mika doing?"

Sierra looked away.

"You know where he is, don't you?"

Sierra did not blink. "No. He hasn't called me either."

"Sometimes I think he takes these missions of yours to get away from me."

Then Sierra's words hit her. For him to call, he would have to be back. He had been gone over a month. And he hadn't bothered calling her on his return. That doubled her anger at him, both for not calling and for exposing the strains on their relationship and her frustration.

"Tomlin checked in. That's how I know they're back," Sierra said.

"When?"

"Eleven this morning."

That was six hours ago. So, he'd been back most of the day but had called neither of them. If she wanted to find common ground with Sierra, Mika had provided it.

She didn't find that thought comforting or amusing.

Amy pulled behind the Jeep that was now permanently parked in front of her driveway. JJ leaned on the passenger door but straightened as she stepped out. Unobtrusive security was an oxymoron, but she appreciated JJ's efforts to minimize the disruption his team caused. He was the dot on Cavana's inner circle, a jovial presence who managed to treat her as Amy or Governor with equal tact.

"Evening, Governor."

"Hi, JJ."

"Governor, you have a visitor."

She caught Mika's silhouette in the living room window before JJ elaborated. Mika stared out, holding half a smile and a glass of wine. He was backlit by the kitchen lights, leaning on the counter that separated her living room from the kitchen.

"Thanks. Go home, JJ."

He flashed a crooked smile. "Emma will kill me if I show up before my shift ends."

She forced a laugh. Emma, JJ's partner, was a fierce fighter herself. But she was also the mother hen of the clan. She had adopted Amy, letting her in to become one of Cavana's crew. Whether Cavana's clan was integrating into New Cal or she was integrating into their circle was no longer clear. "Tell her the tomatoes she sent last week were amazing."

"I will after my shift ends."

She nodded and walked to the porch. There had been a time when she had expected to find Mika when she came home. But he was gone so often she had quit expecting anything. Today, after talking to Sierra, she had hoped. And for once, he hadn't disappointed.

He put down his wine on the counter and hugged her as she walked in. He held on longer than usual, holding her tight.

"What are we drinking?"

He grabbed a glass from the counter and gave her a generous pour. "The first bottle in the wine rack."

She inspected the bottle, a big, high-alcohol monster, one of his favorites. "Good thing I moved the wines then."

That didn't elicit a smile. She lowered her backpack to the floor and sat down on one of the two stools, back to the counter, facing her dining table and the large window beyond. Her dolphin-gray cloth sofa was to her left, facing two black armchairs, delineating a sitting room where no one sat anymore.

"Everything okay?"

He extended the glass to her and sat next to her, resting his head on her shoulder. It was an affectionate gesture that highlighted a vulnerability he didn't display often.

"I've been back a few hours. And just being around people, I'm reminded of how unaware everyone is."

"Of what?"

"Of anything that's more than fifty feet and fifty seconds away."

Mika's life revolved around finding and exploiting what lay beyond those fifty feet, spotting the connections that others didn't even know to seek. And he had never been generous with what he found, neither the little nor the big discoveries.

"And whose fault is that?"

He lifted his head just high enough to nod. "I didn't mean the Purge, but sure, that too." He sat up straight. "I had coffee at the harbor. This guy at the table next to me talked on his tida. He said he was late, though he sat there sipping coffee, that he was cold, though he took his sweater off. He talked for four minutes and said nothing worth saying."

She reached for her wine glass and grasped it with both hands. "Sometimes, it's not about the words. Maybe it was important for him to call. Maybe he cared, or maybe he needed to sound like he cared. Just because the words were meaningless doesn't mean the exchange was."

He grabbed his glass. "There is crazy shit out there. We keep thinking we're one step away and with one more treaty, we'll have a sane world. With one more battle, we'll be safe. With one more truth, we'll know what's going on." He drained his glass. "Well, we're not. The more I see, the less I believe we'll ever get there—wherever 'there' is."

She opened the window, and a breeze blew in, rattling the half-raised blinds. "Listen."

His eyes moved to the empty, quiet street, then found her. "I don't hear anything."

"Exactly. Calm is good. Peaceful is good. But we'll know we're there when you hear children playing in the streets. Ferg talks about long summer nights where kids played ball and whooped and yelled from their bikes. I don't recall anything like that, but I can picture it."

"You're missing noise?"

She chuckled. "Not the noise." She tapped her temple. "We're wired for community. And it'll take time to rebuild that, so you can't quit now."

"I just want a sign, any sign that we're moving in the right direction."

She put a hand on his hair and pulled his head back down to her shoulder. "When I look back to the destruction and the daily fight for survival I grew up in, I know we are."

He shook his head. "Not out there, they're not."

"Where were you?"

"North. Way, way north."

"I don't know what you're looking for anymore, or who."

He sat up straight and shook his head. "You think I'm still looking for Lori?"

She hadn't dwelled on it, but it had crossed her mind with his disappearing for weeks on end, withholding any hints about his whereabouts and coming home all depressed. It didn't paint a healthy picture. She'd found no official Marin mission connecting his disappearances to Sierra.

So, it had to be Sentinel work. But she had let it go partly because she didn't want to put them in danger by drawing attention to whatever they were doing and partly because his spark had returned over the last few months. It was intermittent—now here, now gone—but it was better than the morose, convalescing Mika she had to endure before these missions.

She had watched him come to terms with his new body and accept the consequences of his actions. But he hadn't accepted the consequences of Lori's actions. Whatever he was doing up north, it was breathing new life into him.

But in the process, it was making it harder and harder for her to talk to him. It was as though Mika had died on that hospital bed months ago, and a new Mika was growing in his place: a physically healed but mentally broken one. The cynicism was still there, but the child-like curiosity had been replaced with gloomy contempt. And cynical and contemptuous were not a good combination.

To be fair, it wasn't all his doing. She had been slow grasping the implications of his healing. Accepting that the virus had repaired him and would keep doing so was comforting. Sharing a home with an indestructible partner, one whose definition of safety had been loose to begin with, was not.

But he hadn't denied looking for Lori. "Were you?"

"No."

"What then?"

He stood up, grabbed the wine from the counter, and poured himself another glass. He lifted the bottle to her. She nodded, and he topped her up. "Sierra thinks there are settlements somewhere beyond the Uregs, east of the Cascades."

She thought they were chasing ghosts, rogue agents in the wild. Sierra had never mentioned settlements. She ignored the irony of the vice-chancellor's learning Marin state secrets from an ordinary citizen. Then again, Mika wasn't ordinary.

"Why does she think that?"

"You should ask the chancellor. She knows."

"I'm asking you."

"She got a reliable tip."

She took a deep breath and let it out slowly, not giving in to the frustration building within her. "From?"

He put his palms up as though the answer was obvious, which meant Lori Rose, the woman who had saved Marin, defeated Kern, and pulled Mika out of the grave. Even with nine months gone, she was still her Rome. No matter which way she headed, all paths ended with Lori, making Amy curse and thank Lori in equal amounts.

"And what have you found up north?"

"Not much. But the settlements were real. Beyond that, nothing makes sense."

And that was true for a lot of things. Like how, after not seeing each other for nearly a month, they couldn't share a tender moment. It was easier for them to talk about interminable missions and secret settlements than how they felt. She shut her eyes tight and opened them again. That every conversation turned into a battle wore her out.

"Why are you so mad at me?"

Mika's eyes widened, but he didn't reply.

"Is it because I'm still here and she's not?"

"It's not you I'm mad at."

She sat up straight and faced him. "What do you mean?"

"Lori. It's her I'm mad at."

"What?"

"She promised that in the new world order, I'd be able to take you to her house for wine." He squeezed his eyes shut and reopened them. "Do you recall doing that?"

Amy stood still barely breathing. She wanted to stop Mika from going down this dark path, but he so rarely gave a window to his mind that she didn't interrupt.

"She had no right to do this. To put this on me, to give up her life's work."

"What makes you think she wanted to keep all that?"

"She spent over a decade building that career. Abandoned me in New Cal for it. Happy eighteenth—oh, by the way, I'm leaving, bye."

"Did it occur to you she might have felt the same way?"

His eyebrows shot toward each other. "How?"

"That you had no right to go after Lester. That you should have let her deal with it."

"I thought she didn't care. I was mad at her."

She smiled. "Exactly. You were mad at her for not helping you. And now you're mad at her for helping you. Which is it?"

He took a long gulp, draining half his glass, but didn't reply.

She walked around him to reach the wine bottle and refilled his glass. She sat back down on her stool. "Are you back for a while?"

"A few days," he said in an even tone. The window into his mind was closed shut.

What Mika said about the world applied to them as well. She kept hoping they were one conversation, one gesture, away from making it all better. She feared now that they might never get there either. He walked to the window and stared out, with the same posture as when she had walked in. She had thought he was waiting for her, but she was wrong. They lived in the same house, but on different planets.

"I was hoping for more."

"I can't give you what you want."

She sipped her wine. "What is it you think I want?"

"Noisy children in the streets." He gulped the rest of his wine.

She shook her head. "I said that'd be nice. I didn't say we had to start planning today." When he didn't even try to address her concerns, she blurted out, "You're different."

"Different? How?"

"Cold. Like being here with me, right now, doesn't mean anything to you."

"Cold?" He narrowed his eyes, as though she were a puzzle. "Give me an example."

She shook her head because this was not a game she would play. He would delve into a detail and pretend the full picture didn't exist. If she pointed any particular behavior, he would find a dozen reasons why that was how he had always behaved. And he might even have been right. The problem wasn't his response to any one thing. It was his response to everything. How he dismissed anything disconnected from his current quest.

When she didn't answer, he reached for the bottle and refilled his glass. He waited, but she had nothing—no false promises, no illusions left.

As the silence stretched, he stood up and walked to the door. "Macky's?"

Right, because what this conversation needed was a drunk audience. She had no intention to shout her thoughts in a crowded pub or exchange pleasantries with dozens of strangers who insisted on pretending they were friends. "I'd rather stay in." She raised her glass. "The wine is better here."

He didn't smile. "I need some fresh air." He opened the door but stood there as though he had more to say, as though he was choking on words that wouldn't come out.

She did not speak. She didn't trust herself to not sound mean or weak. The middle ground was eroding away fast. His glass rested on the counter, still full. Mika didn't need fresh air. He certainly didn't need a drink at Macky's.

He needed to get away from her, minutes after returning from a month-long mission.

The saddest part was that he didn't see how different that was.

CHAPTER 6

UNSETTLEMENTS

"We grow neither better nor worse as we grow old, but more like ourselves."

—MAY L. BECKER

On the second hiking day, Mika felt free again. The drive had been consumed by reflection and remorse. He had failed to rise to expectations. Sierra, Amy—both wanted something he could not deliver. The first hiking day was reserved for guilt. He had hurt Amy, again. But now, hundreds of miles from anyone and smothered by the smoke, responsibility no longer tugged at his strings.

They hiked north through the haze of the raging forest fires consuming the eastern slope of the Cascades. A month ago, not a speck of cloud had interrupted the oppressive heat of the cobalt sky. Now, even hundreds of miles from the heat and blaze, the high desert was lost in a dense gray fog with the stench of a thousand campfires. The sun poked through as a ruby disk on graphite background while they set up camp in the evening.

They observed the field with sickly workers for ten days. The place had remained deserted the first night. For the next three nights, the bus brought the workers who dug for ten hours, as though excavating a giant metal dinosaur. Nothing happened the fifth night, then three more labor-filled nights followed. The ninth night was quiet, confirming the three-on, one-off routine.

At dawn on the tenth day, after a quick flybot scan that confirmed the station was deserted, Mika convinced Lin to let him venture into the field. The samples from the buzzard had shown levels of radiation so elevated the workers should not have been able to move, much less labor for ten hours. But whether it was training or punishment, they had kept at it.

Mika pointed his Geiger counter from mound to mound and whispered to his tida as he spoke to Lin who had remained on their observation perch. "Thirty rems per minute on that pile." He moved the counter and held it toward the piles. "Eighty, ten," He moved it again. "Shit."

Lin's voice betrayed forced calm. "What is it?"

"Three hundred rems."

"Get back here, now."

He did a 360 to allow the counter to record the full field. He walked back to the cliff, pointing the counter to the surrounding areas as he passed the mounds. The number shot up on the pile to his left, but he ignored it and kept moving.

"How are you feeling?" she asked as he climbed the rocks toward their perch.

"Fine?"

She picked up the Geiger counter and her face soured. "Five hundred fifty?"

"I wasn't there for a full minute."

Her eyes moved to the field. "Yeah, you were." He sat down and she crouched in front of him, her eyes locked on his. "We heal, but we have no idea how radiation will affect us."

He grabbed a towel, new pants, and a shirt from his bag and walked a few steps away. He stripped and poured water over his head, wiping his head and chest with his bandana. He poured more water and dried off, putting on the new clothes.

"That's not much of a decontamination. We should get back."

He tucked in his shirt. "Most of the radiation had to be in the dust. I should be fine."

"Not good enough."

He gulped the last drops from his water pouch. "Let's just rest for a few hours," he said, wiping his mouth with the back of his hand. "If I feel weak or dizzy over the next few hours, we'll go back."

She nodded, but her eyes didn't relax. Though she pretended to analyze data, she hovered over him for the next two hours. But he felt no ill effect beyond thirst. After an hour, he did wind sprints and couldn't spot any problems.

"I suppose we're tougher than we thought."

She didn't smile. "You don't have a clue what just happened."

"I feel fine. Those poor bastards spend hours in that field and keep ticking. So, clearly, we can handle a fair bit of radiation." He drained his water. "Do we follow the bus tracks now?"

She took a deep breath and exhaled as she nodded. Twenty miles later, he took his bandana off. "What are you thinking?"

Lin kept her eyes on the trail. "Nothing."

They had been climbing for three hours. His mind jumped from topic to topic without lingering on anything that mattered. "Me too."

"Liar." It was an innocuous jab, but there was a kernel of truth in it.

He couldn't coalesce what had been bothering him into a coherent thought. The radiation exposure should have scared him, but it hadn't, which nudged him toward Amy's accusation. Her words haunted him, mostly because he feared she was right.

"Do you feel different?"

She slowed down as she reached another bend. "Different how?"

There was no subtle way of putting it. "Since the training."

Their bodies got stronger each day, trained by poison and mutilation. Their minds didn't. First, they mistrusted their bodies, refusing to believe they'd recover from gnarly injuries. Any tactical edge their bodies provided got lost because they didn't even consider actions to leverage those capabilities.

But then they embraced the transformation and jumped ahead, presuming an aura of invincibility more dangerous than tentativeness. In a few, mind and body caught up, creating aloof but nearly indestructible soldiers like the two of them. But it also separated them from their peers.

She didn't respond, so he continued. "In how you interact with people—do you feel different? Like an observer? An outsider?"

She resumed walking, and he waited for her to think this through as she did with everything. "Not really, yes, and yes," she said fifty yards later. "When I walk into a room, I pay attention to who wants what, who listens, and who postures. So, yeah, I'm an observer, but I don't feel different. I've been on the outside looking in as long as I can remember."

"I never much cared for people. They tire me, and few interest me enough to make the effort to know them. But now, even that's more restrictive, more oppressive."

"Thanks."

"You know what I mean. Those few days in New Cal were hard."

"I thought you'd be glad to be back. To catch up with Chipps."

He looked away, guilt tugging at him for how he had acted with Amy, getting heavier still because he was willing to state it out loud. "Had to run to Macky's the first night."

She snorted. "So, to avoid people you go to the most crowded bar in New Cal?"

"They don't matter. I had a thirty-second chat with Macky and saw no one who mattered after that. The crowd is part of the background, like the tables and chairs." He hadn't known her before her training, so unlike with Sierra, he had no baseline for her behavior. Had she changed too? Become more focused. Less human. "I wonder sometimes whether we were meant to have a finite amount of life."

"It's all finite." She took off her bandana, crouched, and picked up a two-inch stone. "Everything dies, Mika. Fruit flies, flowers, rats, people." She pushed air through her nose, half-snort, half-laugh, holding up the rock. "Even mountains. It all dies, just on different time scales."

"What if life's doled out in precise doses? You have your allotted time, and once that's spent, you're done. Empty. You can keep on living, but you're dead inside."

"That kind of thinking is about as useful as tits on an eagle." She clasped both his forearms. "No, Mika, there is no expiration date. We think we're tough shit, but it doesn't take much to kill us. One bullet, right through the eye." She let go of his arms and snapped her fingers. "And you're gone like this."

It was five miles before she spoke again. "What happened to you?"

The words flew out of his mouth before his brain edited them. "I should be dead."

"You didn't get that much radiation. We'll watch you over the next days, but—"

"Not what I meant."

"The training?" She snorted. "We should all be dead."

He shook his head. "I mean for real. I remember the calm right before. Thinking I was ready, thinking it was okay. Almost welcoming it. And then it hits you. It's not okay, not by a long shot. That all you are—all your thoughts, all that makes you who you are—will become a puddle on someone's sidewalk. And that someone isn't going to wonder about your dreams, your loves, or your fears. No, she's going to wonder whether she can take the bloodstains out of the concrete."

The empty landscape stretched for miles in every direction around them almost as empty as he felt. "They were strange seconds. Expanding and contracting at the same time. You're in transition. Not dead yet, but no longer alive. Imagine my surprise when I woke up."

"You're not dead," she said, rescuing him. "Inside or outside. And I don't think you're changing. But if I had to guess, I'd say you're becoming more and more like yourself. Whatever tendencies you had, they're more pronounced. The feelings you had taught yourself to fight against are back, and they're stronger."

That was an angle that had not occurred to him. Phillips had been blunt and grating. Eva had been peaceful, disconnected from her past. But perhaps they had always been like that and had just given in to their natures. It was possible because they were not converging toward a new type of behavior. Phillips, Eva, Lin—they were all different from each other. Thinking of Sierra, Lin's argument gained strength. Sierra had become more ruthless, more driven—traits that had always been with her.

"I think you're right."

"Glad to help."

"You didn't." The implications sank in. "I spent years becoming someone else. Someone who moved through the crowd without letting them drag me down. Someone who looked people who don't matter in the eye and paid attention to what they said when he didn't care one whiff about any of it." And it had worked. "Now, if you're right, I'm back to square one."

"No, you're not." She smiled. "You're at a whole new square."

That was true. Maybe even on a different board on a different plane. Either way, it left him a long way away from all the other occupied squares, particularly Amy's.

AS THE SUN SET, THEY PITCHED THEIR TENTS A HUNDRED YARDS from the road, behind a bluff. By nine, the bus sped past them toward the field. The next morning, they waited for the bus to leave before starting their hike.

Two days and ninety miles later, the tread marks split, with the Jeep heading north and the bus continuing east. They followed the bus, reaching a settlement by sundown the next day. It was similar in size and layout to the abandoned one they had found on their first outing.

On the last hill, the road dropped down in a dozen switchbacks before hitting the town a mile away. The town was laid out on a grid, five blocks by five blocks of single-story barracks. A square stood in the center with a two-story structure surrounded by a fifty-foot-wide grass patch, the only green in town. East of the last block, goats and chickens were fenced in pens and coops. Cultivated fields stretched in eighteen rows with nets hanging from poles to keep the birds away.

After they set up camp for the night, Mika dug a hole for the fire. The pit not only concealed the flames but also burned the fire hotter, reducing the smoke. In this haze, they would be impossible to spot. He got the airflow he wanted and lit the kindling.

Lin put down her binoculars and sat. She pushed her hands over the glowing hot fire. "What are the odds they don't know we're here?"

They had avoided the road to prevent leaving any tracks and put away their flybot. "Pretty good."

"I hate assuming something so fundamental to everything we do."

They observed for six days, without another word about differences and training and squares. They established the settlement's routines: market, bars, school, traffic in and out. The bus left for three consecutive afternoons, headed for the field near the dotri.

On the sixth day, a truck arrived, and Hatman from the high desert emerged. He disappeared into the two-story building by the square, came out about two hours later, and drove away.

They hiked the two-mile trail to town on the seventh day. Lin settled into a secluded spot at the edge of the tree line, a hundred yards from the nearest building. He walked straight past her and was a quarter of the way in before Lin noticed.

"Mika," she whispered. "Mika," she repeated, without raising her voice. He kept walking. She caught up to him. "What are you doing?"

He spoke as they reached the town. "Observing." They passed three men and a couple, but no one gave them a second glance. The residents were pale, but not the unhealthy gray of the sickly workers. They wore long jackets and gloves, though it was too hot for either.

Mika walked into the first shop. Two mostly empty shelves led him to the back counter. Boots, sweaters, and coats were piled on a bench in front of the counter. The man behind the counter sported a three-day beard. He shut a metal lockbox with his gloved hand as Mika approached him.

"Hey. I was wonder—"

The man motioned them away and disappeared behind a door at the back of the shop.

"Not very friendly."

Lin's frown and pulsating jaw screamed that she was mad enough to murder him. He walked another block to the town square and stood in front of the faded blue bungalow that was the town bar. Over the past week, more people had walked into that establishment than all others combined. And yet it was nearly empty, with five patrons scattered on two of the six tables.

Recessed lights followed the hardwood planks of a bar jutting out from the left wall, bisecting the room. Mika walked to the bar and put a hand on the counter. "What's good here?"

The bartender did not reply. He wore black leather gloves as did all the customers. The man sitting two tables away sneezed then blew his nose on a napkin.

Mika reached for his tida, but thought better of it. He had nothing worth trading he was willing to part with.

"On me," the bartender said and poured two cloudy brews that didn't look too appetizing. But it was the same unfiltered, amber drink that sat on the occupied tables.

"Thanks." He took a sip. It was hoppy, bitter.

Lin stood next to him, but she had far too much sense to touch her beer. The bartender leaned over the counter. "You're a long way from home."

"We're headed north. As far as our legs take us. We'll settle down when we find a spot we can call home. Wasn't expecting to find beer on the way."

"North? Not a good idea."

Before Mika probed that statement, the bartender's eyes darted to the door. He grabbed a glass to wipe, an effort at looking busy. Mika turned at the sound of chairs being pushed back.

A broad-shouldered man stood by the door. He wore a loose, thigh-length brown jacket, a cap, and leather gloves. He waited for the customers to step out and closed the door. He walked in and tossed two sets of home-made leather gloves on the bar. His gaze moved to their beers and then to the barkeep. The barkeep looked away.

He turned to Mika. "I'll escort you out."

"Just as soon as I finish this beer."

The man moved his jacket back, exposing his gun. "It wasn't a suggestion."

Lin put a hand on Mika's elbow. "We were just leaving." She picked up the gloves.

"Custom," the man said and lifted his gloved left hand. His right hand stayed by his gun.

Lin put the gloves on, tugging them to fit.

Mika waved a greeting. "I'm Mika."

The man backed away, eyes on Mika's ungloved hand. "Put the gloves on, and let's go."

Mika grabbed the gloves and ran his fingers over the hand-stitched seams. After glancing at Lin's gloved hand, he shoved them in his pants' back pocket.

The man held the door open for them and pointed to the street. Mika slowed by the table where the man had sneezed. As Lin passed him, he took a glove from his pocket and scooped the napkin from the table, letting it disappear into the glove.

Before they reached the first intersection, a young woman stepped out of a store with shutters hiding all the windows. "Good Morning Mr. Powell."

Lin stopped, letting the man catch up. "Mr. Powell, I presume?"

"Kevon Powell. I'm what passes as law enforcement around here." He pointed forward, and they started walking again.

"What exactly is here?" Mika asked.

Powell picked up the pace. When they reached the edge of town, Powell gestured them out with his gun. "Now go away. And don't come back."

"There is a whole world out there," Mika said.

Powell snickered. "Yeah, yeah, yeah. Marin, Kern, New Cal. War after war. Round and round it goes. Who's invading whom this month?"

Mika's eyes widened in surprise. "You've been down south?"

"Born and raised in South Lake Tahoe. But you don't call it that. Unregulated Territories, you say." He snorted. "Like the rest is regulated. None of you ever cared what happened to us then. Why do you care now?"

"We'd like to know what's going on here," Mika said.

"Nothing that concerns you."

Mika pointed to the settlement behind them. "That concerns me." He moved his hand toward Powell's thin graying hair, "This concerns me."

Powell batted Mika's hand away in one quick motion. "Don't do that."

"There is no reason you should be here."

"This is the only place we can be. Now, go. And if I see you again, I'll shoot." Powell took two steps back and called to Lin. "You sound like the reasonable one. Don't go near people for three days. Not that you're going to find anyone in three days of walking."

"Why?"

Powell pointed to Mika. "If bare hands here is still on his feet in three days, you're good."

They walked to their camp in silence. "Well, that went well."

Lin spun around and grabbed his collar in one motion. "Do you have a death wish?"

"What are you talking about?"

"Dillydallying in the radiation field, walking into that town, that bar, drinking whatever was in that glass?"

"C'mon Lin. It was beer. Why would they try to poison us? You're way too paranoid."

"That's because you're not paranoid enough."

"Other than Powell, they had no interest in who we were."

She shook her head and leaned into him, her hands still on his collar. Her face was six inches from his. "Don't ever do that again. Obsess about finite lives all you want. Contemplate your mortality. But when we hit the field, don't take stupid risks and drag me with you. I'm the only one who gets to gamble with my life. Is that clear?"

It was the most animated he had ever seen her. She had stated the problem without grasping it. He was used to working alone, so his risk analysis had always been flawed. But her point transcended all that. "I'm sorry."

She let go of him and took a step back. "You're going to fuck up one day. And it's going to take a lot more than an apology to fix it."

He relaxed his hold on the gloves and opened them, displaying the soiled napkin.

His contrition must have seemed genuine. She softened. "But you're right. It went well."

"I was being sarcastic."

"I know. But we made contact with locals. We learned that at least some of them are from the Uregs, and that whatever affliction they have," she said, wiggling her fingers in her new gloves, "can spread by contact. It has an incubation period of three days."

She pointed to the napkin. "We may even have a sample." She dropped the napkin and glove into a pouch and sealed it. "There are no other settlements within a hundred, hundred-and-fifty miles. And despite your best efforts, we did not get shot."

He smiled. "So, I guess I didn't fuck up too bad."

"You're bloody reckless." She walked away, grumbling, "This is why I don't think you're up for the job."

CHAPTER 7
BREAKING POINTS

"To be led by a fool is to be led by the opportunists who control the fool."

—OCTAVIA BUTLER

A my leaned back in her mesh chair, the only article in her Marin office she had grown fond of. It was half-chair, half-reminder that some pre-Purge artifacts had earned their hype.

"What can I do for you, Mr. Engelson?"

The morning's executive council meeting had triggered her migraine, partly because she had refereed the bout between Kuipers and Yim, and partly because she hadn't stopped the fight when Kuipers went for the jugular. The few minutes of quiet she had hoped for were now gone as well, most likely sacrificed to another petty quarrel.

"Ms. Chipps," Engelson said, brows tight and lips puckered. His dark brown hair rested in perfect shape around his square face and sharp nose. "Your office rejected our last invoices. I can't partner with a client I can't trust."

Amy raised an eyebrow. "You should talk to the project manager."

"She's refusing to budge. And before you say it, Mr. Cavana has been less than helpful."

Ferg rarely brought up New Cal business on Amy's Marin days, but Amy never questioned Ferg's sense of what mattered. Fred

Engelson owned the company that supplied the seals and valves to New Cal's reconstruction projects and also owned half the mills. As one of New Cal's most powerful residents, he expected to have the governor's ear whenever he chose.

"And you want me to do what?"

"I want you to fix this."

Amy brought up the contract with Engelson on her side screen, scrutinizing the schedule, along with Cavana's notes. She smiled. "Mr. Engelson, you were paid as stipulated."

"For costs and expenses, yes, but I paid overtime to my workers to meet the deadlines. Your project manager refuses to release the bonuses."

"Did you deliver on time to trigger the bonuses?"

Engelson took a deep breath. "Ms. Chipps, you are new, so I don't blame you for being misled. It is customary in our business to be paid in full when the deliveries are close to the deadlines. Otherwise, no rational business owner would pay overtime to stay on schedule."

She scrolled to the delivery schedule. Engelson had delivered half the seals two weeks late. He was using a definition of close that was new to her.

"I'm sorry, Mr. Engelson, but I will back the project manager on this one."

"Ms. Chipps, my company cannot deliver more seals if you do not pay us fairly."

She narrowed her eyes and leaned forward. "Are you saying you cannot fulfill the contract?" She scrolled further down, reaching the legal penalties for the dissolution of the contract. "I hope we don't need to invoke Clause 26."

"No need to be hostile, Ms. Chipps. I brought this matter to your attention so we can avoid further delays and unpleasantries."

She did not reply.

Engelson shifted in his seat. "You are young, Ms. Chipps, and I'm trying to help you. Contracts this complicated require a certain, ah, understanding among partners. In my previous project with Mayor Halsan, for example, we resolved our issues without lawyers enforcing every clause in the contract. The outcome was beneficial to both sides."

The last waterworks contract had been a disaster for Cal City, taking twice as long and costing three times the bid. That Halsan had approved the overruns wasn't a surprise.

"You will be paid according to your contract. Now, if there's nothing else, I do need to run."

Engelson raised a hand, half wave, half a motion to stop her. "I worry that without our seals, improvements to Cal City's infrastructure will fall further behind schedule."

"Are you threatening me, Mr. Engelson?"

"Ms. Chipps, New Cal works differently than Marin. Perhaps, if you were here more, you would notice this. We need a governor committed to New Cal, not Marin."

"Meet your deadlines, and we will honor our payments. Good day, Mr. Engelson."

She swiped the screen clear and leaned back on her chair, massaging her temples. After a morning of Marin bureaucracy, Engelson was almost a distraction. Almost.

Because New Cal's legal system had no teeth, every business transaction and every contract required daily renegotiation. Businessmen like Engelson pushed because they believed she would cave. Every second she spent proving to them that she wouldn't give in stole a second from the real job of fixing New California.

She slid her screen in her backpack and put on her jacket, heading for the door, but she nearly got tackled by Kuipers rushing in.

"I warned you this would happen," Kuipers said, her thin lips pressed flat, her face stretched taut as though every cell were trying to pull away from an imaginary circle's center.

Amy picked up the pace, and Kuipers followed, her quick short steps giving her the determined gait of a stateswoman who was perpetually two meetings behind schedule.

"The body count reached seventeen," Kuipers said. "Seventeen!"

Amy stopped by the stairwell, unable to pinpoint which upset her more: the new body count or that Kuipers got to gloat. Kuipers ran her right hand back and forth on the side of her head, fingers capturing tufts of hair like an imaginary pair of scissors. Her thin, gray, two-inch hair popped back into shape promptly as she withdrew her hand. If only everything Kuipers disturbed could return to its original state so easily.

"If we repeat the mistakes of the past, this time the virus will destroy us."

Hearing about the mistakes of the past made Amy's blood boil. None of them knew what those mistakes were. Twenty-five years ago, the Purge had burned through the population like a brushfire. The full force of Fontaine's fancy world's science hadn't defeated the Purge. She failed to see what Kuipers offered that all those scientists had missed.

"I need you to back me on this," Kuipers said in a low, honest tone. "The safety of Marin, New Cal, and the whole land depends on our actions."

"I hate to make a decision before I understand what we're dealing with."

"We're dealing with a civilization-destroying virus."

Amy cocked her head. "Do you know something I don't, General? Because we still don't have a single sick person. Doesn't that sound strange to you?"

Kuipers joined her palms, her index fingers moving up and down between her lower lip and chin. "More the reason to be cautious. I want answers too. But if we wait for those answers, it may be too late." Her tone was far more conciliatory than the one she had used to browbeat Yim at the executive council.

"How do you propose to do that?"

A quarter-smile appeared on Kuipers' lips. She tapped her tida, and a map of Marin floated up. The blocks where the bodies had been found were marked in red. They did not coalesce into a discernible pattern. "Here, here, and here." Kuipers drew on the major roads, dissecting Marin into fifteen pockets. "We need quarantine zones and test sites in each zone. We erect checkpoints, test all citizens, and if necessary, isolate infected sectors."

Amy stood very still. Testing all citizens may have been an innocent attempt at mitigating the potential damage a virus with a six-week incubation period might cause. It may also have meant Kuipers knew far more than she let on, both about the corpses' origin and the Purge's new activities.

Amy kept her voice steady. "The panic alone will destroy Marin-New Cal."

"Not if we have curfews." Kuipers lowered her voice. "Martial law."

Marin-New Cal was disintegrating before Amy's eyes. The four New Cal towns became their own zones, with Cal City cut off from Marin with a straight line across the Golden Gate Bridge.

"Since we know so little about this new virus, what are we testing for?"

"First, to determine whether this is a new Purge variant. If we can isolate the variant and detect it before it kills, we can prevent another outbreak."

Amy nodded to prevent herself from replying. A test to detect minor changes in virus composition for tens of thousands of citizens wasn't practical. It would take weeks to months to analyze those samples. But a simple test to detect the Purge's presence could be done in minutes. Was it possible Kuipers knew? And if so, who had told her?

"Let's suppose you find some people with a new type of virus. What then?"

Kuipers poked her floating map again. Three areas outside Marin were highlighted in yellow. "We will use these stadiums as temporary staging posts."

"You're building detention camps?"

Kuipers pursed her lips. "Not detention. Quarantine. I am protecting us all."

Amy put a hand on the stairway's wooden railing and glanced out the window. The ordered paths of citizens moving about Declaration Square created a serenity that wasn't real. The window isolated her from the sounds, creating a picturesque snapshot, detached from everyday struggles and realities. It was a framed image much like Marin-New Cal had become. Kuipers was about to take a sledgehammer to that frame.

"Do I have your support, Vice-Chancellor?"

"I sympathize. But I need a clearer threat before I agree to such extreme measures."

Kuipers tapped her tida to an image of bloated corpses piled on top of each other. "This is an existentialist crisis. What's extreme is doing nothing while Marin citizens die by the dozen. If you had backed me up when I recommended these measures two months ago, we could have saved lives."

"That's pure speculation. Transparency and real information will reassure our scared citizens. Roadblocks and curfews? Not so much. Give me something real, and I'll back you up, but I'm not adding fuel to the fire."

"We're fighting for Marin's future. As vice-chancellor, Marin has to be your priority."

"Marin-New Cal, you mean?"

Kuipers rolled her eyes. "I want us on the same side. But if you are this passive, I will proceed without your support."

Amy took three steps down, ignoring the barely veiled threat of a coup. "I'm late, General. Good day."

As she drove to Cal City, Amy tried to pinpoint the reasons for not offering more than token resistance to Kuipers' power grab. She had the clout to prop up Yim's failing chancellorship and push back on Kuipers' council takeover. She also had the power to back Kuipers publicly and prevent endless bickering if and when Kuipers made her move. By eschewing both options, she was relinquishing her responsibilities and passing up the opportunity to wield power in the ensuing order.

Engelson and Kuipers didn't agree on much, but they agreed that she wasn't deferential enough. She was too Marin or not Marin enough, too aggressive or too passive. No balance allowed her to operate in that comfort zone Fontaine had enjoyed. She pushed the impossible task of pleasing everyone away for one day and headed toward the Cal City harbor.

She reached the harbor and stepped out of her Jeep, eyes on the water. The old jetty had collapsed, its remnants sitting as a reminder that nothing was permanent. A smaller jetty built from the debris of the old one protected the docks now. The juxtaposition of the old and new gave her the simple reason she had refused to cave to either Engelson or Kuipers. Marin was about to tear itself apart. Trying to prevent that outcome would simply destroy New Cal.

And for what?

For an entity she had never believed in, one that had been forced on them, on her. When a union started to break, there were two choices: fight to keep it together or go over the inventory to determine what to walk away with.

The fishing boats were coming back, their stands popping up on the docks as they unloaded their catch. A gray-pink tuna loin on display caught her attention. It was equal part food, equal part memory.

Marin-New Cal wasn't the only union at its breaking point.

The one at home, though, deserved one more chance. She picked up the Albacore loin. It had been the first meal Mika had cooked for her, ironically, on another night she had been trying to forget the complications of the Marin-New Cal union.

She would replicate that meal, hoping the seared tuna would rekindle the excitement from that first night.

That is, if he even noticed.

CHAPTER 8

E-TEST

"Failure is the key to success; each mistake teaches us something."

—MORIHEI UESHIBA

Mika sat at the breakfast shop at the harbor with a cup of coffee and a half-eaten egg burrito in front of him. Three white plastic chairs surrounded his metal table. He leaned back, his feet on the chair next to him, facing the water. The boats rocked back and forth in the wake of passing trawlers. After five weeks in the high desert and two more in a makeshift quarantine lab Sierra had set up deep in the Uregs, he needed to see water, to smell brine.

Their hike back had exceeded the incubation time implied by Powell, but Lin had still requested additional tests. They had both gone through quarantine protocol and had given enough blood to reanimate a corpse. All their tests showed that they carried the Purge and nothing else. He had no signs or symptoms of having been exposed to radiation.

On the water, the scream of gulls fighting for scraps tossed from a returning fishing boat reminded him that life went on, that there were no timeouts in the struggle for survival. A gull chased away from the trawler landed on the back of the chair across his table, bold enough to eye his burrito but not enterprising enough to pick at it. The gull gave him a shoulderless shrug, stretching its neck back and forth. Then the gull's eyes darted behind Mika, and it floated up with three powerful flaps and rejoined the battle around the fishing boat.

Mika glanced sideways to catch Eva grabbing the empty chair. She dragged it, spun it to push its back toward the table, and straddled it. "Oh, good, Happy is here today."

He took a sip of coffee. It had gotten cold. "What makes you say that?"

"You're facing the boats. Grumpy faces away."

He took another sip. Some days they were boats. Other days they were reminders of what had started at this harbor, of what he had seen and done, of what he had become. On those days, the boats became unwanted intruders, pestering him with hard-to-dodge accusations.

"Did she send you?"

She bit her lip, disappointment and sorrow rolled into a single expression. "You can fool the others, but you can't fool me. I see right through you."

"What do you see?"

"The calm before the storm. And I can't help you because I don't know what you're after. I'm not even sure you know."

Mika chuckled and took a sip of cold coffee. "Just got back. What did I miss?"

"A lot." Eva picked up his coffee cup, reached behind her, and tossed it in the trash. She went to the counter and returned with two hot cups of coffee. "Sentinel's recruiting picked up."

They were always recruiting and training, though not particularly well or fast. He took a sip of coffee. It was bitter and acidic, but a whiff of smoke and molasses softened the flavor.

"Boss lady visited the Shed. Twice."

It took all his energy to not spit out his coffee. He swallowed and put the cup down. The Sentinel headquarters wasn't called the Shed just because it was a big metal box. What they did to soldiers there brought a whole meaning to "being taken to the back of the shed."

He had a hard time believing Amy would approve anything about the Shed. But times were changing, and so was she. The idealist in her would balk at Sierra's methods, but the pragmatist would value the upside. Which Amy carried the day probably depended on the day.

Eva shook four sugar pouches, tore them open one by one, and squeezed them into her coffee. "She got the tour from Sierra. Second time she came with a Marin expert on the Purge."

He had to hand it to Sierra. Recruiting soldiers to train was survival. Recruiting the vice-chancellor and an expert virologist was ambition. Unless, of course, the definition of survival had shifted. But it was clear from Eva's tone there was more.

"What are you not telling me?"

"The samples from the napkin. The virus they carry is almost like the Purge."

"Almost?"

She sipped her coffee before replying. "The DNA strands were wrecked, but they're convinced it's a Purge variant. By the way, the protective pouch was genius. It kept the virus alive longer than it otherwise would have."

"Lin's idea." She had packed the napkin and glove in a dark, damp pouch to maximize the odds that whatever they contained survived. "Had nothing to do with it."

"Anyway, the scientist says it's most likely the same as the radiation-damaged one from the buzzard. She thinks this virus is a tiny bit longer than the Purge, with symmetric ends. But the DNA is too far gone for anything conclusive."

Symmetric. He had heard that before, how the Purge was almost symmetric. How one end appeared carved off. Phillips had made that point, and it hadn't meant much to him. Still, didn't mean much, except that decomposing in the belly of a buzzard or in a pouch rarely provided the missing part of anything.

"Is that good or—?"

"Bad," she said.

"Why?"

"Because everything about the Purge is bad."

Mika picked at the eggs from his burrito and swallowed a mouthful. "How is Amy holding up?"

Eva took a sip of her coffee and put the lid back on. "If anyone can balance a hostile Marin council, bickering mayors, and rebuilding setbacks, it's her."

"If anyone can," he whispered. "You still check up on her?"

"I don't check up on her. I stop by because I like having wine and talking with her. And yeah, I still do that."

Nothing he said came out right, so he stopped trying. He halved his coffee in two gulps and put the cup back on the table.

She glared at him and pointed to his piping hot cup. "Maybe you shouldn't swallow hot coffee like it's beer?" Her eyes darted around. "Out here, in public?"

He raised the cup to his lips, took a tiny sip, and smiled. She did the same, ignoring his sarcasm. He put his cup down, leaned back, and closed his eyes.

"Are you all right?"

"I'm fine." He opened his eyes to Eva's grimace. "But are you?"

She hesitated. "I'm worried about Marin and New Cal. Last week, Marin closed the border. They claim it's for safety, and Amy says it's all normal, but something isn't right in Marin."

He laughed without humor. "Marin has never been right."

"Fair. But this isn't the usual unease. There is real fear. Not like the fear of a Kern invasion. That was a hazy fear when I was growing up. We knew it'd be terrible if it happened, but we also knew it wasn't likely to happen. This is different."

"Different how?"

"I can't quite put my finger on it. Ma doesn't talk much anymore. Not to me, not to Mom. I visited them twice last month. Same thing both times. Ma comes home, goes to her office, comes out for dinner, says a few meaningless words, and disappears again."

Eva was so unassuming it was easy to forget she was Chancellor Yim's stepdaughter. Mika never saw the connection, even when she blurted it out. "Maybe it was because you were there? Maybe she doesn't know how to talk to you."

She shook her head. "Mom says she's like that every day. Marin is rudderless. So many secrets that no one believes anything anymore. Ma lies to the council, the council lies to the army, and they all lie to the people. It would be funny if it weren't depressing."

"And we lie to all of them," Mika said. "Every day, I lie to Lin. Amy lies to Cavana. Sierra lies to the council. And you…" He wagged his finger at her. "You lie to every Sentinel."

"I don't!"

No matter what she told herself, she had to know that every day she didn't correct what happened in that facility, she lied by omission. "Can you liberate a couple of assault rifle crates?"

She cupped her coffee with two hands. "Should I ask why?"

"You shouldn't."

"From Marin or the Shed?"

Eva didn't know how to hold a grudge. A few seconds after he upset her, she had moved on. The Eva he had met through files and interviews, the Eva he had tried to find in the far reaches of the Uregs, had emanated an impossible-to-believe peacefulness. The indestructible Eva had confirmed and even surpassed that initial assessment. It all confirmed Lin's thesis that they were each embracing their nature. He didn't like what it said about him that Eva's core was so centered and his was so indignant. "I really don't care."

"Marin then." When he didn't reply, she added, "I'll feel less guilty."

"And throw in some light armor and a couple of heavy guns. Fifty cal or higher."

"That's enough to arm a platoon."

Mika smiled. "That's the idea."

She sat up straight. "Sierra wants to talk to you."

He leaned forward and picked up his cup. "So, she did send you."

She bit her lower lip but didn't reply.

He got up. "Let's go, then."

She remained seated. "Doesn't have to be now." She pointed at his half-eaten burrito. "Are you going to finish that?"

Eva didn't eat so much as she picked at her food, moving it from one side of the plate to the other until she got bored and accidentally took a bite. He pushed his plate forward and squinted at her, his disbelief plastered on his face.

She didn't even pretend to want to eat. She stood up and stretched her shoulders, as though the mind of a stern and agile soldier had beamed into her body. The friend was gone, replaced by the protector. What he didn't know was whom Eva was here to protect, Sierra or him.

In the ninety minutes it took them to cover the seventy miles to the Shed, the temperature rose by thirty degrees. The scorching heat of the San Joaquin Valley turned the metal-framed warehouse into an oven. The dozen air conditioning units on the roof fought a good fight, but they had no hope of winning the battle. The musky air turned even walking into exercise, as though gravity were turned up inside the warehouse.

Mika stood by the railing on the second floor, twenty feet above the recruits sweating at each station. With an open floor plan, the converted warehouse was an ideal training center. The east half was a high bay, with four-foot half walls separating three areas for strength exercises, hand-to-hand combat, and aerobic activity, all surrounded by a running track. The walled-off west half housed medical labs and space for tests that needed to happen behind locked doors.

The south corridor, the one on which he stood, was a forty-yard balcony, a viewing platform for the training facility. Four recruits did wind sprints on the track below, alternating going full speed for twenty yards with jogging for another twenty.

Each training day consisted of four forty-five-minute weight sessions, two aerobic sessions, and two sparring sessions. Plus, they all spent two hours in the medical facility.

The routine was effective because of the basic truth about exercise. Working out didn't build muscle. It tore it up. It was the healing between workouts that built the muscle. So, once they healed fast, all they had to do was tear themselves up even faster. After the medical training, the forty-eight hours between workouts standard for mere mortals were reduced to ninety minutes. So, they built as much muscle mass in one week as a Purie would in two months.

They stood above a conveyor belt that took unsuspecting recruits and turned them into fit, indestructible killers in less than a month. Unfortunately, the process didn't work on mental strength. He walked the length of the corridor and reached the west side. Two recruits—a sharp-chinned man in his early twenties and an older, tall woman—stood at the end of the corridor with an instructor, just past a missing section of the railing.

Eva's attempt at delay now made sense. It was test day. Recruits moved through levels, scraping by trials that assessed their progress. Ahead of them, the instructor asked the recruits to jump to the floor below, meaning they had graduated beyond the test where they were pushed down. That stage elicited anger. Today they needed to show they had learned the point of the exercise, which wasn't to break bones but to teach that whether bones will break ought not to guide their actions. They had to move beyond their mental blocks and jump down onto solid concrete. It didn't always work.

Like now. The man was too distressed to let his mind overrule his fear. He moved away twice, avoiding getting between the instructor and the missing railing. After gesticulating back and forth, he walked away, shaken. That was the end of the road for him. He wouldn't become a Sentinel. Once the man disappeared at the end of the corridor, the instructor pointed down again. The second recruit leaned forward. She crouched, palms on the floor, and jumped.

She grunted as she landed. Unbelievable. She had been so concerned about the fall she had not kept her balance, landing sideways, and putting all her weight on the outside of her right foot. That ankle was broken, but it would heal. Whether her mind would, no one knew.

"These people aren't ready."

"Sierra says they need to be. Says we can't recruit and train them fast enough."

Mika ran his fingers over the oak railing. It was warm and rough, but his finger hit a splinter. The railing needed a complete strip and reseal, much like the Sentinel concept. Neither was likely to get what it needed. "Maybe you should stop pushing them down catwalks."

Eva shook her head. He didn't push because there was no need to reignite old battles, particularly since his battle was with Sierra, not Eva. But test day meant somewhere down in the bowels of the Shed, some Sentinels were taking the E-test. He wanted to run away from it and pretend it didn't exist. Instead, he walked down to the basement.

"Let's not do this," Eva said as she followed him down the steps.

"I need to see this, just to remind myself why I can't ever trust Sierra."

It had now become clear it wasn't Sierra Eva had tried to protect. It was him, from himself. Eva was loyal to a fault.

"This is all my stupid idea," he said as they navigated the basement hallways. "I once told Sierra there were different kinds of people: those who can kill and sacrifice themselves for a cause and those who can't bring themselves to do either. And the dangerous ones who can kill, but place too high a value on their own lives."

"Didn't know that."

"I never thought she'd be crazy enough to base the whole fucking organization on that idea. Or devise a test to find out."

"What about the fourth kind?" Eva asked, having done the math. "Those who can't kill but sacrifice themselves for a cause?"

This was psychology, not math. "Have you seen any in the Shed?"

Eva shook her head. "Not yet."

"Martyrs. They're out there, but you sure as hell are not going to find them in here."

"I'm not having this argument with you."

"Don't, then." He stopped in front of a metal door. It was locked, but her access let them into a hallway with a locked inner door. A red light shone on top of the door. Live E-test.

The frosted glass window hid the destruction of another soul. He tapped the screen, and the glass became transparent, allowing one-way viewing. A figure sat on a chair with a hood on his or her head. A recruit stood six feet away with a gun in his hand. He aimed at the seated figure, then brought the gun down, and then raised it again.

Graduation day for someone. Or not.

Lifting weight didn't make them soldiers, much less Sentinels. They were part commando, part spy, all reckless. He conceded Sierra needed to know how far her charges were willing to go for a cause. But this was not the way to find out.

There was no right answer to the E-test. Those prone to self-sacrifice had to shoot to pass. Those good at self-preservation had to avoid shooting.

There was enough psychological mumbo jumbo to make it all sound sensible. But in the end, they gave a gun to a recruit and ordered them to shoot a hooded stranger. That the stranger would heal didn't lessen the emotional impact of pulling that trigger at point-blank range and splattering blood.

He walked out before the recruit made up his mind. He had seen enough real trauma to last three lifetimes. He didn't need to see a staged one. Every E-test broke someone, with the faint hope that they'd be put back together stronger.

Eva followed him out. "I hope we're not training psychopaths." Eva's sincerity was real. She almost sounded remorseful, but she was complicit by silence, by having allowed herself to be the first target and lulling Sierra into thinking what they did was excusable.

"No," he shook his head. "That's not what we hope. We know we're training psychopaths. We just hope our psychopaths are better killers than their psychopaths." He walked away from the test and away from Sierra's office.

"What am I supposed to tell Sierra?" Eva called.

"Whatever you want."

Coming here had been a mistake. He should have trusted Eva and stayed away. Some truths didn't need confirming. He let go of the E-test and Sierra and headed out.

He was so distracted he almost didn't notice the woman sitting in his Jeep. Her bright orange hair, cut above the shoulder, framed a round, vaguely familiar face. She wore a loose wool cardigan that reached mid-thigh. Her eyes never left him as he approached.

He stepped in. "Out."

"We need to talk."

"Make an appointment."

She shook her head to reject his dismissal. "When? You're always beyond the Uregs."

He snapped his head in her direction because his whereabouts weren't public knowledge.

"Are you a Sentinel?"

"No, but I work for them occasionally. Just finished a job."

"What do you need?"

"You're the one who needs me."

"Who are you, again?"

She waved quickly. "I'm Blue."

He nodded, but it was hard to ignore her hair. "What are you, color blind?"

She smiled. "Made you think, no?"

"Seriously, what do you want?"

"I find things. Things buried in dark places where most sniffers won't dare look. And I'm guessing in your line of work, you can use someone with those skills, yeah?"

A hound. Yeah, he needed one of those. Since Kevin Jezek's disappearance, he had muddled through with second-rate hacks. But he had a hard time seeing how this smirking stranger would fix that problem.

"And I'm guessing you're going to say you're good."

She shook her head. "Not blasted good. The best."

"Never heard of you."

"That's because I keep a low profile."

That was one explanation. "Tell you what. Do two things for me, and we'll talk."

She perked up. "Sure."

"Find me something I don't know about the Purge."

She squinted. "That's pretty vague, yeah?"

"Just get me something interesting that's not widely known, say, from the old labs. The kind of shit that's supposed to stay behind firewalls."

"How old?"

"All the way to the beginning."

"Those data have been picked a hundred times over, no? What are you expecting to find that hasn't been found?"

The outcome of the outbreak was here for all to see. But what had been the initial reaction? Not of the scared masses, but of the scientists? Had they expected to find a cure? How had they reacted; what had they tried? Had they understood what they faced?

"Think more metadata than data. Where the data came from, where it was stored, where it went. Whether there was disagreement on the virus' structure or on how it spread."

She licked her lips. "That's still vague."

He leaned across her lap, opened her door, and sat back straight.

"I heard you were strange."

"From?"

"Sentinels, others, you know? I work with a lot of people. I hear things."

"Most of it is probably true."

She closed her door. "What's the other thing you want?"

"A T-shirt."

She shifted in her seat, putting her back to the door, crossing her left leg, and sitting on it. "You're joking, yeah?"

"I'm very serious." He described the exact design and size of the T-shirt he wanted.

"Fine," she said, her shoulders dropping with her enthusiasm.

That raised a warning flag. Good hounds had no regard to the objective value of the item their client sought. It was the subjective value to the client that mattered. If she hadn't mastered that yet, she was no use to him.

"What did you expect working with me would be like? That we'd eat tacos by the harbor and talk about old times?"

"I also heard you were an asshole."

He laughed. "Probably also true. But your interview skills need work."

She shook her head, pushed the door open, and stepped out. But she didn't slam the door, which won her points.

He leaned toward her seat to make eye contact. "Tell you what. Convince the guards at the gate that I'm supposed to leave, and we'll talk again."

"Now?"

"Yeah, now." He would rather leave without having to shoot anyone.

"Sure." She sat on the ground and grabbed her screen from her backpack.

He put the Jeep in gear and headed for the gate. As he approached, the gate lifted. The guard got out of her seat, eyes on him, but the screen under the canopy chimed and she went back to it, perplexed. He waved and gunned it, grinning at his new ally's audacity and skill.

His detour by the Shed and the episode with Blue had distracted him enough to forget he was back in town. But it was duty time and there was no avoiding his next stop.

Water the plants. Reconnect with acquaintances. Get sniffer updates. Pay the bills.

Pay the emotional bills.

CHAPTER 9
WEDGE

*"You keep your pain in harbors, and that's
why all your ships are sinking."*
—ERIN VAN VUREN

The meal went as well as Amy had hoped: civil, with sparks that hinted at something more. Or were they embers? Mika was content one moment and bouncing around like a caged tiger the next. They had become strangers again, which wasn't necessarily bad. It gave her a path forward, an opening to get to know the new Mika without comparing him to her expectations.

He sipped wine. "I've given a lot of thought to what you said."

Her eyes flickered as she tried to find context. She hadn't said anything of note.

"How I'm different," he added when she didn't reply.

She had gotten used to Mika's completing conversations interrupted hours earlier. Now he was completing one that had started over a month ago. Still, that he had cared enough to think about it was promising.

"You were right."

She smiled to encourage him. "And?"

"Having a mission, a purpose, helped. I went through a reset, and some of my reactions were unfiltered. I can work on it."

"We can work on it together."

He grabbed the dishes and headed to the kitchen. He set them down and grabbed the half-full bottle. "Wine?"

She nodded and he refilled both their glasses.

"I hear you've made new friends in the Uregs," he said.

She took a sip. "Still trying to figure out what to make of Sierra."

He sat back down in his chair and leaned back. "I'm surprised you are. I'd have thought you'd have steered clear of anything to do with the Sentinels."

She traced the rim of her glass with her index finger. "It's complicated."

He smiled wide, letting his ebullience escape through his gap tooth. "It always is. It's just that you manage to find a way to simplify it all."

She reached for his hand and squeezed it. "I need to ask you something." He squeezed back. "Do you know what Kuipers is up to?"

He withdrew his hand and reached for his wine. "I don't," he said after taking a sip. "But I'll tell you what I know, and maybe that'll help you connect the dots."

He described his long missions north and the settlements they found scattered beyond the Uregs. They did not paint a picture that made sense and did not provide any link to Kuipers.

She put her right foot under her left hamstring. "They told you they were from the Uregs?"

"That's what Powell, one of their leaders, said. He had no reason to lie."

"I'd love to know how much of this Kuipers knows."

"Would knowing the existence of these settlements explain Kuipers' behavior?"

She cocked her head. "Not really."

"That's too bad."

"Why?"

"Because we haven't been back long enough for the news to affect her actions. So, if she knew, it'd have meant she has other sources."

"I can't explain Kuipers' actions."

He took another sip. "Why do you react to her moves? You won't understand what she wants until you push her out of her comfort zone. Push her on the corpses and see what she does."

"And what if she doubles down on the quarantine and locks down Marin?"

He shrugged. "Then you'll know."

She took a sip. "I rip Marin-New Cal apart up to see what makes Kuipers tick? I don't think so."

He stared at her, with his mouth open. "If she knows where the corpses come from, she's using them to lock down Marin and consolidate power. If she doesn't, she'll lock down Marin to prevent more corpses from coming in. It's not whether she locks down Marin. It's how and why she locks down Marin."

She shook her head. "Your mind works differently from mine."

"Trust me, that's a good thing." He tapped his temple. "You don't want to live in here."

She smiled and drained her glass. She shook it to request more.

He took the wine bottle and reached toward her glass. He tilted the bottle, ready to pour, but his grip slipped. He caught the bottle mid-flight and swung it up to prevent it from spilling. The whipping motion sprayed wine straight up. A glass' worth landed on the table, splashing in all directions.

"Fuck." He straightened up but had spots on his shirt.

She reached for a towel and contained the wine before it spilled over the side of the table. Mika stood on tiptoes with bottle in hand, paralyzed. He waited for her to take care of the mess with an expression too sour to be caused by a wine spill. She dumped the towel in the sink. "Are you good?"

"Fine," he said too fast.

He was back to the distant Mika as though the previous hour hadn't happened.

He walked around the counter, took the dirty towel from the sink, and tried to wipe his shirt. He was spreading more wine on his shirt than he was taking off. It didn't feel as though it were the shirt he was trying to clean. He gave up and came back to the table. He sat down and took a large gulp, swallowing half his glass.

"Mika, I don't mind that you're different. But you gotta let me in."

"Don't know what that means."

"Talk to me."

"Don't know what to say."

"Then listen." She moved her chair to sit next to him and leaned forward. "You have to stop blaming yourself. The Uregs aren't your fault. The Marin-New Cal mess isn't your fault. You did your best."

"Did I?"

She reached for his hand. "You did." He remained silent. "Talk to me, Mika."

He took another gulp. "In this fucked-up world, there is nothing to talk about."

She wanted to scream. She had given him room to heal from his injuries. Then she had given him room to deal with the implications of what had transpired. But along the way, the person who defused volatile situations with a simple remark had disappeared, replaced by a person who created volatile situations by choosing exactly the wrong word.

"What are we doing then?"

"I don't know anymore." He refilled his glass.

"I need you to know."

"You're the one trying to save the world. You're steering this boat. I'm just a passenger."

"A passenger I can handle, but you're becoming an anchor. That I can't deal with, not now." She met his eyes. "You need to get your shit together."

He straightened up, and a sad smile crossed his face. "People are dying left and right from what we don't know. Some strange force is gathering beyond the Uregs, ready to unravel everything in Marin and New Cal. And you're worried about my shit?"

"I've never not faced shit odds. People die. People break things. You fix them. Some asshole breaks them again. And you fix them again. None of that external crap worries me."

There was something buried in his expression, between sympathy and pity, which disturbed her more than his hostility. When he spoke, his voice was softer, calmer.

"There was a boy who used to hang around the same orphanages I did. Teddy was tall, scrawny, and about three years older. By then, I'd figured out how to get what I needed. I grabbed what I could and took it to Lori. Teddy knew, and I'm sure he thought I was trading it for something else. In a way, I was. Some days, what I took made the difference. To me, the orphanage was a tool I needed for survival. And survival became a game, and every day we made it we were winners.

"Now Teddy, presented with the same picture, came to a very different conclusion: survival by itself had no meaning. That it wasn't one person's survival, but the survival of the whole clan that mattered. He was swallowing a large serving of sermons with the food. Most kids just listen to that shit, and few ever take it to heart. But Teddy, he went all in. He became Theodore. He kept harping on and on that to find meaning, we had to dedicate our lives to others.

"And to his credit, he practiced what he preached. He cooked, he cleaned, he chased kids a few years younger than he was. He taught the little he knew. All because he wanted to feel like he mattered. I could never decide if he was crazy or stupid."

"What happened to him?"

"Don't know. Don't care. Probably dead. That's what happens when you dedicate your life to a cause."

Her mind drifted to Fontaine, the man who had built New Cal from the ashes of a broken world. He had dedicated his life to New California. And now he was dead. She accepted Mika's premise, but not his conclusion. Because checking out had never been an option.

"And to you it's still a game? Take what you need and survive?"

He leaned back and extended his legs, putting his right ankle over his left. "Still here."

She got up and put her fists on the table, leaning forward. "Good for you. And it's fine if you don't care about what happens to the world. But some of us do." She shook her head. "That little insight about Kuipers hadn't occurred to me. I like the way you look at the same things as everyone but see something different. But lately, you don't even look at the world, much less see anything interesting."

He took two gulps of his wine but didn't reply.

She sat back down. "I'll tell you a story too. There was a field, at the edge of the compound where I grew up. It was only thirty miles east of here, but it may as well have been three hundred. The summers were so blisteringly hot and dry that nothing grew there. But every spring, with the little rain we'd get, wild poppies cropped up, along with weeds. I was fourteen when I spotted Justin spending an hour each morning in that field, whacking weeds.

"Seemed pointless. Weeds as far as the eye could see. But Justin was sixteen and strong, with dreamy eyes that sucked you in and made you forget what you were going to tell him. I had a huge crush on him, so I had to understand. I followed him one morning, and after twenty minutes of Justin pulling weeds, I asked what he thought he was doing. He said he was working out. I mentioned that was easier to do in the compound gym."

She lifted her index finger and pointed to the wall. Mika's gaze followed her hand, though there was nothing to see. "He pointed to the field, and said, 'There's a battle between the flowers and the weeds. Everything I do or don't do helps one. So, I have to choose sides.' That field went for miles. I pointed out that there was no way what he did helped or hurt anything.

"He swung his pick, and a lump of dirt came loose, attached to a two-foot weed with shallow roots. 'I didn't help this one,' he said, and swung again, uprooting another. 'Or this one.'"

"Let me guess: you end up with a beautiful weed-free field of flowers."

"That was not the point. He knew the score. That field was never going to be one or the other. But he preferred the poppies. And once you do that, you have to believe every bit helps. And when you look at it that way, it's easy to see the obvious."

"Which is?"

"You're either part of the solution, or you're part of the problem."

"So, is Justin part of the solution?"

She took a sip. "He settled down with Elise, a broad-shouldered, big-hipped farmer built for childbearing. Sure enough, by the time I left, they had a toddler who told stories in a language no one but she understood, a baby permanently strapped to Justin's chest, and a new bump in Elise's belly."

"So, he isn't."

She flicked a hair behind her ear. "Depends. I'd say we need that as much as we need anything. In the end, we all need to do our part."

He grimaced. "You're always recruiting, aren't you? Always lecturing. Sometimes you remind me of Teddy."

She narrowed her eyes. "The one you called crazy and stupid?"

He was ready to deny it, but she didn't let him. It was bad enough he felt entitled to put down her ambitions. She wasn't going to let him pretend it was in good fun.

"I'll give you a pass, this once, because your head isn't in the right place. But you don't get to call me that ever again. Pick your words carefully. I'm not here to take your resentment at the world."

He didn't say anything, which a month ago would have been progress. But today, it was the final nail in the coffin—one more indication that not only they were going in circles, but they were spiraling down. Silence hadn't helped. Talking certainly didn't. She had run out of options.

She was reacting to him, just like he said she was to Kuipers. And his advice to dictate rather than react was equally valid here. She exhaled, hating the implication.

She picked up her wine glass and walked to the bedroom, leaving the wine stains and mental strains behind. The wedge that had worked its way deeper and deeper between them for months had finally accomplished its mission. She didn't see any connection left, nothing to use to repair what she thought they had. She closed the door with the certainty, deep in her bones, that he wouldn't be there when she came out.

And for the first time, she was glad for it.

PART II
DOWNPOUR

CHAPTER 10

RIDDLE

"Memories are the key not to the past, but to the future."

—CORRIE TEN BOOM

Mika brought the rear of their single-file convoy of five Sentinels, trying to ignore the idle chatter he had endured since they had landed. Kristin, a well-drilled Marin soldier, walked behind Lin and kept to herself. Yasuo, a Santa Cruz militia and a recent graduate of Sierra's program, chose to broadcast every thought that crossed his mind.

The final Sentinel was a gung-ho Marin soldier whose name escaped Mika even after their four-hour flight. She encouraged Yasuo's chatter, and the two of them managed to comment on every rock, bush, grouse, and rabbit they passed on their three-hour hike to Powell's settlement.

The rising body count from the new virus had shattered Sierra's patience, sending them out with a team and a scout transport. The scout was an agile transport with a cargo bay that held a truck, a motorbike, a small lab, and a galley. With two tilt turbofan engines on its stubby wings and two more on its aft winglets, it could land vertically on any terrain, including the square at the center of Powell's settlement, but they continued with the charade of stealth a while longer.

They needn't have. The settlement was empty. They paused by the edge of the tree line, the spot from which he had walked into the compound four weeks ago. They dropped their heavy gear and Lin went through her last instructions. She aimed to convey the insights they had gained by months of living, breathing, and smelling these parts.

The exuberance of the two young Sentinels implied that Lin's caution was falling on deaf ears. Their excitement would have been uplifting were it not depressingly predictable and fanned by ignorance. They felt invincible because they had left the known dangers behind. But out here, what killed people wasn't the dangers they expected, but the ones they never suspected even existed.

Lin tolerated their nonsense in the name of team building. The occasional irritation Kristin showed to their reactions endeared her more to him than any action she took. They donned gloves and trekked to the main gate.

"Feels strange," Mika said as they approached the square, following the same path Lin and he had taken.

In each building they searched, the same scene repeated: enough chaos to hint at some disturbance, but not enough to imply a catastrophe. In the second apartment, dishes and pans were stacked on kitchen counters, but nothing was broken. In the third, clothes were piled on chairs and beds in heaps. It was as though the occupants had been interrupted while folding laundry and had left the room with the intention of returning shortly.

Lin pointed to three more buildings ahead of them, and a Sentinel disappeared into each. She approached him. "I've seen this before."

He hadn't. He had seen Uregs compounds after skirmishes. He had seen abandoned compounds. But those always came with blood and bodies. He had never seen an empty settlement of this size without signs of violence.

"Where?"

"During the Purge." The blood drained from her face. "This is what most towns looked like. Abandoned in the middle of the night, with people running away with just the clothes on their backs and, if they were really lucky, a few personal things."

She was no longer in the present. He put a hand on her forearm. "Are you okay?"

She shook her head. "I never thought I'd see this again. It's just…." She shook her head. "This isn't right."

It was the first time he had seen her shaken, so he heeded the sign. "Let's head back." When she didn't protest, he turned to the crew. "Wrap up all the sniffer feeds. We're done here."

Kristin waited for Lin to nod and started packing. She was too well-trained to argue, and for once the other two took their cues from her and didn't talk back.

Ten minutes into their silent trek back, Yasuo approached Mika. "What happened there?"

"Wasn't safe. The place was abandoned too hastily."

Yasuo's eyes widened. "Do you think we've been exposed?"

Mika shook his head. Yasuo, with his limited concerns, had asked the wrong question. The real question was why the settlement had disappeared soon after they had made contact.

Over the next day, they made three more trips to the settlement, in teams of three. The beer tap was still functioning in the bar. The general store's shelves were empty of canned goods, but the storage room reeked of rotten tomatoes and decomposing squash. The bungalow that passed as the town hall had three empty file cabinets and a collection of records strewn across a desk that painted a mundane, peaceful community. If there had been any medical records, they were gone.

Their flybots picked tread marks and let them plot the exodus paths. They caught up in a day because a thousand people, with a limited number of trucks and a fair bit to carry, did not move fast. They flew low and landed on a bluff overlooking a creek on the convoy's path.

It took the convoy the rest of the afternoon to reach the creek and set up camp. Lin pointed to a clearing half a mile east of the settlement camp where the creek did an S bend.

"Mika, Kristin, with me," she said, back in the skin of the confident leader. Whether she had shaken the ghosts from her past or temporarily shelved them, she took control.

They followed Lin to the bend and took up positions one hundred feet apart along the creek. Half an hour later, a man walked toward the creek. He had a double chin and small eyes that almost shut when he squinted. Beads of sweat speckled his forehead as he carried two five-gallon buckets. He put the buckets down and stretched his back.

Mika walked in his path. "Don't be alarmed."

"I figured you'd eventually find us."

Mika approached him. "Find you?"

The man sat down on a rock. "No one walks north for a thousand miles to settle. I don't know what you're after, but you're no settler."

Mika now recognized the man. He had been in the bar, nursing a beer when Mika and Lin had walked in.

"No, I'm not a settler. But I'm curious."

The man opened his arms. "And I'm fed up with this shit. Living in a monitored environment, not being able to leave except when you're forced to leave. Of being a lab rat."

"Maybe we can help each other."

"I have a wife, a daughter, Lise. She's twelve, and she deserves more than this."

"I don't see why that's a problem."

The man spoke faster and faster. "I tell you what I know, and you take us away from here? All of us?"

Mika nodded.

The man approached and reached for Mika's forearm with intent and desperation. A shot rang out and the man collapsed. Mika moved toward the man on the ground.

"Do not touch him." Kevon Powell stood forty feet away, at the edge of the tree line, holding a pistol. He walked closer. "Told you this would happen if I ever saw you again."

"I thought you meant you'd shoot me."

"I still might." Powell strode toward them. "But Martin was a problem."

Martin didn't move. The bullet had hit him a few inches to the left of his breastplate. He breathed in short, quick rasps and spit blood.

"What are you, his keeper?"

"Close." Powell stopped ten feet away. "We all have our niche in life." His eyes moved from Martin to Mika. "You know what a lion is?"

Mika gave him one nod.

"Back in the day, lions in the wild were revered. They were powerful, majestic animals. When they strayed close to human settlements, they were feared. But when they killed people, they stopped being lions. They became man-eaters. You know what they did to those?" Mika shook his head. "They hunted them and put them down, that's what. Once they acquired a taste for human flesh, they'd keep coming for more no matter what you tried. And Martin was obsessed with going back. No matter what we did, he wasn't going to give up."

"And the problem?"

"Eleven hundred lives depend on that not happening. And you, if he'd touched you, there's a good chance you'd have never been able to go back home."

Martin had stopped moving, his empty eyes pointing to the sky.

"If you touch him, I'll shoot. This time, I do mean you."

Lin walked out of her hiding spot, with her gun aimed at Powell. "I wouldn't do that."

"Figured you weren't far."

"You're about as understanding as mama-bird whose chick fell out of the nest, aren't you?" Lin asked.

Powell shook his head. "If he touches Martin, I'll shoot."

"So will I."

"I believe you, but I don't have any choice here."

"Okay," Mika said. "How about I back away, and no one shoots? And perhaps you can tell us what has got you so spooked."

He took several steps back. They stood in a triangle now, with Lin being out of Powell's aim as long as Powell kept his gun pointed at him.

"I'll tell you what I know, and then you have to leave." Powell lowered his gun. "They gathered us from different towns, about two years ago. Infected us with something. Some died. Most didn't." He lifted his gloved hand. "We're contagious. We can never go home."

"Spreads by contact?"

Powell nodded. "Body fluids." He pointed to Martin. "Sweat will do it. With how many times he touched his face," he shook his head. "If I were you, I wouldn't let an ungloved stranger touch me or pick up a glass at a bar for that matter. But hey, you're still here."

"What is it you're infected with?"

"How the hell should I know? You think we have a lab? I'm telling you what I see."

"And those who died. Did it look like the Purge?"

Powell nodded.

"How about we take some blood."

He shook his head. "No. Too dangerous."

"No one will know."

"Not what I meant. Can't let you unleash this thing back home."

Lin stepped in. "We have containment protocols. I'll handle it myself." Powell didn't look convinced, so she pushed. "It'll be worse if this virus reaches our shores, and we're unprepared."

"Don't fuck it up. I don't know what it is, but it killed over forty of us."

Lin took a kit from her backpack and approached Powell who pulled his sleeve up. She put on her gloves and drew two vials of blood. She sealed them and locked them in a metal container. She knelt down and repeated the procedure with Martin's body.

Mika pointed at Martin. "What's the deal with him?"

"He's tried to escape twice already. The last time, I caught him fifty miles south and barely made it back before a full census."

"That does not make him crazy. I'm surprised more haven't tried. Or that you haven't organized some sort of uprising."

"You don't get it. If any of us leave, they kill everyone. And some of us are pretty hard to kill, so they're very creative. I've seen it once, and I still have nightmares." Powell tapped his sidearm. "Two of my deputies have pistols as well. That's it. I'm not about to fight armed transports with sticks and stones and three pistols."

Lin was back on her feet, holding the two metal boxes. "Who are they?"

"No clue. Our handlers stop by once a week to drop supplies and pick up samples. Once a month, they come in large numbers, trucks, transports, just in case we're not scared enough. It's a full curfew, census, and batteries of tests."

"What are they after?"

"How we respond to this virus. How it spreads."

Mika tapped his tida, projecting faces from the men they had monitored in and out of the settlements. Powell gave him a hard look, as the depth of their surveillance became obvious. Mika pointed to Hatman from their first sighting.

"That's Gibson," Powell said. "He's a tough son of a bitch. You don't want to cross him."

"How many people did you lose over the last year?"

"Not many, but we lost one last month. There's a group of us that stay at the edge of the settlement. They leave on a bus every day. Sometimes one doesn't come back, you know."

"Do you know how many settlements like yours there are?"

"Four that I know."

"Based on?"

"Bits of conversation, merchandise in the back of the delivery trucks, the timing of Gibson's visits. The few others I met at Gibson's compound every three months or so. There were eight of us there, two from each town."

"Where?"

"Two hundred miles northwest." He looked away as though he wanted to say more.

"What is it?"

"Three weeks ago, we had another gathering. The thing is, there were only representatives from three settlements, not four."

"What do you make of it?"

Powell crouched by Martin's body. "You need to get out of here before someone else shows up."

"What about Martin?"

"I'll bury him." Powell closed his eyes. "And find something to say to his wife."

Mika gestured to Powell. "Walk with me?"

Powell did not move.

Mika pointed toward their hidden transport. "Just to that cliff."

Mika walked and Powell followed. Mika stopped twenty yards into the bush and pointed to two metal-framed molded-resin containers and a three-foot tan duffel bag sitting on top of them. "These are yours."

Powell opened the duffle bag, exposing tidas, antennae, screens, and servers. He put it down and unlatched the first container. Sixteen short-barreled, air-cooled M4s sat in two layers of foam. He opened the second container. Magazines and ammunition hid eight more M4s.

Powell closed both containers. "Why?"

Mika shrugged.

"I'm not signing up to be your foot soldier."

"I'm not asking you to. Shit's changing fast out there. If you decide you're fed up, maybe you won't have to use sticks and stones."

They flew straight to the makeshift lab in the Uregs. The trailer where they had done Mika's blood work the previous month now had a twelve-foot-high, forty-foot-long companion. They formed an L and created a courtyard, with their awnings providing cover between them. The space was lit by three down-facing LED lights on eighteen-foot aluminum poles, with wires disappearing to the diesel generator behind the first trailer. As the centrifuge and sequencers in the lab came alive, the generator wheezed louder, spewing a musty stench into the cool air.

The lab was now permanently staffed by a Sentinel and a technician. Lin handed them Martin's and Powell's samples, then closed the metal box containing two more of each sample. The early results confirmed that Martin and Powell had the Purge: in trace amounts in Martin, larger amounts in Powell. As they set up camp, Mika took advantage of the communication link to contact Blue, who appeared on the screen wearing a white cap backward, splitting electric blue hair into two cascading tangles.

"How's the interview going?"

"Nice to see you too."

"So?"

"Halfway done."

"So, I have a T-shirt?" It was the perfect present for Amy. Then it hit him. He no longer needed a present for her.

"Not exactly, no."

He blinked at the screen and leaned forward. "Can you shield this conversation?"

Blue's image shifted to a cartoon and laughed hysterically, the chin dropping to double the face's size and closing shut in quick succession. Blue's real, bemused smirk replaced the cartoon.

"You did not just ask me that, did you?"

"What have you got?"

"Interesting data protocols. Files containing Purge data are encrypted, yeah? Like 2K-bit, AES encryption."

"But you can crack it?"

"No." She glared at him as though he were slow-witted. "But based on headers, context, traffic patterns, and time stamps, I spot two different protocols. One is consistent with known Purge activity and stands at the center of all the furious exchanges when the outbreak started. The other is more subtle, and I only spotted sporadic traffic. Those files have older time stamps."

"Older? Are you sure?"

"You can't ever be sure of anything. But yeah, I'm pretty sure."

"You're hired," he said. "Now, I need you to work on something else."

"Oh goody." She smiled. "Not a fishing expedition but a real job?"

"Find Lori Rose."

Her smile faded and her lips parted. "She's alive?"

"Figuring that out is your job."

"No one has heard from her in nearly a year."

"If we had, what would I need you for?"

"Any leads? Or am I starting cold?"

"Find Kevin Jezek. He'll lead you to her."

She licked her upper lip and then clamped her lips together.

For hounds, very few names brought a reaction. They were all too eager to prove they were the best and ready to take down the previous top gun. Not so with Kevin. It took her ten seconds to reply. "You know what happened to those who tried to find him, yeah?"

Kevin had left a warning to leave him alone. Of course, not every hound had listened. So, Kevin had made an example of the two who had gotten closest. He had corrupted their sniffers, dug up their pasts and shady deals, and exposed their secrets to the world. One had turned up dead within a day. The second was still missing, and Mika doubted it was because he was good at hiding. No one had bothered Kevin since.

"I'm not suicidal," she said when he didn't reply. Then, five seconds later, "Why Rose?"

Because every piece of evidence was pointing to a larger, more complex problem than they had ever grasped. Because Sierra was emotionally bankrupt, unable to inspire her troops when the odds stopped favoring them. Because Yim was intellectually bankrupt, unequipped to chart a course forward. Because Kuipers was morally bankrupt, powerless to recognize anything beyond her political ambition. Because Amy....

"Not a question you should ever ask a client."

"True for most jobs. But you want Lori blasted Rose."

"That makes not asking that question even more important."

She rolled her eyes.

"One final thing."

"Yeah, boss?"

"What do you need from me?"

"What do you mean?"

"This is expensive shit. People who can evolve sniffers for what I'm asking charge a lot. You're working for free. Why?"

"I'll let you know when I need a favor."

"I don't write blank checks."

"The going rate for what you're asking is clear, yeah? I'll stay in the ballpark."

"Fine. And it goes without saying but keep everything you find to yourself."

As the link cut off, her cartoon flashed again, this time rolling her oversized eyes.

CHAPTER 11

IRRADIATED

"You can't say that civilization don't advance... for in every war they kill you in a new way."

—WILL ROGERS

Lin leaned forward on the low folding chair with her hands clasped together and her elbows on her knees. Her coffee cup sat on the three-legged stool next to her, listing toward her by ten degrees. The flames from the fire at the center of the courtyard flickered on her face, keeping the chill of the desert morning at bay.

Mika picked up a folding chair and set it next to her.

"I thought your obsession with coffee was borderline insane, but I have to admit I got used to this routine," she said.

He filled his cup and sat down, clutching the coffee that provided the warmth he needed and the caffeine he did not. A dry twig crackled as it caught fire. "Obsession?"

"You carried pounds of it in your backpack for weeks. Now, I find a bag in every nook on the transport. If I didn't know better, I'd think the bags were multiplying."

"Nothing good comes out of a day that starts without coffee."

She gripped her cup with both hands. "Coffee isn't going to fix today's problems."

"Won't make it worse either." He smiled. "It can't be bad this early in the morning."

"Got new orders from Marin." She took a sip. "We are to destroy any samples we've acquired and return to Marin immediately."

He sipped his coffee. "You don't look pleased."

"We've spent four months chasing ghosts. Now that we have a lead, we need to stop?"

"It means we got their attention."

"I want answers, not their bloody attention."

Yasuo swiped at his screens while Kristin inspected crates in the transport's cargo bay. Mika's eyes drifted in their direction. "Did you tell them?"

She shook her head. "I called Rendon for confirmation. She did not contradict the official orders. But she did reiterate how critical our mission was."

"She wants you to disobey a direct order?"

"Of course not. But communication channels can be unreliable out here."

He put his coffee on the table, holding it for an extra second to ensure it wouldn't slide off. "Well, it was bound to happen. You can't be a Marin major and a Sentinel forever."

She drained her coffee and walked to the pot by the trailer. She refilled her cup, then walked over and topped off his cup.

"So, what's the play?"

She sat back down. "We stay with the mission."

He nudged his head toward the transport. "Are you going to tell them?"

She shook her head.

"They'd stay, you know."

"I know."

"Well, then, we should probably get going soon. You never know when those pesky comms might start working again."

BACK BEYOND THE UREGS, MIKA TOOK A BACKSEAT TO LIN. Their equal partnership had turned into a hierarchy that had to accommodate five Sentinels, now unmoored from the formality of Marin. They surveyed hundreds of square miles a day, but whatever claim they had had on being discreet was gone. They now waited for whoever was pulling the strings on the other side to show their hand.

The next settlement they found had the same organization as Powell's. They observed it for a week, establishing activity patterns and traffic in and out, but did not make contact. The third settlement they approached had no sign of activity. "This one looks abandoned," Yasuo said. "Need a flyby?"

"No," Lin said. They had established early on that they wouldn't fly over settlements, occupied or not. Lin wasn't going to modify her rules for expediency.

Two warehouses with corrugated metal roofs lined the eastern perimeter of the compound. They landed half a mile from the warehouses. He caught Lin out of the team's earshot. "I can take this one," he whispered.

She shook her head. "Kristin, with me," Lin called. She pointed to Mika. "You too." She turned to the transport. "Yasuo, set up camp."

The double-wide steel door to the warehouse was padlocked. Though they were confident the place was empty by now, Mika banged on the door. When nothing happened, Kristin pointed her gun to the lock. Mika nudged it away. It took him twelve seconds to pick the lock. He held it up. "These things are for amateurs," he said and pushed the door open.

He hit the light switch, but the warehouse remained dark, so they turned on their flashlights. Six cylindrical shells filled the warehouse, twenty feet tall and fifty in diameter. He pushed the door open to the first one. A large turbine-like device stood in the center, attached to the concrete floor with fist-sized bolts. A thick pylon reached out to the ceiling and three metal-framed spokes spun out from the pylon, ending in small cabins by the inner shell of the cylinder.

"Centrifuge?" he asked.

Lin hopped on the first cabin and opened its hatch as a response. "Yep."

He stepped next to her. The cabin contained two rows of three seats. She tugged on the seatbelt and stepped off the cabin, running her hand on the tapered metal spoke. "From how sturdy these belts and struts are, I'm guessing this thing could hit twenty Gs."

"Pilot training?" he asked.

"Haven't had a plane that could pull that many Gs in two decades," Kristin said.

"Document all this and move on," Lin said and snapped images of the key parts.

Twenty minutes later they were in the open, facing a settlement unlike any other they had seen. The soot on surfaces, the broken windows, and the bullet-marked walls all pointed to violence. Glass and furniture littered the side streets. There were crisscrossing grooves on the unpaved street, as though heavy objects had been dragged. And then they hit the blood.

First, it was in small stains, as though an injured person had rested here and there and then in an eight-foot semi-circle of dark dirt at the intersection. Similar stains adorned the other side of the street. The blood was leading them to the town square.

"Here," Kristin called, and Mika stood up from one more coppery stain he had stooped to inspect. He walked to where Kristin stood. The house's front door was off its hinges. Bullet marks peppered the walls. Dried blood speckled the floor, and copper smears pointed to where a body had been dragged to the door. Two sets of brown stains on the porch marked where two residents had lost their bowel control. The lack of offending smells and the desiccated remains put the date of the cataclysm at three to four weeks.

"Don't touch anything," Lin said, though for once, her warning was unnecessary. They all had their gloves and masks on. Lin stood behind him. "Where are the bodies?"

They continued their scans, moving toward the square one block at a time. Mika reached the square first. There were two pits, one ten feet by twenty and one about double that. Beyond the pits, two nine-foot square structures jutted out of the square as though concrete walls had been ripped off and stacked next to one another with rebar connecting and interlocking them.

Mika walked to the small pit. What he had expected. Kristin caught up to him as he walked to the larger one. Her eyes widened as though she had just grasped what the pits were for. She stood at the edge. "Holy shit."

The understatement of the day.

Charred bodies filled the large pit. The bloodied bodies in the small pit were covered with a granular blue-white chemical whose purpose must have been to ensure nothing living remained in or on those bodies. The lack of rotting corpse stench meant they had done their job.

The bodies were misshapen and squat, but the nightmare Powell had warned him about wasn't in the pits. It was in the concrete contraptions in front of him. Each of the two structures contained a body, crushed between the concrete sheets. A dozen pieces of rebar went through the bodies at different angles, including one through each jaw, anchoring them to the concrete.

"The radiation is off the charts," Kristin said, reading her screen. "Based on these readings, I'd say those metal bars are highly radioactive."

He approached the trapped bodies when a twitch startled him.

Fuck.

They were still alive. Had they been in those things for weeks?

Lin and Kristin stood behind him. For the first time in his life, he was glad there was someone in charge and that that person wasn't him.

"Get a cutter," Lin said, though it wasn't clear how that would help. There were no gaps for a cutter to work its way in.

He kept his voice down. "No way we can get them out of these without tearing them apart."

Then again, that they were still alive meant they had activated and trained the Purge. So perhaps, there was a way to get them out and have them recover.

Kristin put a dozen sensors around the first man and a few outside of the concrete to create a 3-D image of what they faced. The density scan didn't make sense. It showed a spot far denser than tissue or bone inside the man, about his midriff. Mika grabbed a cutting torch and a four-inch circular saw and put his hand on the concrete.

"One piece at a time," Lin said and turned to Kristin, who was monitoring the operation on multiple spectra ranging from Gamma rays to microwave. "You're the kill switch. At the first sign of trouble, freeze it all," she said, linking their instruments to Kristin's tida.

Mika cut a six-inch strip of concrete. He pushed the saw closer and severed two of the bars that pinned the man in the structure.

"Stop," Kristin shouted, as his saw cut off.

Kristin had their undivided attention. "His pulse picked up," she said. "I'm detecting radiation."

Mika put a tida on the man's exposed side to collect his vitals. The man was so desiccated, he didn't even bleed. The acute radiation syndrome was at a point where virus-enhanced or not, there was no way this body could recover.

After Kristin gave the go-ahead, he resumed cutting. He removed over a quarter of the front sheet from the man, exposing his head and the top of his torso. The more concrete he removed, the more disturbed he became. The man was emaciated, with skin stretched so thin across his frame he looked like a translucent drum and probably weighed no more than eighty pounds.

How long had they been in these things?

"Stop!" Kristin yelled as Mika's saw hit one more rebar. "The penetrating Gamma radiation spiked." Her face was ashen as though she had seen a ghost. "Enough to fry us all."

"Everyone back!" Lin called, and they hustled around the corner, though it was far too late for that. "What the bloody hell happened?"

Mika huddled next to the screen. The source of radioactivity wasn't the bars, but the dense object in the man's torso. It had released enough penetrating Gamma rays to kill anyone in its path. On their screen, the man's gray skin turned red, then his vitals dropped one by one.

"How much did we get?" Lin asked.

"Almost nothing." Kristin pointed to the reconstruction: the concrete had shielded them. The radiation had spread out on a plane squeezed between the two sheets of concrete. None of them had stood in its path.

"I didn't touch the thing," Mika said, and the footage confirmed it.

"It was the pressure," Kristin said. "I queried for pressure changes, and there it was. On the last rebar you cut, the pressure the concrete sheet exerted dropped."

"You didn't accidentally release the radiation," Lin said. "You hit the booby trap. There is no way to free them without irradiating them in the process."

Kristin's eyes were still glued on her screen. "Now what?"

"Now, we get what we came here to collect," Lin said. She pointed in the direction of the second trap. "But first, we take care of that poor bastard."

Mika walked to the second man then circled the concrete contraption. By the time, he came around, Lin stood at the gap, gun out. She extended her arm and pulled the trigger.

She turned to Mika. "Take samples, and let's get the bloody hell out of here."

THEY ATE IN SILENCE. THE CURIOSITY OF THE TWO WHO HAD stayed behind waned quickly as it collided with the sour mood of the exploration party. "I could use a drink right about now," Mika said once everyone but Lin had retired to their tents.

"You're a good guy."

"That's a minority opinion."

"I need to know you're okay."

He had been worried about her. Why was she worried about him?

"I'm fine."

"You say that, but you're not. That was an easy call today. No moral ambiguity. But you couldn't bring yourself to do it."

"I wanted to double-check that he was in the same pickle," he lied.

"That man was already dead."

He gripped the lip of his water cup between thumb and index finger. "No bar within hundreds of miles."

Lin sat next to him. "I'm going to guess you never took the E-test."

He stopped playing with his cup. "It's a stupid test."

"No, you never took it. No way you'd pass. You are so ready to sacrifice yourself."

"I also killed a lot of people."

She shook her head. "Didn't take you for one with too much empathy."

"That's not what the E stands for."

She raised an eyebrow.

"I never took it, but I named it. It's the Eva-test."

Her eyes opened wide, turning her amused glance to a confused one.

"An asshole shot Eva in the Uregs. Point blank, in the chest, as she sat on a chair with a hood on her head. When Sierra had the bright idea that this stupid test would tell us what the recruits were made of, all I could see was Eva's chest exploding. I meant it as a putdown, so she'd back off. She didn't, but the name stuck."

"Call it what you want. But that's not the problem. The problem is that you're not here. And I can't have that. Is it that hard to work with a crew?"

He gave her half a nod.

"Or is it trouble with Chipps?"

He stood up. "That's done and dusted."

"You sound like a monkey, fist still in the jar, insisting he wasn't stealing nuts."

"Give it a rest."

"I need your head in the bloody game."

"Don't worry about me."

"I do. Because though there aren't many guarantees about life, you and I do have one. We're going to have a violent death. In our line of work, there are no other options." She stood up as well and put her right hand on his. "I need you to promise me one thing."

"What?"

"If..." She stopped. "If it's me in that thing, I want you to—"

He withdrew his hand. "Let's not do this."

"Listen to me." She pushed without raising her voice. "I need you to promise me you'll do what you need to do if it's me in there."

"Fine."

She grasped his hand. "Promise me."

"I won't leave you in there."

She gave his hand a light squeeze and let go. "Thank you."

He retreated to his sleeping bag wanting to scream. He kept pointing out how fucked up their world was, but both Lin and Amy insisted on finding reasons to argue with him. And here he was, receiving thanks from a new friend for promising to shoot her.

Fucked up didn't even begin to describe it.

CHAPTER 12

UNTRUE

"The truth will set you free. But first, it will piss you off."
—GLORIA STEINEM

Two days removed from the atrocity they had witnessed, they were perched atop a hill, spying on a compound run with military precision.

Three hundred feet below and half a mile out, a perimeter fence topped with barbed wire delineated a narrow, rectangular space that could have contained four city blocks. A dirt road bisected the compound on its short axis and dead-ended at a carport near the back of the compound. Three barracks stood perpendicular to the road on the west side, a voluminous white tent on the northeast corner. A heavy transport squatted between the tent and the carport, and just south of it across the road from the barracks sat a prefab lab similar to the one they had observed by the sickly workers. Three trucks and two Humvees sat in the carport.

Mika took a sip of water, gargled it, and spat it out. Closer to the cascades, they breathed in the harsh scent of pine and fir forests smoldering to their west. The haze had intensified with soot covering every device left exposed for more than a few minutes. He put his bandana back on and ambled to his sleeping bag as Kristin took over the watch.

He had not spoken more than two words to anyone in days. In battle, trust was their strongest ally, but trust came from a personal connection. He had offered nothing, so he received nothing. He spotted the gung-ho Sentinel near the transport, inspecting screens. He lowered his bandana and approached her.

"What do you make of this compound?"

She tapped the screen. "Center of all the spokes."

It was a good analogy. Geometrically and organizationally, the compound sat at the center of the six settlements they had found: two abandoned, three occupied, one destroyed.

"How long have you worked with Lin?"

"Two years. Major Tomlin was the commanding officer on my first mission."

It was probably some milk run in the Uregs. Nothing like what they faced here. Had Lin requested this team or had Sierra picked it for her? It bothered him that he didn't know and that the people on whose skills he had to rely were strangers to him. "What's your specialty?"

"I'm Special Forces," she said with pride, which told him she hadn't been at it long enough to have one yet. He couldn't think of anything to say, so he walked away from the forced conversation.

Their camp was hidden under a tarp topped by branches; their generator hummed deep in a cave, shielded for noise and heat signature. The observation schedule and notes they took reminded him of his market runs as a kid when they had watched the merchants' habits with Lori. They had recorded the patterns on Lori's old tida that worked one day out of three and scratched them on concrete with stones when the tida refused to cooperate.

Recon work boiled down to one thing: people created patterns, and the better he grasped the pattern, the better he could use their routine to his advantage. And this compound ticked on pattern. Every morning, two trucks left at 11 a.m. to return after sunset. Another left by late afternoon to return by lunch the next day. Every other day, a transport left at dusk to return the next afternoon.

For eight days they watched, their existence a stream of observations occasionally interrupted by strategy meetings. The compound housed Gibson and sixteen mercenaries, nine men, and seven women. A man with a well-trimmed goatee and deep cheekbones came on the second transport run and stayed one night. On day four, one returning truck didn't go to the carport but toward the tent. Two mercs in hazmat suits came out of the truck and carried four bodies to the tent. Then sprayed the truck and left it by the tent.

The central barrack had to be the mess hall and community room because they all gathered there during meal hours and evenings. Only Gibson, the goateed man, and two others ever entered the flat-roofed lab across the barracks, usually after lunch every day. The rest of the time, that structure stayed empty.

When the sun dipped behind the ridge on the ninth day, they were ready. Gibson was on his night lab tour, most likely supervising the sickly workers. The other two trucks had not yet returned, and with the transport on its tour, the compound was at its emptiest. The sentinel whose name floated in and out of his consciousness stood next to him. Beth? Tess? One moment she was real and had a name. The next, she was a nameless stranger, the quiet Special Forces soldier to whom he had spoken four sentences in two weeks.

Lin went over their mission plan, their approach, and their exit in enough detail to fill the next eight minutes. The only part that stuck with Mika was the Sentinel's name: Bess. He looked Bess in the eye and repeated the name to himself. Bess. He was glad that nugget wasn't going to gnaw on him all night. The rest of the briefing consisted of instructions: "Don't talk unless you have to, get as much data as you can, and don't get shot." All and all, it was a sound strategy.

"Any questions?" When none of the solemn faces answered, Lin nodded. "Okay, then." She pointed to Bess. "Bess with Mika. The rest with me."

Mika and Bess moved to the north perimeter and slit the fence with twelve-inch bolt cutters. They hadn't detected any electronic surveillance except for cameras by the front and back entrances to the lab. He didn't expect the mercenaries to be sloppy, but there was little reason for an abundance of caution when they were a thousand miles from potential hostiles.

As they approached the back of the lab, Mika deployed his best intrusion sniffer, a legacy from Kevin. Though Kevin had been gone almost a year, his sniffers were better than anything he could get on his own. This one overtook any surveillance equipment and replayed random, empty segments from the previous hour, adjusting it all for time and light conditions. Unless they analyzed the footage with special tools, they would never know the feed had been tampered with.

They stepped into the lab, and Mika put a hand up to stop Bess. He deployed another sniffer to shield them acoustically as well as visually while inside. "Keep an eye out," he said.

Two abutting desks sat in the middle of the room. Benches ran along two walls, covered in electronics, scopes, and centrifuges. An RNA-sequencer with a smooth, black front and a forty-inch screen monopolized one narrow wall. The fourth wall alternated with metal shelves and stainless-steel refrigerators.

He moved toward the desks and swiped the main screen on. He put the drive next to the screens and tapped his tida to clone the database. As his tida displayed the process, he rummaged through the three metal shelves full of blood samples, with dates and codes he couldn't decipher.

Twenty-five minutes later, his tida lit in soft green letting him know they had it all cloned. He stashed the drive into a Faraday bag, sealed it, and stuffed it into his zippered jacket pocket. They retraced their steps and had just cleared the fence when the hum of a light transport intruded on the silent evening.

Ten seconds later, its lights poked through the haze, and the transport landed behind them, between the tent and the fence. Two mercs in hazmat suits loaded six bodies from the tent to the transport. Three mercs stepped out of the mess hall and walked toward the tent, chatting with the pilot. As the transport took off, most likely destined for Marin, the mercs turned south and strode inside the perimeter toward the gate.

Lin's team hadn't checked in, most likely because they were pinned outside of the gate by the transport's arrival and current activity. Across the compound, the lights of a truck that bounced toward the gate appeared, poking through the brown dust cloud that disturbed the gray fog for a few feet before merging with it.

Mika hoped Lin's team would stay put until the activity ceased, but his job was to get the drive to safety, so he and Bess picked up the pace. They were halfway to the wooded hills when shouting rang from the entrance. Mika crouched and whispered, "Down." Bess complied. He crawled toward Bess on his elbows, brought his index to his lips, and moved away.

Gunfire rang in the distance. Two shots were followed by a three-second silence, then two more shots pinging off metal. Uninterrupted machine-gun fire followed. Two bright spotlights appeared above the fence by the gate, and mercenaries spilled out. Six mercs hopped into the two Humvees and sped out, others ran toward the gunshots.

One Humvee screeched to a halt by the gate but the other circled the perimeter, with four roof-rack lights blinding anything in its path. When they reached the slit on the fence, they stopped and turned the Humvee to face out. Two mercs stepped off, semis drawn; the third stayed in the driver's seat. One inspected the fence; the other walked out, straight toward Bess, stopping thirty feet short. Then he advanced again, but Bess remained still as a rock.

When he was three feet from Bess, Mika tossed a pebble toward the Humvee. The merc turned around, his rifle aimed at the disturbance, but instead of heading toward the sound, he backed away, tripping over Bess. He fired into the air as he landed on his back.

Bess rolled up to one knee and fired at the guard's face, but the muzzle flash gave her away. The Humvee turned a few feet, and its roof-rack lights found Bess. A spray of gunfire followed with bullets tearing into her.

Mika went up on one knee and fired, hitting the merc standing by the Humvee. He then fired four times, taking out the roof-rack lights, and rushed forward to shoot the driver as he stepped off his vehicle. Mika scrambled back to Bess, put a finger to her jugular, and found her pulse. He lifted her by her collar, shouldered her, and ran toward the tree line.

A spotlight flickered around them—a random search from inside the camp—but by the time it reached their path, they were in the thick. Bess was bleeding from two wounds to the chest and one each to her thigh and shoulder. He gave her a stick to bite and cut into the wounds. He dug the bullets out and inspected her bleeding thigh. The bullets had missed the bones and artery. She would be good to go in ten minutes, but he couldn't wait that long. He took the bag containing the cloned drive from his jacket and pushed it into her hand.

"Head to the transport and wait."

"I'll be fine in a few minutes."

He closed her hand around the Faraday bag. "Bess, one of us has to take this back. This is where the bodies in Marin come from. This drive has more data than we've gotten in months. Go to the transport, and if we're not back in an hour, head back to Sierra."

She gave him one nod.

He ran toward the lights on the compound's south side. Four strobe lights lit the dirt road and clearing. A Humvee stood in the middle of the road, front tires blown out, steam escaping from the engine grill. The driver and passenger doors were open. Three faces stared out the back seat, and three armed mercenaries stood in the cab, partially hidden by the tarp that covered the Humvee's side.

A Sentinel had been shot in the head. Not Yasuo, who was sprawled a few feet away, bleeding from what appeared to be knife wounds. Mika exhaled as he found Lin. Two mercs held guns to her head. Gibson stood a few feet from her, blood from two fresh bullet wounds staining his shirt.

Gibson turned away from Lin. "I know you're not far," he yelled. "And if you come out now, I won't shoot these two in the eye."

Mika walked toward them, his left hand under his right, steadying his gun as he approached. The lights found him.

"Put the gun down," Gibson said.

He had once made the mistake of giving up his weapons before walking in to talk to someone he didn't trust. It had ended with a lot of bodies and a much closer call than he wanted to repeat. "Not a chance. The first sign of trouble, I'll fire. And I'm a good shot."

Gibson smirked. "If that's the way you want to play it."

Mika got within thirty feet of Gibson and forty to Lin, who had bruises on her forehead and blood on her cheek and chin. Kevon Powell was in the back of the Humvee, eyes moving from Gibson to Lin to Mika.

"I'm Gibson," the man said, taking three steps toward him. "But you already know that."

Mika planted his feet wide and kept the gun pointed at Gibson.

"And you're Mika Bayley. Phillips' pet project."

Mika's whole body rose, all weight on the ball of his feet. He made eye contact with Lin but didn't reply.

"Yeah, we go way back with Phillips. Waaay back, if you know what I mean."

Phillips had mentioned associates going back to the first days of the virus. Mika's gaze wandered around the clearing, connecting with Kristin's body. "A little late to be friendly."

"Unfortunate. I lost soldiers too. In fact, more than you, and I wasn't the one who came for an assault."

"What do you want?"

"I want answers. But short of that, I'll settle for more heads."

Mika doubted he could explain their presence here, but he could buy time for Bess. "We're trying to find out where the bodies in Marin come from," he said. "And now we know."

"Forget the bodies. If you know what Phillips was up to, you're on the wrong side."

He didn't know whose side he was on, or what the sides were, so he remained silent.

"You're aware of the Puries' power grab last year. They were misguided and delusional, but they weren't wrong: one side is going to control the other. Unlike the Puries, we have a winning hand."

Mika glanced at Lin. Her lips were pressed so hard against each other they had nearly disappeared. "How about you stop pointing a gun to her head."

Gibson nodded, and his soldiers brought their guns down. Lin stood up and took two steps toward Yasuo who was unconscious, lying in a pool of blood, along with two other bodies.

"Don't touch him," Gibson said. Lin kept her eyes on Yasuo for five more seconds, then turned to face them, which meant his injuries weren't lethal for a trained Sentinel.

"The Puries are still stuck on Marin and Kern," Gibson said. "They've lost Marin, but they've got leverage in Kern."

"And you still work for them."

Gibson spat his next words. "I do not work for them."

"So how are your infected bodies popping up in Marin?"

Gibson grimaced. "You need to get your head out of your ass. Puries are done in Marin. Let them go. They're a dying species."

Mika had come to hate that word. And such grandiose statements always led to mass graves. "How do you figure? Marin is already tearing itself apart."

"Not tearing apart at all. More like applying a tourniquet before you start bleeding. Because the truth isn't going to ooze out. It's going to explode."

"I still don't get the point of sending bodies."

"There's little harm to Marin. The virus is inert twenty-four hours after the host dies, and these bodies have been dead a lot longer than that. But it's enough to get Marin to wake up."

"What are you after?"

"Isn't it obvious?" Gibson groaned. "To figure out who made the viruses."

"Somebody made it? You're saying it wasn't from the comet?"

Gibson's eyes widened, as though his intentions had been self-evident. "Those two thoughts are not mutually exclusive. It's so much more interesting than what Phillips suspected, what the viruses were trying to do. And who fucked it up. But we need to be sure, so we need more data. And we can't do this while the Puries are playing their asinine games and threatening us all with Kern's military power."

"Who is this 'we'?"

Gibson smiled. "Me and my partner, Tulum."

"And the settlements are just data?"

"Some are."

"We saw what happened to your data down south."

Gibson scratched his cheek with two fingers. "I don't like those any more than you do. Sometimes when you face two bad outcomes, you have to choose the lesser evil." Gibson took his silence as a license to continue. "We're close, very close. You and your gang—you're like us. So, don't get in our way, and we'll be done in half a year."

"And what is it that you're close to?"

"Finding the makers of the viruses. The why, the how."

Mika's jaw slacked and Gibson smiled.

"Yeah, exactly. Stop playing games and look at the real threat."

Mika exhaled from his nose to prevent himself from speaking. He wanted to know what Gibson knew and how he knew who the makers were. But any of those questions would have given Gibson the leverage he wanted. "Right now, you are the threat."

Gibson put two fingers on his lips and his eyes moved from Mika to Lin. "This is a one-time truce. If you get in my way again, I won't be held responsible for the consequences." Gibson brought his index finger above his head and swirled it. As his team fell back, one of the mercs brought a Mylar blanket and dumped it on the ground next to Yasuo.

Mika approached Lin and put a hand on her shoulder. "Okay?"

She nodded. He kept his gun aimed at Gibson but put his left arm around to support her.

"He needs to stay in isolation for seventy-two hours," Gibson said, pointing at Yasuo. "So, should you, and if you want to stay here, we have the facilit—"

"No."

"Suit yourself. Don't touch him without gloves and don't let him cough on you."

"What does he have?"

"Nothing good," Gibson said and walked away.

Mika carried Yasuo wrapped in the Mylar blanket, and Lin brought up the back. They made it to the transport minutes before Bess was set to leave. Ten minutes into their flight, Lin let Bess take the controls.

She turned to him. "So," she said in a neutral tone without taking her eyes off him. "What was that all about?"

He didn't know where to start, so he didn't. They had been on a recon mission. But the first shot had come from Lin, or perhaps Kristin. And they hadn't shot at guards, but at Gibson's Humvee, blowing out its tires. It was a miracle four of them were still alive.

"You tell me. You're the one who shot their Humvee."

"I knew you had what we came for. When Gibson's Humvee appeared, I gambled that we could grab him. That asshole was the secondary mission. If we captured him or his partner, we'd know what they want with the Marin Council."

It all snapped into place: Sierra's distance, Lin's caginess, the new team with new loyalties. Marin's order to recall them. Even Gibson's words now made sense. He should have been mad, but Lin's deception didn't measure up to the whopper he had been keeping from her.

"And all this time I thought we were a data collection mission."

She didn't back down. "We were. This was an opportunity that presented itself. And it would have worked had he come back alone as he did for the last eight days. Instead, we stumbled on the bloody day they hosted the settlement leaders."

That was the problem with patterns. As soon as you trusted them, they bit you. "What happened to Yasuo?"

"Got into a knife fight with two mercenaries who jumped out of the Humvee. One tackled him. Turns out a knife fight between hard-to-kill soldiers gets bloody fast. Now Gibson thinks he contracted whatever those folks had—whatever Powell's people had." She tapped the dash rhythmically with her fingers. "Now you. What was Gibson talking about?"

"He was trying to rile me up."

"That's a bigger pile of shit than a herd of elephants can generate after finding a soft-bark-tree grove."

He stayed silent.

"I lost a soldier tonight, one I've known and respected for years. So, I'm not in the mood for games. Who the fuck is Phillips, and what the fuck are Puries?"

Phillips was secret. The Puries were secret. "It's complicated."

Lin jumped out of her chair, grabbed his forearm, and pulled him to the cargo hold, out of Bess' earshot. "Don't fuck with me."

He shook his arm clear. Kristin was gone, and not because she had made a mistake, or Lin had been careless, or Mika had missed a clue. She was gone because there was no beating the odds, not if they kept playing this game. In their line of work, they played against the house. They occasionally got ahead, but in the long run, the house always won.

"Okay," he whispered.

He flipped the hot water dispenser switch and walked to Yasuo who was strapped to a cot, still sweating, still nonresponsive.

He came back and sat across from the galley. The dispenser chimed and Lin poured the near-boiling water over two coffee capsules. She handed him one and sat down next to him.

"Talk."

"Met Phillips nearly a year ago. I'd been searching for Eva after she'd disappeared from the hospital. I dug into miracle recoveries, where they happened, who it happened to, and what caused them. I went after hospitals, but records were incomplete as though someone was erasing key parts. Phillips nudged me in the right direction and provided what was missing."

"The bloody drug."

He took a deep breath as though his long exhalation would soften the impact of his words. "There is no drug."

She snorted. "Of course, there is. There is nothing natural about us."

"No, nothing natural. But it's not a drug. It's the Purge."

"What?" She was squinting now with her eyes pushed beyond focus.

The nutty, oily coffee scent filled the cabin. He took a sip. It was more bitter than it should have been.

"The Purge. That's your miracle drug. Many survivors still carry the virus."

"In trace amounts. Everyone knows that."

"Once you activate it, it learns to repair you, and it's no longer trace amounts."

"So, you still need a drug to activate it."

"No drug. Injuries and poison. If they damage you at the right pace, it keeps getting better at it. They weren't training you. They were training the Purge."

She opened her mouth and closed it again before saying, "That's a bit hard to swallow."

"Phillips was a scientist and one of the first trained ones. His life's mission was to uncover the secrets of the Purge. Why it killed so many, and why it repaired a precious few."

She raised her hand, and he stopped. "So, what does Gibson want with the bloody Purge?"

"Not sure."

She took a sip. "And where is Phillips now?"

"Not sure about that either. He's been gone a year."

Her head moved in short, quick jerks, most likely cross-referencing every bit of data while matching every date and every event to what she had heard. "Puries?"

"Pure humans. Those who beat the virus, those who can't heal. They've been manipulating Marin and Kern for years. Lester was one of them. I thought they were behind all this, but now I'm not so sure."

"This is too much," she said, putting a hand up. "Puries, virus repair, Gibson." She shook her head. "When the fuck were you going to tell me?" The rage in her eyes was too raw to be assuaged by words, so he stayed silent. "You weren't going to."

Her eyes widened, then narrowed, progressing from dismayed to disappointed to betrayed. "Rendon knows all this?"

He nodded. "I thought Gibson was helping the Puries grab power in Marin and Kern. That is probably what Sierra thought, considering your mission. But that's gone now, and we need to figure what he's after because it sure as hell isn't helping the Puries. But first, we need to get out of here without getting shot."

"I'm so pissed right now I can shoot you myself."

"Let's not do that." He softened. "Lin, nothing changed. We still have enemies out there. They're still trying to kill us. The only difference is that what you thought was a chemical was in fact a process. Everything else you were told is true."

"I don't like being used. And I don't like being lied to."

"Focus on the big picture. Everything is exactly as it was ten minutes ago: your friends, your allies, your enemies. They're exactly the same."

"No." She put her still-full coffee cup on the counter, walked to the cockpit, and put on a headset. "Not my friends."

CHAPTER 13
SIX FLAVORS

"The best way to find out if you can trust someone is to trust them."

—ERNEST HEMINGWAY

On day three of their quarantine, Yasuo slipped into a deep sleep bordering on a coma and snored like a tea kettle running dry. Though his wounds had closed, he sweated as though he were melting, and his exhalation reeked like a rotten-egg-rubbed tuna can dunked in a slaughterhouse gutter.

Mika raised his collar in a futile attempt to keep the desert chill away. It was almost dawn, and he had the last watch of the night. He put gloves on and lifted Yasuo's eyelids. Yasuo didn't react to light. He took a kit from the med lab, rolled up Yasuo's sleeve, and drew three vials of blood. Yasuo didn't stir at the needle going in. Mika marked the time and sealed two vials.

He plugged the third one into the med unit and disposed of his gloves. He washed his hands before heading to the transport's galley to set the water to heat. He unsealed the oatmeal bag and scooped a large heaping into his bowl. Bess had woken up and was sitting in her sleeping pack, stretching.

He held up the bag. "Oatmeal?"

She nodded, put on a long-sleeved shirt, tied her hair in a ponytail, and headed his way.

He dumped oatmeal into a second bowl and poured hot water over both bowls. He stirred them with a plastic spoon and handed her a bowl.

She took it, sat down on the transport's ramp. "Thank you."

"You're welcome."

"I meant for the other night." She took a spoonful and chewed.

"Don't mention it."

She swallowed and produced a smile that may not have been forced.

"Yasuo is not going to heal," he said.

"What do you mean?" She squinted in surprise. Even a few months were enough to alter her reality and to enforce the belief that sickness and injury no longer applied to them.

"His wounds are closed but he's got flu-like symptoms." Which also meant Purge-like because the Purge mimicked a bad flu up until his lungs liquefied and came out in little red chunks as he coughed.

The med unit gave three short beeps followed by a long one. Mika swiped to push the results to the screen. The Purge activity was high, which he had expected. It had partially repaired his knife wounds, but it wasn't doing anything to his lungs, which were full of fluid.

He scarfed down his oatmeal and tossed some protein bars and two bottles of water in his backpack. He walked to the transport and took a set of Yasuo's vials going back twelve hours, along with the samples they had collected from the settlement and the cloned drive. He packed them into a padded box and stuffed them in the case of the motorbike.

"What are you doing?" Lin frowned as though he had stepped on her kitten.

"The shitty port-a-lab here," he said, pointing his thumb to the transport, "says there is nothing wrong with Yasuo. Except, clearly, there is. I need to get to a real lab."

"No."

He didn't want to argue with her. But he also didn't want her anger at him to prevent them from doing what needed to be done.

"We're stuck here. We don't know what Yasuo has or whether we have it too. Let me find some answers."

"Too bloody risky to break quarantine. You can infect anyone you meet."

"I'm only going to the Uregs lab. I won't touch anything."

"Yeah, that'll protect you as much as a mesh condom."

He tossed his backpack in and closed the latch of the bike's case. "Let's not do this."

Bess put down her bowl down and moved closer, standing in the path where he would have to roll the bike, about ten feet out. Her smile vanished, and she reached for her sidearm, though she kept it holstered. They were all on edge and ready to go off at the first hint of a spark.

"Let's really not do this."

Lin ratcheted the pressure down by waving her hand downward to Bess, who let go of her gun. "Not saying I agree to this, but assuming I do, what's the play?"

"I take one set of samples to the lab. See if any of it links to the deaths in Marin. Use the communication link there to contact Blue and hand her the samples and the drive."

"Who is Blue?" Her voice went up, steeped in suspicion.

"A hound. A good one. She'll find answers and better yet, she'll know if anyone is monitoring these searches."

"And you trust her?"

"As much as I trust anyone I've known a month."

Lin laughed in small coughs, and the cloud of mistrust dissipated. "That's not much of an endorsement."

"It's all I got. And right now, we need her. If anyone can break into that drive, it's her. We also need her to cover Sierra's deficiencies."

The edges of Lin's lips edged upward. "Didn't know she had deficiencies."

"She's assuming Gibson works with the Puries, which means every action she takes is the exact opposite of what she needs to do. Also, she's put way too much faith in the Sentinels."

Bess' head spun in their direction, and the remnants of laughter left Lin's face. "That's a deficiency now?"

"After what we heard from Gibson, yeah. Not only are we watching the wrong people, but dozens of bodies are getting into Marin undetected. Do you trust Gibson? Or his partner? Or whoever in Marin or the Shed is working with him?"

Lin's silence told him he had hit a nerve. She stood there, pensive, but the defiance was gone. He grabbed the bike's handlebars and kicked its leg stand but didn't push it forward.

"Fine," Lin said after ten long seconds. "But don't touch anything or anyone."

"I'm not going to fuck Blue."

Lin didn't blink. "Too bad. It might do you some good."

Bess stepped back as though twelve feet of air would act as insulation.

He reached the Uregs lab by mid-afternoon. The large trailer was gone and the smaller one was locked up. The recall order Lin had ignored must also have been sent to the lab. He relaxed, relieved to have avoided awkward conversations and virus containment protocols.

The communication antenna was still there, so he powered up the generator and informed Blue he had samples for her. He had expected she would set up an encrypted channel and come pick up the samples after he left. But she told him to stay put because she did not trust the lab's security measures for what she had to show him.

It would take her most of the afternoon to get there, so he settled under the shade of a four-trunked sycamore and slept for two hours, trying to erase the bumpy hours he had spent on the bike. He woke to his tida chiming that Blue was thirty minutes out. He picked the trailer's lock and rummaged through the cabinets. The Sentinels must have left in a hurry because they had left supplies behind, including coffee. He plugged the kettle into the battery rack of the trailer and dropped a coffee capsule in the cup.

He was sitting on a tree stump sipping coffee when a Jeep appeared in the distance. It stopped forty yards away, and Blue hopped off, pink hair blowing in the wind. She put on plastic gloves and a jacket that sealed at the waist. She grabbed an insulated bag from the cab and strutted toward him. She set the bag down and stepped back.

"I'd offer coffee, but I don't think you should touch or drink anything from here."

"So, you're contaminated?" she asked.

"Don't think so, but no harm in being cautious."

"I hate coffee anyway." She pointed to the box next to him. "That's the package, yeah?"

He nodded. The images from the burned and chemically cleansed bodies in the pits of the destroyed settlement floated in his vision. For Yasuo's sake, he hoped there was another option.

He doubted it.

"Samples and an encoded drive. If you can break into that, we might get some answers."

She went back to the Jeep and came back with a clear box. She put it on top of the samples and the bottom gave way, swallowing the smaller box, and sealing itself. She eyed the Faraday bag containing the drive. "Who is that for?"

"For now, you and me. If I'm not back in a day or two, give it to Eva."

"Not Sierra?"

"Eva can decide, based on…." He shrugged. "She'll know."

She nodded and put the drive in a second pouch, then took both the pouch and sealed box with samples back to the cab. She came back and sat on a log across from him eight feet away.

He reached into the insulated bag and grabbed a tightly wrapped burrito. He tore the paper and sniffed the flour tortilla. Whiffs of fresh cilantro and onion caused him to salivate. He took a bite. It was cold but tasted rich with eggs still soft and potatoes still firm because they hadn't spent weeks in the vacuum-packed container of a transport cargo hold.

"Nice," he said as he chewed. He rummaged through the bag and found a bottle hiding below the burritos. "Nice," he repeated.

"Eva said you'd like that."

As usual, Eva was right. Which brought him to his problem. "I need you to dig into the communications in and out of this lab."

She licked her lips and pressed them together. "This connects to the Shed."

"Are you working for the Sentinels right now?"

She shook her head.

"Good. I need you to dip into Sentinel communications. Particularly at the top."

She didn't reply, but the lines on her forehead deepened, broadcasting her discomfort.

"Is there a problem?"

"No," she said, finally relaxing her eyes and forehead. "I'm just trying to figure out whose side you're on."

"Me too." He forced a smile and took another bite of the burrito. "So, why are you really here? Why did you ask me to stay instead of dropping the box and heading out?"

"The last set of samples you brought caused a lot of commotion. The Marin Executive Council freaked out at the news."

"How do you know that?"

She winked. "I keep an eye on them too. With the bodies in Marin, I thought they might find something interesting. I mean, they should be looking into the Purge, no? But they're more interested in who's looking into the Purge."

"Do they know you're looking?"

She cocked her head. "Puhleeze."

"So, what do they have?"

"They're convinced it's a new variant," she said with an exaggerated fake smile.

"But you don't agree."

Her cheeks relaxed. "Nope. It's an old variant." She tapped her tida. Numbers and charts popped up between them. "Remember the different data protocols I mentioned? Turns out there was something there." She pointed to his left. "The numbers in this column are the file sizes for all the virus samples, averaged over years of traffic." She pointed to the rows. "These are from labs scattered all over the world, yeah? Ninety-nine percent of the files are the same size. But these," she said, pointing to four highlighted rows, "are larger."

"Can it be the different encryption?"

She gave him a saddened look. "Like I didn't think of that."

"Sorry."

"The question is: Why are the viruses from those labs longer?"

"Are they all the same length?"

"Not quite, but those are within the encryption errors."

"So, this is where you tell me you've decrypted them?"

"Told you, I can't access the files, much less decrypt them. They're physically sealed."

"Where are the special labs?"

"That's where it gets interesting. I sniffed data from over thirty labs. Live Purge samples never moved, yeah? The labs only worked on the samples from their regions. There were four cases of physical movement. All originating at the Tromso comet site. One went to a lab in Siberia, one to Sweden, one to China, and, ta-da, one to Shasta."

"Shasta?"

She spoke faster and faster. "Yes, to a lab under the mountain, under that irradiated wasteland. Here's where things get interesting. Those longer versions of the virus? They came straight from Tromso and predate the Purge outbreak."

There was just enough data to spin any story they wanted. "What does it mean?"

She grinned, displaying all her teeth.

"You got something else?"

She reached inside her jacket and pulled out a folded piece of paper. She put it between them, put a round rock on it, and retreated to her spot. "From Shasta."

"I thought you couldn't get inside their systems."

"I can't. But someone inside sent this from a personal account. It's out of the secure servers, but not out of the last filter. It's been stuck there for twenty-five years."

He picked up the paper and unfolded it. His eyes moved from the picture to her, then back to the picture. "What the fuck?"

"The older data are organized over a pattern of six. Six dedicated servers, six data protocols, and logistics to support six teams." She pointed to the picture. "You do the math."

He looked at the picture again. "I don't want to offend you." He drew a breath through his nose instead of finishing his sentence.

"But you're going to anyway, yeah?"

"Look, there were hundreds of good hounds sniffing around this shit for decades."

"Not that many competent ones, but yeah."

"And by now, with the shitty way Marin handles information, there must be dozens who know where we got the new virus samples."

"The old virus samples."

"You're telling me no one found this in twenty years? People have been after anything Purge-related forever."

"What are you asking?"

He waved the picture. "How did you stumble on this shit?"

She interlocked her hands, the webbing between her index and middle fingers on each hand pushing the gloves tighter. "You're right. Maybe a hundred hounds have the skills for this, and maybe a dozen know enough to dig. But only one spent decades trying to hack her way into Shasta."

"Why?"

All playfulness was gone from her eyes. "My mom worked there. Back before..." She tugged at her right glove, stretching it and letting it snap back into shape. "She's probably still there."

"You know it's been twenty-five years, right?"

She squeezed her eyes nearly shut. "This asshole thing—do you work at it, or does it come naturally?"

He folded the picture and tucked it in his shirt pocket. "What were you doing in my Jeep, and what do you want from me?"

She sighed and her eyes reset. "Nothing. I'm repaying a debt to Eva by helping you."

"How do you know Eva?"

"She lived with my little sister."

Past the gaudy hair, the resemblance reached from the back of his mind and slapped him for his sloppiness. Blue was an older version of Eva's friend from the orphanage, the martial arts instructor whose sorrow had convinced him that Eva had not left on her own.

"Jen?"

A sad smile stretched across her lips but did not reach her eyes. "Jen loved to push boundaries. Eva softened her. When she was with Eva, she was the adult. After that, she didn't think I was mothering her so much, you know?" She stood up and looked into the distance past the trailer. "I tracked the gang that hit the orphanage. Eva took care of the rest."

He sipped coffee, letting her take her time. He cupped the mug in both hands, absorbing the warmth. When not cooled by the chilly bay breezes, coffee stayed hot surprisingly long.

Her gaze returned to him. "She did it for me. She didn't see the point in revenge. And you helped her apparently with one of the tougher guys. So, see, you don't owe me anything."

He didn't recall. He had helped Eva take care of assholes without asking what it was about.

"Anyway, when I was trying to find a way into Shasta's systems, I found a Uregs compound that made a living trading old information. Their barely competent hounds hooked the backup power grid of a data center to solar panels to get servers up and running. Unlike Shasta or the real labs, their encryption wasn't worth shit. Took me half an hour to get in. They have secondhand accounts like old news shows, police reports, comedy routines, and political spats. Mostly nostalgic shit, but that's the thing with data. Once you get enough, you can reconstruct the hidden event by observing its ripples and by how everyone reacts to it. And it all points to one place."

"Shasta."

She licked her upper lip. "I first spotted the repetition of six in their data banks. They even had six-week cycles on supply schedules and maps for the settlements you visited. I finally put it all together when I found that," she said, flicking her index finger to his breast pocket. "Six test tubes can't be a coincidence, yeah?"

He took the picture from Shasta from his pocket. "The one who tried to send this—was it your mom?"

She shook her head. "She'd never have done that. She was IT security—too straight, too by the book. I learned a lot from her and then added a few tricks of my own." She chuckled. "See, I'm in the family business. Unfortunately, her team did their job too blasted well."

His eyes drifted to the image. He tried not to think and not to speculate. But it was impossible to not let his imagination run wild. The picture was a close-up of a blue aluminum, ten by four test tube rack. The right-back slot had a sealed tube with PRG written in black marker over the tape. Three tubes occupied the front row, starting from left, followed by a gap, and two more tubes on the fifth and sixth slots.

The markings on the tapes read PRG-1, PRG-2, PRG-3, PRG-5, and PRG-6.

CHAPTER 14

FIGHT OR FLIGHT

"The single and most dangerous word to be spoken in business is no. The second most dangerous word is yes. It is possible to avoid saying either."

—LOIS WYSE

The fragrance of Chancellor Yim's tea, a mix of bergamot oil and citrus that harmonized with the intricate wood trim on every door and window, overpowered the council room. Amy sipped her coffee, whose flavor and scent intruded on a tea temple. Her presence in the hallowed executive council was probably as much an affront to Yim and Kuipers as her coffee was.

Amy's clutch on her coffee cup tightened.

She again sat away from the window across from Kuipers and Yim. To her right sat Harding, the judge who spoke only to agree with Yim and was as much a part of the décor as the molding. Their fifth member, General Dabiri, was absent. Dabiri supported everything Kuipers proposed, though more forcefully than Harding ever supported Yim. Not that it mattered because Yim had given up the pretense of running Marin and let Kuipers get her way on every issue.

Amy rested her elbows on the soft leather armrest and brought her chin on her interlaced fingers. General Kuipers continued to bore them, talking for fifteen minutes about the reduced military budget and another ten on the decline in military recruitment. She almost sounded as though she missed the "good ole days" where a Kern attack was imminent. Harding listened with intent and occasionally took notes even though Kuipers said nothing worth remembering.

"The main reason I convened this meeting is to discuss a new alliance," Kuipers said. "I have been contacted by an individual who has knowledge about the virus that has killed many of our citizens. Aiden Tulum, the leader of a compound northeast of us, has studied this new virus for nearly two years. He has provided preliminary information that our scientists have corroborated. He is willing to share all his knowledge with us."

Amy waited for the cacophony of senseless questions to cease. "What does he want in return?"

"In return for medical records, he is requesting our approval to relocate his settlements."

"Relocate?"

"North of us, to areas that we neither developed nor plan on developing. He wants to set up a new town and, in due time, join the Marin-New Cal federation. I am not concerned with the details of what such an incorporation entails. We have a roadmap with what we signed with New California. We can settle the details when appropriate. What I want is an agreement to enter in good faith negotiations with Tulum in exchange for what he knows about this new virus."

"Proceed," Yim said as though Kuipers needed her assent.

"We haven't discussed anything," Amy said.

"All our analysis shows that this virus is similar but not identical to the Purge. We have the best scientists and the best laboratories. They do not yet understand how its incubation cycle works or how it spreads. I have no doubt that in due time our scientists will uncover this virus' secrets. But I'm not willing to waste a chance to team up with an expert," Kuipers said.

"It is convenient for Tulum to arrive just when we need him."

Yim grimaced. "We had inklings of new settlements a year ago. I shared it with General Rose, but she was convinced they were hostile."

"To Lori Rose, everyone was an enemy," Kuipers said. Yim and Harding nodded.

The statement was most likely accurate. But given the choice of trusting Lori's or Kuipers' judgment and motivation, Amy's vote was for the person who wasn't here.

"But they're not our enemy. We need to stop looking at the world with warrior eyes."

Harding was too meek to speak, and Yim had nothing to say. Amy had no expectation of winning an argument because it was clear Kuipers had already made up her mind. But Amy pushed to test Mika's theory that what Kuipers reacted to might shed light on her motives.

"A new alliance requires senate approval, then council approval. If we follow the constitutional process, how do we promise an outcome we can't predict?"

"Good points, Vice-Chancellor. But we are out of options. With over thirty recorded deaths in four months, we can no longer use the 'wait and see' approach. We must act now, and I, for one, want to act with as much information as I can gather. Tulum offers information at a reasonable price. There is nothing but radiated wasteland to our north."

"Then why does he want it?"

Kuipers pursed her lips. "What?"

"If there is nothing of value to our north, why does Tulum want to build a city there?"

"They are isolated. They'd like to move closer to trade partners. Also, they're in arid lands. This move gets them more rain for crops. Is this the topic we should be discussing?"

"I'm simply trying to understand their motivations."

"They're offering help. Is that so hard to believe?"

It was. It was too convenient that a magical solution had presented itself so soon after strange corpses had appeared.

"The first step is for us to implement the quarantine plan I drew up," Kuipers said and moved to detailed logistics.

Amy had to hand it to Kuipers. She had mastered the art of hiding big revelations in long and boring tirades. As Kuipers droned on, Amy moved her attention to the window and the square below. The activity had picked up with soldiers moving in crisp lines. Some were moving out toward the city, but too many were moving toward their building.

Two urban-combat transports buzzed the square.

"I am asking for a vote," Kuipers said, snapping Amy back to attention. "And we cannot untangle these questions, so we need one vote on all three issues: Accepting Tulum's offer, setting up the quarantine, and implementing martial law."

"Where is General Dabiri?" Amy asked, as the fifth member of the council was absent.

"General Dabiri has voted in support of this move," Kuipers said. "She is downstairs, convening with senate leaders, top judges, and mayors. They are discussing the tactical implementation of our plan while we discuss the strategic decisions."

Amy did not point out that Kuipers had overstated the level of discourse they had shared.

Kuipers took a deep breath, and her gaze moved around the room. Harding had been picked to make up the numbers and to punish the judiciary for Lester's stupidity. Yim had already given all control to Kuipers. So, the vote was a sham; Kuipers had already won.

That Kuipers had gathered the executive council, as well as all leaders across the three branches of government in one building rang alarm bells in Amy's mind. Anyone who may have dared oppose Kuipers in public was, at this moment, in this building.

"I need this vote to be unanimous," Kuipers pushed. "For this transition to occur as efficiently and safely as possible, we need to show it is the will of the entire council."

"I will think about it," Amy said.

"I'm asking all of you to vote with me."

"I said, I'll think about it."

"There's nothing to think about. We must protect Marin. The council must be unified."

"Telling me how to vote is not the way to unify the council."

The movement outside of the window intensified, and three Humvees stopped in front of the senate. Amy put her fingers on her temples and squeezed, shutting her eyes. "I need some cold water," she said and stood up.

She opened the door to face a guard who did not budge. Kuipers waved, and the guard moved aside. Amy stepped into the twelve-foot-wide corridor. Two soldiers to her left guarded the main hallway and elevator. To her right, the corridor dead-ended at a three-pane, knee-to-ceiling window. The bathroom was to her right across the corridor, halfway to the window.

Amy walked to the bathroom door, but the guard stepped in front of her. "Allow me," the guard said in a polite tone. She walked into the bathroom and pushed open all three stall doors. Satisfied the bathroom was empty, she stepped out and pointed Amy in. "I'll be right outside Vice-Chancellor."

Amy did have a headache, but it wasn't the migraine she pretended to have. She leaned forward over the sink and turned the faucet on, washed her hands with the citrusy soap, then splashed water on her face, rubbing her eyes and forehead. She shut the faucet off and stepped back, barely recognizing the tired politician who stared back from the mirror.

The gathering of the entire Marin leadership in this building, Kuipers' tone, and her frequent use of "I" broadcast Kuipers' intention. She wasn't declaring martial law. She was staging a coup. Amy stood straight, tucked her shirt in, and pulled the door open, ready to face her dwindling options. The guard who'd escorted her was no longer there.

The door ten feet to her left across the corridor was ajar. Eva opened it wider and brought her index finger to her lips, then put her palm forward, instructing Amy to wait.

Fifteen seconds later, a woman in a knee-high skirt and a flowery blouse approached the soldiers in the elevator end of the corridor. "I need to see the chancellor."

"No one is allowed in or out of this floor," the first soldier said.

"It's important. I need to—"

"Turn around and go down, now."

"Please, I'll be fired if I don't get in there," she pleaded.

One of the soldiers moved toward her, and the woman dashed forward. The soldier grabbed her wrist and slammed her to the wall. The second soldier pinned her head to the wall while the first cuffed her wrists behind her.

Eva motioned her forward, and Amy traversed the corridor in four long strides. The guard who had escorted her sat crumpled on a chair facing the desk and window. Eva caught her eyes dwell on the guard and winked. "She'll be fine."

"Now what? There are guards at every exit."

Eva pointed behind the desk. Amy stepped forward to find a two-foot-diameter hole in the floor and a larger square hole where the drop ceiling of the floor below should have been. A metal ladder with orange plastic steps stood below them. Amy stepped on the metal frame between the floors and lowered herself to the ladder.

Cavana held the ladder.

"Aren't you meeting the mayors and other district leaders with General Dabiri?"

"I got lost and never made it to that meeting."

Eva slid the desk back, dropped down, and put the ceiling tiles back. She handed Amy a blonde wig, black, thick-rimmed glasses, a military uniform, and a tida. "ID should hold."

"Major, really?"

"It's a high enough rank to gain you respect but not so high that soldiers will expect to recognize you."

Amy motioned Cavana to turn around. She put on the pants and jacket in thirty seconds, bundled her hair into the wig, and they were out in the hallway. The commotion around them had increased, which made it easier to hide in plain sight. They took the elevator down to the parking garage. Amy's new ID opened the door, and the guard waved them forward. Eva walked toward an already revving Humvee.

Eva, now wearing her Special Forces beret, said to the soldier, "I'll take it from here." The soldier saluted and stepped out. Eva waved Amy to the driver's seat. "This one's yours."

Amy pointed to the ramp leading up to the street. A gate blocked the way out, with soldiers setting a slalom course behind it with concrete blocks. "This ID won't work there."

"Fair," Eva said. "But they only chase the first truck. So, make sure you follow me."

Eva took off her beret, stuffed it in her pocket, put on sunglasses, and dashed to a Jeep parked thirty feet away. She hopped on, started it, and gunned it toward the exit, horn blaring.

The soldiers by the gate fired at her but jumped out of the way as Eva crashed into the gate, swerved around the first concrete block, smashed sideways into the second one, and skidded away. More gunfire erupted behind her as she flew up the ramp. Blood exploded from her shoulder and back as bullets found her, but Eva didn't slow down.

A Humvee flew out in pursuit as an officer shouted for them to follow Eva's Jeep.

"Let's go," Amy snapped, putting her Humvee in gear. Cavana jumped in the back, and Amy gunned it. Not only did the guards not shoot at her, but they waved her on.

Amy followed the Humvee pursuing Eva's Jeep. Declaration Square and the Senate disappeared in her rearview mirror almost as fast as the Marin-New Federation was dissolving. Another Jeep appeared behind her, creating a convoy speeding toward Richmond Bridge at breakneck speed.

"She will not make it to the Rim," Cavana said, hopping from the back seat to the front.

"She's not going to the Rim. She's going to take Canal Street toward San Rafael and disappear in the backstreets. The first Humvee will follow her. We'll go straight as though we're trying to cut her off but continue to the bridge."

As if on cue, Eva veered left, and the Humvee followed her. Amy raised her arm above the frame of her Humvee and motioned forward to let the Jeep behind her grasp what she intended to do. She drove straight past the turn, but the Jeep turned behind the others.

"How did you know?"

Amy smiled. "You know what we did all those nights you worried I had dinner with Eva? We talked a lot. I know how she thinks."

They sped over the bridge and turned south when they reached the Rim.

Cavana frowned. "I cannot believe she kept driving. Those bullets ripped her shoulder; we should not have left her there."

"She'll be fine."

"That was a lot of blood, Governor. Those shot—"

She slowed down. "Nando, I haven't been honest with you. I need to tell you something."

"Can it wait until we are back in New Cal? I'd rather you focused on driving right now."

She slammed on the brakes and took the first right. She pulled to the side of the road in front of rotting, boarded-up bungalows. Each house had one oak tree, no doubt planted when this subdivision had been planned. She rolled to a stop in the shade of one.

"No, it can't wait. We need to talk now."

He squinted. "You are not dying, are you?"

"We're all dying Nando." She laughed, but it hit her. Even that platitude was a lie. "Well, not everyone is dying. I'm sorry... I should have told you this months ago," she said and launched into the virus, the healings, and why the last thing they had to worry about was Eva getting shot.

CHAPTER 15

FORGIVEN

*"It ain't what you don't know that gets you into trouble.
It's what you know for sure that just ain't so."*

—MARK TWAIN

Blue left late afternoon to make it to Cal City before dark. Mika slept by the tree, under a starless sky because everything but the half-moon was cloaked by the distant fire. This far east, the smoke was more haze than threat, a reminder that large forces were eating half the forest in the west. It wasn't death the blaze brought. It was rebirth, a topic he knew a thing or two about.

His ride back felt longer. On the way to the lab, he had a mission to deliver data and tease out the secrets of the virus. Now, he returned to a team that no longer had a purpose with hard-to-process clues that offered more questions than answers.

He reached camp in the early afternoon, stored the bike in the transport, and took off his helmet. Bess stood behind him, not hostile, but not offering to help either. "How's Yasuo?"

"Worse."

The man had recovered from four knife punctures to the chest and three bullet wounds. If he were going to recover from this new virus, he would have by now. He didn't know Bess well. But they had been through a firefight. He figured he was entitled to a little candor. "How's Lin?"

"Major Tomlin is fine."

"How's she handling Yasuo?"

"You think we sit by a fire and pour our hearts out when you're not around?"

He had figured wrong. He walked to the campsite. Lin sat on a folding chair next to her tent, jotting notes on her screen.

She spoke without lifting her head. "Anything from the samples?"

"Just dropped them. Blue has a few leads on another matter."

"And if that was something important, you'd tell me, right?"

"When it's more than a lot of maybes, I will."

She lifted her eyes when he kept standing there. "What?"

"Are we okay?"

"I decided to forgive you."

He didn't argue that he didn't need her forgiveness. That restraint triggered a realization. His polish was returning, allowing him to overcome his urges—urges to avoid people, and urges to argue for unnecessary accuracy. So, perhaps, he hadn't landed in a square too far from where he had been.

"What are you grinning about?"

"Nothing," he lied as his epiphany wouldn't have survived an explanation.

She put her screen on her lap. "You were right. Nothing changed."

"Even the friends?"

"Even those."

The rest of the day dragged on. Mika sat by his tent, trying to make sense of Blue's lab data. As twilight turned into darkness, he lay in his sleeping bag, spotting the few stars that dared poke through the smoky haze.

"I've been trying to figure something out," Lin called.

He had just closed his eyes. He lifted his head, inviting the analysis.

She dragged her chair to his tent flap and sat down, facing in. "You pretend to be aloof and detached, but you do care. And you do have mood swings. You were in a dark place when we met. As we worked you opened up, and I saw another side of you. Still guarded, but a bit more playful. But this last trip—"

He pushed himself on his elbows and waited.

"Something happened," she said. "You're back to that dark place. Is it the trouble you keep hinting at with Chipps?"

He shook his head. Leaving Amy's house that night had carried a finality, but it had been coming for months. Being disappointed by the expected was foolish. No, what had gotten to him was missing Lori's birthday for the first time in over two decades. Lori had been a strong teenager but taking care of him had taken its toll on her. He had seen her cry once, in secret, only to find out that it had been her birthday. And there hadn't been a soul who had known about it. He had made a solemn promise—as only a ten-year old can—to always be there for her.

And he had kept that promise until now. Even after she moved to Marin, leaving him behind, they managed to meet every year around her birthday. But now, he had no idea where Lori was, or even whether she was alive. He had let the year slide past him, recovering and tearing himself and others apart. But deep down, he had hoped and even expected a message with a Uregs address and a date that would have put the world on hold for an evening, just like old times.

But it hadn't happened. "I was expecting to hear from a friend. I didn't." He sat up cross-legged on his sleeping bag. "I don't have many friends. Not real ones. I landed on the wrong side of the border with one. But we still met once a year come hell or high water. But not this year."

Lin raised an eyebrow. "Is this friend the mysterious Phillips?"

He shook his head. "A childhood friend. I hadn't admitted to myself that she was gone. Despite all the evidence, I really thought she'd show up."

"How is Chipps handling this lady friend?"

That was such a small part of the problem that he didn't bother figuring out whether it mattered. He took too long to answer, so she pushed.

"Is that part of the trouble between you two?"

"Told you, there is no trouble with Amy. We're done." He stood up and walked to the transport. He opened the case on the back of the bike and grabbed the bottle of bourbon and two cups. He sat back down. "This conversation needs help."

He couldn't tell whether she was pleased or disturbed. "Where did that come from?"

"Small distillery north of the Rim. Pete grows his corn, so it is actually bourbon." She kept her eyes on him, eyebrows squeezed tight. "Oh, you mean, how did it get here?" He laughed. "From Eva through Blue."

"Is that why you insisted on meeting her?"

"No. But I wasn't about to turn down such a generous gift."

"Jeez." She shook her head at his apparent glee. "You crave it that much?"

"If I did, I wouldn't be sharing it with you." She smiled half in agreement and half in apology. "Besides, your premise is wrong. Chemical dependence is no longer a threat or an option. Neither is impairment, so drink up. You'll be good as new in a few minutes."

"You know a lot about this."

"Testing limits is what I do. Mine, the world's." He smiled. "Yours." Amy's. He pushed that thought away. "You must have noticed that drinking no longer affects you."

She nodded.

"We can't drink fast enough to get drunk. Trust me, I've tried. It's not a question of how much; it's a question of flow rate. It's not even of how fast you ingest it but of how fast it hits your bloodstream. Turns out chemistry is too slow. Now," he said, lifting and shaking the bourbon, "the first few times you down a bottle, you'll get a buzz for a few minutes. But it'll be a real waste. By the fourth time, even that won't work. Kinda sad if you ask me."

She chuckled and took a cup. "I've never seen anyone oscillate between pragmatic and ludicrous as fast or as often as you do."

He smiled. "I do what I can."

"Or between infuriating and charming."

Now, she sounded like Amy eight months ago before she had concluded that infuriating won. "Lately, I hear the charming part is missing."

She raised and shook her cup. "You have your moments."

"Want to see a neat trick?"

She gave him a distorted smile, with only half her mouth stretching up.

He took her cup and put both their cups on the box between them that pretended to be a coffee table. He opened the bottle and poured. She reached for her cup, but he put his hand up. "Not yet." He took his knife out and put it next to the cups. "How well do you heal?"

"What?"

He touched the tip of his knife to his forearm. "How long before a cut here is good as new?"

"Few minutes to close. Ten, fifteen to disappear."

"Lucky you." He smiled. "This will work even better on you." He reached into his tent and took a small navy towel. He extended his left hand. "Do you trust me?"

She put her hand out after a few seconds. He held her forearm in his left hand and took the knife in his right. "Relax." He pushed it in half an inch in one quick thrust and cut for two inches. He put the knife on the towel and gave her the cup.

She took a sip and grimaced. Her eyes bulged out. "What just happened?"

"The Purge is distracted. Seems liquor isn't a priority when you have a gash to fix." He took his switchblade knife and cut his forearm, going higher. He drained his cup. "Burns going down, doesn't it?"

Her eyes stayed on his forearm where the wound had already closed, the blade's intrusion erased. "Wow, that's bloody impressive."

"More work. You get to sip for ten minutes. I get maybe two before I need to cut again."

They drained their cups in silence. He poured another round and waved his hand across the empty landscape. "Do you think we'll ever know how this all happened?"

She took a sip, taking her time swallowing and chewing her drink. "Does it matter?"

"Most of the time, no. Sometimes, I can't shake the feeling it's the only thing that does. The initial outbreak started in Tromso, right? Because some activists got past the quarantine."

"Yeah," she said. "I was in college."

He had been in first grade. The gulf between them hit him. "Wow. Did you always look this good, or is it the virus?"

"Why, if I didn't know better, I'd say you were coming on to me, young man." The mischief in her smile implied she was only half-joking, or maybe a quarter.

He smiled back. He hadn't meant anything by it, but there was a warmth to her amber eyes that cut across her cold stare. Past the acerbic soldier, an attractive woman sat by the fire.

"What were you studying?" he asked to avoid dwelling on her words, his thoughts.

She raised her cup. "Drinking. I was getting bloody good at it too."

She took a sip and frowned. She tapped her arm, and he handed her the knife. She put a three-inch gash, took another sip, and savored it.

"Finance," she said after she swallowed. "Or public policy. Hadn't decided yet whether I wanted to make money or make a difference. So many possibilities that I didn't want to have to pick." A distant look snared her as though she fought the pull of another world. "I sure as hell wouldn't have picked chasing freaks across this desolate landscape."

And yet, they both had just done that. Even in their decrepit world, most folks stuck to a simple routine. They did their chores, took food to their tables, and forgot the world outside of their doors and gates. Apocalypse didn't reset the human psyche; it shuffled wants and needs.

"I remember it all like it was yesterday," she said, the playfulness gone from her voice. "The claims that the Purge had come from the comet. The counterclaims calling that nonsense—going back and forth like a game, like all that counted was to find a good argument. But it all became a sideshow once people started dropping by the millions."

He took a sip. The Purge used the exact same set of nucleotides as life on Earth. Extra-terrestrial origin was a statistical impossibility, or so the experts claimed.

"The conspiracy theorists claimed one of the governments created the virus in a lab. Others swore it was a bad mutation of some virus that had always been with us," she said.

"But you don't believe that last one."

"That always sounded unlikely. But if it repairs us? No way that was a bloody mutation."

He didn't buy it for a second that a scientist had found the fountain of youth right after comet fragments had landed at Tromso. He pulled the folded image of the test tubes from his pocket and placed it next to her glass. She unfolded it, stared at it, then pushed it back to him.

"Blue says that's twenty-five years old."

She exhaled. "Figures."

"What do you think it means?"

"Who knows? Created in a lab? From the comet? A weapon? Guessing at this is like figuring out which of the buzzing flies to blame for the large pile of horseshit on the road. It's probably all true. Comet, labs, conspiracies." She shivered. "There's no way whoever fucked with this knew what they were doing. Because the way the Purge spread?" She stopped. "It's not where the bloody thing came from that caused the problem."

He would have bet good money that the labs at the center of the conspiracy theories were those with the original samples.

Shasta.

"What now?" she asked.

He refilled their glasses. "Yasuo is shivering with a fever of one hundred and four. His skin is blue because there isn't enough oxygen in his blood. His heart is pumping like crazy, trying to compensate, but it can't because his lungs are full of liquid." He stopped to let that sink in. "Bodies show up in Marin by the dozen, looking a lot like Yasuo. There's a settlement out there, abandoned in the middle of the night. There's another burned to the ground. Does any of this ring a bell?"

She drained her drink, shaking her glass for more as an answer. He reached over and filled her glass. He was too young to remember the beginning. But it didn't take much imagination to reach the same conclusion she had.

The Purge, or a close cousin, was back on the prowl.

CHAPTER 16

ADRIFT

"Guilt is not a response to anger; it is a response to one's own actions or lack of action."

—AUDRE LORDE

As he waited for the kettle to boil, Mika dropped the coffee capsule into his cup much like he had done at dawn the day before. Then, he had downed it quickly, alone, before a long day of riding. Today, he had time and company but nothing to do. The coffee didn't care, and he didn't have to look at the colossal, ageless rock behind their camp to share the long view. Even his simple, day-to-day actions proved that simple repetition was the basis of existence.

Mika drained his cup but didn't replenish it. With so little to engage his mind, he was going stir-crazy. Their defenses were up, but anticipating an assault hid their real burden: they were waiting for Yasuo to die. He now coughed blood, slipping in and out of consciousness. He had reached the end stage of the Purge.

Mika found Lin in the cargo hold, lost in canyon maps. "I need to go for a run."

Lin grimaced. "We're not exactly in friendly territory."

"You're welcome to join me."

Lin's eyes move from Bess to Mika and back. "Not today," she said. "Go. Short loop."

He was off before she changed her mind. On the first mile, he settled into a zone, and then he pushed, sprinting until his lungs burned and his muscles screamed. The pain only lasted a few seconds, but it channeled his frustration on the gray, hard-packed soil. He traced eight half-mile-radius circles around the camp at his five-minute-per-mile pace.

As his damp skin cooled, it sucked the dust from the air, coating him with a gunmetal film. The alkaline dirt on his lips tasted almost as bad as the pungent smell of the decaying sagebrush. His surroundings screamed the same warning with every step he took. He didn't belong here. And he had no arguments to offer to the contrary, not with the haze blurring everything around him into a vague mirage. The thousands of burning acres were very real, though, shrouding the western horizon under a granite cloud.

He spiraled in, jogging the last quarter mile, bringing his breathing to normal before reaching camp. He had known what they had to do all along, but the run had crystallized it. He gulped water, sat down, and waited for Lin to lift her eyes.

"We need to take Yasuo to the lab."

Lin put her screen down. "What do you think we can do for him there?"

That was the wrong question. When the Purge decided to kill, people died. Either Yasuo died pointlessly here or while his last breaths yielded some clues to the virus' machinations. Collecting samples from dead bodies was one thing; observing a living patient was another.

"No," she shook her head. "Can't risk the exposure."

"We need to find what Gibson is after, and we can't do that with Yasuo in tow. And someone needs to study Yasuo while he's still alive."

"Give it a rest." He must have gone back to being infuriating because she waved to dismiss him. "And clean up. You look like you just wrestled three pigs in the mud."

It took him fifteen minutes to dip into a stream and get dressed. Lin sat alone at the edge of camp in her folding chair when he got back. "Okay," she said without looking up, "that asshole has been shipping bodies to Marin for months. Why is he doing that?"

"Not why. How." He dragged a chair and sat next to her. "No way Gibson can bring these bodies into Marin on his own. He needs collaborators on the inside. And high up."

"That's a bloody short list." She strolled to the transport. "Bess."

Bess came out in five seconds.

"Take Yasuo to the lab. Use the truck. You're leaving as soon as you're packed. Once there, call Rendon and ask for a specialist and full isolation."

"Yes, ma'am."

"You don't move from the lab till you hear from Rendon, and you follow full quarantine protocol." She turned to him. "Happy?"

That was not a word to describe any of this. "It's the right call."

"That remains to be seen."

The dust cloud from the truck shrank as it moved toward the horizon. The rest of the day passed in dissonance, with Lin restless from having too much pent-up energy and nothing to apply it to and Mika peaceful after flushing his adrenaline in his run.

They ate dinner in silence, gulping down their spiced, flavored proteins that approximated chicken in look and smell but not in taste or texture. The safe play had been to accompany Yasuo to the Uregs, contact Sierra, and wait for instructions.

Mika put his plate on the ground. "I'm guessing it wasn't my charming personality that convinced you."

She studied him as though he were an unwelcome present, one she had to either find a use for or discard. "You're right. We do need to know what Gibson's up to."

"What's the plan?"

"The plan is to have a good night's sleep and then go ask Gibson what he's up to."

As plans went, he had heard worse. He had also heard better because Gibson was not their normal type of threat. When two indestructible forces met, one always found out it had been wrong. Some claimed that contemplating one's mortality focused the mind.

It didn't.

It made him wish he had rationed the bourbon. It wouldn't have helped with his introspection, but it would have given them a reason to sit and talk. His body didn't crave or react to the alcohol, but he still needed the social lubrication a drink provided.

He tossed and turned for an hour in his tent, his mind too active to sleep. He had just stopped pining for the empty bottle when his tent's Velcro crackled. That's why he preferred Velcro to zippers. There was no way to sneak in. Lin's hand slid down, separating the sides. She stepped in and resealed it, there to stay.

The faint moonlight lit her silhouette. She crouched next to him, her hand wandering on his chest, his belly, but no further.

He reached up and took her hand, massaging her palm with his thumb. That was all the signal she needed. She straddled him, sitting on his thighs, and leaned forward. Her free hand moved over his face. She grabbed his chin in a strong grip and kissed him.

She pulled back and took off her shirt. When she arched her back, her small breasts stretched and disappeared between her toned abs and pecs.

He surrendered himself to the moment, letting her guide both their hips.

Mika could just about make out the mountains in the distance from his tent's side window. The sky had turned soft red, with hazy gray slowly spreading and erasing the dark, foreboding red it had been minutes ago. With the wind shifting, the smoke smell had eased, almost letting him believe the sky would lighten in a few more minutes.

He stepped out of his tent to find Lin clutching an empty coffee mug and facing the mountains. He had felt relieved when she had gone back to her tent, but he had fallen asleep while debating whether that was good or bad. Despite his misgivings, he had slept better than he had in a long time. He poured himself a cup and walked over to her. He squeezed her shoulder and held the pot. She extended her cup. He poured, put the pot back, and sat next to her.

She sipped her coffee and greeted him with a lost-in-thought half-smile.

"What do you want out of this day, Mika Bayley?"

He took a sip. "Blue skies and clear direction. I'll settle for strong coffee."

She pushed a breath from her nose, more of a chuckle than a sigh. "Why are you here?"

"What do you mean?"

"I'm a soldier. I follow orders. You're more like a volunteer. So why are you here?"

"I thought I'd find some answers."

Now, she chuckled for real. "There are no bloody answers here."

"Maybe not. But I needed to find out what I'd become."

She took a sip and grew serious. "Your answers are back in New Cal."

"And what are they?"

"How the hell should I know? I only know there is nothing here but misery."

"And why are you here?"

"Rendon is convinced Gibson holds the key to what's happening in Marin."

"Gibson or his partner?"

She shrugged. "They're holding the strings to someone high in Marin."

"Snatching him for an interrogation was her solution? Brute force, really?"

"You sound bitter."

He took a sip. "I just expected more from her."

"Maybe you shouldn't expect so much."

"I don't expect anything from you."

She flattened her lips. "Now you sound defensive."

He sipped his coffee but didn't reply.

"Wow, you went from bitter to defensive to guilty in ten seconds flat."

He swirled his coffee, letting it reach the lip but not spill over. The heat bled out with each revolution of the mug. "Of what?"

"You can't even be honest with yourself."

He reached over to pour himself another cup and leaned back on his chair, extending his legs. "I don't regret last night."

"That's not what I meant."

He stared at the mountains.

"You want some free analysis?"

He took a sip before replying, "That's the worst kind."

"Your problems aren't with Chipps."

"We really don't need to talk about that." He stood up and walked toward the bushes. The sun had just cleared the horizon, fighting the smoky haze to spread pale blue across the sky but not succeeding. He was not going to get blue skies or any clarity out of this day.

"You keep saying you two are through every time we get near that topic. I thought you were trying to convince me, but that's not it. You're trying to convince yourself."

"I don't need convincing. I know where we are."

"And where is that?"

He lifted his arms. "I'm here. Which is pretty much nowhere."

"You've been moping about for months now, but you know what? You haven't said one unkind word about Chipps. Not one. Do you have any idea how unusual that is?"

He came back, sat down, and sipped his coffee without replying.

"I've listened to a lot of friends dissect their love lives. They all complain about their exes, bitch about how incompatible they were, how they gave all they had, and it wasn't enough. They grumble about how they had to live up to unrealistic expectations, and how they drifted apart as they didn't have anything left to share. But you, you're like a mole in daylight. Not blind, exactly, but you can't see shit because it never occurs to you to open your eyes." Her lips flapped as she pushed air through them.

"So, you know all about me now?"

"I know enough. And the problem is with you. When you're at peace and content, love comes easily. When you're not, you think the love is gone even though that's rarely the case. It's just that the fog of doom and gloom makes it impossible for you to see it's still there. And you, you're not in a happy place. Whatever the hell happened to you—whatever you went through—it left a hole in you. You have to patch that hole before you can move forward or be with anyone."

People talked about love like they talked about sailboats: wistfully. Most had no idea how much work it took to paint that cheery snapshot of sailing into the sunset. The hours spent with wrench, brush, mop, drill, and needle all had their equivalents in emotional tools. He was willing to admit the fault may lie with him but did not want to autopsy his relationship with Amy. He took a sip of coffee. "You figured all that out after one—" He paused.

She squinted, cheeks stretched tautly into a disappointed smile. "I knew you'd say something like that. But, no, I figured it out before. This morning just confirmed I was right."

There was neither hostility nor malice in her voice. "Even if you're right, I have no idea what any of it means." He took a deep breath. "We might die today."

"We might die any bloody day."

"Today's different." Her impulse last night and her words now were a reaction to that truth.

"So, today calls for more honesty," she said.

"I've had enough honesty for one morning."

"That friend of yours, the one whose birthday you missed. Who is it?"

He turned his cup upside down, letting the drops trickle to the rim, circle it, and land on the dusty ground. "I told you the first day we met. Why I'd gone on that mission with Sierra."

She threw her head back. "I can't believe I spent five months with the childhood friend of Lori Bloody Rose. What was she like?"

He shrugged. "She liked her coffee too. But you'd say she was obsessed."

"Seriously?"

"We'd scored a bag from a warehouse. And I don't mean beans from Santa Barbara like this stuff," he said, raising his cup. "But from a place called Colombia I'd never heard of. I couldn't have been more than twelve. She brewed it every morning and dumped enough sugar in it to turn it into syrup. But not me, no. I drank mine straight." He chuckled. "Hated the bitter flavors at first, but I had to show her how tough I was. I believed that as long as we had coffee in the morning, everything would be all right."

She took a sip. "There's not enough coffee in the world to fix the mess we're in."

"Not supposed to fix the mess. Just me."

"We were talking about Rose."

He traced the rim of his cup with his finger. "We were?"

"She's a myth, not a person in Marin. I will pester you till you give me something."

"She is a very real person to me. Pragmatic, serious, but also funny." He took a deep breath. "I was there when she took the first step in turning into a myth. I walked with her to the clinic she worked at in Cal City before the border went up, when it was little more than a big Uregs compound with delusions of statehood."

"She worked at a clinic?"

"Yeah, she started as an aide and became a good medic. Anyway, the place had been torn apart by a gang, and from the look of things, they were after more than drugs. I don't know whether they had a beef with the doctor or what, but they left nothing. They killed the doctor and the aide who was there, took all the medicine, and destroyed all the equipment."

Lin ambled to the coffee pot and refilled their cups. He took a sip as she sat back down.

"I remember two things from when we walked into the clinic. The pungent smell of antiseptic and the certainty that I'd lost Lori. Everything she'd worked for, the entire life she'd built, was destroyed. That was the day she gave up on Cal City, the day she gave up on fixing things one piece at a time. Soon after, she moved to Marin and joined the military."

"And you stayed in Cal City?"

"She asked me to go, but that would have never worked. Can you imagine me in Marin?"

"No, not really."

"She never would have become General Rose had that clinic remained intact."

"I can't picture her in a clinic."

"And I never pictured her in the military. I guess we were both wrong. I appreciate who she's become, but I do miss the caring teenager who helped me grow up." He chuckled. "She had a dry sense of humor."

"I don't think I've ever seen her laugh."

"That's Marin's fault."

"There's plenty of blame to go around." She stood and tossed the last of her coffee, along with a few ground beans, into the dirt. "You think she's alive?"

"I really hope so."

"Me too," she said and sat back down, staring into the smoke in the distance.

"Funny how we're peeling away my present and my past," he said. "And I know so little about you. Basically, you didn't know what you wanted to be in college, and you became a soldier to protect Marin from raiders. And somewhere along the line, you learned to shoot."

"Not much more to me."

"I don't believe that."

"Okay, what do you want to know?"

With the sun up about ten degrees, it was now bright red, forcing its light across the smoke. But he couldn't count on celestial motion to brighten their mood.

"I don't even know where to start. But that first day we met, I asked you one personal thing." She thought for a moment but didn't grasp what was he was asking. "In Sierra's office." She still stared. "Nameless Major Tomlin."

It took another few seconds for her to force a crooked smile. "Seriously?"

He waited with his eyes on her. She leaned over and whispered in his ear.

"Wow, they named you after an island?"

She raised a finger and widened her eyes in mock threat.

He smiled back. "It suits you. Not in the simplistic definition captured in drawings, but in the old, menacing, don't-fuck-with-me one."

She sat back down. "You will never say that bloody name out loud."

Her words and actions only gave him random access to who she was. Like staring at a painting through a colander, the whole was reduced to a sampling of shapes and colors. What she wanted out of life and what she ran from were locked away, hidden from sight. But she had given him a slightly larger aperture to look through. She had run away from a graceful name.

But she was right.

No matter which definition one picked, that name was not of this world.

CHAPTER 17

BODYGUARD

"A leader takes people where they want to go. A great leader takes people where they don't necessarily want to go, but ought to be."

—ROSALYNN CARTER

"Are you reconsidering?"

Cavana led her through the concrete-walled corridors of the basement to the large storage room that had become their new headquarters. Three four-inch metal pipes ran along the long wall across the door at knee height, bending up and disappearing into the ceiling. A fake-marble laminate counter left from pre-Purge days lined the back of the room with strips that had peeled off near the small sink.

Amy plopped onto a rolling chair and tried to shut out the musty scent of the stains that marked years of leaks in shades of gray, from nearly white to the dark of still-damp spots. She turned on her screens and put her feet on the plastic-top folding table that had become a desk.

A year ago, when she had been unsure of her first steps into leadership, she might have taken Cavana's words as a criticism of her indecisiveness, but not today. Cavana had shown a loyalty she hadn't even earned in those early days, and his questions were meant to prepare for all the eventualities.

Amy pressed her temples. "Dissolving the union is not just a political blow. It's also a psychological blow."

"The ink is barely dry on the treaty. It will be just like eleven months ago."

"Eleven months ago, we were on the second floor with windows overlooking the bay."

"I would rather be safe right now. You are the only senior Marin official outside Kuipers' sphere of influence."

Amy pushed her chair away from the table and stared at the concrete ceiling.

Cavana put his rucksack on the counter and pulled out a napkin. He took out a loaf of bread and a wedge of gray-white, semi-soft cheese and put them on the napkin. "Hungry?"

Her stomach growled at the nutty cheese aroma, answering for her. She nodded.

Cavana reached for the cabinet above the counter, and the door came off as he pulled. He caught it with both hands and put it on the floor, resting it against the lower cabinets. The exposed shelf had sagged, only holding because the half-dozen plates and randomly colored cups on it were thin aluminum. He picked up two plates, inspected them, and put them back with a frown.

"For almost everyone in New Cal, the union was an abstract concept," he said.

She shook her head. "If you promise your neighbor a bottle of wine but don't deliver, she'll be upset, but she'll forget it in a day. If you give it to her but take it back the next day, she'll remember it for the rest of her life and hold a grudge. We gave them a taste of a new life, and now we're taking it away."

He spread two more napkins on the counter. He cut two slices of bread, put them on the napkins, and picked up the cheese.

"Governor, you overestimate how attached your average citizen is to this treaty. Most just want to eat, drink, and get the plumbing to work."

"We've just built some sort of stability. But if we do this, Marin won't be charitable. They'll make this as painful as they can. Deport hundreds of citizens. Cancel hundreds of contracts. It will disrupt a lot of that eat, drink, and flush routine."

Cavana put the cheese on the counter, wiped his hand on the edge of his napkin, and approached the screen. Numbers floated up when he tapped, superimposed on a map. He pointed at the first row. "New Cal has twenty-one business contracts with Marin. A little over three hundred of our citizens live or work in Marin." He pointed to the Cal City side of the map. "Fewer than a hundred Marin citizens are in Cal City, and about fifty in Santa Cruz. Dissolving the union is not a disruption; it is canceling a bus tour."

"I'm not worried about those who moved. Those are the resilient ones. But for many, the idea that they *could* move was uplifting. They had the option to do something new. Most would have never moved, but we gave them a new normal."

"Governor, I know people. Trust me on this; it will not be as hard as you fear."

He cut four slices of cheese and placed two on each bread slice. He lifted one napkin from its ends, forming a basket, and put it on the table in front of her.

"Thanks." She picked up a cheese slice and bit into it. It was softer than she expected. The sharp, rich flavor exploded in her mouth. "This is good," she said as she chewed. "Goat?"

Cavana smiled. "Sheep."

"Just so you know, I'm not reconsidering leaving. I'm mulling over how to leave." She nibbled at the second cheese piece.

"I thought you would announce it in public like you did last year at the Capitol."

"Yeah." She chuckled. "See if lightning strikes twice. But what motive do I give?"

"Discrimination. Tariffs. Bad faith. You have the pick of the litter. Marin promised two thousand new citizenships. We barely hit three hundred. They have not satisfied any part of the treaty." He bit into his open-faced sandwich.

"I meant constitutionally."

"I do not follow."

Amy had studied the terms of the union in the fine print. Their chief negotiator, Andrea Wender, had brought decades of government experience to the negotiating team, ensuring both parties had leverage. And she told Amy about all the details. In the end, it wasn't even Andrea's forward-thinking that bailed them out. It was the hawks in Marin who insisted on simple mechanisms for dissolving the union.

Article 7 outlined a long list of economic, political, and social rules that had to be followed to remain in the union. The peaceful transition of power and democratic elections were a critical component of the union, along with transparency in business licenses and immigration laws.

Then realizing that New Cal may adhere to the letter of the law, they added Article 0, named so because it had been inserted after all other items had been agreed to. That article allowed either party to leave unilaterally by executive decree in the first two years or leave after a referendum and executive endorsement in the first ten years of the union.

She finished her second piece of cheese and bit into the bread. "We can use the 'It's not you; it's me,' line by invoking Article 0. We can also hold their feet to the fire and invoke Article 7 and list our grievances," she said after she finished chewing.

"Do you really want to piss Kuipers off?"

"This is not just about tomorrow morning. It's about next month and the month after that. How does Marin view their leadership? Are we the ungrateful kids who ran away? Or should they look more closely at their government?" She took a deep breath and exhaled. "I'm not sure Kuipers will get the subtle message. Anything beyond the rebuke of her seizing power will be lost on her. She might lash out."

"Our militia has come a long way, but I would rather not face the Marin military."

"About that."

Cavana pushed the last of his sandwich into his mouth and swiped his screen. A map of New Cal, with entrenchments, guns, and militia numbers floating over different spots.

"Defensive options?" Amy asked.

Cavana pointed to the northernmost spots on the peninsula as he finished chewing. "The gun batteries over the cliffs will stop most anything coming our way. The surface-to-air missiles are top-notch. I am still shocked General Rose installed those and gave you the codes."

"Don't guess at Rose's motivations. Are you saying we can stop a Marin assault?"

Cavana ran his fingers through his hair. "I am saying they cannot waltz in here like they could have a year ago. We can cut off access from the north by removing six pieces of roadway from the Golden Gate. We can push back light transports. But we cannot prevail in a prolonged battle against heavy transports."

"Food?"

Cavana pointed to newly lit spots on the map: farmland, supply lines, warehouses. "Covered. Each city has a three-week supply. Cal City is closer to ten days because we have more to feed."

"Power?"

Four power plants lit up, one for each city. Then four more, the secondary plants. "They have always been fortified. They were designed against attacks and disruptions, and we have a solar backup for most essential installations."

"From the Uregs, not Marin military."

"Short of a full-out Marin attack, there will be power."

"I don't want plans short of anything," she snapped.

Cavana took his time replying. "Governor, we can defend the cities. We can defend the streets. We can make it costly for Marin to invade. But I cannot upgrade our air defense systems to survive a full-on Marin missile barrage. If they want our grid down, it is going down."

Amy closed her eyes and rubbed her temples again. It was a simple headache, nothing more. One advantage of being in a skunky basement was that she didn't have to worry about random bright reflections triggering her migraines. She reopened her eyes and blinked.

"Mayors?"

"You know the count."

She did. Mountain View had gone through a succession of three mayors in ten months, losing one to resignation and two to council politics. They had a baroque system of representative democracy, and any slight or askew glance in the council triggered a no-confidence vote. But she polled higher there than any of their cities, well into the seventies, so all the mayors went out of their way to support her. They would back her no matter what she did.

San Jose was a different story. Amy butted heads with their mayor, Meghan Heath, on many issues. But that's because San Jose had always disliked Marin and the union, and they resented being forced into it. Heath viewed Amy as a Marin representative and showed her contempt at every opportunity. But unlike Halsan, Heath was consistent in her politics. Leaving the union was the one topic on which she had enthusiastically endorsed Amy.

She had a harder read on Santa Cruz. Sumit Joy had turned into a good leader, generally supporting her policies on the council. But this wasn't some random topic, and Santa Cruz had benefited the most from the Marin partnership. They didn't always see eye-to-eye, but she trusted Joy to do the right thing for the benefit of New Cal.

The rivalry between Joy and Halsan had become the running joke of New Cal politics. Joy was probably the one person Halsan hated more than her. He viewed Joy as both a political rival and an outsider, though Joy was far more Californian than Halsan would ever be.

"You think we can get a unanimous vote?"

Cavana ran his fingers through his beard. "I would be happy with Joy or Halsan. I do not see both voting yes."

"Not if Sumit votes first." She chuckled.

"Halsan does dislike the union," Cavana said. "So you never know."

"He dislikes me more." She popped the last morsel of bread in her mouth.

"It would not surprise me if he challenged you."

"Into the union. Out of the union. Our governor cannot make up her mind. New California deserves better," she said, mimicking Halsan's cadence.

"Exactly. He will use the confusion and discontent to have another grab at your seat. We cannot allow that. When—" he said and caught himself. "If we break, we need a simple message. Everyone has to be on the same page; everyone has to back you. If the mayors, people, or militia waver, we will all end up in a Marin jail six hours after we start."

"I know."

"I can handle Halsan and his gang, but I cannot do it with kid gloves."

"I know," she repeated. "Do not worry about my commitment."

"Governor, I do not question your commitment. But you are fond of peaceful solutions. Sometimes, with some people, you need to choose a less subtle approach. While we are at it, we need to bolster your security."

Two of his best men followed her everywhere. She picked up bread crumbs from her napkin, rolling them between her index and thumb. "I think you've got that covered."

He shook his head. "I respected your privacy up to now, but I cannot anymore. After this, you will need round-the-clock bodyguards. And I do not mean in your street or in front of your house. I mean inside your home, twenty-four seven."

"JJ is not going to watch me pee."

He winced at her crudeness. "That is why I am bringing a new member to your detail."

The idea of a new face in her house made her skin crawl. "A stranger in my house, right now? I don't think so."

Cavana's smile widened, and he went to open the door. Eva walked in. Bloodstains painted the front of her gray jacket, and her left sleeve had a darker, coppery hue.

"I'm so glad you're okay." Amy walked to hug Eva. As she let go, she addressed Cavana. "How long have you been plotting this?"

"She will not let our doctors look at her." Cavana ran his finger through his mane again.

Amy moved her eyes from the blood on Eva's jacket to Cavana. "I told you about this."

Cavana had a confused look as though he hadn't grasped Amy's words' implication. "How fast is fast healing, exactly?"

Eva's eyes darted toward Amy. She nodded and Eva took a few steps back and unsheathed her hunting knife. She put her left palm up and cut across it.

"Whoa!" Cavana jumped back.

"No worries, Mr. Cavana." Eva lifted her hand, letting the blood run down her already blood-stained sleeve. She wiped her knife on her sleeve and stashed it away. She rubbed her hand on her jacket. Beads of blood appeared, but the flow had stopped. She wiped the blood again and raised her hand for Cavana's inspection.

Cavana hesitated, caught between inspecting Eva's hand, and avoiding it. He got closer but did not touch the hand.

There was a red welt on Eva's palm. Eva squeezed her hand into a fist, and when she reopened it, the welt was a scar. It turned into a scratch, and within seconds, it was gone.

"This," he said and stopped. "Wow."

"Very few are like her," Amy said. "Most just heal faster, as in hours instead of days for minor cuts, or days instead of weeks for serious injuries."

"Even better," he said. "Governor, meet your new bodyguard."

"No." Amy shook her head. "No, Eva, I appreciate what you did in Marin, but you cannot do this."

"What? Why not?"

"If you do this, you're done with Marin. I can't ask you to do that."

"I don't care about Marin. But I care about you. And you're not asking me to do anything."

"Eva, Marin forces may come after me. What Nando is asking—it's mutiny. You don't owe me anything."

Eva covered the distance between them in two quick steps. She clasped Amy's forearms right above the wrists.

"When I came back from the Uregs after what I went through, you were the only one who treated me like a human being. Not a weapon, like Colonel Rendon did. Not a party trick, like my peers did. Not a lab experiment, like my doctors did. Not a wounded pet, like my mothers did. But as a real person with real needs. It's the only thing that kept me sane and kept me going."

Amy freed her left hand and raised it to eye level. She dug her left thumb into the tip of her index finger and displayed a quarter-inch scar for Eva's inspection.

"Remember when I broke the glass over a week ago?"

Eva moved her finger over the tiny scar. "Yeah." She smiled. "Don't let the boss lady wash wine glasses."

"You don't owe me anything," Amy repeated.

"You think I care? I'm here because you're my friend."

Amy's shoulders dropped. She tapped her index on her thumb. "Eva, do you understand what this scar means?"

Eva grabbed Amy's shoulders and pulled her closer, hugging Amy tight with her non-blood-soaked arm.

"Yeah," Eva whispered. "It means I need to be extra careful protecting you."

CHAPTER 18

BREATHLESS

"If you gaze long enough in an abyss, the abyss will gaze back into you."

—FRIEDRICH NIETZSCHE

The honest night, the guarded morning, the tender minutes, the harsh words: all fell away once they went airborne. Mika shuffled to the cargo hold to check their magazines and clips for the third time. Satisfied they were properly loaded, he bolted the gun case and sat back next to Lin. The canyons carved by the Klamath River stretched below them, eerily empty, as though canyons, mountains, and plains had been pushed away from each other in an expanding universe.

These forests drew attention to the need for isolation while still allowing for the occasional coming together in the form of a long, twisting river. The clues were subtle, but these lands told the recipe of life to all who would listen. He'd put all the distances he needed around him. Now, all he had to do was find his river.

He let go of his musings as they neared Gibson's compound. Lin brought the transport down low, skimming the rustling treetops like a speedboat riding the surf. She landed in the clearing a mile in front of the compound and hailed Gibson. When they received no response, they flew within half a mile. After another ten minutes, they took the last hop, landing just outside of the wide-open front gate.

Lin pushed open the unlocked chain-link gate. "I don't like this."

Mika walked to the patch of grass where they had faced Gibson four nights earlier. The transports and Humvees were gone. He crouched where Kristin had been shot. All that was left of her were the brown patches on the short grass where the blood had dried and been sun-bleached. He had barely known her, his memory of her no more solid than these fading stains.

They walked into the courtyard between the lab and the barracks. The door to the lab was ajar. He pushed it open. The screens were gone, and all the metal shelves were empty.

Lin crouched where the heavy transports had stood. Four large indents of broken and torn grass marked the landing pad. "I really don't like that asshole."

Mika walked back and put a hand on her shoulder. "They're not coming back."

Neither spoke on the walk back to the transport, as though Kristin's memory was so fragile that words would shatter it.

"Time to head back," Lin said.

Then it hit him. "Our makeshift lab, Bess, and Yasuo—they're on Gibson's way to Marin."

Her eyes narrowed as she tapped the coordinates. She flew hard, but with the half-day head start Gibson had, they were never going to catch up.

"So, what's Sierra's beef with Gibson?"

Lin engaged the autopilot and leaned back. "She thought he or his partner was blackmailing someone on the executive council. I'm not so sure it's blackmail anymore, but he bloody well has someone's ear in Marin."

They had been disconnected from Marin and New Cal for so long he had no insight. "Yim?"

Lin shook her head. "No one with these resources will hitch his wagon to someone that ineffective. It'd take him ten seconds to figure it out."

"The one who replaced Lester—what's her name?"

Lin rubbed her lips with her hand. "Harding." She let go of her lips and chuckled as she talked about the judge who represented the judiciary in the executive council. "She makes Yim look like a heavyweight. No way she's involved."

He doubted Lin knew of Lester's involvement with the Puries, so she didn't grasp why he would be suspicious of anyone from Lester's branch. But he accepted her conclusion because Sierra was savvy enough to vet the person who had replaced Lester on the council.

He focused on the barely moving horizon as Lin pushed the transport hard. At forty thousand feet, he had no sense of speed. In a metal shell, the higher he went, the less he was connected to his senses. It seemed as though human brains had evolved to view distance from the ground as distance from reality. The same detachment occurred as one moved up in politics.

"I have to ask," Lin said, breaking his trance. "Could it be Chipps?"

"Cloak-and-dagger isn't her style."

"It would give her the upper hand in the council and pull one over on Kuipers. Take over Marin, or for that matter, turn Marin into an annex of New Cal."

"I really don't see it."

She grimaced. "I need a bit more than that."

"Trust me on this. One, she won't be seduced by someone like Gibson."

She laughed. "See, not one unkind word."

He waved her off. "Nothing to do with it. And two, Gibson won't go to her. She's not—she's not the profile he's after."

She drew a deep breath but didn't argue. "Kuipers, then?"

"Likely."

"Then we're bloody well fucked."

As they cleared the last hill, wisps of smoke from a dozen fires around the lab filled their view. Lin jumped out as they landed, and he followed. They were greeted by the pungent smell of the still smoldering tires and heat radiating from the torched trailer shell. Gray-white ash floated around them, propelled into the air with every step they took, as though they moved through old, haunted grounds rather than a recent crime scene.

Yasuo's charred body lay to the side of the lab. Bess' body had been dumped face-first into a shallow ditch a few feet away, along with two other bodies, most likely the lab specialists Sierra had sent. All three were covered in the blue-white chemical that emitted an acrid whiff, barely registering against the burnt-rubber stench. Bess had burn marks on her legs, her left arm had been broken in at least three places, and she was missing three fingers on her right hand.

"What the fuck did they do to her," Lin hissed.

He cupped his hands into a shovel and dumped three batches of dirt to bury Bess' hand. It was a futile gesture as no amount of dirt could erase the image of the offending hand from their minds.

"They probably figured out we cloned their drive and wanted to know where we put it."

Her jaw pulsated faster and faster, ready to go critical. He slapped his hands to shake the dust, wiped them on his thighs, and reached for her shoulder. She jolted away, looking at footprints, but it was pointless. People like Gibson didn't leave clues they didn't want found.

"Did Kuipers order this?"

"This is what 'containment' means. Those with the new virus burn. The rest get chemically cleansed. If she's working with Gibson, she did so implicitly."

"I'm not letting him get away with this."

"Look, Gibson is not your run-of-the-mill freak."

"Yeah, I gathered that," she snapped.

He pulled her away from the transport door. "I promise you we'll deal with Gibson when the time is right. But right now, we need to head back."

Her pulsating jaw slowed its rhythm, and she may have been ready to agree when a call crackled from the transport. She hopped in and tapped the screen.

"Are you stupid or are you purposefully trying to contaminate Marin?" Gibson's voice booming from the transport's speakers erased any hope Mika had of appeasing Lin.

"Talk. I'll trace it," Lin said before reaching over and tapping the transmit key. He shook his head, but she pointed to the cockpit and leaned on the back of the pilot's seat.

Mika sat in the co-pilot seat and tapped the screen to unmute the cockpit. "What are you talking about?"

"I said quarantine, and you sent for a doctor and a tech?"

"What the hell did you do this for?"

"Containment. For some reason, my partner Tulum still wants you on our side. Me? I'd bury you too, but hey, I'm a team player."

Lin swiped her tida in an attempt to isolate the comm towers that linked them to Gibson's broadcast. She didn't look up, so he pushed on. "There was no need for this."

"You left us no option. You can't play with this virus."

"Says who?"

"We spent a lifetime studying this virus, as did your buddy, Phillips. So, when we say we know more about the Purge than anyone alive, it's not bragging. When we say you can't play with it, you shouldn't fucking play with it. These deaths are on you. Operating an unauthorized lab right here, how reckless can you get?"

"Unauthorized?"

"Marin didn't authorize it. I didn't authorize it. Biohazard protocol wasn't followed. Civilians can't handle a dangerous biological weapon. You're lucky you didn't kill thousands."

Lin's mouth formed the word "weapon."

"You killed a sick man, a nineteen-year-old, and two specialists. What weapon were they handling?"

Gibson gave a throaty groan. "Don't be obtuse. They were the weapon."

Lin gestured for him to keep talking as she studied her tida.

"Tell me something. Was there ever a Purie state in these parts?"

"You only thought that because you have tunnel vision. For every action, there's an equal and opposite reaction. Puries pushed. We pushed back. Puries reached for Marin, we reached back. There never was a Purie state here or anywhere else. They operated from military bases in the fringes to infiltrate Marin and Kern. If you idiots thought these experimental settlements were a state, that's on you. But now, yeah, there is a Purie state. It's fucking Kern."

Lin swirled her index finger again for him to keep going. "What happened in Shasta?"

"Ah. Good, you're not totally clueless after all. They screwed up, that's what happened. Like monkeys playing with fire and getting surprised when they burn down the neighborhood."

"And that dotri? What's underground in that irradiated field?"

A burst of static crackled. "I need to go now," Gibson said. "And I'm guessing you've triangulated our signal. Do not come this way."

The line went dead. "So?" Mika asked.

She pointed to the map. A narrow cone edged southwest, then fanned out into a wider westward cone. Lin was in the pilot's seat punching coordinates.

Mika stood. "Can we talk about this?"

"What's there to talk about?"

"I thought you didn't gamble with your life."

She tapped the autopilot on. "I said I'm the only one who gets to gamble with my life."

"This mission is done."

She pointed to the ditch where Yasuo's and Bess' bodies lay. "They say otherwise."

"Lin, he's got a small army." She didn't budge. "We need to warn Sierra."

"You gave the drive to Blue. There's nothing we know that won't be on that drive."

"This is crazy."

She activated the takeoff sequence. "You're welcome to step off."

"Not a chance. You're not going anywhere." She took her fingers off the controls and stood up. Her eyes narrowed into pins, and her hands pressed into fists. "Alone," he added.

The tension in her shoulders released. She undid her fists and jumped to her seat, strapping herself in. She pointed to the seat next to her and punched the ignition before his back hit the seat. He remained silent as she pushed them forward, her gaze burning with the determination of winning the next battle. But the real win would have been avoiding this particular battle, and he'd already lost that one.

This was their third flight over these old-growth forests. Each trip had been painted by their expectations. On the first one, they had been unemotional, all business, and the scenery had been oddly soothing. On the second one, hope and worry had mixed evenly, allowing him to notice the majestic beauty of the forest pushing for every inch of nonvertical rock. Now, Gibson's savagery and Lin's fury tainted every action. Below them, the indifferent forest amplified their mood. Jutting rocks became belligerent, even angry.

Lin tapped the main panel on the dash between them. "Conversation mode on."

The panel beeped. "Scout Delta-One-Six online and listening."

She put her palm on the screen and stared into the panel to her right. "Code 2450104. Confirm match."

"Major Tomlin, confirmed," the autopilot said, authenticating her voice, face, print, and code.

"Authorize new pilot," Lin said and pointed at Mika to do what she had done.

He put his hand on his screen and stared at the panel. A green light flashed signaling his facial recognition had been completed. "State your name."

When Lin didn't offer any advice, he said, "Michael Rose."

She raised an eyebrow and gave him a side glance, but the autopilot spoke before she did. "Michael Rose accepted. Select a seven-digit code for activation."

"2037929"

"Repeat code."

"2037929"

"Michael Rose confirmed as authorized personnel and pilot."

"Do you know how to fly this thing?" she asked.

"You ask the autopilot nicely?"

She answered with a sidelong glance.

"Yeah, I do." He gave her a crooked smile. "Didn't know it talked, though."

"Gets way too chatty. First thing I do in any transport I take command of is to turn off the conversation mode."

"Never met a chatty autopilot before."

"Wait till you break it. Then it's nag, nag, nag."

"You know it can hear us, right?" he said, pointing a thumb to the screen.

She ignored him. "Autopilot, maintain course." She walked to the cargo hold and unlocked the gun case. He followed her. She put two handguns on the short shelf and stuffed three magazines in her jacket. She slid open the sniper rifle case and lifted the rifle. She moved the bolt, pulled the trigger, and put the rifle back down.

"What's the plan?"

"The plan is we take out Gibson, then find Tulum, and take him out too."

"Can you be more specific?"

She snapped the rifle case shut and opened the assault rifle crate. "No." She walked back to the cockpit and pointed to the map on the large screen between the two seats. A sixty-mile radius cone was highlighted. "That's a large footprint. We should spiral in from the northwest."

Forty-five minutes later, as they completed half the first outside loop, Mika's tida chimed. He flicked his tida to the screen, and the highlighted cones on the screen shrank and disappeared. A bright red dot appeared on the map about twenty miles west and forty miles north. The dot did not get larger as Lin zoomed in, pinpointing an old mine at the edge of a cliff on the Klamath River.

"How?" she asked.

"You carelessly gave control permissions to Michael Rose, and he accessed the comm link."

"Rose? Really?"

He grinned. "You think that's going to be the problem if this goes south?"

She squeezed her eyes shut for three seconds, jawbone clenched, and then reopened them. "How did you get a bloody location?"

"I sent your triangulation info to Blue. She's been chasing virus transmissions and dipping into Marin communications for a while. She had narrowed down compounds linked to *old* virus experiments, and she decrypted one of the eight partitions on the drive. With all that bundled together, she isolated the transmission towers."

"So." She put her finger on the dot on the screen. "Gibson is here?"

"He went that way. There's something there connected to the settlements."

She waved her hand toward the windscreen. "I thought you didn't want to do this."

"I still don't. But if you're going to insist on doing it, we might as well get proper intel."

She zoomed in and out of the compound, overlaying satellite images, isolating entry and exit points. They were headed to an old silver mine that had been repurposed into a hidden lab.

In another half-hour, they had the workings of a plan.

They flew low, hugging the canyon walls to avoid detection, and landed in a cave carved into the cliff. They climbed to the edge of the bluff, hiding behind three eight-foot boulders and a dozen smaller rocks. The clearing by the largest entrance to the mine stood three-quarters of a mile out and a hundred feet down. Two military crates were stacked on each other with a third to the side halfway between the mine and the road. Two heavy transports stood menacingly in the clearing fifty yards from the entrance, like two dragons protecting their den. The still air and absence of birds or other animals created a deep silence that heightened the incongruity of the military equipment.

Mika dropped and hid a dozen remote-trigger grenades under moss mounds in a hundred-foot-radius semi-circle and returned to their hideout. Below them, gray slate dulled by erosion rose straight up from the mine's entrance. The occasional green jutted out of cracks but didn't soften the harsh rock.

A Humvee was parked at the spot where the road narrowed and lost its tar right before diving into the mine. Two twenty-by-thirty shacks with single, slanted tin roofs rose to the right of the entrance, tucked into the side of the hill. The roads leading to the secondary entrances had disappeared, eaten by the sagebrush and tall grass. Other than the structures by the main entrance, nature had healed the decades of mining, leaving no scars on the landscape.

Lin stopped cleaning her rifle and nudged her head toward the grenades. "You know if we're ambushed, those will be as useful as a dick on a mule, right?"

"A mule's gotta have his fun." He pointed to the screen that displayed the distribution of grenades around their transport. "There's no path without getting near at least two of these."

She traced the pattern. "You're good at this."

He swiped the screen off. "If I were, we wouldn't be down to two out of a crew of five."

She didn't offer any words of comfort, which was good.

"We really should talk about this plan," he said.

"Look, I appreciate that you're here, but I don't need a lecture."

He looked through the scope again. There was no activity around the entrance. He stood up. "I don't like this. Finding them was too easy."

"You think Blue is compromised?"

He shook his head. "No, but they stayed on the line till we got a direction. Why?"

She ignored him and tapped her tida to float the mine's entry points between them. "That's the main entrance," she said, marking the spot with the heavy transport. "Here and here are two other entrances." She pointed to a tunnel leading up to the side of the cliff. "And this looks like an emergency exit."

"If those plans were accurate. If the tunnels haven't been modified."

She swiped the plans away, stood up, and put her assault rifle on her shoulder. "Let's pick an entrance and go then."

They hiked to the southernmost entrance in twenty minutes. A half-dozen overgrown false cypresses blocked the entrance. Even knowing it was there, it took them three tries to reach the opening behind the branches. He turned his headlight on and pushed forward.

The jagged walls sloped in as they rose, reaching a dimpled roof ten feet above them. Sixteen-inch-thick pine timbered the adit. The pine had bowed but held firm under pressures that would have long ago broken harder woods like oak. Mika caressed the rough, splintery timber.

The rusted mine rail track surfaced fifty yards in. It faded in and out—now here, now buried, like the century-old vestige it was. A hundred yards later, the tunnel sloped down sharply to a cave-in. Loose rocks in small mounds blocked half the tunnel. Debris had been cleared from the other half, creating a narrow passage. A quarter mile later, the tunnel split with the rail track veering left. They followed the rail, which did an S-bend a hundred yards in. Another quarter mile later, the rail went straight into a pile of rock that blocked the tunnel completely.

To their right, a five-foot opening led to a chamber with a domed ceiling he could reach by raising his arm. The walls became flat and smooth, almost glass-like, as though the rock had melted.

"This turn isn't on the plans," Lin said.

Mika didn't reply, having made his views on the ancient plans clear, but he followed her. A hundred yards later, he slowed and crouched next to a form by the tunnel wall. He nudged the shape with his foot, and a decomposed body rolled over. It produced no smell, and no soft tissue remained. The heavy coat had been reduced to strips. "A year, maybe two."

Lin didn't comment as they pushed further in.

With the tunnel bending and diving deeper into the rock, Mika stopped. "We haven't seen many air shafts, and the ones I spotted were too small for a tunnel this size."

"Was probably fine for old times."

He shook his head. "This would have been too small in any era. Why bother putting tiny vents when you know it's inadequate?" He then put his hand on the wall. "And this isn't old. Not only wasn't this section in your plan, but these walls are too smooth. This was dug by high-temp tunnel-boring machines, not old-timers."

The second corpse appeared another hundred yards in and with the same state of decomposition. He turned to Lin to comment, but she wasn't there.

"Lin?" He took eight quick steps, moving his head side to side for his headlight to spot her. She was leaning on the tunnel wall with her forearm, head bent. "Lin?"

She breathed heavily and collapsed.

He supported the back of her neck and shone his light on her face. Her eyes had rolled back, and her lips were blue. He put an arm on her waist to support her, and she sagged further. He lifted her on his shoulder and strode back the way they had come, leaning forward to keep a brisk pace.

Halfway back, his eyes burned, and his head throbbed as though his skull was about to explode. His breathing grew ragged, but he pushed on, reaching the rail at the old adit. Instead of slowing, he went to a light jog, his lungs bursting like he was sprinting. He kept his legs moving, settling into a rhythm, chewing up the yards. He hopped through the narrow passage of the cave in, relaxing only when he spotted the cypresses standing guard by the entrance.

He put her down between the bushes and the entrance. She stirred, taking quick, shallow breaths, and opened her eyes.

"That was stupid," she croaked and cleared her throat.

"There was no radiation," he said as he unclipped his water bottle and extended it to her.

She sat up and took a swig. "There was no oxygen either."

"We weren't deep enough," he said. But then, he thought better. "Unless—"

"Unless the tunnels are set up to not circulate air. Unless the small pipes are on purpose."

"Why?"

"To trap idiots like us?"

He took three deep breaths. "This was stupid. Really, really stupid."

"You were okay, though," she said, half-questioning, half-observing.

"I feel like an idiot."

"Good thing you take this hard-to-kill shit seriously." She chuckled and shook her head. "You'd think we'd have taken a hint from the bodies."

"I thought they were put there to scare trespassers." He took his water bottle from Lin and took a sip. He extended it back to her, and she took it and put it in her lap. "Rest for a few minutes. I'll grab oxygen masks and be right back."

He bolted at his five-minute-mile pace. This should not have happened. They had established a balance that had served them well. He pushed the limits, and Lin tempered his more dangerous tendencies. But when Lin's anger clouded her caution, they steered away from their roles and landed at an unstable point.

He disabled his grenades and reached the transport. He grabbed masks and two oxygen cans and rushed back, arriving twelve minutes after he'd left.

"That was quick," she said, sitting in the same spot.

He handed her a mask and an oxygen can as an answer. They donned their equipment, clipping their lights to their masks, and ventured back in.

"This doesn't make any sense," Mika said as they reached the spot where Lin had fainted. The oxygen levels had dropped from 21 to 19 to 15 percent at the point the track hit the tunnel wall. A few hundred yards into the new section, it hit 12 percent and hovered at 10 percent where he had spotted the second corpse.

A hundred yards later, the tunnel widened to a twenty-foot chamber and ended on a green metal door. Mika tried it, but it was bolted and sealed, more like a submarine door than a gate. Three rows of shelves lined the chamber. He pulled one, and it came out like a drawer. It contained a pillow and blankets. "Sleeping pods?"

She pulled two others, and they were the same. With ten on each shelf and three shelves on either side, there were sixty sleeping pods. "What do you make of it?"

He tapped his tida. "Eight percent oxygen. This is where you go to sleep if you don't intend to wake up."

She shivered. "You were right. This was a stupid idea. Let's get the hell out of here."

He followed her but stopped under one of the narrow intake vents. "Ten percent here too." He walked twenty yards to the vent that was supposed to bring good air into the tunnel. "Eight percent. The carbon dioxide is also at eight percent. What a pleasant mix!"

She unholstered her gun.

"You're going to shoot carbon dioxide with that?"

She spun her head in his direction, blinding him with the light on her mask. "I don't think we're alone."

The *thud* of a metal door closing shut behind them stopped him from replying. They picked up the pace, retracing their steps. They scurried back past the fork and slowed when light from the entrance filtered into the tunnel. Two soldiers with assault rifles dangling from their shoulders guarded the entrance.

They doubled back to the fork and took the side path. A hundred yards in, the tunnel veered right, and sunlight appeared in the distance. The tunnel narrowed to ten feet with smooth, straight walls and ended on a cliff.

The river flowed 140 feet below. Mika snuck his head out. They were fifty feet from the top. He did not find a single crack or handhold, not one plant larger than a fist to even consider climbing. The way down was even less inviting, the cliff sloping away from the river.

"Fuck!"

"I guess we fight our way out," she said.

"For that, I'd rather be in the wider tunnel."

As they reached the fork, they were greeted by a hiss. "Oxygen levels are dropping," he said with eyes on his tida. He took a step into the main tunnel, and shots rang out around him, one connecting with his shoulder. He jumped back into the side tunnel.

Lin took her assault rifle from her shoulder and slung it forward. She pressed her lips together. "Three," she said, pointing deep into the tunnel toward the green door, eyes on her tida.

"We're not going to fight our way out while they have us pinned from the back."

"We're kinda pinned now."

He turned his light to passive infrared. "I got this." Lin lifted her hand to tell him to stop, but he ignored her. "Cover me," he said and ran across the tunnel.

As Lin fired into the dark, Mika moved up with his back to the wall. With luck, they wouldn't spot him until he got closer.

He edged up. A shot hit him in the thigh, which meant they had infrared vision as well. So much for luck. He let go of the side and ran toward their assailants. Shots hit him, but he didn't slow. His goggles displayed two orange-red silhouettes crouched on either side of the S bend. He fired as he got to within fifty feet. Their shots tore into him, but he returned the damage.

The first one crumpled forward and stopped firing, and Mika tackled the second one, smashing him into the wall. He stood up and fired into the eye of each collapsed soldier. He took two steps and came face-to-face with the third soldier, who came around the bend, aiming at his head. Before she pulled the trigger, her head exploded.

Lin stood thirty yards behind him, rifle in hand. "You're okay?"

He leaned on the wall. "Be fine in a minute."

"We don't have a minute." She walked toward him, with her eyes glued to her tida. He must have looked bad because her face soured when her light hit him. "Fuck me!"

Blood stained his chest and chin. His right thigh was shredded, flesh hanging to the side. His left knee bent out twenty degrees out. He put his thigh together and pressed the flesh in.

She examined him, from shoulder to chest, to thigh, to knee. He must have been a mess because her eyes retracted to pinholes. "How?" She kept a hand on his elbow. "Can you walk?"

He limped three steps. His knee sent jolts of fire up his spine at each contact with the ground. "Yeah."

She kept her eyes on him for a few more seconds and then moved ahead. "I'll take point."

He breathed in, out, in, out with every step because that knee wouldn't work properly for half an hour. Twenty steps later, he could push on his thigh, and his shoulders stopped warning him that they were about to drop. As long as he didn't need to run hard, he would be fine.

They plodded toward the entrance. His knee registered every change of elevation, first up, then down, then up again. He struggled with the unsteady soil by the old cave-in when they had to trek over loose rocks, his bad knee screaming at every step.

Lin slowed down, then climbed down the other side of the cave-in. He stopped and put a hand on the wall as he slid over the loose rock. "Damn knees," he huffed. "Muscle, bone, cartilage, ligament—all have to operate just right for the fucking thing to work at all. Everything else degrades smoothly."

An armed squad stood by the entrance. Her eyes moved from the entrance to his knee. "We need to move."

"Where to?"

She didn't reply because they were trapped between the metal door of an underground installation, a 140-foot drop down a ravine, and an entrance guarded by an armed squad. He should have been afraid, but he felt tired, tired of fighting, tired of pushing for answers. The last time he felt at an end, he had found many things he still had to say to Amy and to Lori. Today, he felt empty. He straightened up, ready for whatever was coming their way. "They weren't wearing oxygen masks," he said.

She stopped scanning the tunnel and turned around. "What?"

"The three back there. They didn't have masks." He tried to flex his knee by trying to sit on his heels but gave up after halfway. "Well, you did say I was going to fuck up one day."

"You haven't yet."

He chuckled. "My knee begs to differ."

She put a hand on his shoulder. "This one's on me." She offered him his water bottle, the one she kept when he had gone to the transport. He rested his back on the wall and took two sips. He handed it back to her and she also took a sip. "Just how did you get this indestructible?"

"You know the routine."

"No, no, no. It's one thing to get the cut on your arm to close faster than mine when we do bourbon shots. This is something else. If I'd been shot half as many times as you just were, I wouldn't be moving at all. You didn't surprise me; you surprised them. Their tactics were based on my type of healing. Even though they can handle low oxygen levels, they can't heal like you."

He didn't point out that they hadn't gotten anywhere. He took a deep breath, letting it out slowly. "I had a few serious kicks to the system rather than the slow process you went through. Mostly out of desperation."

"How serious?"

"Lots of ricin to fix bad internal injuries. And then some AHtX."

"What the fuck?"

"I broke my neck in two places, severed my spinal cord. Phillips figured out a way to use AHtX to keep me going. So, I'm not exactly a reproducible model."

"Bloody hell."

He stood up. "Definitely bloody. Hell, we'll see." He smirked. "Not good as new, but good enough."

Lights moved on the walls and the hum of an engine sound filled the tunnel. He peaked to find a dozen soldiers advancing behind an ATV with bright lights and a fifty-caliber gun mounted on its hoods. Lin moved over the cave-in, and Mika followed.

As they approached the fork, lights turned on ahead of them. Another ATV sat fifty yards past the fork, near the spot of their last gunfight. Lin ran to the fork and dove into the side tunnel as gunfire erupted. He limped behind her, hopping hard on his right leg, letting the left leg hit the ground every three hops to stabilize his gait. As he collapsed, she grabbed his collar and dragged him into the side tunnel.

Daylight trickled in from the end of the tunnel, teasing them with the possibility of a way out. "There's only one way out of this," he said.

As spotlights drew closer, they sprinted to the cliff. She did so with elegant strides, her legs pumping, knees high, he like a bowling pin tossed down a curving slide. She jumped first and with force, reaching high to clear the rocks below. He didn't jump so much as tipped over.

A heavy transport rose from the canyon as he cleared the cliff wall, cargo bay doors open with two Gatling gun-like devices protruding. The guns fired simultaneously, and dozens of arrows flew toward them. Lin's path was straight toward the transport. She slammed into the arrows as much as they struck her. He counted eight tearing into her, with four going straight through her torso.

The ones coming at him were too high because he had barely cleared the cliff wall. One arrow pierced his right arm below the elbow, but the rest flew harmlessly past him. As his arm got yanked around, the lines came into view. These projectiles were more harpoon than arrow.

The line on his arm snapped, pulling him a little closer to the middle of the canyon, but he still was not going to make it to the river. He fired over a dozen rounds to the cliff wall. Though the bullets weighed little, they moved fast. The recoil of the bullets and secondary recoil of the expanding gas bought him a few more feet of clearance, and he needed every inch.

The water was coming at him at breakneck speed now, but it wasn't the sight of dark submerged rocks that petrified him.

It was that Lin had sprung back up, tangled in the tension of a wire and arrow contraption, dangling from the transport.

CHAPTER 19

ANGEL DOWN

"True friends stab you in the front."

—OSCAR WILDE

Mika coughed himself awake, spewing out water from his lungs. His frozen left cheek rested against wet dirt. He pushed himself on his hands and knees and coughed again. He crawled a few feet and sat up. He was on a soft dirt patch on a river bend. Ahead of him, short sage bushes jutted from a rocky shore. Across the river, rolling hills covered in juniper led to firs in the distance.

His head throbbed, and his chest burned as though it contained tiny explosions. He took a deep breath, and his lungs screamed. He took three more breaths, and the pressure let up. He reached to wipe the dirt from his lips with his right hand and spotted the arrow stuck to his arm, the shaft broken. The broadhead had four three-inch spikes embedded in his arm, more like an anchor than an arrow. He tugged on the shaft, and the flexing spikes dented his flesh to yank his arm. Eight or ten of these would support an adult's body. He pulled out the head, removing the shaft.

He put the shaft into his jacket pocket and tapped his tida to check the time. They had gone over the cliff five hours ago.

Shit.

He pitched a small, dry branch into the water and counted the seconds as it moved away. The flow was about three knots. His tida informed him he was six miles from the compound, meaning he had floated for two hours and washed up about three hours ago.

He was surprised Gibson's team hadn't fished him out, but then he remembered the transport exploding as he hit the water, or rather, as he hit the river bed, after being marginally slowed down by the water. He checked his thigh and shoulder, spotting no damage from the bullets that had torn into him.

He stood up and tested his knee by bending forward and twisting side to side. It was good as new. He was on the wrong bank, but he still took a dozen steps, leaving indents on the soft dirt. He walked back to the water, stepping into his footprints. He swam downstream another three minutes before finding a branch on the opposite bank extending to the water from a rocky outcropping.

He climbed the branch to the rock and disappeared into the brush. He ran away from the river for five minutes, then up the river for thirty, reaching the cave where they had left the transport. He needed food before his body shut down. Repair took a lot of energy, and he had abused his body, first during the attack, then during the jump, and now running back. He did not trust himself to think straight, much less fight.

He approached the cave from the hills, the arrow shaft in his fist. He used caution, but the cave and transport were unguarded. He tapped the codes, and the cargo door hissed open. He swallowed three full dinner packs, stripped out of his filthy clothes, and put on clean pants and a shirt. He reached down to pick up the shirt he had discarded as he gulped two quarts of water. It was torn to shreds with multiple puncture marks on the back and side. He tossed it away and reached for a jacket. He stuffed two handguns in his pockets, strapped an assault rifle on his shoulder, and headed out.

He approached the main entrance from the forest, but his caution was again unnecessary. Both transports were gone, though the Humvee was still there, next to the two shacks. Three soldiers sat around a crate in front of the shacks, in the open. They chatted and played cards, not the least bit concerned that he might be tracking them.

Then he saw it.

A concrete coffin stood to his right, at the back of the clearing, baking in the sun, the bright blue mold still visible on one side. The first time he had seen these contraptions, he found them revolting. Now he was consumed with enough rage to start another fire in the Cascades. His burn wouldn't be concerned with rebirth, though, just death.

He circled the clearing but found no activity other than the three soldiers. He perched two hundred yards out at an angle that turned them into sitting ducks. He set up his rifle on the low bipod and settled into the sniper position, eye on the scope.

He put the rifle on a three-shot burst and aimed at the soldier closest to the entrance. He pulled the trigger, moved, pulled, moved, and pulled. He waited for ten seconds, and when no one moved, he put the rifle on his shoulder and trotted to the clearing.

He had hit the first and the third clean but only hit the second in his neck. He fired into his eye and headed to the concrete coffin.

"Lin!" he called as he reached it.

A grunt came from inside.

He reached in and grabbed her hand. It tightened around his.

"I'll be right back," he said and headed to the first shack. A low bench ran the length of the back wall with tools strewn across it. He picked up a circular saw and moved to his right. The benches held lab test equipment, centrifuges, and small fridges. On the shelves above, he spotted two field medical packs containing saline bags, IV tubing, Y-connectors, and more. He grabbed them and sprinted back.

He cut the concrete vertically first, then horizontally, dropping one-foot sections. The back piece was solid. The front was only 90 percent cured, so he focused on that one until he reached her face. He cut through the rebar to free her jaw then removed the piece down to her neck. Her face was ashen. He poured water onto her lips, and she held it in her mouth before swallowing. She coughed, spitting blood.

"You promised," Lin whispered when her coughing fit stopped.

She wheezed as she breathed because the rebar holding her in place went straight through her lung. He took two catheters from the medical pack and inserted them into her veins. He drew blood from the first one, draining three pints. Her eyes fluttered, but she stayed conscious.

He spiked the saline bag and hooked it to the second catheter through a Y-connecter, hanging the bag from a rebar stump over her head. He nicked the vein in his forearm and pushed in the IV tube directly as his flesh sealed around it. He had never been more grateful to be a universal donor. He shoved the tube to the Y-connecter, switched it from the saline solution to his blood, and raised his arm above hers.

Five minutes later, color returned to her face, and she opened her eyes. "Didn't think you'd make it."

"Huh?"

"You hit the bottom so hard the river ran red."

"I don't remember."

"Good thing."

"I guess that's why no one was watching the cave."

"You need to go."

"Not a chance."

"You're wasting time."

"Shhh."

"They let us follow them."

"Just rest."

"Listen, they did this to keep us here."

"It's working."

"You need to go back and warn Rendon and Chipps."

"You're coming with me."

"Stop." She rasped with all the energy she must have kept in reserve. "I'm already dead. I received a lethal dose many times over."

"You're tougher than most."

"You think they don't know that?"

"Once you're stronger, you might fight the radiation."

"Can't fix this. And I'm not letting you cut that thing to kill us both with the trap in my chest."

He tapped the concrete on her back. "This is cured." He tapped the one he had just cut. "This one still has wet spots."

"And?"

"It means the pressure on the device had to be set. Which means it can be unset."

"I'm a little heavy to carry."

"We'll find a way."

"You're a terrible liar."

"I thought I saw an explosion as I floated downriver. What happened?"

She took three shallow breaths. "When I saw you shatter into a red mist, I thought we were both done. Had an unused grenade. Didn't want to waste it."

He smiled and reopened the valve to let new blood flow. "I bet that surprised them."

"They weren't very happy with me."

He caressed her face, pushing her sweat-soaked hair from her eyes. "They shouldn't have messed with an angel," he said, fighting back his tears.

"You're really bad at keeping promises."

The analyzer showed elevated radiation in her blood, so he increased the flow. The radiation dropped but then started to climb again in fifteen seconds.

"Just do what you promised," she said.

He closed his eyes, trying to erase her pained expression from his mind. "We're going to get you out of this."

She closed her eyes. "I told you. I'm already dead."

"You don't know that."

As a response, she bit hard, clamping her jaw, and pushed her lips out with her tongue as though she were chewing or generating spit. She then ruminated and pushed her tongue out, exposing a tooth. She spat it out, though it just dribbled down her arm. "Just do it," she said.

Before he countered, a shot tore into his shoulder. He pulled the tubing out of her arm and spun behind the concrete as the gunfire intensified. A heavy transport appeared overhead with chains dangling toward the concrete coffin as he climbed the hill.

He sped toward his transport at a full sprint. Now, there were two guards at the mouth of his cave, sitting on two rocks. He fired at the first one before she had a chance to stand up. The second drew his gun, but Mika tackled him and slammed his head to the ground. Mika stood up and fired a shot into the man's face.

He hopped in the transport and punched the activation code. The transport shot out of the cave and was on top of the heavy transport hovering above Lin in thirty seconds. Because they had already attached one of the chains to Lin's concrete box, the heavy transport couldn't maneuver out of the way. Mika let a full salvo fly into it. The transport snapped the chain and tried to gain altitude to no avail. Mika launched a missile that connected with the transport.

The dozen or so soldiers on the ground took cover as rotors, wing parts, and fuselage flew in all directions; the carcass turned into a fireball and crashed into the trees.

"Six heavy transports on approach," the autopilot said.

"When will they be here?"

"Five minutes, twenty seconds."

That was an eternity for what he had to do. Mika pitched forward, opening with his chain gun, hitting the soldiers scattered around Lin.

"Incoming."

He rolled hard to his right, but he was too low to avoid the surface-to-air missile. It tore into his port wing taking the wing, engine, and aft winglet out. He spiraled out of control.

"Autopilot on."

"Copy."

"Land straight down there." He pointed to the back of the clearing, thirty yards from Lin. He picked up another handgun and opened the cargo doors, waiting to jump out.

The spot to which he had pointed spun out of his view as the autopilot fought to bring the craft under control. They landed hard on some trees, but mostly on their landing pads a hundred yards from the clearing.

"Are you damaged?"

Chatty indeed. "No," Mika said. "Status?"

"Incoming transports are four minutes out."

"I meant your status."

"Port wing and engine are gone. Starboard engine damaged but operational at sixty percent thrust. Starboard aft at thirty percent."

"Can you take off?"

"In normal mode, no."

"What does that mean?"

"There is not enough thrust for a conventional takeoff."

"What other type is there?"

"Rocketed vertical takeoff is available, but it is not advisable."

"Why not?"

"In vertical takeoff, all engines are at full thrust. Without port engines, we will damage starboard engines."

"I see. Prep vertical launch. I'll be right back."

"Copy." Three seconds later, it beeped again. "Warning."

"Yeah?"

"At this pose and orientation, we are unlikely to clear the tree line."

"Good to know," he said before it beeped again. "What?"

The autopilot was making up for weeks of silence. "Once we burn starboard engines on take-off, we cannot land again."

"Just get ready for launch and stop with the warnings."

He lifted the sniper rifle from its case, snapped in a five-cartridge magazine, and ran out. He didn't run to the clearing because whoever had shot him down still had to be there. He didn't have time for another fight. He settled on the first hill that gave him a clear look at Lin.

A dozen bodies were scattered in the clearing. One soldier stood by Lin, scanning the tree line. Another soldier crouched from casualty to casualty. They were the only two moving.

The autopilot chimed through his tida. "Two minutes."

He put his gear down and raised the rifle to look through the scope. Lin's face filled his crosshairs. The sun reflecting from his scope danced on the rib steel roof of the shacks. Her eyes darted to the reflection, then the sun, then toward him.

"Do it," she mouthed.

"Ninety seconds," the autopilot called.

"Stop talking," he snapped.

One bullet scrambles that brain of yours beyond anything the Purge can do.

True or not, those were not the words he wanted to remember Lin by.

I'm already dead.

Neither were those.

He exhaled to empty his lungs. He caressed the trigger. When his finger tightened, the imperceptible motion would unleash irrevocable violence. She looked his way, and her lips stretched as though she attempted to smile. His brain only registered a face contorted in pain.

He emptied his mind of everything except Lin's true nature, captured in a name. A name that didn't belong in their world, a name he would remember her by.

He exhaled and squeezed the trigger, keeping one promise. He figured she would forgive him for breaking the other one and whispered, "Good night, Angel."

PART III
FLOOD

CHAPTER 20

DIVORCE

"It took me quite a long time to develop a voice, and now that I have it, I am not going to be silent."

—MADELEINE ALBRIGHT

After two long days in the basement, reclaiming her office offered a positive spin to an otherwise miserable week. Because Kuipers had suspended the council and claimed emergency powers, Cavana had objected to her moving upstairs, but Amy couldn't govern if she hid in the basement.

Four rows of sticky notes littered her desk, huddling to the back and right with their reminders as though they cowered away from her screens. She dreaded the day they would run out of sticky pads—not because it would sever one more link to a more prosperous past she had never known, but because she would miss their disposable practicality.

Her office was bigger than necessary, with a white, round table, three wire-back chairs in the far corner to her right, and a row of bookshelves on the wall to her left. Her single wood-framed armchair sat behind her desk right across from the door to the antechamber occupied by Ferg and Eva. Twenty feet separated her desk from the door covered by a rug whose colors had long washed away by the sunlight from the square window to her right.

Fontaine's books still lined the shelves. Beyond those, only his metal-rimmed glasses had remained in the office. The ones he had worn during the summit had shattered, but the spare ones had been on the desk. They pleaded to be left alone, and she avoided touching them for months. Now, they had reached a truce. The glasses sat on the bookshelves next to their old master's books, within view of her desk, but without infringing on her workspace.

She put her pen through the bottommost note that reminded her to link her comments to Fontaine's last speech.

Not today.

She resumed her recording: "And therefore, New California must accept responsibility for…." She tapped her tida, leaned back on her chair, and rubbed her temples. The words didn't capture her intent, didn't allow her to express her disdain for Marin's new direction. And they certainly didn't inspire anyone to follow her.

It was so easy to set up a position against Kuipers. But when she had to spell out what she stood for, the subtleties tripped her, and she sank into a stream of hopeful word soup that meant little.

She stood up and walked to the bookshelf, lifting the glasses by their temples. Fontaine would have known what to say. He would have found just the right word that would excite New Californians without antagonizing Marin. But would he have wanted to say any of this? She doubted it. She was struggling with the words because she was struggling with her direction.

She put the glasses back and tapped her tida. "The sovereignty of New California requires…" she started but tapped her tida again, her thoughts drifting to Marin.

What would a wise Marin chancellor have said? It would have been the opposite of what Amy wanted. Perhaps she should write that speech, the one that took the exact opposing position to better test her arguments? But she didn't have time for games.

Somewhere between what a Marin chancellor or Governor Fontaine or Cavana would say lay what she had to say. But it wasn't what she wanted to say.

She ambled to the window. The increased militia presence was the new normal. She hopped on her desk, away from the sticky notes, and listened back to her narrative. It was worse than she feared. Her words were forced, clunky, bludgeoning the moment.

Then it hit her. The problem wasn't the words; it was the audience.

She had been apologizing to the old guard for what she had to do. Instead, she needed a new audience. She headed to the antechamber that separated her office from the corridor. It was a square room with two desks on either side of the walking path connecting her door to the hallway door. Eva had nudged her desk toward the corridor to shove a gray sofa on the wall behind her. She sat on the sofa with her arms on top of the backrest, smiling at something Ferg must have said.

Eva and Ferg were thirty years apart, one a soldier and one an assistant. Different in a thousand ways, yet whatever they'd wanted or aspired to had led them here. They were her intended audience, those who had chosen to stay, not the ghosts from her past.

She went back to her desk without a word and recorded the message in one go. She still hit all the points listed on her sheet, but the tone had shifted. Satisfied that she had something to work with, she instructed her tida to transcribe the message.

She put her elbows on the desk and rubbed her eyes with the heels of her hands. When she opened her eyes, Ferg was standing by her office door, eyes narrowed in concern. Ferg closed the door and sat down in the armchair across Amy's desk with the weariness of someone who had spent a lifetime fighting against insurmountable odds.

Interesting, Ferg wasn't here as her able, wonderful assistant. She was an old soul, a witness from the past here to share wisdom. She must have noticed Amy observing them by the door and waited for an extended silence to interrupt her.

"Every choice I make leads down a path I don't want to go," Amy said. "I know where I want to go, but do I know the steps that will get me there? Not so much."

Ferg poured a glass of water from the pitcher on the desk and placed it by Amy's hand. Speaking nonstop for twenty minutes had dried her throat, so she took three gulps. "We're about to go backward."

"Sometimes it seems that way."

"It's like we're unraveling last year. Going back to that fork in the road and taking another path."

Ferg smiled, eyes warming up. "Oh no, dear. There is no unraveling the past. It may seem that way, you may even give ground on the progress you made, but you're always moving forward."

"The past doesn't have a hold on me. But I know what it meant to those around me. I know what I have to do. And yet, I…." She fumbled for the right words. "I don't want to sever another link to Fontaine's legacy."

Ferg took a long breath and exhaled through her nose as though she were about to betray a trust. "He was a great man. He built this city from nothing. He built the state from even less, as Marin and Kern tried to trip him at every step. But he didn't see the full path to the destination either. He kept going because that's what we do. He struggled with most of his decisions."

"He seemed so sure of himself. He made it look easy."

Ferg gave a shrill laugh. "It was anything but. Just so you know, this union was never his goal. It appeared out of nowhere, and he made it work. And that's what you have to do."

It was good advice but hard to follow because it required a leap of faith. She needed to understand Ferg, not the wonder assistant but the wise old-timer who'd chosen to stay in Santa Cruz. "Early on, why didn't you pick Marin?"

A sad smile appeared on Ferg's face. "It was a strange time. You can't imagine what it was like. We went from the most prosperous time on the planet to death and chaos. From tapping a tida to summon a driverless car to take you to the trendy restaurant by a hip new chef, to stepping over corpses to get at food scraps. All order broke down. Marin today sounds like a fine place, but then it was just another compound with a hard-to-swallow message to boot."

Her eyes narrowed with sorrow and joy. "I was lucky. I married my best friend. He sent me messages throughout the day, silly little things that didn't mean anything. It was our little game against the world. We had a dozen years together, so I can't complain. Many people never get any of that."

Ferg stared straight into the wall. "I lost him in the third year. One week we were hopeful, the next he was in bed, and the one after that he was gone. Marin wanted me to buy into the fiction that he didn't matter. That he had never mattered. I wasn't willing to do that. And by the time that faded, the work to build New Cal was underway, so I stayed with Fontaine."

Both Ferg and Fontaine had lost their spouses. Had there been more between them? She pushed the thought away. "What I do next is going to turn us into targets. Me. You. Nando. Everyone in this building and this city."

"Don't worry about us. Do what you need to do. We've been through worse."

"This path I'm about to take, I don't know if anyone will follow me."

"They will."

Amy took another sip of water. "How can you be so sure?"

"I've seen it before. These last few years, people followed Fontaine out of habit. It didn't occur to anyone to not follow him. It wasn't always like that. In the early days, he was full of passion. We followed him because we believed in him and that he'd take us to a better place even if none of us knew where that place was."

"I don't know how to do that."

Ferg smiled again, eyes warm. "You already did. I see something I haven't seen in years in faces I cross in the street. And I feel it too."

"What?"

"Hope. Ever since your speech last year. They, we, believe in you not because we should, not because we have to, but because we want to. We believe you will take us to a better place. Trust me when I tell you this: do what you have to do. New Cal is behind you."

"Thank you," Amy said, allowing Ferg's belief to lift her mood like the incoming tide.

Ferg leaned across the desk and reached for Amy's hand, giving it a squeeze. "No, thank you for giving an old woman new hope."

Ferg had plenty of passion of her own. "Why didn't you want this?"

"Not for me," Ferg said, her voice disappearing into a whisper as though wishing for an unattainable prize or fearing waking up a deadly monster. "I organize. I advise. But I'm not a leader. I can't ever find words like you do to inspire."

Amy smiled. "You're doing great now."

"One on one with you, I can say what I feel. But crowds petrify me. Confrontation melts my resolve. Negotiation exhausts me. Put me in front of an audience, and I turn into a blabbering idiot. I wouldn't last two days in politics."

Amy reached over to her desk and took her tida. She rotated it between her fingers. "Till I broadcast this message, we can still back out." Ferg remained silent. "But should we?"

Ferg stood up. "That's for you to decide. Either way we're behind you."

"Thank you," Amy said as Ferg walked out.

By the time Cavana arrived an hour later, she had completed her recorded announcement. "Are we ready?"

"The team is in place," he said.

She joined Cavana by the round table next to her door. The mayors of Santa Cruz, Mountain View, and San Jose had been briefed. They hadn't been thrilled, and though each had expressed reasonable concerns, they now supported the move.

Heath had wanted to leave since day one, and Joy wanted assurances that Santa Cruz wouldn't bear the financial burden. In the end, it had worked, not because of the arguments but because they had dealt with reasonable people. A distinction that wouldn't apply to her next call.

"How's what I'm doing different than what Kuipers did?" Amy blurted out.

"What do you mean?"

"I told them I wanted their public support. That's exactly what Kuipers told me."

Cavana shrugged. With his wide chest and broad shoulders, it looked like half his torso was moving up and away from his arms. "There is a major difference."

"What?"

"You are right, and Kuipers is wrong."

Amy chuckled. "Let's hope so."

"Are you sure you want to talk to Halsan? I can brief him on the procedural matters first."

"Get him on the line."

Halsan appeared on her screen. His face, too close to the camera, hounded her from the get-go, giving the pleasantries no chance to set a softer tone.

"I thought you'd be happy," Amy said after they'd gone three rounds.

His cheeks reddened in protest. "It's not your conclusion that worries me; it's that we got here without proper discourse."

Amy took a deep breath. "All three mayors and the vice governor are in favor of independence. If you agree, we can announce a unanimous New Cal decision."

"I cannot support this move."

"Mayor, you've never wanted to be in a union with Marin. Why do you oppose leaving?"

"I oppose your approach. You've talked to each mayor, talked to the public, and swayed them to your way."

"I made a case. They supported it. That's how democracy works."

"Is that what you call this? I'd say you're acting unilaterally and increasing your personal power at the expense of what's in the best interests of New California."

"I'm not going to debate this. I wanted to give you the option of joining us in a unified front. But my decision is final."

He shook his head. "No."

"If we look indecisive, we will invite a stronger Marin response. There will be violence."

"That's on you. If you insist on this path, I will oppose you publicly."

Cavana grimaced from across the table.

She softened her voice. "What would make you support this announcement?"

Halsan leaned over his desk and smiled. He must have meant it to be friendly. But his unblinking eyes and cheeks, unaffected by the smile, gave him a creepy look, as though two entities competed for control of his face. "If you were to give more autonomy to Cal City—"

"What do you want?"

Cal City was already semi-autonomous and the seat of power in New Cal. She blinked away her irritation.

"If you were to, say, name me vice governor, I might be able to give you public support."

"No."

"Don't be hasty. I can be a strong ally. Or…" He flashed his shit-eating grin again. "I can leak this, making it impossible for you to strike the deal you want."

"All right, we'll do this your way. Here's a simple choice. Either you support me, or you'll be in house arrest till the Marin response is under control. But I cannot have you undermine every decision I make while I'm negotiating with Marin."

He laughed and leaned back in his chair. "I will leak this if you don't agree."

She tapped her tida, authorizing it to send her decree to Marin headquarters, and sixty seconds later broadcast her prepared statement to all of New Cal and Marin.

"You're too late to leak anything."

CHAPTER 21

POINT OF NO RETURN

"No one changes the world who isn't obsessed."
—BILLIE JEAN KING

Mika rolled to his left and slipped his right hand under his pillow. After ten breaths that did nothing to quiet his mind, he opened his eyes and rolled onto his back. He had a ceiling, and it was the wrong height. For months he had slept either outdoors or in a tent. A ten-foot ceiling upset his depth perception.

He forced his mind back to this room, a nine-by-nine square with a narrow bed, a single nightstand, and a barely screen-wide desk in the corner. The sterile room occupied his mind for all of six seconds before Lin's image through his crosshairs took over as though projected on every wall.

He shut his eyes, visualizing flapping sails and ocean swells, but his mind wouldn't be tricked that easily. He opened his eyes again and reached for his tida.

4:10

He may have shut his eyes for half an hour at some point, but he wasn't going to get any more rest tonight. He had turned in early to avoid talking to anyone, and Sierra had given him space on his first night back.

He got out of bed, put on a T-shirt, and sat at the desk. He scrolled through the news articles his sniffers had labeled as of interest, catching up on Marin-New Cal events. All in all, a lot had happened, and nothing had happened.

He ventured out of his room, strolling the hallways, and stepping out into the north-facing courtyard. In their absence, the Shed had grown, acquiring two new buildings—one complete to his right and the other straight ahead, a shell with an embryonic roof. He went back to his room and changed into his running shorts. Being indoors, being in a group, eating in a cafeteria all emphasized the transition to a new life, drawing a thick line under the last six months. He had to delay that at least for a little while longer.

He ran for two hours on the dirt roads, first south then east. The temptation to keep going wherever the road took him was strong. But he hadn't agreed to come back to the Shed because he believed in Sierra or because he was ready to get back in the fold. He was here because it was the best way to find Gibson and Tulum.

He slowed to a walk by a lone oak tree with long, knotted branches that could have cradled a warehouse. Each branch spread at a different angle in its fight for sunlight, but together they formed a cocoon that shielded him from the mid-morning sun. A branch as thick as his torso stood under the tree, out of the fold, dead. He sat on the branch, running his fingers over the dry, rough bark, and letting it transport him to another branch, hundreds of miles away.

What happened at the mine wasn't his fault. It was his fault.

He had supported Lin. He should have stopped her from chasing Gibson.

He had done all he could. He most certainly hadn't.

He had killed Lin.

He withdrew his hand as though the last thought had come from the dead branch. He started back, consuming the miles with his pace. As he approached the Shed, his tida chimed, picking up the tower's signal. Sierra was calling him insistently. He tapped it off.

He went into the facility, avoiding eye contact with the guards at the security cabin that had replaced the canopy by the gate. The showers were empty because only loners who didn't follow orders took showers at 11 a.m. He cleaned up, grabbed a quart of water, and headed to Sierra's office.

Sierra stared at him with a clamped jaw and tapped her tida, which informed them both that it was 11:28.

"I called you nearly two hours ago."

"Well, I'm here now."

"You do realize I'm the commanding officer while you're in this facility, right?"

"Command away."

She shook her head and pointed to the screen. "I'd have liked to have a context before he got here."

Mika walked around Sierra's desk and leaned forward to see her screen. Gibson's truck was half a mile away from the compound.

Sierra motioned him off the camera, and Mika moved across the desk and plopped on one of two chairs. He extended his legs, crossed his ankles, and sipped his water bottle. Sierra spun her screen sideways to let him watch. One guard stood behind the gate in front of Gibson's truck. The other was talking to Gibson, whose frown signaled his unhappiness. After a Gibson monologue followed two more guard explanations, Sierra tapped her screen.

"Anjali," she said, and the guard's hand went to her ear. "Patch me directly to him, I'll take it from here." She then tapped the main screen on the security panel to talk to Gibson directly. "What seems to be the problem?"

"Who is this?" Gibson moved toward the checkpoint.

"I'm Colonel Sierra Rendon, the commanding officer of this facility."

"Ah, good. As I was explaining to your sergeant, I need to talk to you."

"This is a restricted area."

Gibson spoke a little faster, unable to hide his rising irritation. "Colonel, I am here to inspect your progress on orders from the Marin Council."

"That won't be necessary." After a pause, she added, "Who are you again?"

Gibson produced a fake smile that didn't warm up his eyes. "I am Gibson and an associate of General Kuipers. I've been sent here directly by General Kuipers to oversee your progress." He put two curled fingers on his lips and his thumb under his chin. "I also have reliable information that the person who crash-landed with a damaged aircraft was taken here."

"I cannot confirm that."

"Do you deny it?"

"I cannot confirm that."

Gibson smiled again, this time with a hint of amusement. "If you let me in, we can—"

"I'm afraid this facility is restricted to command staff only."

"I am the representative of General Kuipers," he said, voice rising, unable to contain his irritation. "As such, I am command staff."

"It doesn't work that way. I report to General Kuipers. If I receive a direct order from her, I will follow it. Till then, you are a civilian who is trespassing."

"I was led to believe this facility was... uh... outside of the usual channels."

"That is a fair assessment."

"We're all on the same side. We all want the same thing. If you allow me in, I can prove this to you."

"Mr. Gibson, this is a restricted area, and I am busy. When I receive orders through proper channels, I'd be happy to discuss your contribution to our cause."

Gibson's guard stepped off the truck, but three more Sentinels came out of the cabin, with hands on their assault rifles. Sierra leaned toward her screen. "I don't recommend testing the resolve of my security team."

Gibson's smile faded, and he motioned his guard back in. "Very well."

"He'll be back," Mika said as Gibson's truck completed its three-point turn and headed back out.

"I know."

"He won't ask nicely next time."

"I know."

Mika chuckled. "I hear Amy was here. Now Gibson. Clandestine organizations are not very effective if they're not clandestine."

Her eyes stayed on his. "Before Gibson returns, I need to know everything about him."

Mika narrowed his eyes in surprise. "Didn't you know that before sending Lin to snatch him if the situation arose?"

She shook her head. "I knew Gibson and Tulum were mixed in Marin politics. I first thought they represented the Puries and that they would turn Kuipers or someone else in the council into another Lester."

Mika took a deep breath to prevent himself from jumping out of his chair. There was ill-informed, and there was criminally ignorant. Sierra had stepped pretty far over the line. Her assumptions had not changed over the last months even as the evidence and bodies mounted. She had kept her head buried in the past.

He pointed to the screen. "This asshole works with Tulum. And based on what I've read about what's been going on in Marin and Gibson's current antics, I'd say they've already influenced Marin beyond anything you can fix."

Sierra put her elbows on her desk and cradled her head in her hands. After thirty seconds, she lifted her head. "You shot Lin, really?"

Mika kept his gaze on Sierra but did not speak.

"That's what you said on the transport. I listened to it three times to make sure I hadn't misheard."

"I need some coffee," he said though it wasn't strictly true. Coffee had become a pleasant, aromatic hot drink with no physiological impact, another casualty to the Purge, just like bourbon.

Sierra sighed. "I gave you space last night, but I need to know." She swiped her screen. "Jill, can you get us a pot of coffee? Thanks." She stood up, walked around her desk, and sat beside Mika. "I'll go first. Whatever you read this morning, whatever you think is going on, it's worse. Yim is out, not that she was ever in. The union is on life support."

"The union was never alive."

"Yeah. Marin is split into fifteen districts, and you can't move from one to another without biometric IDs, which you can only get after a full scan. They're storing blood records and monitoring every zone crossing. Marin is a total mess with the checkpoints disrupting everything from food deliveries to work schedules to school attendance."

"What is Kuipers after? She has to know those bodies pose no danger."

"I thought they were hunting for Puries."

He shook his head. "Doesn't track. You don't need quarantine zones for that. What is she bracing for?"

"Another outbreak?"

"Fuck." He slapped the table. "The settlements up north. The versions of the Purge they carry are different. Powell, my contact, said they lost over forty people when they got infected."

Sierra's eyes widened. "What fatality rate are we looking at?"

"They had a little over a thousand people. Assuming there's nothing special about them, that's roughly four percent."

She pushed air out of her mouth and cringed. "That will cripple Marin. The chaos and panic will bring life to a halt. Curfews will paralyze life. I can't blame Kuipers, not for this."

He waved, ignoring and disputing the statement in one motion, but was saved from a comeback by the knock on the door. The aide brought a pot of coffee and two metal mugs and placed them on the coffee table between them.

"Thanks, Jill," Sierra said.

Mika filled his cup and leaned back. "What was Amy doing here?"

Sierra paused, pot in hand. "She wanted to know where her militia was disappearing to."

"What did you tell her?"

"All of it." She filled her cup and added a touch of cream.

He sipped his coffee and grimaced at the empty, bitter flavor. "How is she doing?"

Sierra took a sip as well and seemed to enjoy the terrible coffee. "I honestly don't know. I haven't heard from her since she left Marin."

"Left Marin?"

"My sources tell me Amy is in New Cal. She walked away from a critical meeting two days ago, and the official line is that she rushed back to New California for personal reasons. I'm still piecing what happened, but it seems there was a shootout involving Eva and a chase, but it's not clear who was chasing who. Amy left in the confusion. Kuipers downplayed it, but since she claimed emergency powers, I doubt she was happy that Amy slipped out."

"I don't like this at all. This means Amy didn't agree to Kuipers' power grab, which means she'll oppose her."

"I don't think she'll publicly go against Marin."

"Then you don't know her at all." Amy would not back down, not when she believed she was right. And Kuipers wasn't the kind to retreat either. If they let them posture and talk across the bay, the sparring would graduate from words to weapons in a hurry. And to say the balance of power favored Marin was an understatement. "We need to get them to talk. Here."

"You overestimate my influence."

"It's not about influence. We need to give them each a reason to listen. For Amy, it's a neutral site to talk, a site she can go to without caving into Marin's demands. For Kuipers, it's deniability. Nothing that happens here needs to be on the record."

"I'll give it a go. Kuipers has two major headaches. Puries consolidating power in Kern and the new Purge variant getting loose in Marin." She sipped her coffee and lifted her head as though a new thought hit her. "Actually, it might work. Kuipers believes we still have Purie spies in Marin and the Sentinels.

"Do you?"

"Kuipers believes it."

"But do you?"

"What are you asking?"

"Are there really Purie spies, or is Kuipers sowing a culture of fear and mistrust so she can bypass the rule of law?"

"She already has all the power she needs," Sierra said.

"Will you shoot a random Marin citizen if she asks you to?"

"I need more information to answer that question."

"If your answer isn't yes, she needs more power."

Sierra finished her coffee and poured herself another cup. She extended the pot to Mika. He shook his head, having had enough of the over roasted coffee. She needed a better supplier.

"Tell me," she said as she put the pot down. "What happened out there?"

Mika walked her through it all, from the abandoned settlements to Powell and his forced migration and to the missing settlers. He spent a full minute describing the settlement with the two pits with the bodies disposed of in two different ways. He stopped twice while describing the concrete coffins but pushed through. His eyes blurred, having acquired a thin wet film.

"Anyway, we then found Gibson's command center." The more he delved into the detail the more dispassionate he became. He told her about Kristin's death and Yasuo getting infected from fighting radiation-hardened soldiers. How Yasuo deteriorated over forty-eight hours and how they found the lab destroyed.

Sierra shook her head in disgust. He moved to the mine and their deliberations to explore it. "So, in the chamber at the end, we found this strange dormitory."

"In the oxygen-deprived section?"

"Yes. At around ten percent oxygen. And some of the soldiers who attacked us didn't have oxygen masks deep in the mine at the same oxygen levels."

"And then?"

And then, they had fucked up. He described the traps, the cliff, and Lin's capture. "By the time I got back, they had her in one of those concrete coffins."

"Fuck."

"I got to her, but there was no way to get her out." He clasped his empty coffee mug. "With the radiation she received, she knew she was already dead. I tried to convince her we'd find a way, but every word and option I offered was a lie. She was gone. And then while she was still pinned in there, six transports came our way."

"That's what you mean by 'shot her'?"

"I'd made her a promise. I couldn't leave her." A tear drop slid down his cheek.

Sierra reached out and put her hand on Mika's forearm. "I'm sorry."

Mika withdrew his hand and wiped his cheek.

"Was Tulum there?" Sierra asked.

"How the fuck should I know? He was probably in Marin, messing with Kuipers." When she didn't reply, he added, "You underestimate his impact."

"And you underestimate Kuipers' ambition. She won't let Tulum dictate her agenda."

He squeezed his mug harder, bending the circular metal frame into an oval. "I don't give a fuck about her agenda."

Sierra softened her tone, but she didn't convey empathy well. "Let's not lose sight of the fact that Kern and the Puries are our real enemy."

"So, Tulum is our friend now?"

"I didn't say that."

"You kinda did."

"Mika, I said, I'm sorry. The threats are changing fast."

"I tried talking her out of chasing Gibson, but she wouldn't hear it."

"How about you take a few days off? To clear your head."

Mika got up. The anger he had been trying to contain spilled over. He flicked furiously at his middle finger with his thumb. "A few days? You think that's going to fix anything?"

Sierra stood up as well. "You're blaming yourself. You're blaming me. You're blaming Tulum. You need to let the blame game go." He moved to the door, but Sierra took two steps and pushed the door closed. Her voice rose as she spoke. "You're not the first one who's lost someone in the field."

Her tida chirped before he formulated an answer. "What?"

"Governor Chipps is making an announcement," her aide announced, as Amy's picture floated on the screen. Her lips were pressed thin against each other. She pushed her hair behind her ear with her right hand and narrowed her eyes.

Mika chuckled. "Uh-oh."

"What?" Sierra's eyes moved from Amy's image to him and back to Amy's image. He never got to answer because Amy's voice pushed from the screen.

"In response to the illegal seizure of power in Marin and the suspension of civil rule of law, New California invokes Article 7 to unilaterally dissolve the union binding New California and Marin. As of this moment, New California is an independent state and will…"

As Amy's image continued on, Sierra's lips curled up, showing confusion and irritation. "She can't do that, can she?"

"She just did."

CHAPTER 22
NEUTRAL GROUND

*"Memories warm you from the inside.
But they also tear you apart."*

—HARUKI MURAKAMI

Eight heavy transports hovered silently at the edge of New Cal on Amy's screen, two hundred feet above the bay—high enough to be seen for miles and low enough to be intimidating. They stood still, almost peaceful, only betraying their destructive power when the feed panned out. The downwash of their turbofans scarred the bay and formed thirty-two dimples with white-capped circumferences from which even the water struggled to escape.

Amy waved the sound on, and the swishing of high-speed turbine blades merged with the hissing of compressed air to create the perfect white noise. The transports had arrived at dawn, threatening but neither attacking nor advancing. It worked wonders as a display of force, but it was an unnecessary reminder of Marin's military prowess.

Amy's attempt at reaching Chancellor Yim had been fruitless with her calls being redirected to General Kuipers' office. In turn, Amy had declined Kuipers' invitation to appear side-by-side for a joint announcement.

Cavana appeared at her door, and she muted the sound, relegating the metal monsters to hover in silence again. "What did you tell Kuipers?"

"I didn't talk to her. Why?"

"There is a Marin arrest warrant for you."

"Every time shit happens in Marin I end up on that list."

"This is not funny."

"Well, I did turn down Kuipers' invitation to Marin."

"I certainly hope so." Cavana dug his fingers through his hair. Amy had learned that the farther he went, the more concerned Cavana was. He went all the way back and cupped his neck.

"Kuipers is right about one thing. I need to talk to her, or this is going to end badly."

"Governor, you cannot go to Marin."

"And Kuipers can't come here, not without accepting New Cal's autonomy."

"Looks like we are at an impasse."

"Not necessarily." She swiped to a new screen. "I got another invitation this morning."

Cavana listened to the message in which Sierra had invited her to the Sentinel headquarters to find a diplomatic solution.

"The last time Marin invited you to mediate, things did not go too well."

A year ago, she had been abducted by a Marin-Kern collaboration that had, at the time, defied all logic. All because she hadn't known about the conspiracy trying to keep the Purge's secrets. She had fallen for then-Chancellor Lester's lure because she had been too eager to solve a problem whose parameters she hadn't fully grasped.

She had a lot to learn, but the maelstrom she had been thrown into was a meticulous teacher. The world she faced today was different, but the problem was the same. She had to grasp Kuipers' angle before jumping to solutions. "This is interesting though because Sierra can't mediate shit. The concept wouldn't even occur to her."

"So, it is a trap."

"Or it's a way out for Kuipers."

"Or it is a trap," he repeated. "I do not think anyone in Marin was thrilled with the way you slipped out of there or with your declaration."

"It all depends on who's feeding Sierra her lines."

Cavana only offered token resistance to the Sentinel trip for the rest of the day. They headed east and then south in a convoy of two Jeeps, three militia trucks, and a bus full of New Cal officials. The rains had not come yet, so the hills had reached the hue that drove her aides to endless conversation. The optimists called them "golden hills," but the pessimists leaned toward "dirty" or "brown." Amy saw sawdust, so she kept her opinions to herself.

The construction's dust came into view as they approached the outer gate, and the roar of metal drilling into stone resonated as they pulled into the compound. They did the same thing inside, damaging and rebuilding flesh and bone to produce the Sentinels who needed the housing. The only difference was that out here, the construction workers knew what they were doing.

The original warehouse stood to their right, its long side running along the road. The new construction straight ahead had now acquired a roof and siding on all sides. Pile drivers worked the rock a hundred yards to their left for the third building, which consisted of four corrugated-metal walls and a roof. That shell was the New Cal headquarters, and with trenches running inside the frame to accommodate future plumbing and electrical needs, they would be closer to camping under a canopy than being indoors.

Sierra had offered rooms in the main building to her and Cavana, but that wouldn't do. The New Cal contingent had to stay together, both for security and for bonding. Besides, the half-built shell presented as good a metaphor for the state of their union as any.

Sierra met them as they unloaded their supplies. "You brought your drinks," she said, as barrels of beer and cases of wine were carried in. Two members of Amy's crew assembled five-hundred-gallon bladders by the metal gates to store the water they were about to treat. Another two brought a folding table and six chairs.

"We did not want to be a burden," Amy said, though Cavana's arguments had focused on safety and security more than resource sharing.

Sierra accepted a plastic cup of white wine. "Your declaration made things hard for us."

Amy sat down and poured herself a cup as well. She wanted to like Sierra, but she had never gotten past the soldier, the awkward formalism, and the casual adherence to rules that turned every conversation into a drudgery. "That was not my intent. Or my concern."

"General Kuipers never visited this facility. But she will be here tomorrow."

Amy sipped her wine but didn't reply.

"Our operation relied on being out of sight." Sierra's brows pushed toward each other. "I guess we're not hiding anything anymore. Kuipers knows about the Purge and what it does."

"From?"

"Tulum. The scientist from the Uregs group. Not only Kuipers knows but she's aggressively hunting Puries. They've arrested and interrogated over a dozen high-ranking military officials last week."

"Interrogated? I haven't heard anyone being arrested."

Sierra winced. "It's not official. Kuipers uses hidden Special Forces compounds in the Uregs where Marin law doesn't apply."

"Unbelievable. Wait, I thought you'd rooted out the threat last year."

"I pursued those with suspicious activities. Kuipers started widespread Purge testing."

Amy extended her lower lip and exhaled. Kuipers had gone off the rails and Amy needed to know whether she had been pushed. "This Tulum guy, what do you know about him?"

Sierra nodded and drained her wine. "Looked like a scientist to me. More interested in the virus than the people who carry it."

"In my experience, that's never a good thing."

Sierra refilled her wine cup and sat back down. "Mika's back."

Amy flicked her hair behind her ear. "How is he?"

"He got back yesterday and kept to himself, not that he has many friends here."

Amy took a sip and filed Mika away. "What does Tulum want?"

"Unclear. He knows what we're doing here, and he's advising General Kuipers."

"That's a problem."

"Why? Tulum understands how the virus works. We're taking stabs in the dark."

"Biology isn't the problem. It's what Tulum is after that worries me."

"And what is that?"

"I don't know, and neither do you. When someone whispers in the ear of the most powerful person in Marin, and shortly after, officers are interrogated in secret compounds, we should all be worried."

"If they're loyal to Marin, they'll be fine."

"This is how it begins." Amy shivered at how willfully Sierra had turned a blind eye to Kuipers' actions. She took a deep breath. "We should have told them about the virus to get ahead of this mess. Now we've even weaponized the truth."

"Weaponized?"

"Yeah. It's no longer a question of whether the secret will hurt anyone. It's about who it'll hurt when it comes out."

Sierra winced. "How about we grab some dinner at the cafeteria? It's not the best food, but it'll be better than anything you can heat up on these stoves," she said as she pointed to the outdoor cooktops Amy's crew had stacked by the half wall.

Amy didn't agree with Sierra's assessment of their food options but stood. They walked toward the old warehouse. "I need to know what happens when Kuipers arrives tomorrow."

"What do you mean?"

"What happens when Kuipers' orders you to deploy the Sentinel for her agenda?"

"I honestly don't know," Sierra said, looking away. Her words implied there was wiggle room, but her tight shoulders and pulsating jaw said otherwise.

"You need to know."

"I'm not handing this organization to you if that's what you're asking."

"I'm not. But if you want me to trust the Sentinels to be the neutral arbiter between New Cal and Marin, I need to know you're not just a branch of the Marin military."

Sierra sighed and opened the door to the cafeteria, her every motion screaming that she wasn't ready to defy Kuipers.

With tables cutting it in three rows, the room held over eighty seats. The low tile ceiling and heavy smell of frying oil made it seem smaller and stuffier. The food sat under heat lamps on a counter running half the length of the back wall, with two taps in the corner. "Just how many Sentinels do you have?"

"Forty trained. We just took in another forty last week."

"I thought you were going ten at a time."

Sierra spooned black beans on her plate and topped it with chicken pieces. Amy took two chicken thighs and a spoon of mashed potatoes and followed Sierra to a four-person table by the corner. Eva sat down next to Amy at an angle that allowed her to watch both doors and the counter. The lone piece of chicken on her plate rolled around but did not fall.

Sierra took a mouthful of beans. "Unless we grow, we become irrelevant."

Ten minutes of idle chatter later, Eva's eyes shifted toward the door. Mika walked in alone and took a stutter step as though he contemplated disappearing. He must have concluded he had been spotted because he walked toward their table.

"Good to see you," Amy said.

"Hey." He made no move toward her, so she didn't attempt to hug him.

Sierra pointed to an empty chair at their table. "Want to join us?"

Mika's eyes darted from Amy to Sierra to Eva and back to Amy. "I'm really beat. Maybe tomorrow?" He rubbed his left middle finger with his right hand, as though trying to take off an imaginary ring. He wasn't gentle, tugging at it as though he wanted to take the finger off.

Amy put a hand on his forearm. "You're okay?" He let go of his finger. "If you want to talk, you know where to find me."

He nodded and ambled toward the food counters and then to a table across the room. He didn't pick the farthest table but the one hidden behind two occupied tables.

She turned to Sierra. "Does he always eat alone?"

"He declined to join me last night."

"Not like him."

Sierra glanced toward Mika. "I need to tell you something."

Amy put down her fork and leaned forward, bracing for bad news.

"He had a difficult crash landing. His craft was badly shot up. To be honest, I still can't believe he managed to land, by some definition of land. But near the end, when he'd lost control, he didn't bail."

"Were the chutes damaged?"

"There were two functional ones in the cargo hold, it should have been a no-brainer. He implied he wanted to protect the live virus sample, but it's a variant we already have, and he knows it."

"Was he trying to protect against contamination?"

"From a crash site? No, besides, we have containment protocols. No one would have been exposed to it."

Amy looked to the drink counter. "Any wine here?"

Sierra shook her head. "Beer."

"That'll do." They walked to the beer tap, and Amy filled her pint glass. "He thought he'd survive anyway, so no reason to bother with getting into a parachute?"

"I might have bought that. And then I listened to his conversation with the tower. If I didn't know better, I'd have said he was goading them into shooting him down."

Amy gulped the IPA. It was bitter, as though the brewmaster wanted to test how much hop she could pack into each pint. She clenched her teeth and cringed, thankful that the ale gave her a cover for doing so.

"He needs to talk," Sierra said. "About that, about other things."

Amy didn't trust her voice to respond, so she took another sip.

"So, do you have a drink with him or do I?" Sierra asked.

Amy shook her head.

Sierra turned to Eva. "How about you?"

"I'm not leaving the governor's side."

"Even here?"

"Especially here."

"Fine." Sierra put her tray on the rack at the back of hall and walked toward the beer tap. She filled one glass, half-filled a second one, and headed toward Mika.

Not that it was going to help. Sierra had waited till today, hoping Amy would address her Mika problem for her. She didn't know how to help Mika because she didn't understand the root of the problem. Sierra handled Kuipers with the same lack of finesse along with every other problem she couldn't solve by shooting at it.

Amy drained her beer and headed to the door as Sierra sat down at Mika's table.

Eva bit her lower lip, then said, "I'll talk to him tomorrow."

Amy walked out with half a smile, thankful to have one person who understood, one person she could count on, no matter what.

CHAPTER 23
ADVICE

"The man who views the world at fifty the same as he did at twenty has wasted thirty years of his life."

—MUHAMMAD ALI

The dining hall occupied the southwest corner of the hastily built addition to the Shed. The rectangular room featured three-foot-square windows, designed to maximize the area for the minimum cost. The inner walls undulated like the shell of a hot air balloon, the lath and plaster unable to resist the warping caused by the heat trapped inside. The baseboards had already parted where the cracks in the walls reached the floor, as though creating pocket doors as a peace offering to the field mice that had been displaced with this monstrosity.

The aesthetics weren't the only deficiencies. Entrances, windows, tables, and counters were in the wrong place. The two doors stood too close together, causing congestion at mealtime, the windows faced south to turn the place into a greenhouse, and the food counters, placed under the air intake, forced the stench of burnt vegetable oil into the first floor. The facility's design and build screamed that no one expected it to exist in another year.

None of that mattered, except that the entire organization had been built with the same attention to detail as this hall. Mika tapped the table with his fork as he chewed another roasted chicken thigh.

The flesh had developed a leathery second skin from sitting under the heat lights, and it was as juicy as a rock. He washed it down with his ale, the only palatable portion of the meal.

Sentinels came and went in groups, oblivious to the futility of it all. It galled him that Lin had died so this shoddy, can't-frame-a-wall, can't-cook-chicken organization limped on.

He shoved the last piece of chicken in his mouth and pushed his nearly empty plate toward the middle of the round table. The Sentinels separating him from Amy's table stood up and left, leaving him exposed. Sierra talked in hushed tones and jammed a spoonful of beans in her mouth. Amy nodded with a frown. She put a wayward strand of hair behind her ear and spoke, leaning forward.

He drained the last of his ale and slumped in his chair as he kept his eyes on Amy's tense shoulders. She alternated between leaning back and rocking forward and putting her elbows on the table. A permanent frown adorned her face, but that didn't narrow down the list of topics that Sierra must have been droning on about.

They lived in a world devoid of good news. Lori had met that truth with force, even pushed it back a ways before succumbing to it. Lin had ignored it but that hadn't helped in the end. Amy confronted it head-on, with an optimism whose source he had never been able to locate, though she wasn't making much progress either. Attempting to fix their clusterfuck of a world meant wasting their lives on a pointless cause either figuratively or literally.

He wished he could get Amy to accept that, but he had failed enough times to stop trying. He was still brooding when he spotted Eva by the door. Amy stole a quick glance in his direction, but her gaze didn't linger. She blinked and disappeared down the hallway behind Eva.

Because he had kept his eyes on Amy, he missed Sierra sitting down across from him. She had two beer glasses—one full, the other half full. She pushed the full one in front of him, which was the only reason he remained seated.

"Thanks, but I'm fine, really; you can entertain your guest."

"I'm just finishing my beer."

He raised his pint glass up to hers and took a large gulp. Sierra did the same but held on to the glass, rotating it slowly around an imaginary circle's center.

"I've seen this before, you know," she said when he didn't speak. "After the battle of Anderson. Many soldiers had trouble jumping back into the swing of everyday life. They'd done things and seen things that made them wary of the simplest sounds or the gentlest touches."

He gripped his pint glass in both hands because as far as everyday life went, what surrounded them left much to be desired.

She took another sip and put her glass down. "It takes time to shake the guilt survivors carry from those battles. Not because of anything they did, mind you, but because they're alive. And their buddies aren't."

"I'm fine."

"No, Mika, you're not. And that's okay. You're irritable and disconnected. But what happened out there isn't something you shake off by pretending it didn't happen."

He pushed his fork toward her. "Stick this in my eye and see how fast you shake it off."

"None of this is your fault."

"That's one opinion." He drained his beer. "I replay it over and over, looking for the play I missed because there had to be another option. There had to be."

"Sometimes there isn't. You're in the field. You react. You can't go back and scrutinize every decision you made."

He walked to the beer tap and refilled his pint glass. "Are we done?"

She didn't reply, so he sat down, leaning back and stretching his legs along the table.

"I need you, Mika, and I need to know you're okay."

"Why?"

"I need someone to run ideas by. Someone who understands the big picture."

"Try me."

She took a sip that barely wet her lips. "For starters, I'd like to know what we do when Tulum and Kuipers get here."

He smiled wide with teeth and all. "I'm guessing shooting them both is not an option?"

"See, this is why I worry."

He looked at his feet to find something to distract Sierra. "I'd ask them one question."

"Why Tulum wants to settle up north?"

"Nope," he said and took a gulp of beer.

"What they're doing with the radiation-hardened virus?"

"Nope." He took another gulp. "Kinda boring as a drinking game."

She extended both hands, palms up. "What?"

"Where did they get the rad-hardened virus in the first place?"

"Huh?" she said, intrigued enough to let go of her intrusion into his state of mind.

"Well, you can now go entertain your guest."

She sighed. "It's okay to say her name, you know."

"Good night." He drained his beer and headed toward the door.

She followed him. "I think I know you pretty well by now. You keep people at arm's length, so you don't have many friends. But the few you have mean the world to you. And you'll go to any length to protect the ones you really love."

He lowered his voice. "It doesn't end well for anyone I try to protect."

"That's bullshit. Anyway, all this time, I've never commented on your personal life."

"But you're about to."

"Just to say that I know you care about Amy. And frankly, you're never going to do better than her."

"Yeah, I know, she's a saint."

"No, but she's real, she's here, and she cares."

He started to walk away. "I really don't need advice."

She grabbed his sleeve to stop him. "I don't have any advice. All I have is an observation. Take it for what it's worth." She leaned forward and whispered, "You're an idiot."

CHAPTER 24

NEARLY UNITED

*"That's the real trouble with the world,
too many people grow up."*

—WALT DISNEY

Amy stopped by the door, letting the air-conditioning cool her face. The corrugated walls radiated heat, and as the air rose from the large open space, it got trapped between the roof and the second-floor walkways. Amy wiped her brow while two fans on either end of the corridor fought a losing battle against physics.

All she had to do to escape the fetid air was to step in, but she took her time, soaking in the scene. Sierra sat on the far side of a racetrack conference table, chatting with a man to her left sporting a goatee. He wore a plaid gray-green shirt, with the sleeves rolled to his elbows. The man's hands rested on the table, his short fingers intertwined. Amy forced herself to not dislike the man before they met, but only half-succeeded. The way he leaned forward, head slightly cocked, as he listened to Sierra radiated privilege.

Amy stepped in and spotted Mika in the back of the room, sitting away from the table on one of the four chairs lining the wall. He was lost on his screen but smiled and waved at her as she entered. She returned his smile.

"Governor Chipps, this is Dr. Aiden Tulum," Sierra said from across the table. Tulum partially stood, waving across the table in greeting. Sierra pointed to Eva. "And Eva Asher."

Tulum sat back down, though Amy remained standing. Tulum's eyes stayed on Eva too long, betraying that Sierra must have briefed him on her past.

"Colonel, I was under the impression we were here to discuss the status of the military transports hovering over the bay, a quarter-mile from Cal City's populated core," Amy said.

"Of course, Governor."

"Wouldn't General Kuipers need to be here for that conversation?"

Sierra winced, broadcasting that Kuipers' absence was more than a simple delay.

"I do not want to waste your time, Governor," Tulum said. "So, I will get to the point. I'm here to discuss a broad alliance."

Amy's eyes floated from Tulum to Sierra and back to Tulum. "Between?"

"You, General Kuipers, and me."

"Who do you represent?"

"An alliance of settlements."

"I see. When will the general join us?"

"She was detained in Marin. She will be here tomorrow. I am here to brief you on the situation in Marin and on the threat the discovered bodies cause and their origin. I briefed the Marin Executive Council, but unfortunately, you were not present."

She would have liked to attend that meeting, but with all the nonsense Yim and Kuipers had put her through, it had been impossible to determine when anything of value might be exchanged in the Marin Council. Still, he was a stranger who had not earned his seat at the table. "I have matters to attend in New California."

Tulum stood and took a step toward her. "You really should hear what I have to say."

Amy smiled. "I'm looking forward to it, Dr. Tulum. You can brief us as soon as General Kuipers arrives tomorrow."

Tulum took another step toward her, and Eva stepped forward, coming between them. Tulum's eyes narrowed, darting from Amy to Eva. "Governor, who do you think keeps General Kuipers' tendencies in check?"

Amy put her hand on the handle but did not open the door.

"Who, say, keeps the transports hovering over the bay, instead of engaging your defenses?"

Amy let go of the door and faced Tulum. "Why would you have an interest in keeping New California safe?"

Tulum sat back on his chair. "I don't, really. But I have an interest in preventing distractions. And both an uprising and the suppression of that uprising are huge distractions."

"Declaring independence as dictated in the constitution is not an uprising."

"I don't disagree with you, but the general does. So, I'd like to prevent either of you from taking actions that can't be taken back. Hostility between you two will set my agenda back. So, you want to know my motives? Why I want the north if there is nothing of value there?" Tulum smiled as he spoke the words Amy had uttered to Kuipers days earlier.

"Okay, then, what is your agenda?"

"To build a lasting state, one that values science. One that will uncover what the Purge was and how it got loose."

"And how do widespread testing and quarantine zones help with that?"

"Those are precautions."

Amy approached the table, pulled a chair, and sat. "You have ten minutes."

Eva stood to Amy's right, two feet back, eyes on Tulum, body between Amy and the door. Her feet were shoulder-length apart, left foot a hair ahead of her right. She looked bored but was ready to strike. Tulum didn't notice. Mika tapped the chair next to his and smiled at her. Eva did not move.

Tulum leaned back, bending the back of his chair. "First, let me say I'm very impressed with this operation. To put all this together in under a year and to train as many soldiers as you have, that's something, particularly since you did it with little to no scientific help."

"That praise is for Colonel Rendon."

"I'm here to accelerate that progress. You're doing well, but you need a better mix of bioagents and a more interspersed injury schedule."

"Dr. Tulum, stopping Kuipers' hostility is a selling point. Accelerating the program here? Not so much."

"We're at a critical junction, Governor. It's imperative that we work together." He took a sip of water. "I've been studying the Purge for two-and-a-half decades, but I discovered the combination to trigger it intentionally only three years ago. At first, I did exactly what Colonel Rendon is doing here. When my mercenaries showed their worth in battle, my client base broadened to include Kern generals. One turned out to be an intermediary for the Puries. I reached out to two former colleagues to expand the operation."

Mika nodded to corroborate the timeline. She would have liked to ask him what he thought of all this, but his distant eyes did not invite a question.

"A year and a half ago, the Puries kidnapped some of my medics," Tulum said. "Soon after, I discovered extensive Purie experiments in the north. They collected people from the northern Uregs and distributed them into settlements of about a thousand each. We couldn't get too close because they were protected by Puries in Kern, but we did observe that each settlement had a different routine and activity profile. Something fundamental was different in each."

"Did you find out what?" Amy asked.

Tulum gave a condescending smile. "Some, yes. When the Kern Purie bases were destroyed last year during the last stages of the Kern-Marin war, the military protection of the settlements was cut off. We overpowered their command center and uncovered their schemes. Two of the settlements had been destroyed."

He shook his head. "It took months to dispose of the thousands of bodies. Whatever happened at the end must been sudden because they couldn't wipe it all out.

"You just picked up where they left off? Instead of, say, letting them go."

Tulum grimaced as though the thought caused him pain. "I'm afraid that's not possible. They all have variants of the Purge, and they're contagious."

"Variants?" Sierra asked. "As in mutated versions?"

"Not exactly."

Amy leaned back and crossed her legs. "Contagious how?"

"We're still working on potential spread vectors and effective containment protocols. But if the infected get loose in Marin, they can spread it with devastating effect."

Amy shook her head in disgust. "What are we looking at?"

"For those of us carrying the Purge, hospitalization rates of 20 percent. Fatality rates are 3.4-to-4.2 percent based on the variant. With the right medical treatment, we might be able to drop that to 2 percent."

"How does it spread?"

"Body fluids. Blood, saliva, sweat, vomit. To infect, it needs to come in contact with broken skin or mucous membrane in eyes, nose, or mouth. It can live a day or two in bodily fluids like blood, but not long outside the body."

Amy clutched her tida tight. "What's not long?"

"On dry surfaces like doorknobs and countertops, an hour or two."

Amy cringed, as every interaction, every object became a hazard: screens, utensils, door handles. "Why would anyone release this virus?"

"The Puries' immunity extends to these versions. But in some of us, whatever stopped the Purge can't handle the variants."

"And you still shipped bodies to Marin."

"Dead ones, well past the viability period of the virus. There was no danger."

"Why?"

"To get Marin to stop pretending that the world had suddenly become safe. That the Kern threat had been neutralized by defeating them at Anderson Valley last year. That the Purie threat had been neutralized by dismantling Lester's Marin network. The bodies got you to remember it's a dangerous world out there."

Mika's head swiveled to Tulum. He didn't speak, so she forced her eyes back to Tulum. "Quarantine and martial law? They help how?"

"The Puries might still release the new virus. They don't control the settlements anymore, but we have reliable evidence they have live samples."

"You let them escape with samples as you took over their labs?" Sierra asked.

Tulum shook his head. "No, nothing of the sort. But two residents were abducted from a settlement last week."

"Infected?"

Tulum nodded. "As you might know, our team was attacked recently." His eyes moved to Mika and narrowed accusingly. "While we were addressing that problem, a commando team reached into our southernmost settlement and grabbed two residents." His eyes returned to Amy. "The quarantine in Marin is to at least save parts of the city if this variant is released."

Amy's eyes shot daggers at Sierra. "I thought you contained the conspiracy in Marin."

"I did," Sierra said.

"Irrelevant. We have strong evidence it was a Kern unit."

"Kern is behind this?" Amy asked.

"Have you looked at Kern?" Tulum asked. "Spindler is on the run, his hold weakened."

"Good," she said with venom.

"No, not good. What happens when the Puries win the Kern civil war? You get the belligerent Kern war machine with a Purie agenda. Add to that the Kern army camped in the Uregs, also under Purie control, and now what? Marin is on the back foot again. And somewhere out there, they have two live patients with a virus that can kill thousands and cripple all the manufacturing and economic base of Marin."

Amy narrowed her eyes. "Why are you telling me all this?"

"I don't want you," he said, moving his eyes from Amy to Mika, "any of you, to treat me as an adversary. We are on the same side."

"What side is that?"

"The side that doesn't want the brutes in Kern to turn this state into a reenactment of the sixteenth century. The side that doesn't want the Puries to wipe out those who carry the Purge."

"Why can't we handle these new variants?" Sierra asked. "Are they that different?"

"They're similar enough and provide cell repair as well. One, for example, fights radiation damage." He spoke in the tone of an excited scientist. "I don't mean like the Purge does with everything, but like it was designed to erase radiation damage at the genetic level."

"Designed?" Amy asked.

"It is really too good at it to be an accident."

"So, they designed this in a lab?"

"Not likely. It's beyond anything ever speculated."

"What then?"

He pressed his lips together. "If I were guessing, I'd say these are the original virus samples from the comet. The Purge is a variant of this virus with a few genes carved out. It lost its specialized tools but can still perform a generic repair job."

"And kill nine billion people."

"I'm guessing that whoever removed the end didn't know it would do that."

"No shit," Amy said.

"The alteration must have removed a safety mechanism and turned it airborne. I'm guessing the fatality rate would not have exceeded four percent in the general population if no one had mucked with it."

Amy pushed her lips together. "You're guessing a lot."

"These are hypotheses, supported with decades of experimental data. But no, I do not have definitive answers." A forced smile appeared on Tulum's face as the politician displaced the scientist. "I need you to believe me when I say these things are very elegantly constructed for very specific purposes."

"You talk about them as an engineered system."

Tulum took a sip of water and let the implication sink in.

"You said no one could have added the extra bits. Which is it?"

"I didn't say who it was engineered by."

"What does that mean?"

"It came from a comet."

Amy stood and reached for the iced tea pitcher at the edge of the table. She poured herself a glass. "I'm going to need something stronger if this turns into an alien invasion story."

"No, I don't think that's it. Considering how sophisticated these viruses are, if they wanted us dead, we'd all be dead."

She dropped a lime wedge in her tea and sat back down. "We almost were."

"Through our own stupidity. Also, almost dead is very different from dead."

Sierra leaned forward. "How does this help with training soldiers?"

Tulum rolled his eyes. "It doesn't. I help you train your soldiers. You help me by playing nice with Kuipers. We go to Shasta, dig under all that irradiated rubble, and find out once and for all what the origin of the viruses was. That is what I want."

Mika leaned forward, and his eyes narrowed, but when Sierra spoke, he sank back in his chair. "That's why you have radiation-hardened soldiers."

"Exactly. The tunnels have collapsed in Shasta. There is no way in or out. The radiation levels are so high, even the well-trained among us wouldn't last half an hour in that environment. But with the radiation-hardened workers, we can clear up the rubble. Through high-altitude radiation labor, we've increased their resistance by 800 percent. They can dig through that mess in two-to-three weeks."

Amy took a long sip of her iced tea. "So why are you here?"

"I don't want to dig in Shasta to come out and find a Purie and Kern occupied state. If you and Kuipers cannot get along, that's what will happen. And then all of this is for nothing."

"I'll consider it," Amy said. "But I have one question."

"Yes?"

She wiped the condensation from her glass with her index finger, going up and down rhythmically. "How did the radiation-hardened virus make it out in the first place?"

"Some of the scientists deduced the Shasta lab was slated to be nuked. They infected themselves to get a leg up in case they survived the blast. It's also very likely they had human experiments. In the mayhem that followed, they were the most likely to survive."

She kept his eyes on him. "Were you there?"

"Oh no." He shook his head, "I was nowhere near Shasta when this happened."

"So how do you know this?"

"We've traced scientists and subjects from Shasta to the settlements."

"What happened to them?"

"Most are still there. One is a town doctor. Another is in charge of their power plant. They're getting by."

Amy cocked her head. "So why haven't we heard about these viruses before?"

"They knew they were contagious. They stayed in their towns deep in the Uregs. They knew how it spread so they took precautions and kept it under wraps."

"But someone found them."

"The Puries wanted isolation and distance to test the Purge. They came across these towns by accident and overpowered them. Once they figured out what they'd stumble upon, they split the infected into settlements and turned the whole thing into a field experiment."

Amy shook her head. "Unbelievable."

"So, how about we work together? I'm not asking much. Just do not antagonize Kuipers for three more weeks."

"Then what?"

"Then we'll finally understand what this virus was meant to do."

"Then what?"

Tulum raised his eyebrows in confusion.

Amy drained her iced tea. "Dr. Tulum, how does any of that help New California? Help keep Kuipers in check? Make Kern less belligerent?"

He shrugged. "If we understand, truly understand, what the Purge was, what it did, and what it was meant to do, does it matter whether it's you or Kuipers in charge?"

"If you can guarantee that there will be no more threats from Kern or others and that Kuipers will restore the rule of law, then no, it doesn't matter. Can you do that?"

"I'm afraid I can't."

"Then it does matter." She stood up and put her fists on the table. "It's all well and good to talk about the meaning of life, but I need to think of the lives themselves. Right now, our citizens are worried about whether they'll have food tonight, or whether the lights will come on. Chase the Purge all you want, but I'm not sacrificing our citizens' well-being for your cause."

"Our job is to look beyond those mundane concerns."

Amy didn't return the patronizing smile. "I will stay till I talk to Kuipers. Beyond that, I can't promise anything."

"How about the Sentinels?"

Amy took three steps toward the door and stopped. "What about them?"

"If we adjust their training, we can have stronger soldiers in a week."

"With Marin already committed, I think we can work together," Sierra said.

"Who represents the Sentinels?" Amy asked.

"I do," Sierra said.

Amy put her hair behind her ear. "So, this was a branch of the Marin military all along."

"No, we're an independent organization."

"And yet a Marin colonel speaks for it."

Sierra put her hands on the shaky table. "What do you suggest we do?"

Tulum pointed to Mika before Amy spoke. "How about him? He's high on the Sentinel leadership, isn't he?"

"We're a flat organization," Sierra said.

Tulum's gaze moved between Sierra and Amy, locked in a silent tug-of-war. "I'm fine with his decision."

"I don't see how accepting Tulum's help is anything but good."

Amy didn't reply. Sierra had inadvertently revealed the trouble with her leadership. She did not see particularly far, and she did not analyze how and why most endeavors failed.

Mika, who had daydreamed in the back for the last half an hour, asked Sierra, "Are we going to shut down the Sentinels if we turn this offer down?"

"What?" Sierra's shoulders tightened, and her head jerked forward. "No!"

"Then we work with Tulum."

Sierra leaned back, the tension slipping away from her shoulders.

Amy shook her head. "Why?"

"If we're going to do this anyway, we might as well do it right."

"There we have it," Sierra said.

Tulum stood up with a broad smile, waved at Mika, and headed for the door.

"How did you know?" Sierra asked as she followed Tulum out.

"I'm a good judge of character," Tulum said before disappearing into the hallway.

Amy waited for Mika to move as well, but Mika stayed seated. She walked around the table toward him. "Is this what you want?"

"I don't want anything."

Amy rested her chin on her knuckles. "I'm a little disappointed."

"You always expect too much from people."

"You're not *people*." She reached for his forearm. "You're better than this."

He pulled his arm away but did not reply.

"You've really changed."

"Yeah," he said. "I grew up."

She straightened up and attempted to smile but she doubted she kept the disappointment from her eyes. "You shouldn't have."

CHAPTER 25
FULLY DIVIDED

"Maybe all one can do is hope to end with the right regrets."

—ARTHUR MILLER

"I miss the harbor," Mika said, as he chewed his burrito under the dining hall's lights that were two shades too blue. "As they dip in and around the boats, the gulls remind us that there is life outside of our control. Here, it's all artificial."

"That's Grumpy talking," Eva said. "He complained plenty at the harbor too."

That she was right didn't help his mood. He took another bite. "Look at this. It doesn't even hold together without the paper." He put it on his plate and pulled a piece of tortilla, bringing it to his eye. "It's so thin, you can see through it. A real burrito doesn't need a wrapper to hold together. And don't get me started on the eggs. They're the consistency of rubber and taste like chalk. No self-respecting chicken would lay these."

"The burrito? Really?"

Mika smirked. "The coffee sucks too. It's too watery but making it stronger wouldn't help. The beans are so shitty it'll just get bitter and smell more like burnt plastic."

"You know, you used to have two moods. Happy, the relaxed dude who made everyone feel better, and Grumpy, the somber one who was lousy company. I don't know what to do with this fake cheerful one. I'd call you Dopey, but you talk too much for that."

He sipped his coffee and grimaced.

"How are you holding up?"

He raised his coffee mug. "Splendidly."

"C'mon, Mika."

"Look, I really don't want to talk about any of it. Can we let it drop?"

"Sure. I get it. It's too soon."

"Does it help, talking? Because I don't see how words are going to make the nightmares go away or how they'll make me forget her face."

Eva took a sip of her coffee. "It's not meant to make you forget anything. But it helps a little if you do it at the right time with the right person. Any jackass who tells you that you need to move on, you can ignore them. Or you can deck them; that works too."

He laughed despite himself.

"In the end, whatever happened is part of you. You have to find a way to live with it, and sometimes talking helps with that."

"Good to know, but right now, I don't know what to think, much less what to talk about."

"Fair." She took a bite from her burrito and chewed. "You know the shit I've been through. Early on, I got pissed off, but that didn't help. Then I tried to let go, and that didn't help either. Then I found a trick that let my mind disconnect. That helped when I was at the Purie compound, but it also helped when I got back. It still helps."

"What do you mean?"

"I find a place in my mind that lets me get away from it all. I visualize rolling on a non-ending dojo mat. The key is to put in all the detail that makes it real, so your mind has to engage fully to recreate that scene. I lean forward with my right arm out, protecting my head. I pitch forward and land with the blade of my hand, distributing the pressure from hand to forearm to elbow to shoulder. I come out of the roll with the right foot planted and the left leg folded under me. I push up on my left knee, with the right knee and hand pointing forward and shoulders relaxed. Then I roll, leading with the left arm and on and on."

She raised her open right hand and tapped the blade of her hand to her left palm, stretching every muscle in both hands. "You have to focus on every muscle. How hard the ball of the foot pushes, which part of the hand makes contact with the ground first, and how much force the shoulder absorbs. If any of the detail is missing or if the roll isn't perfect, you start counting from one."

"How do you know if the roll is good?"

"They're all good. They need to be perfect to count."

He smiled, impressed.

"Once in the Purie compound where I was held, I reached 748. When I realized I wasn't actually rolling, I found a thigh-full of nails in my right leg."

Mika winced at the memory of how Eva had become this indestructible. "Rolling is your thing. I guess I need to find my own activity. Sails flapping in the wind?"

"Might be too chaotic. The predictability of the repeated motion frees the mind."

"Seagulls," he said as though he had gotten the answer to a complex formula. "Gulls flapping wings."

"Might work." She took a sip. "You're right; this coffee sucks."

He took another sip of coffee and chewed it, letting it coat his mouth before swallowing. "Enough about me. Heard from Blue recently?"

Eva shook her head. "She's working around the clock on something. She said she was halfway in, whatever that means."

"Good, good." He pushed his cup away. "What are you up to these days?"

She sat up straight, pushed her shoulders back, and announced, "I'm a bodyguard."

Mika kept his lips from parting. "Who pays you enough to put up with that?"

"It's Amy, dummy!"

"That's great." Then it hit him. "What the hell are you doing with me, then?"

"She's with Cavana."

He narrowed his eyes. "Did she ask you to talk to me?"

Eva reached for the coffee she had given up on to fill the silence but didn't bother lying.

"Tell her I'm fine, will you? She has enough to worry about without adding my shit to her plate."

"You don't have to be this tough. We're here for you."

"I know. I know. How's she handling Sierra?"

"How do you mean?"

He drained his coffee. "Sierra is loyal, and she's tough. But she's rudderless right now. She needs to find someone to be loyal to, and she needs to do it fast."

"Fair. She's stuck between Marin and the Sentinels."

"I don't think she sees it that way. She hasn't yet grasped that those two aren't on the same page. Between Kuipers and Amy, she's about to get run over."

"She does need help," Eva said. "And she trusts so few people so it's doubly hard."

"Well, she's not the kind to ask for help."

"She trusts you."

He tapped the rim of his empty cup. "Right now, she's not high on my list of people to help."

"It might help you both. If you accepted she made a mistake and agree this wasn't the outcome she wanted, maybe you can forgive her."

"Not anytime soon."

She bit her lower lip and shook her head.

"Look, I pulled the trigger," Mika said, raising his voice. "Talking isn't going to fix that. And if I pretended it was all okay, she might even think it was. And she has no right to think anything is okay."

Eva let out her breath slowly. "Not everyone who needs help knows to ask for it."

"Not Sierra's strong suit."

Eva stood. Her unwrapped burrito was not even half-eaten. "I wasn't talking about Sierra."

Two hours later, Mika sat at the end of the long table in the conference room, absorbing the exchange between Tulum, Sierra, and the scientists Sierra had recruited to monitor the impact of the virus and advise on improving training schedules. He made every effort to be cooperative, though he didn't push the friendliness too far.

His backing Tulum's involvement with the Sentinels had bought him more goodwill than it should have because Sierra was desperate for allies. Tulum confirmed everything Powell had deduced about how the radiation-resistant Purge spread. He didn't have a good answer for why the Puries were immune to this version as well, but they all knew the crass response: the Purge had culled the population so heavily that seeking further answers was pointless.

Having agreed on a new training regimen, Sierra and her scientists stood and headed for the door. Mika waited for Sierra's back to turn before slipping the picture of the test tubes with multiple PRG samples to Tulum. He then stood up and followed Sierra to the door.

"Mika," Tulum said, eyes on the picture in front of him. "Can you stay a minute?"

"I'm headed upstairs for the briefing."

Sierra stopped by the door. "What is this about?"

"It's between Mika and me," Tulum said.

"Sure." Mika sat back down.

Sierra called the Sentinel guard who had been stationed at the door and pointed to Mika with her head. Mika stood up, and the guard patted his arms and chest.

As the guard moved to his legs, Mika took his tida out of his pocket and dropped it on the table.

The guard stood up and said, "Clean."

"Jerry," Tulum said to the broad-chested man with short-cropped hair and a permanent squint. Everything about the man screamed military.

Mika's eyes moved between Tulum and Jerry. "Seriously?"

Jerry patted him as well, finishing by squeezing his ankles and calves. Sierra turned to Tulum as Jerry backed away. "Keep it short. I need you both upstairs in ten minutes."

Tulum lifted the picture the instant the door closed. "Where did you get this?"

Mika took the picture, folded it, and put it in his inside pocket. "This one is from Shasta."

"You have others?"

"A few more. And some data, but you already know there are six PRGs."

Tulum reached for the water pitcher on the conference table and poured himself a glass.

"Six settlements. I know you can count," Mika said. "The radiation-fighting version. The low-oxygen one you're testing in the mines. The one with—"

"Yes, the high-gravity version. So, you visited the centrifuges."

"And the last two?"

Tulum pressed his lips together. "Well played. For a moment there, I thought you'd understood. But if you think the Purge is one of these, you don't understand anything. And you don't have samples because if you did, you'd know how they're related."

He drank half his water and wiped his mouth with the back of his hand. "Doesn't matter. We don't have to play games. There are three other versions, and for a moment there, with that picture, I thought you may have uncovered something interesting."

"Three more?"

"The Purge is not one of the six. The four we've studied all are the same length with symmetric ends. The Purge is shorter and is the common stem of all four. Early on, I wracked my brain on why radiation repair might be useful. It's not like a lot of folks would survive a nuclear blast. But then I found the other three, and their real purpose dawned on me. PRG is the Swiss army knife of repair. It does a lot of things, but nothing very well. You and I are resilient, but that's nothing for what you may face out there," he said waving his hand to the sky.

"Out where?"

"Whatever skipped through our atmosphere was no comet. Whatever landed in those sites were no fragments. It was an invitation with instructions."

"Invitation?"

He pinched his forearm, capturing skin between his thumb and index finger. "We're too fragile to be space-faring. Out there, radiation is the real enemy. Over time, there is no way to overcome radiation damage. Even going to Mars is tricky. The concept of colony ships was always a pipe dream. You can sleep all you want, but you can't prevent accumulated radiation damage."

"But if you repair that, you can."

"And that's just the start. If we'll ever become a multi-planet species, we need to handle different environments. Different-sized planets mean different gravity wells. Different chemical compositions mean different oxygen content. Different suns and orbits mean different atmospheric pressures and temperature swings. Not every planet will have a strong magnetic field, so we need to tolerate higher radiation levels."

"Trying to kill us all is a pretty shitty invitation."

"That was us. The dimwits in charge figured out that all the viruses shared a common stem. They isolated that part to produce a generic repair virus because, let's face it, the appeal of near immortality is too strong. But they didn't know what the hell they were doing, so they accidentally removed some sort of equilibrium mechanism."

"Phillips always suspected that."

"Yeah, he did, but he didn't want to do what was needed to find out."

"What was that?"

"Push on with the real work. Push and push and push until you get to the result."

Tulum acted as though they had met the day before and as though they were on the same side. It was one thing to be so lost in his work that he saw DNA before he saw a human being, but it was another entirely to forget about what his henchmen had done to a particular human. Then again, as far as Tulum was concerned, nothing had happened. Lin had never existed.

"Think of the possibilities. One increases bone density and heart capacity. One repairs radiation damage. One increases hemoglobin count and efficiency. One protects against extreme pressures and temperatures. I cannot wait to find out what the others do because we are redefining what it means to be human. We will conquer the stars with these."

Mika leaned back and pushed his legs under the table. "What did Kuipers promise you?"

"Labs with full resources of Marin. And no interference from Kern."

"What did you promise?"

"Stronger soldiers and sharing my findings." He smiled. "I'm glad you are past our misunderstanding."

If Tulum had wanted to pick a word to remind Mika that he was dealing with a monster, he couldn't have picked a better one. Tulum had perfected his act, always sounding helpful, concerned, while running over anything and anyone that got in the way of his quest.

Mika gave him a cold smile, keeping his lips fully closed. Tulum misinterpreted it. "It's good to be on the same team and to talk like civilized men."

Mika swallowed his snort because Tulum was not a civilized man. Entitled, yes. Privileged, certainly. Used to getting his way, definitely. Tulum's outward politeness masked a superiority that no words could mask. No, he was not civilized. Then again, neither was Mika.

"Civilization is overrated."

Tulum laughed. "Not so, but I'm still glad that you're no longer angry."

Any notion of letting his vendetta go dissipated. "I'm not angry."

"Good to hear." He frowned and spoke with the practiced sincerity of a man used to getting his way. "I'm sorry about your friend. Things like that happen in the heat of battle."

"Did you come up with those concrete contraptions?"

"No, no. We found molds in every settlement. Turns out they used them in the early days to control the scientists after two spoke against the official policy. Gibson believes they're necessary as a deterrent to an uprising."

Control. Necessary. Deterrent. Tulum used words with little regard for their impact, most likely because no one had called him on it in a long time. "So, it was Gibson's fault?"

Tulum shook his head. "We're partners. He doesn't question my science, and I don't question his methods."

Pushing Lin's death on Gibson hadn't been a defense mechanism. It was the way Tulum operated, passing on responsibility and absolving himself without even trying. "Must have been great for morale. Sounds real ethical too."

"Morale? Ethics? You don't understand, do you? They saw the end of the human race. They did whatever they had to do and however they had to do it to stave off extinction. Order and obedience is what they were after."

"They failed."

"We're still here."

"No thanks to them. And they're wrong. There's no point saving the human race if it's to put people in those things."

"As long as you and I are here to argue about it, they'd claim they were right."

"And they'd be wrong."

"They did what they had to do to keep order." Tulum took a deep breath. "Just as Gibson did. That night you attacked our compound, Gibson was hosting settlement leaders. And you and your team crashed the party and started shooting." He closed his eyes and shook his head.

"She shot Gibson, in front of everyone! If we don't respond to that, we look weak, and we can no longer keep order. What's to keep a settlement leader from thinking they can do the same and get away with it? Still, I was willing to let it go, but then you showed up at the mine and—" He shook his head again. "You killed sixteen of my people. Sixteen!"

"So, the idea was to turn her into a living statue to scare the others?"

He must not have kept the contempt from his voice because Tulum leaned back and spoke softly. "Gibson can be impulsive, but in this case, you did not give him any choice." Tulum pushed his chair back and stood. "Let's go. Rendon is waiting for us."

"Just to be clear, I said I'm not angry. I didn't say I wouldn't kill you."

Tulum forced a laugh, half-exhalation, half-chuckle. "That's funny."

"You think I'm joking?"

Tulum waved a lazy hand, as though to chase the doubt from his face. "Don't be silly. I know every tactic the Puries used for a decade, I know dozens of Purie operatives in deep cover inside Marin. Kuipers has literally named me her personal advisor. I know the optimal training schedules to turn this place into a conveyor belt for indestructible soldiers. Kuipers won't let you touch me."

He smiled, showing enough teeth to bite Mika's head off. "Forget Kuipers. Even Rendon will give me your head on a platter."

"I wouldn't bet on it."

"Let's," he said, the arrogance back in his voice. "I'm curious now. Aren't you? What's your head worth?"

Tulum's words transported Mika to another day and to another conversation with a zealot. Once he abstracted away on which side of the Purge fence they sat, Tulum sounded exactly like Lester. The Purie chancellor had held the same conviction that she had all the answers and held all the cards.

They were the ones who deluded themselves that they were doing the necessary work that others didn't have the stomach for. They were all out there to save the human race. Except they were the ones doing the destroying because they defined victory in narrow terms. Worse yet, they infected all those around them with their madness. Kuipers had already bought into Tulum's plans. And Mika believed him that, given time, so would Sierra.

This was a man who had survived the apocalypse and government sweeps by playing a simple game: information for power. He would be in control of the Marin Executive Council in no time if he wasn't already. "We're never going to find out."

"What do you mean?"

"I mean, I believe that you own Kuipers. And that you'll own Sierra soon."

Tulum snickered. "Yeah, in a few minutes when we talk next."

"Except you won't."

Tulum laughed again though traces of nerves replaced the taunt. "I think we established that you're not armed. What are you going to do? Bore me to death?"

"You got it all figured out, don't you?"

Mika played with his tida, flicking it with his thumb and catching it again and again.

The smug smile returned to Tulum's face. "You're going to stab me with a tida?"

Mika grabbed a chair and walked to the door. He put the chair down and banged on the door. "Open up," he yelled. He took a step back and threw the chair against the door. "C'mon!"

Tulum stood up and approached as Mika kept banging on the door. Mika turned to him and grabbed him by the lapels. Tulum swung at him, and Mika didn't duck or parry. Tulum's fist landed on Mika's nose, splattering blood.

Mika pushed him away as the door opened. The Sentinel guard burst in, braced for battle with feet wide, hips low, and right hand on her holstered gun. Her eyes moved from Mika to Tulum, trying to reconcile Mika's agitated words and bloody nose with what she must have expected.

"He attacked me," Mika said.

"What's going on?" Jerry, Tulum's bodyguard, jumped into the room, shoving the Sentinel toward Mika.

Mika put his left forearm on the Sentinel's throat and moved behind her. He stepped back, taking her balance, and making her lean back. As her hands gripped his left arm, he reached to her holster and grabbed her pistol with his right hand.

He let go of her and took a step forward. He put his foot on her stomach and shoved her out of the room, with little impact but the full momentum of his coiled body. As she stumbled out, Mika fired three shots into Jerry's back, then two into his knees as he turned around.

The way Jerry fell, trying to wrestle Mika, meant he was trained and would be fine in a few minutes. But with his knees buckling, he was incapacitated now. Mika grabbed the man's collar and dragged him out. The Sentinel was up, ready to charge.

"Don't," Mika said, pointing the gun at her. He nudged his head to the room. "He's not worth it." She didn't move. Mika shut the door and touched his tida to the handle, locking it. He pointed the gun at Tulum. "You were saying?"

Tulum took a few steps back. "Let's not do anything rash."

Mika had no intention of doing anything rash. Like talk. He took two steps in Tulum's direction and fired three shots into Tulum's chest. Tulum stumbled back and collapsed.

The banging on the door now came from the other side. "Open up!"

The lock had come from Blue. And he had come to appreciate that genius came in all shapes and sizes and colors. They could break the door down in a moment, but that lock wasn't going to budge in the meantime. And he didn't need more than a moment. He fired into the back wall at hip height to punch through the plaster and kicked the lath to create an opening to the adjacent room. He then covered the fifteen feet between him and Tulum in four quick strides.

"Let's talk about this," Tulum pleaded.

He put his knee on Tulum blood-soaked chest. "Too late to talk."

Tulum had recovered from the shock of the bullets but was still too weak to push Mika's knee from his chest. "C'mon man. Think of the big picture."

Tulum liked playing that card. He felt untouchable, protected by his information and connections. But while Mika had made a promise to Lin, he had also made a promise to himself: that if someone ever forced him to keep his promise to Lin, he would find them and put a bullet through their eye too. Sure, Gibson was the one who had put Lin in the concrete coffin. But Gibson was a tool in Tulum's toolbox.

The irony that Lin wouldn't have approved wasn't lost on him. She would have put the needs of Marin ahead of her own. But she wasn't here. If Tulum had wanted to deal with someone reasonable, he should have gone after Mika instead of Lin. No rational thought allowed him to look into the man's eyes and not see Lin trapped in a square, irradiated, concrete coffin. He weighed in the big picture against the tiny picture of Lin through his crosshairs.

The big picture came out wanting.

The banging on the door grew louder. Sierra called his name, saying something about being rational, about talking, and about thinking this through. That she sounded like Tulum didn't help her cause. But none of it mattered. He kept his promises.

As the door behind him split open, he brought the gun to Tulum's eye and pulled the trigger.

CHAPTER 26

OVERBURDENED

"The search for a scapegoat is the easiest of all hunting expeditions."

—DWIGHT EISENHOWER

"You left them alone?"

Amy stood by the conference room she had left so disappointed the night before. She didn't let her real worry show on her face, flashing the concerned governor façade she had perfected over the last year. She tightened her hands into fists by her side as two medics carted Tulum's body away on a stretcher and stepped out of the way as they wheeled it out.

Another day, another body. This was one more step in the wrong direction, no matter their destination. The human cost lay in front of her covered in plastic as though the corpse were apologizing for offending her sensibilities. The political cost hovered half a day behind, with Kuipers ready to unleash her fury. The emotional cost had waltzed away with Mika's leaving.

"Tulum's the one who asked to talk to Mika alone," Sierra said, half in frustration and half in apology.

Amy relaxed her fingers, letting them extend before Sierra spotted her fists. "You know what Mika's really good at? Making his ideas seem like yours. Tulum picked Mika to make the call on whether the Sentinels should work with his team, and Mika told him what he wanted to hear. 'I'm a good judge of character,' that idiot bragged. Unbelievable."

"Didn't realize you cared so much about Tulum."

She didn't. But with each step Mika took in this direction, with each wave of casual violence, he lost a little more of himself. Had she talked to him last night or had a drink with him, could she have prevented this? She doubted it, but that she hadn't tried burned deep in her gut like a stab wound.

She took a deep breath. "It's Mika I worry about."

Sierra motioned for the guard who had been by the door. "Louise, what happened here?"

Louise hesitated, her eyes moving from the blood on the floor to Tulum's guard by the door. The guard sat with his back to the hallway wall while a medic inspected his wounds.

"There was shouting and commotion," Louise said, "and banging on the door. I opened it, and Bayley rushed out with a bloody nose. One chair was broken."

Sierra picked the gun from the floor. "Yours?"

She accepted and holstered her handgun. "Bayley grabbed it."

"You didn't stop him?"

"I tried. He threw me down."

Amy allowed herself half a smile. He had shown restraint by not harming Louise. She had to cling to any shred of evidence that somewhere in there, the real Mika still lurked.

"And he didn't shoot you but shot him," Sierra said, eyes on Tulum's guard who was now sitting back with a medic removing the bullets. Amy still struggled with this new normal, this flippant disregard for flesh by medical staff when attending the wounds of trained soldiers.

Louise's shoulders tightened. "Yes, ma'am."

"Why do you think that was?"

She lifted her eyes to face Sierra. "It's possible Tulum attacked him first."

Sierra chuckled. "Really? You don't find it odd that Tulum even touched Mika, who's not only trained but one of the best martial artists here?"

Louise didn't reply. Sierra turned to the guard on the floor. "Anything to say?"

The guard's eyes moved from Sierra to Louise and then to the medic by his side. He gritted his teeth as the medic put tape around his chest. "No."

Sierra turned to Louise. "I want every detail of every instant between that door opening and shutting again. My hound says the video systems were down for a few seconds. So, you're it." She turned to the guard. "The same goes for you too."

Sierra's tida chimed, and her attention moved to it. "Yeah?" Sierra nodded, closed her eyes, and nodded again. "Keep looking," she said and tapped her tida off.

"Let me guess; Mika is gone," Amy said, eyes on the damaged wall. Louise and Tulum's guard, supported by the medic, disappeared down the corridor.

Sierra nodded.

To be fair, knowing Mika, he probably had half a dozen escape routes from the building and the compound. "Why do you think he did it?"

Sierra's brow furrowed. "They had an encounter in the Uregs. It's complicated, but Mika blames Tulum for Lin's death."

Amy's eyes widened. There was negligent and there was stupid, and this wasn't even close.

Sierra closed her eyes and tilted her head back. "Kuipers is going to be pissed."

Amy's chief concern was still Mika, but Sierra was moving up on her list. With just those words, Sierra had reiterated why she was in over her head and so ill-suited for command. She had lost a key asset. She had let Mika betray her trust and disappear. And instead of dissecting how they had ended up here or what they had to do, Sierra was worried about Kuipers.

"Was Tulum really that influential in Marin?"

"I thought he was dangerous before I realized he was an ally."

"You may have been right the first time," Amy said.

"Kuipers is on a rampage to root out Purie spies. She'll never let this go."

"We both know that's not what happened."

"Yeah, that's not how Kuipers is going to see it," Sierra said. "She'll tear this place apart till she finds a Purie or a scapegoat."

CHAPTER 27
WALKABOUT

"If one does not know to which port he is sailing, no wind is favorable."

—SENECA

Mika had never expected to be in this dingy Uregs bar again, but then, the last year had become one long list of what he had never expected to do. The middle of the trio of naked bulbs hanging over the counter had gone out, darkening the narrow room to match his mood. A year ago, he had spent half an hour here without touching his drink, killing time before he met Lori. It was early afternoon, and he was on his third pint today and well past caring whether the brew had improved or he had lowered his standards.

Blue sidled up to the gap between him and the stool to his right, her deep purple hair the only thing in the bar intentionally out of place. She flagged the barkeep to order a beer.

Mika kept his eyes on the wall behind the counter. "Can't help you. I'm not a Sentinel anymore."

She climbed onto the stool and spun it to face him. "If I'd wanted a Sentinel, I'd have gone for the two who followed me here."

Mika met her gaze. "Followed you?"

"When I refused Sierra's insistence to track you, she put two Sentinels on me. She figured I'd find you, yeah?" She took a sip from the beer the barkeep pushed in front of her.

"Should I even ask where they are?"

She held her beer in one hand and waved toward the back wall of the bar with the other. "About eight blocks that way, getting mixed up in a weapons deal with a local gang."

He laughed, shoulders shaking. "You're funny."

She put her beer on the counter. "Not to them."

"This place stinks."

She took a sniff, nose flaring out in a quick inhale and eyes drifting to the sixty-gallon trash can behind the counter.

"I don't mean the leftover lunches that didn't smell edible to begin with. Now, the Red Spider was a proper drinking establishment. You drank for fun, before sex, or after business. Each option had its area with its character so there was no confusion. This," he said, waving his hand, "whatever this is, isn't a proper establishment. No soul."

"Are we talking about the blasted soul of the Red Spider?"

"No, ours." He finished his drink in two gulps and motioned the barkeep for another one. "Can't even get drunk anymore."

"I can," she said, taking another sip.

The barkeep refilled his pint glass. He took a sip. "What do you want?"

"You look like you can use a friend."

He spun his stool around to face her. "Still paying your debt to Eva?"

"Now you're just trying to be an asshole. No, we're all square with Eva. So, if you want me to work with you, you gotta pay me now."

"You're the one chasing me."

She sipped again. "I'm having a drink."

He reached for his drink and spun it, the glass tracing a widening spiral over an imaginary point on the bar. He didn't take a sip.

She pushed her stool out and stood up. "You need to have some fun, yeah?"

"What do you have in mind?"

"I'm driving," she said and headed for the door.

Twenty minutes later, they were driving east in the Uregs, but he resisted the urge to ask where they were going. "So," he said, "anything interesting from the cloned drive?"

She took one hand off the wheel and tapped her tida sitting on the dash. She swiped one of the dozen colored icons toward him. "It's best if you see it for yourself."

He skipped the logistics reports that confirmed the existence of six variants for now. Because the drive had come from Tulum's labs, it didn't have any more information on the two variants from the destroyed settlements. But it contained detailed quantitative analysis about the other four.

"That's amazing," he muttered as he glanced at the data from the settlement they had observed from a distance, the one he knew the least about.

"Yeah?"

"Response to an extreme environment is pushed beyond anything I've seen. These folks can handle crushing pressures in the deep ocean." He pointed to a curve. "A first-degree burn would feel like handling a warm cup. Frostbite wouldn't be an issue for another fifty degrees."

She nodded, both hands on the wheel. "Isn't that how you are too?"

"Not exactly. I'll recover, but I'll burn. Then I'll get into repair. This looks like it won't even burn as the heat will be dissipated before it becomes a problem."

"What does it all mean?"

"Not sure. Tulum thought this was meant to make us hardy for space colonization."

She gave him a furtive glance. "About him."

"You don't approve."

Her knuckles hardened on the wheel. "All this data and all these experiments… they say Tulum was the scientist. He was interested in finding out about the Purge. Genuinely interested. His pitch about space travel may have been real."

"How do you know that?"

"All the experiments and all the procedures have the originator listed, yeah? Tulum's are all about science. He tested everything a million times on mice, pigs, monkeys, and primates before moving to humans. Gibson's? They're all about manipulating the Purge, the vectors, the patients, and the settlements. He wants the secrets of the Purge too, but to rule it all. He's the one in contact with Marin, manipulating the Executive Council."

He swiped the data away. "Your point?"

"You shot the wrong man."

He put his feet by the windshield. "I'm not done yet."

He flipped his tida on again and went back to the data. An hour later, they reached the foothills of Mt. Diablo. The dry, golden hills turned to majestic valley oaks and, in the distance, forests. She pulled into a trail that climbed for three miles, and just as it looked as though she was going over a cliff, a pine-needle-covered driveway appeared. She parked and stepped out.

"I come here to clear my head. Maybe it'll work on you too, yeah?"

The hundred-foot firs hid a one-story wooden cabin nestled at the foot of the rising hillside. A shed stood to the right and back of the cabin, locked by a short metal farm door.

Blue strolled past the cabin and flicked her tida to the lock on the shed door. She swung the doors open to expose enough firepower to arm a platoon. A wooden bench lined the left wall, ending at floor-to-ceiling metal shelves containing hundreds of boxes of cartridges. Two reloaders were clamped to the bench. The green plastic one displayed settings for four different caliber cartridges. The scent of the gunpowder in the conical container filled the shed. Below the bench, buckets of casings stood accompanied by gallon-sized containers of powder. Bullets and boxes of primer lined up the bottom of the next bench.

"Correct me if I'm wrong, but this isn't standard-issue hound equipment."

"You're not wrong." She moved to the locked shelves lining the wall to their right. She lifted the shutter doors exposing eight rifles and five pistols, hanging on the wall. She grabbed two ear muffs, tossed him one, and picked a bolt-action hunting rifle. She waved at her collection. "Pick one." She walked out, carrying a bucket of cartridges.

He picked a heavier bolt-action rifle and followed her. They skipped the thirty-yard opening to their left that ended on the rocky hill with metal targets that formed a handgun range. She stopped under a makeshift canopy that stretched between two tall firs with a hunter green tarp covering a shapeless mass to their right. Straight ahead, round steel targets ranging from two feet in diameter to what must have been a few inches hung at fifty, one hundred, and two hundred yards.

She took the tarp off to expose a damp, worn-out wooden rack, a camping table, and a wooden bench. She flicked her tida, and a rendering of targets floated above the bench, including some at four hundred yards Mika hadn't spotted. She put her bucket next to the wooden bench, loaded her rifle, and took three shots to the steel target at two hundred yards. The pings informed him that she hit all three. The screen pinpointed that each shot had hit dead center.

He loaded his rifle, leaned into his scope, and focused on the steel, pizza-sized target. He hit the center on first and third, but the second was off by half a foot to the right.

She pointed to the far target and fired. "How about ten shots?"

They took turns firing. He hit six cleanly. She hit nine of the smaller targets with the tenth off-center by a few inches. She refilled a five-cartridge magazine and popped it into her rifle. She shot, pulled the bolt to eject the casing, locked it into place, and shot again until empty, all within ten seconds. She alternated hitting the targets at two hundred and four hundred yards, all in the center.

"That's incredible."

She sat cross-legged, rifle resting in her lap. "Practice. I shot every day growing up."

She reloaded and took another shot. "You're perfectly still," he said.

"It clears my mind."

"Your breathing is just right."

"It's the only time I freeze. Mind and body, yeah? It's all in this one moment, focused on nothing, then on the target, and then on nothing. That's how I see things."

"See things?"

She smiled and blinked. "I'm not getting weird on you. A hound's approach is not that different from a sniper's. You have to freeze and shut out your thoughts and preconceived ideas, yeah? Let the moment lead you to the scent. That's how I find patterns and design my sniffers. When everything stops, I see paths that weren't there seconds before."

"And with all this ability, you decided to be a hound?"

"Pays better."

"Yeah." His eyes moved toward the spartan cabin. "I see that you chase wealth."

A shy smile displaced the confident hound for a second, and in that split second when her eyes warmed up, she broadcast that she was too soft to use this skill.

"We should get back," he said.

She shook her head. "Sun's almost down. These paths are tricky in the dark." She grabbed the bucket. "Let's eat; but first, we collect these," she said and crouched to pick up the casings. "I shoot too much to waste them."

He helped her with the casings. They dropped them in the shed and stepped into the cabin. An open kitchen took the right wall, a dining table stood in the middle of the room, and a couch hid to the left. A door straight ahead led into a small bedroom. A second closed door to the left must have been the bathroom.

She walked into her bedroom and came out with a sleeping bag. She tossed it at him, and he tossed it on the couch. They turned in early after dining on the squirrels Blue hunted and Mika cleaned and cooked.

Mika jolted himself awake, disoriented for a second, not sure whether he was still camping with Lin. The wood-paneled walls brought him to the present. He tapped his tida. The forest air, the swishing of the fir needles in the wind, had allowed him to sleep uninterrupted for two hours. He forced himself to stay in the sleeping bag with his eyes closed. In his mind's eye, a seagull took flight; one stray feather on its left wing swayed in the wind. He lost his concentration after a few flaps, so he started again, and again. He declared victory when he reached triple digits and got up.

Sunrise was still a half-hour away. As he rummaged through the cabinets, Blue opened her bedroom door. "Where do you keep the coffee?" he asked.

She rubbed her eyes. "I don't have coffee."

"How's that possible?"

She yawned. "It's blasted disgusting."

"Don't you have to drink coffee to become a hound?"

She walked into the bathroom and shut the door as a response.

He headed out into the brisk morning. He sat on a tree stump that stood like a small island on a dry pine needle sea, a few yards to the left of the makeshift shooting range. The wind had shifted, blowing in a light haze from the north. It tickled his nose as though he sat by a smoldering fireplace.

Ten minutes later, Blue came out and sat next to him. "Everybody complains about this smoke. But I like it."

"You like inhaling ash?"

"I like the patterns in the sky and how the reds are deeper and change from dawn to late morning to afternoon. It's like we're on a different planet with a different sun."

"Well then, you need a better view." He walked to his Jeep, which had a full charge, courtesy of Blue's generator. "You don't have anywhere to be tomorrow, right?"

She shook her head.

He picked up the sleeping bag she had given him. "You have another one of these?"

She headed to her bedroom and came back out with a sleeping bag and a cardboard box about a foot square. She held out the box. "Here."

He tossed his sleeping bag back into the back of the Jeep, opened the box, and lifted a heather gray T-shirt with red art and lettering that was the perfect present for Amy. He smiled, "Nice."

His smile vanished when it hit him that he no longer needed it.

CHAPTER 28
CORE BREACH

"Learn from the mistakes of others. You can't live long enough to make them all yourself."

—ELEANOR ROOSEVELT

A my stepped out of their warehouse shell to take the short walk to the old, central dwelling. The transformation of the place in the two days since they had arrived was a testament to how people built communities whenever they could.

A makeshift kitchen had sprung up along the back wall frame. Crates lined one long wall, while sleeping bags carpeted the ground, separated by backpacks. The metallic scent of newly oiled heavy guns signaled their intent, while the aroma of frying onions reminded them there was still some living to do between battles.

Cavana and Eva flanked her, while JJ, and Isa, a Cal City militia she recognized but didn't know, walked behind them. The courtyard buzzed with the precision of Marin military operating procedures. Three light and two heavy transports stood watch in the distance to their left, blending together to form the outline of a squat new building completing a quad. They crouched like a family of giant metal birds: mom, dad, and three little chicks. That Kuipers had arrived with two platoons made the Sentinels neutral territory in name only.

A dozen armed Marin soldiers lined the door to the conference room as Amy made her way into the corridor. A booming male voice drifted from the open door, punctuating insults with bangs on a table or other solid surface that assaulted them with reverberating thumps.

"That's enough," Kuipers said, five seconds before appearing in the corridor, uniform crisp and tight. A man Amy assumed to be Gibson popped up behind Kuipers with his jawline stretched tautly and eyes narrowed followed by a beet-faced Sierra.

"The more answers I hear, the angrier I get," Kuipers said.

Amy stopped halfway down the corridor, forty feet before reaching Kuipers.

"This is incompetence at a scale I have not seen in a while." Kuipers waved in Amy's direction and flicked her hand toward Sierra. "You two are incapable of running this operation. I warned you there was a Purie inside, and you did nothing."

"With all due respect, General, we don't believe a Purie was responsible for what happened," Sierra said.

"You don't believe?" Kuipers shook her head.

Sierra looked at her feet, unwilling or unable to offer counterarguments.

"This is your fault," Kuipers said, eyes on Amy. "Puries took over New California and you did nothing. And I'm supposed to believe this is all a coincidence?"

"Believe what you want," Amy said in an even tone. "Just don't invent facts."

"Halsan is working with Kern."

Amy stayed silent.

"Are you incompetent or are you actively working for them?"

"General, Governor Chipps was not in the room when—" Sierra said but paused when Kuipers spun around and glared at her.

"Of course not, she's too smart for that." Kuipers took a step toward Amy. "How do I know you didn't ask your lover to do this?"

"You don't know when to stop, do you?" Amy asked.

She started to walk away but stopped when Kuipers raised her voice. "Your declaration dissolving the union had every legal scholar occupied and every general questioning our path. You wasted our time and resources for days on a stunt. Then you show up here, and my strongest ally is murdered. Do you see a pattern here?"

"You want me to sit here and listen to your accusations? I don't think so."

"Major Vandi," Kuipers said to the officer standing next to her. "Arrest Chipps for sedition and working with the enemy."

Vandi stood next to Kuipers, eyes wide in shock and indecision because Amy was either the governor of a sovereign state or the vice-chancellor. Disobeying her commanding officer was not an option. Arresting the governor was not a good option. She looked like a robot that had broken down from conflicting instructions. It took her a few seconds to step forward, but there had been no doubt. In a crisis of indecision, the safe path was always to follow a direct order.

Cavana stepped in front of Amy. "You do not have jurisdiction here."

"Arrest him too," Kuipers said, and the Marin soldiers drew their guns. Vandi left her gun holstered but ambled toward them in short, slow steps, as though if she only took half the steps needed, the problem would go away. If her still-wide eyes were any indication, she was going to run out of corridor before she completed her internal debate.

Isa and JJ also went for their guns, resulting in two sets of soldiers facing each other from forty feet in a narrow hallway. Unless Kuipers acted quickly, this was going to end with a lot of blood.

Gibson shoved Sierra aside and stepped forward, gun drawn, overtaking the major in three quick strides. His tight eyebrows and narrow eyes broadcasted his murderous intent.

Eva stepped in front of Amy and pushed her behind with one arm.

"Lieutenant, step aside," Kuipers called to Eva, which made Gibson stop.

Eva did not move.

"I am ordering you to step aside."

Cavana stepped forward, flanking Eva. "We all need to take a deep breath," he said.

Kuipers' gaze moved from Cavana to Eva and back to Cavana. "If I need your advice, I'll let you know. Now ask your soldiers to lower their weapons."

"I will, as soon as you do so as well."

One of Kuipers' soldiers took a step forward to her right, gaining an angle on them. Isa tracked her with her gun.

Cavana put his hand on Isa's gun and nudged it down thirty degrees.

"Stand down," Kuipers said in response.

The Marin soldiers brought their guns down, but Gibson straightened his arm and fired, as did Isa. Eva spun around and tackled Amy to the ground, cradling Amy's head in her arms as gunfire erupted around them.

"Stop!" Sierra yelled, but the gunfire went on for another four seconds.

When the ear-popping staccato stopped, Eva got on her knees. Amy lifted her head to see around Eva, but the corridor slipped out of focus as though she viewed it through a thick, shifting smoke. She couldn't make sense of the shouting or Eva's agitated face.

Cavana crouched to her side, calling her name, and with his booming voice, it should have been deafening, but she barely heard him. The caustic whiff of spent gunpowder jolted her mind and the sound of Sierra shouting for a medic penetrated her fog. Eva's bloody hands were pressed against her left side. Shit, why did Eva have to smear blood on her?

It took Amy a few more seconds to pinpoint the source of the searing pain in her gut. The blood was hers.

CHAPTER 29

ROGUE

"We meet the people we're supposed to when the time is just right."

—ALYSON NOEL

They had covered three hundred miles toward Oregon when Blue asked, "Did it help?"

Mika kept his eyes on the empty road, letting the rattle of cracked asphalt and the occasional jolt of dirt-filled potholes fill his silence.

"Tulum," she said two bounces later.

He tapped the steering wheel with his thumb for a few more seconds. "Not really."

Blue remained silent for another three miles. "Me neither. I thought I'd get some satisfaction, knowing that asshole couldn't hurt anyone again, but I didn't. Jen is still gone. They say time will help."

He didn't tell her it didn't. Since he had nothing to offer, he let her talk, trying to find meaning in something that didn't have any.

"Sometimes, I feel guilty," she said.

"Don't."

"Since Jen isn't back, I feel I've added to the violence, you know?"

"What you've added is a drop in a fifty-gallon container."

"All the same," she said and rested her head on the back of her seat.

They rolled to a stop when the dirt road ended on a semicircular clearing fifty feet across. The forest rose thousands of feet in the north and east. To their west, bushes led to dense fir. He set two folding chairs and a cooler, twenty feet from the ledge and sat down.

The light gray sky darkened to a dull gunmetal with a red silhouette sinking over the hills. The heavy air smelled like pine needles tossed on a campfire. Mika sat on the chair and stretched out his legs, ankles crossed.

She set a cooler between them as a side table. "Where is the fire?"

He pointed north. "About seventy miles that way."

"I can't believe the scale of this." She stood and walked to the edge of their outcropping, looking north. "How will it stop?"

He took a sip from his water bottle, the only potable liquid Blue had kept at her cabin. "Not sure. Either the rains will come, or it'll run out of fuel."

Her eyes widened and scanned the horizon, green in all directions. "Run out of fuel?"

"Bare strips, a quarter-mile-wide, crisscross these forests. Bands of old, cracked concrete meander around them, like runways carved by a drunk deity. The old timers must have put them here to keep fires from getting out of control decades ago. Even with young trees shooting up, they'll do their jobs."

"You're saying this happens often?"

"Seems like it. We've come across cleared-out dark patches fifty miles that way," he said pointing northeast, then to the east, "and two hundred that way. It's like an alien landscape for miles, with broken down charred trees and then green bushes and saplings pushing through."

He extended his hand out, rotating his wrist. "It's so still I have to do this to remind myself that we're still alive." He chuckled. "There is a fire raging seventy miles away with violence, infernal heat, and cracking trees the size of your cabin. The smoke has blotted the sky. But underneath it all, it's calm. No wind here, and nothing moves."

She didn't reply but kept her eyes on the horizon.

He spun around to the creaking of a pine cone and spotted a slight movement in the bushes to their left. He stood up to find the red dots of laser sights on his chest. And on Blue's back.

"Don't make any sudden moves," a voice said from behind the bushes.

As Blue turned around, Mika stepped between her and the laser beam. But they probably had multiple sights on them. New dots on Blue confirmed that their new foe was not alone.

A soldier with a brown leather jacket over combat fatigues walked out of the bushes. Her long forehead disappeared into half-inch-cropped hair, her face hidden behind a bandana. She stopped six feet from him. Her eyes moved from his Jeep to Blue's purple hair to the chairs, and she lowered her bandana, exposing deep dimples that ended on round cheekbones.

"You're not Kern," she said.

Mika fought the urge to laugh. "Impressive."

"The fuck are you doing here?"

He smiled without letting his lips part. "Camping."

She halved the distance between them. "Don't fuck with me."

"I'm not. We've come to watch the red sun."

"Don't move," she said and took another step. She patted him through his jacket, reaching for his belt and back. She pulled his jacket where she had nudged metal. She reached in and took his hunting knife. She pointed to the piece of folded paper in his pocket. "What's this?"

He grabbed her wrist.

One of the red dots on Blue's chest moved to her forehead, and Mika let go of the wrist. She reached in and took the paper, unfolding it. Her eyes went wide and moved back and forth between the picture and Mika. "What are you doing here? And if you say camping, I'll deck you."

"It's a long story."

"Walk with me." She took three steps before stopping and turning around.

Mika didn't move. "Put the guns down."

She waved her hand down, and the red dots on him and Blue disappeared.

He reached for Blue's forearm and squeezed. "Inhale, hold, exhale." Blue looked like she hadn't taken a breath in four minutes. He turned to the soldier. "If anything happens to her—"

"I'm not in the business of hurting unarmed civilians."

She walked away and this time Mika followed. She stopped twenty yards later where the bushes opened up to the ledge of their hill and raised the picture. "What does this mean?"

"I wish I knew."

She still clasped his knife in her right hand. She pocketed the picture and held out her left hand in request. He extended his right hand. She grabbed his forearm and turned his palm up. She brought the knife to his palm. "A nick?"

"Nick away."

She pushed the knife tentatively, giving him a shallow half-inch cut with the tip. The cut closed, exposing only a few drops of blood. She cut deeper, and the same thing happened. She slashed his palm, cutting all the way across. The blood bubbled up hiding the cut. He reached with his left hand and wiped the blood, exposing a closing wound.

"Hot damn," she said.

"You, now."

"What?"

Mika pointed to her palm.

She cut an inch. The wound turned into a red weld, then turned into a deep scratch. It stayed that way.

"So," he said, "you don't work for Gibson." She frowned. "Because if you did, you'd heal a lot faster."

"I thought I did," she blurted out and then laughed. "I don't know who the fuck you are, but you're all right." She took a handkerchief and wiped her cut hand. She moved his knife to her left hand and waved with her right hand. "I'm Josie Eze."

He wiped his hand on his sleeve and waved. "Mika Bayley."

Her eyes grew wide. "Hot damn."

"What?"

"I have heard that name before."

His shoulders tightened. "I hope I didn't piss you off in a different life."

"You kinda did."

"Look," he started, but her deep, throaty laugher cut him off. He waited.

"You pissed me off by flying out of the chancellor's fifth-floor window."

His face went slack, and he took a step back.

"Relax. Chancellor Lester was a snake. I tried to look you up after that. But you know what? Not a single account of the events that night mentioned you. Why might that be?"

"Because I wasn't there?"

"Oh, you were, but that's not the interesting part. The interesting part is how General Rose reacted when the initial report came. She didn't want to know how the chancellor was doing. Oh no, she wanted to know how you were doing."

Mika couldn't keep his lips from parting.

"Yeah, exactly. I was the one who received the report. I was the one who told her. So how did you disappear from the record?"

He kept still. "How would I know? I was in a coma."

"Yeah."

"What now?"

She laughed again. She walked to where her team and Blue stood. "Ease up," she called. "We have guests for dinner."

Eze's camp was three miles north. Rows of tents lined the west side of the camp with three fire pits surrounded by folding chairs and crates in the middle. Humvees and trucks were parked to the east in front of four light transports that faced out. Dozens of soldiers buzzed around the fires. Eze talked to two soldiers before coming back to him.

"So, you worked with Lor—General Rose?" he asked.

"She was my commanding officer."

"These parts?"

"Not exactly, but yeah."

"What does that mean?"

She chuckled. "Not sure what to make of you. But considering the general's reaction, I'll assume you're not hostile. Don't disappoint me." She chuckled. "Imagine that; we might be on the same side."

He kept his eyes on her. "Which side is that?"

"The not-Marin, not-Kern, not-New Cal side who'd like to prevent Puries and those fighting the Puries from killing everyone."

It was his turn to laugh. "Yeah, I can roll with that." He turned serious. "Have you seen the general, since…."

She shook her head.

He pointed to his palm. "How did you find out about this?"

"The general briefed me and my partner. On her orders, we went after Kern bases that supported those who set all this in motion. Eliminated their threat."

He pointed to her nonmilitary jacket. "That's not a Marin officer uniform."

"I'm retired."

"Since?"

"Since our attack in the Uregs caused the release of a biological weapon in Marin."

"That was you?"

"That was me." There was more regret than pride in her trailing voice. "Let's say I wasn't welcome in Marin after that, and I didn't want to explain anyway."

If anyone deserved to know why he healed so well, it was Eze. But a year in the field shifted allegiances, particularly since these days there were more sides in the Uregs than on a die.

"You've been in the Uregs this whole time?"

"You wouldn't believe me if I told you about the things we saw."

"You'd be surprised."

Her broad smile said he didn't know what he was talking about.

"Settlements of about a thousand people?"

Eze's eyes widened.

"Maybe even one with a thousand corpses? Burned or chemically cleansed?"

"So, you've been southeast?"

He shook his head. "Straight north."

She let out a whistle. "Who is Gibson?'"

"He replaced the Puries' role in the settlements. Same experiment, different agenda."

She took the Purge vials picture out of her pocket. "You really don't know what this is?"

"I know there are other versions of the Purge. One helps combat radiation. One reduces oxygen need." He pointed to the picture. "This implies there are more. Anything like that south?"

"Everyone in every settlement down south was dead by the time we found them."

"A year ago?"

"Yeah, right after we took out their last base. Some of it was recent, with charred corpses piled into ditches, still smoldering. Haven't run into anything like that since."

She extended the picture. He folded it back and put it in his pocket. "The lab this came from? It's in Shasta."

"Irradiated?" she asked.

He nodded.

"If you're serious about this," she said, waving at the test-tube picture, "we can help each other. I have equipment and soldiers who can gather more info."

"That sounds—"

"Mika!" Blue shouted, alarm in her voice.

He spun, as did Eze, but Blue sat on her folding chair, head buried in her screen. Mika covered the distance to Blue at a jog. "I thought we were out of tower range."

"They have access," Blue said sheepishly. She stood up and leaned toward Mika. "There was a scrap at the Shed. Amy was shot."

"Fuck."

"They're apparently looking for a Purie spy." She chuckled. "She's fine, Mika."

No, she's not!

"You need to get me in there, now."

Blue tapped her screen. "How serious is this?"

"What do you mean?"

"I can use every trick once. Some tricks are better than others."

"Do whatever you need to do to get me in and out unnoticed."

"Okay, then, we'll use my best card," she said and went to pack up her equipment.

Mika turned to Eze. "I need to leave now." He grabbed his chair, folded it, and tossed it into the back of the Jeep. He jumped in, started it, and backed up toward Eze. "Say, you don't have a light transport I can borrow, do you?"

Eze chuckled. "I barely know you."

"I can stay here," Blue said. Her backpack hung low on her shoulder.

Eze's eyebrows shot up. "That helps how?"

"For starters, you need better security for your network."

Eze pushed her breath through her nose. "That's not exactly worth a transport. Not to mention, letting you into our systems requires even more trust than handing him a transport," she said, jabbing her thumb in Mika's direction.

Blue licked her lips. "I'm already in."

Eze's eyes moved from Blue to Mika back to Blue.

Mika cut in before Eze spoke. "Look, it's important, and I'd owe you big."

Eze motioned him to come. He stepped off the truck and approached her.

"Tell me one thing, just one thing that'll make me trust you."

"Lor—Rose didn't socialize with her officers but liked her wine. The cabinet next to her desk was full of wine."

"So, you might have ended up there during an investigation."

"You think she offered wine to witnesses and suspects?"

"Okay, so you knew Rose. That's not enough."

"Were you at the battle of Hollister?"

Eze nodded.

"You used a really good hound to freeze the Kern forces. That hound was a personal friend of Rose."

She tapped her lips with her index finger. "Don't make me regret this, Bayley."

They walked toward the transports, with two soldiers trailing them. Eze opened the transport side door. Unlike the other three, it was a lightly armed cargo-troop carrier hybrid, with one seating row and a cargo hold. "Thank you."

Eze added him to the authorized user list, talking through the transport's idiosyncrasies.

Mika stepped off to find Blue. "You're good?" She nodded, and he leaned closer, "Can you disable any trackers in this transport?" She nodded again, and he straightened.

He sat in the pilot's seat and set a course for the Shed, but let the autopilot fly. His thoughts drifted to Kuipers' witch hunts then to Sierra's struggle for clarity. Sierra's world contained allies and enemies, but her ire was reserved for those she thought were allies but weren't. Her reaction to betrayal, true or imagined, was not hard to predict.

Fuck!

PART IV
PUDDLES

CHAPTER 30

ONE OF A KIND

"When one door of happiness closes, another opens; but often we look so long at the closed door that we do not see the one which has opened for us."

—HELEN KELLER

Amy sat in bed, listening to Sierra drone on about whom to include at their next meeting. The sharp smell of iodine didn't protect her against Sierra's monologue or keep her at full attention. The screen she had been reading lay by her side, displaying the origin of Sentinel equipment. She was tempted to reach for it, but she did not want to be rude. In any event, New Cal's contributions were a short list. They had supplied a quarter of the recruits, so they had human capital but not much else.

Pain shot through her side like she had touched a live wire as she reached for the glass of water by her bedside. She steadied her hand to let the jolt pass and took three sips while Sierra talked. The strong painkillers dulled her mind, so she made do with the weak ones. Sadly, painkillers were an on-off proposition and hers were set to off.

She put down the glass and rested her head on the wall. The bullet had ripped through her gut and left kidney. Dr. Cossa had stitched her intestines and saved the kidney. Her back ached from the soft mattress, a hazard of convalescing in a medical facility for trained soldiers who had forgotten about pain.

Eva sat on the armchair in the corner to her left, past the foot of her bed. From that spot, she scanned the bed, the narrow corridor to the door, and the bathroom. The room had been a rectangle into which they had dropped a bathroom to her right, creating the corridor to the door.

"I'm fine. You don't have to check up on me," Amy said.

"It's the least I can do." Sierra leaned on the wall. "I'm still investigating the altercation. If a Marin soldier shot first, I need to know."

"It was Gibson," Eva said.

Sierra took a deep breath. "There is no surveillance footage in the corridor. I will look at what you're saying, but Major Vandi claims one of your people shot first."

"I'm sure we'll all feel better if we can blame this on Isa," Amy said.

"That's not what I meant. But I need to follow all the leads."

Amy pushed a strand of hair behind her ear. "How many factions are there in Marin right about now?"

"Factions?"

"Kuipers. Yim. Tulum's people. I'm guessing some officers are still loyal to Rose."

"They're all soldiers. They'll follow orders."

Amy smiled. "You told me once to not trust anyone, not even you. You might want to take your own advice right about now."

"Trust and mutiny are two different things."

"All the same. Many factions, many agendas. Just make sure you account for all that when you follow orders. You might also consider whether your orders are legal."

Sierra took two steps forward and lowered herself, sitting on her heels, back flat against the wall. "Look, I'm trying to prevent you two from tearing Marin apart. You're both pulling. Something is going to give. I tried to calm Kuipers down about Tulum, but she's still cross with you. She's convinced there's a Purie here, and she's testing everyone. She even suspects you. Once I get your results and convince Kuipers you're not a Purie, we can all get on the same page."

Eva shook her head, but Sierra didn't spot the motion. Amy remained silent.

"I really don't understand what's taking this long." Sierra stood up, "Actually, I'll head there now and get to the bottom of this."

After Sierra left, Eva stood and then sat on the foot of the bed.

"I'm a little surprised they haven't figured this out yet," Amy said.

"I asked Dr. Cossa to keep your results to herself."

Amy dropped her chin to her chest. "And she agreed?"

"She was one of the doctors who studied me when I got back. Most didn't know what to do with me, so they avoided me. But Dr. Cossa was different. Her wife had been at the front lines in Anderson Valley. She died on the first offensive. When Cossa found Jen had also been killed, she opened up to me. We talked a lot. She won't lie or falsify data, but she agreed to not volunteer your test results until she gets a direct question."

"Which she's about to get."

"Do you really think there's a Purie in the Sentinel?"

"I doubt it. They'd be exposed pretty quickly. It's most probably a cover. Kuipers is using the oldest trick in the book: create a credible threat, arrest a few high-profile officials, and everyone becomes much more accommodating and much more likely to follow whatever order she gives."

"We need to get you out of here. Sierra doesn't do ambiguous. She's torn between her loyalty to you and Kuipers. She'll welcome anything that makes her inner conflict go away."

"Yes, I'm beginning to agree with you. But aren't we under lockdown?"

The lock cycled again, and the screen on her bedside displayed the ID: Sierra.

"That was quick," Amy said.

Eva stood and put her right hand on the gun in the small of her back. She took three slow steps toward to door and stopped before the bathroom protrusion, facing the door. Her wide stance anchored her to the floor, and her face went slack. As the latch released, she drew her gun.

The door closed with a thud, and Eva relaxed her arms and put her gun back to its holster. Her voice rose. "Are you insane coming back here?"

Mika waltzed past Eva into the room. "They won't look here."

"They're tearing this place apart, searching for a Purie on base."

"Good thing I'm not a Purie then." He turned to Amy. "Are you okay?"

Amy stood up. The room spun around her, so she sat back down on the bed. She reached for her pants and put them on one leg at a time, arching her back to get the waistband up. Pain shot through her scar, and she folded forward, resting her forearms on her thighs.

Eva put an arm on her waist.

"I'm fine," Amy said, sitting back down on the bed.

Eva turned to Mika. "Kuipers or Sierra will get Amy's results any time now. We need to get her out of here, but they're watching my every move."

"Good."

Eva frowned. "How's that good?"

"As long as you stay put, they'll assume Amy is still here."

He pointed to the screen on the wall that still showed Sierra having entered the room.

"For how long?"

"Maybe fifteen minutes," Mika said.

"I said no more than ten. Don't push it," a voice said from Mika's tida.

Mika smiled. "Just checking, Blue."

Amy took a deep breath and stood up again. This time the dizziness subsided. She reached for the stool next to her bedside table and picked up a long-sleeved shirt and her burgundy leather jacket. She sat back on the bed and put on her clothes.

"We have control of what happens in this room. They can't hear or see, but Blue can," Mika said.

"What's the plan?" Eva asked.

"You stay here. Make a call or anything else that'll actively reinforce that you're here. Meanwhile, Amy and I walk to the loading dock, hop on a bike, and ride toward the New Cal building. We drive right through it."

"The fence?"

"Has a hole to let us pass. Cavana saw to it."

"How far are you going on that bike before Kuipers sends everyone after you?"

"I have a transport three miles out. As long as you can delay them for a few minutes, we'll be long gone by the time they search for us."

Eva leaned back on the wall. "Might work."

He put his hand on Amy's forearm. "Can you move?"

"Slowly."

Eva grabbed his elbow in a vice-like hold and spun him around. "If I'm letting her go with you, I need to know you're up for this. That you can protect her."

"You know I can."

"No, I don't. I know the old Mika could." She waved at him. "This one, I'm not so sure."

He leaned in and whispered in her ear. Eva's eyebrows lifted in question. "A hundred and twenty," he said, and Eva let go of his elbow.

Amy stood up and zipped her jacket up to midriff. If she didn't move, the pain was tolerable. She suspected the next steps required her to move.

"We need to go now," he said.

Eva bit her lower lip but let go of Mika's elbow. "Six days' of antibiotics," she said and packed IV pouches into a cooler by the side of the bed. "The infection is under control, but you need to continue with these."

Mika extended his hand to give her a lift. "Ready?"

Amy put a hand on the wall. No, she wasn't ready for any of this. She wasn't ready to let Eva deal with the aftermath of her deception. She wasn't ready to take Mika's hand into the unknown. She pushed off the wall and stepped forward, almost bumping into Mika. She stopped by the door and kissed Eva. "Stay safe."

Eva's eyes shone with tears that didn't flow. "You too."

Mika jammed the cooler into his backpack and slung it over one shoulder. He stepped into the corridor and signaled her to follow. The corridor was cooler than her room, and even with her jacket zipped up, she shivered as she shuffled behind him. They had almost made it to the loading dock when Harry Ge, a former Cal City militia, popped out of a door to their left. Mika nudged her into the first door opening.

"You're back," Harry called.

"Yeah, tracking job for Sierra."

Harry chuckled. "Didn't think you'd be back in the fold so fast. I guess all is forgiven when there's a Purie spy on the loose."

Mika grinned, "I guess."

"That's Rendon for you. Results are all that matter, am I right?"

"What can I say?"

"Did you see Chipps?"

Mika's cheeks tightened ever so slightly. The tension was unmistakable from Amy's side angle, but there was no chance Harry would notice it. "No, why?"

"She's in medical lockdown. Rumor is she's not healing well, if you know what I mean."

"If I get around to it, I'll pay her a visit."

"Gotta run. Stop by for a beer after dinner?"

"Sure."

"See you later," Harry said.

Mika waited another five seconds and motioned her forward. Isa was waiting for them in the loading dock with a motorbike. He took the handlebars and turned to Amy. "How are you feeling?"

"I'm feeling like I have seventeen stitches in my gut where they fished out a bullet that tore up half my left kidney and spilled bacteria from my gut into my blood."

He winced and half-supported, half-lifted her onto the bike. "It's just for three miles."

Isa pointed to the New Cal occupied building shell. "Slow down as you enter. Ramon will wave you through when the camera sweep passes. You have twelve seconds before the camera returns."

"Got it," Mika said.

Isa turned to Amy. "Stay safe, Governor."

He started the bike, and they rolled between the two loading docks. As they approached, Ramon held his hand up, his eyes on a screen. Mika slowed down. Then Ramon waved furiously, and Mika gunned it.

They flew toward the fence at a speed that would have been fatal to her if Mika missed the opening. He didn't. The chain-link fence parted as they hit it. Amy clutched him with all the dwindling strength she had left because she didn't want to fall and because she wanted to believe the old Mika was back.

Six minutes of bumps, agony, and gritted teeth later, they reached a transport. She stepped off but leaned on the bike, not trusting herself to take a step. Mika put an arm under her shoulder and guided her to a seat in the back of the transport.

This was a multipurpose transport with one row of seating right behind the pilots' seats, a cargo hold to the back, stacked storage crates, and a two-foot galley. A heavy gun mounted on a swivel completed the semicircle behind the seat. She put her head on the back of her seat, not budging when the ripped leather scratched her neck.

He started the engines, then stepped out to roll the bike in and strap it to the cargo hold. They flew low, barely skipping over the treetops to avoid radar. She leaned back and unzipped her jacket. An oval bloodstain covered the right side of her shirt.

"My stitches didn't like that ride," she said.

He engaged the autopilot and stepped back. He frowned as he lifted her shirt. She looked down as well and winced. The ooze leaking out of her torn stitches was thin pumpkin orange, not the thick, red of healthy blood.

"You there?" the screen chimed.

"Blue?"

"Yeah. Sierra just got to Amy's room. Eva's still there. Wanna hear?"

"Put it on."

"… And you didn't tell me Mika was here?" Sierra hissed. "Did you know?" Ten seconds of static followed. "Did you know?" Sierra insisted.

"Know what?"

"That Amy is a Purie?"

"She's not."

"So, she fooled you too."

"No, she didn't," Eva said.

"It's going to be a long time before you recover from this betrayal."

"I didn't betray you."

"What do you call what just happened?"

"I made it very, very clear that my top priority was protecting Amy. If you were surprised by my actions, you weren't paying attention," Eva said in a voice so calm it was comical.

"I thought you were smarter than this."

"Than what? Than blaming Amy for something she didn't do? For who she is? Sure, Amy does not carry the Purge. But she's not with the Puries."

"You're naïve. But the world doesn't work that way."

"How does it work?"

"You follow orders."

"Yeah," Eva said. "That's the moral equivalent of 'just because.'"

"You follow orders," Sierra repeated, "because your superiors know more than you do."

Eva chuckled. "Clearly not in this case. But that's not how loyalty works."

"Oh?"

"Why didn't Blue help you when you wanted her to track Mika?"

"Because she's an untrained punk, not a soldier."

Eva snorted. "Fair."

"But you, you're supposed to be a soldier."

"Not anymore."

"You are a soldier. And though Amy may have fooled you, you still owe Marin."

"Yeah? What exactly do I owe Marin for? Letting me be abducted from the hospital? Not even looking for me? Treating me like a weapon after I got back? I don't owe Marin shit."

"Get out! You're nothing but a spoiled, ungrateful excuse for a soldier."

"You..." Eva said in disgust but didn't finish the sentence.

"What? Looking for a good insult? Don't bother, I've heard them all."

"You're just like my mother."

"Patch me to—"

"That's all, folks," Blue cut in. "I've burned the link, and I'm burning this one too, yeah? They can't trace this, but I don't want to take chances."

"Thanks, Blue. And did you take care of the trackers in this transport?"

"All burned to the ground. Take care," she said and was replaced with static.

"Well, that was fun," Mika said. He turned to her but winced as they made eye contact.

Her head became heavy, and she folded sideways to rest her head on the seat. She spotted more blood dripping to the seat but didn't have the strength to push herself away. She closed her eyes and reopened them. Mika's concerned face hovered around hers. He rearranged her head and put her legs up on the seat, whispering that all would be fine.

She tried to smile at him but didn't think she succeeded. She didn't want to let the irony that he had become the optimist pass, but she couldn't form the words.

When a blanket dropped on her, she gave in and let sleep take over.

CHAPTER 31

DECLINE

*"Between two evils, I always pick
the one I never tried before"*

—MAE WEST

Mika completed his walk-through of the perimeter sensors. He would get at least an eight-minute warning if anyone approached their hideout, though the benefit of that information was dubious. His defensive strategy relied on a quick retreat with three escape routes. Now, none of that mattered because Amy was in no condition to walk, much less run.

They were six miles from the Mendocino coast, within Marin, and forty miles north of a seaside fishing town. The property was tucked behind a winding driveway that ended at a brick courtyard separating a two-car garage and a three-bedroom bungalow. The tarp-covered transport sat behind the garage, with enough fuel left for fifty miles, which would get them nowhere.

In the weeks that Amy had suspected he was searching for Lori, he had gone to all her safe houses he knew. She hadn't been at any of them, but he had taken the time to replace and treat the diesel-fuel drums, inspect the propane tanks, and maintain the generators and solar panels. He removed the cap from the thousand-gallon propane tank that sat in the covered side of the garage like a grounded submarine. He primed the generator that coughed three times before shaking into life and switched the circuit from the solar panel to the generator.

He stepped into the garage, which reeked of diesel. In the dim light of a single exposed bulb hanging from its cord, he siphoned the blue diesel from the drum into a five-gallon container. He walked to the side of the garage and pulled the gray-white tarp from the truck. The red at the bottom of the doors implied the truck had not always been this dirty gray speckled with rusty blisters as though it had the measles. The front fender was missing, but the truck's engine had turned eight months ago.

He poured the diesel and capped the tank. Blue diesel was for the Marin military, and the penalties were severe for those caught with it. Then again, if they ran into a Marin official, the color of the diesel would be the least of their worries.

He marched back toward the bungalow. The siding had bubbled and separated in patches, and flocks of dark aluminum flashing shingles that had slid off littered the ground. The roof, though, was functional. He closed the door behind him, inhaling the damp fetor that reminded him of a poorly aerated sailboat, a mix of decaying cloth and rotting wood.

He sat next to Amy's bed and wiped the beads of sweat speckling her forehead. He cleaned her surgery scars, but the visible pus wasn't the problem. Her dry lips and pale complexion signaled a deeper infection, and the antibiotics Eva had packed were not working. In two days, she had gone from weak to feeble to frighteningly frail.

He heated the soup to lukewarm and walked back to the bedroom. She stirred, opening her eyes and yawning. She lifted her head, and he helped her to sit up in bed. He fed her the soup, but she barely swallowed three half spoons before giving up.

She rested her head on the headboard. "I was doing better before you rescued me."

"That's not funny."

She took shallow breaths and took the bowl, swallowing three more spoons of soup. "Where are we?"

"West of where they think we are."

"West?"

"Outskirts of Marin, past Mendocino."

"Why?"

"This is the last place they'll look for people hiding from the Marin military."

She flashed a shallow smile. "I missed your logic."

"Well, you're stuck with it for a while."

She wiped her forehead with her napkin. "How... how long have we been here?"

"A little over two days. You've mostly slept. You're holding in soup, but not much else."

"I remember Eva, the motorbike." She cocked her head. "What did you tell her to convince her to let me go with you?"

"I described a seagull flying over the bay, head retracted, one feather out of place, flapping its fully stretched wings a hundred and twenty times."

She narrowed her eyes. "I'm the one who's supposed to be delirious."

"I also reminded her how stubbornly single-minded I can be when I protect someone who matters to me."

"And I matter again?"

"You've always mattered."

She broke a sad smile. "The bike, and then did we fly here?"

"Yes, at very low altitude and through their blind spots. If they had spotted us, they would have been here by now. We're only three hours west of the Redding base."

"We have a transport?"

"Stashed away."

She straightened up. "What did you think Sierra was going to do when she found out I don't carry the Purge?"

"Kuipers is arresting officials without the Purge and Sierra is confused. She's not equipped to handle Kuipers, new players, new viruses, and Marin under martial law."

"She was doing fine with the Sentinel last year."

"That was a clear mission: find Puries beyond our borders. And even that one, she inherited from Lori. And bungled it."

"So, I'm a *Purie* for her now?"

"She doesn't do well with ambiguity; she's a follower. I was hoping she'd latch on to you for guidance, but it seems Kuipers' Marin credentials won out."

"Kuipers isn't my biggest fan."

"I know. So, it's not what Sierra would have done. It's what Kuipers would have gotten her to do. And I didn't like the options."

Amy closed her eyes and hung her head. "I'm afraid you're right." She rested her head on her pillow. He reached for her hand. She didn't squeeze back but didn't withdraw it either. She was gone in minutes. He pulled the blankets over her and turned off the lights.

He took her bowl to the kitchen and dropped it in the sink. He came back, sat on a low chair that allowed him to stretch and put his feet on the end of Amy's bed. He dozed off a few times, but only for a few minutes. As the night wore on, Amy's breathing became more ragged, every breath turning into a struggle. Every time she became quiet, he got up to make sure her chest still rose and fell.

As morning light filtered through the south-facing window, he stood, stretched his shoulder, and checked on Amy. She was curled into a fetal position, so pale and so delicate. He made oatmeal, but she couldn't hold it. She vomited far more than she took in, the viscous bile a deep green with a putrid stench.

When she slipped into a deep sleep again, he hopped on the truck and drove down the coast. He stopped ten miles from the town and hid the truck behind bushes by the side of the road. He was running out of antibiotics—not that they were doing much good.

The Pacific stretched to the west, a smooth dark blue in the morning calm with a wispy haze floating above it, burning up and disappearing by the minute. By midday, the whitecaps would display the ocean's playful side. The menacing anger the storms brought was weeks away.

He tapped his tida and initiated a call using Blue's sniffers.

"Didn't expect to hear from you," her cartoon said. Three seconds later, she appeared, puffy eyes and ruffled hair signaling that she had just woken up.

"I'm close to a town, so my signal should blend in." She nodded and rubbed her eyes. "How's our new friend treating you?"

"Like a rock star. And her team? It's like I have my own private army, yeah?"

"Don't let it get to you," he said. "Are we secure?"

"Took care of that before answering. What's up?"

"Amy's not doing well. These antibiotics are not enough."

She squeezed her eyes shut and rubbed her cheek. "What do you need?"

"An emergency room. New Cal can't keep this quiet, and they don't have the facilities anyway. You need to find me someplace they can handle blood poisoning and potential sepsis."

She went quiet for half a minute. He guessed she was searching for medical facilities. "Not many options. Mild cases, maybe four locations. But if it's serious, it has to be Marin." She added, "Or a Marin base. Two Marin bases have what you need."

"Who are the commanders?"

She took another ten seconds. "Elana Simon in Portola and Maria Lambert in Redding."

"Who was the chief commander when they got their current command?"

She was quiet for another minute. "Simon was appointed six months ago, by... General Kuipers. Lambert was appointed a year ago, also by Kuipers."

"Fuck."

"Interesting," Blue said.

"What?"

"Lambert was General Dey's chief of staff."

"Why is that interesting?"

"A year ago, she was in the inner circle of the most powerful person in the Marin military. And now she's in charge of a base of a few hundred in the middle of nowhere? That's not much of a promotion, yeah?"

He perked up. "What are you saying?"

"Just because she was appointed by Kuipers doesn't mean she's on team Kuipers."

"I guess that'll have to do. Send me all you can on her and the base. Thanks."

"Sure thing. And if you keep it short, you can use this tida without trekking to a nearby town. I've downloaded sniffers that'll actively detect and fight any intrusion."

"Are you saying you just hacked my tida?"

"Of course not. I've gone through your firewall and deposited sniffers on the top layer."

"Take care, Blue."

On the drive back, he debated the wisdom of smuggling Amy to a Marin base three days after smuggling her out of one. It took one step into Amy's bedroom for the debate to end. Amy hadn't moved. In three hours, her face had turned from pale pink to a bluish-white. He took her hand, resting his index and middle finger on the inside of her wrist. Her pulse was over a hundred. Her heart was pumping hard, but no blood was reaching her skin or her organs.

He brought her soup and woke her. She barely opened her eyes and didn't seem to recognize him. "Where are we?"

"We're safe, in a protected house."

She pulled the covers over her chest. "This is not my room. Why am I here?"

He held her hand. "You were ill, but you're getting better."

Her eyes darted from the window to the door to the ceiling. She twitched as though she wanted to bolt toward the door, but she just collapsed to the side of the bed. As Mika caught her, she spasmed and retched, leaving green-brown drops on his sleeve.

He put her back to bed and caressed her forehead to relax the creases on her brow.

Lambert's allegiances no longer mattered. For Lambert to have any decision in the matter, he had to take a living Amy there. That meant he had to go now.

Because Amy was not going to live through another night.

CHAPTER 32

BOUNTY HUNTER

"You only have to do a very few things right in your life so long as you don't do too many things wrong."

—WARREN BUFFETT

The Marin base's perimeter was an obtuse trapezoid with a two-mile stretch to its south. Mika approached the security gate at the northwest corner. He had left the truck three turns and two miles ago and had avoided the sentries for the first mile. He no longer wished to hide his steps, so he walked down the middle of the cracked asphalt. He raised his collar to protect against the early night chill, but it didn't help.

As he neared the gate, he lifted his bandana to cover his face. Two guards came out of the cabin and waited for him. The short, stocky one had her rifle trained on him. The taller one with the narrow face placed one hand on the semi hanging to her side, but she didn't point it at him.

"I have information," he said as he came within thirty yards. At southern bases near the fringes of Marin, Uregs bounty hunters were common. This far north, he had no idea how often their paths crossed, but he gambled that they would be familiar with the routine.

"So, you've been broadcasting." An officer walked from behind the cabin and approached him. Under the lights of the gate tower, she cast a shadow that reached halfway to Mika, a thin scrawny alien form. "What's this information you're selling?"

"It's sensitive."

She put her palm up, instructing him to stop. "You are not getting closer."

"Colonel Lambert will want to hear what I have to offer."

She shook her head. "I decide that. So far, I'm not impressed."

"I have information on the whereabouts of a target on your wanted list." He waited for her to pay attention. "Very high on the list."

"Let's hear it."

"I need to talk to your commander."

"My sergeant called me when you flooded our network with your bullshit. So far, I see a con artist and not a good one. So, do you have something or are you wasting my time?"

He walked to within ten feet from her and spotted the stripes on her jacket. "Lieutenant, this is time-sensitive, so how about we speed things up."

He reached for his jacket's right pocket.

"Slow," she said, and the two guards moved closer with guns pointing at him.

He reached in with his index finger and thumb, took a pendant, and brought it to his chest to hide it from the guards. He opened his palm to expose it. A silver piece, shaped like California, dangled at the end of it.

He leaned forward, speaking in a low voice as the pendant that had become synonymous with Amy, going back to her speech in Cal City, dangled between them. "I can deliver her."

She flashed a sarcastic grin. "Every asshole in the land has been after her for three days. Why would I believe you?"

He pointed to his pocket again. She nodded. He took a tida at a pace that implied his hand moved through molasses. He flicked his tida, sending a list of bounties. Blue had concocted the list to match a top quarter bounty hunter, a list comprised of mid-to-high level fugitives, a mix of gang leaders, and Kern commanders. The list painted a bounty hunter good enough to be credible, but not so good to have acquired a reputation.

"This is supposed to impress me?"

"I'm not trying to impress you. I'm trying to convince you I know what I'm doing."

"So far, it's not working. 'Cause any two-bit jeweler can make one of those."

They were wasting time Amy didn't have. He closed his fist around the pendant and raised it. "This is real."

Her gaze moved from the pendant to his bandana. "And who are you?"

Mika tried to look bored. "I'm just a bounty hunter."

She blinked twice, took two quick steps toward him, and grabbed him by the collar. "Go away, before I shoot you for trespassing." She let go of him and clutched her pistol.

He expected they would be suspicious, but he hadn't expected this level of hostility. "Doesn't the guards alerting you get logged? What do you intend on telling the commander?"

She shoved him in the chest. "That a crook was wasting my time and wouldn't take no for an answer." Her speech sped up to let her fury out. She pointed her gun toward his chest. "That I shot him after he became aggressive and reached for his gun."

He had miscalculated but didn't understand how. As he debated tackling her, the lights of a vehicle appeared in the distance. The lieutenant brought her gun down but kept her eyes on his for the twenty seconds it took for the Humvee to reach them.

The Humvee stopped in front of the gate, and the newcomer rolled down her window. "That'll be all, Lieutenant Scall." She turned to him. "Step in."

As he did, the driver turned to the lieutenant. "You will forget everything this bounty hunter said. Is that clear?" Scall nodded, and they took off before he closed the door. Fifty yards past the gate, the road split into a Y, one heading south, the other east toward the barracks. The occupied section was smaller than he expected.

For a second, his chief concern turned to whether they would even have the facilities he needed. He exhaled that worry away. He had to trust Blue on this one.

They turned south toward a three-building cluster. Two square, brick, two-story buildings were separated from each other by a narrow ramp that dipped toward their basements. Across the street stood a three-story rectangular building that matched the length of the two square buildings combined. The rectangular building was dark except for the lobby and two windows on the top floor, left of center.

"Stay put," the driver said as she stopped in front of the building to their right. She got out, walked in front of the Humvee, and opened his door, pointing to the frame of the Humvee. He exited and put his hands on the frame. She frisked him and stood back.

"You can take that silly bandana off now, Bayley." He lowered his bandana, letting it hang on his neck. "Colonel Lambert will see you."

They stepped through double lobby doors into a stairwell. They hiked to the third floor and emerged into a dark, narrow corridor. Light spilled from the first office in the hallway.

His escort knocked on the open door and pointed him in. Lambert sat by a narrow desk. She had short-cropped hair and an upper lip so thin it was barely there. She didn't get up when Mika walked in.

She had a full view of the outer gate and an even better view from the two screens to the left of her desk. "So, you know the whereabouts of Governor Chipps?"

"That's what I said." He sank into the closest of the two stiff chairs across from Lambert's desk without waiting for an invitation.

"Thanks," Lambert said as the officer who brought him in walked out, closing the door. "That doesn't surprise me. What surprises me is that you're offering to turn her in."

"Why is that?"

Lambert tapped the screen closest to him and spun it toward him. Images flipped by, covering most of the last year of him and Amy in and around the Capitol. The shots exhibited one constant:

a healthy and strong Amy. He moved his eyes to the window to avoid the painful reminder of Amy's current condition.

"I find it hard to believe you are about to turn Ms. Chipps over to our custody."

"We had a falling out."

"It still doesn't add up."

"How about we talk about the reward?"

Lambert leaned back on her chair, but her eyes never left him. She pressed her lips out as though she was disappointed. Good. "Talk," she said.

"I want the full credits deposited here." He tossed a tida on the desk. "And I want medicine. Antibiotics in particular."

"Not an option. We have little, and what we have is for emergencies."

"I need a little, and this is an emergency." She didn't budge so he pushed. "It's nonnegotiable."

She jumped out of her chair, fists on the desk, leaning forward. "Let's get one thing straight. You are a wanted man; you don't get to negotiate."

He was willing to accept the premise but not the conclusion. They were all wanted, just by different sets of people. The question was to which of those groups Lambert was loyal. Not that the answer mattered. He still needed the meds, and Lambert was the only one with them for hundreds of miles in any direction.

"Still, those are the terms. I get the reward, plus the antibiotics, and you get Chipps."

"How about I arrest you, and our interrogators make you tell us where Ms. Chipps is?"

He smiled, but his lips didn't part. "Now you're being predictable. Chipps will be long gone by the time you get that info. I'm your only shot at getting her."

"I can arrest you when you bring her in."

He had accepted that possibility. "If you arrest bounty hunters after they deliver, you can forget about any of them ever showing up here again."

"You don't think I'd risk my reputation for Chipps?"

"You're getting her anyway. I'm betting you won't risk it for me."

She rubbed her chin. "Deliver Ms. Chipps, and you'll get your reward and the medicine."

"When I get close, if you can guide me to the clinic, it'll be best. We can do the exchange there." He stood up and took one step toward the door before stopping. "And don't follow me. If I sense a hint of a tail, I'll just keep driving, and you won't see either of us again."

"Major Cox, my chief of staff, will meet you at the perimeter gate. Keep Chipps hidden. She has sympathizers even here."

He stood motionless, parsing Lambert's words. Did that mean Lambert wasn't one of those sympathizers? Or was it a hint that she was? Why had she revealed this to him?

She waved him out. "Go."

He reached the door but didn't step out. "One more thing. I'm holding you personally responsible for what happens to Chipps while she's in your custody."

Lambert took three quick steps in his direction. She was half a foot shorter than him, but she got right in his face. "You don't get to hold me responsible for anything."

He pulled his head back. "Fine. Just as long as we understand each other."

"I don't understand you at all. I hope whoever needs the meds is worth it."

"She is," he whispered and walked out.

As he approached the Mendocino bungalow, he built the fantasy that he would find a healthy Amy, that they would just drive away and forget the whole episode with Lambert had ever happened. His fantasy evaporated with his first step.

Amy's lips were dry, cracked, and blue. Her sweat was beading on her forehead and had created a dark, wet spot on the pillow. She was curled into a ball on her side, shivering. She had not touched the water bottle he had left by her bedside. He lifted her head and brought the water to her lips. She took two sips before her head fell back to the side, too weak to take a third sip.

He rested her head on his shoulder, caressing her hair. He put the bottle down and lifted her. She was so light he held her with one arm as he opened the truck's door.

He had gone over the risks and had analyzed each path five steps ahead. And though there were too many unknowns in the loop, he didn't have a better option. Once Amy was back on her feet, he would worry about everything else. The alternative was to stay here, which didn't lead to risk but to a certainty he couldn't bring himself to contemplate.

He drove straight to the base without any attempt at stealth. The bungalow was another casualty now, used and discarded, not worth the extra minutes that he would have needed to keep it hidden. He rolled to a stop at the gate but didn't offer an explanation.

Cox got in the passenger seat and craned her neck to inspect the back seat. Her face soured at the balled up, shivering form with cracked, white lips and a sweaty pale face. Nothing that resembled the fiery governor they were after. "What's wrong with her?"

He put the car into gear. "Can we go now?"

Cox gestured him right, then left, to follow the streets toward the three-building cluster. As they approached, she pointed left, down the ramp between the two square buildings. He stopped halfway down the ramp where three crates blocked his way. Two guards stood on either side of Lambert who waited for them by the inner door. Mika stepped out and opened the back door. He pulled Amy to her feet, and put his right arm around her waist, half supporting, half carrying her. One of the guards approached Amy with wrist cuffs.

He pushed her away with his free arm. The guard hesitated but stepped aside when Lambert stepped forward and spoke to the guard. "Get a gurney, and wake Lucy up."

Before they took a single step, Amy collapsed forward. Mika caught her with his left arm and lifted her. He walked up to the doorway. "I'm going to need the antibiotics now."

"What happened?" Dr. Lucy Dunn asked as she walked into the infirmary with her eyes on the gurney. She shined a light into Amy's eyes. "Alcohol? Overdose? Trauma?"

"She was shot four days ago. Had an infection that seemed under control but deteriorated over the last two days."

"Shot where?"

"Abdomen."

Dunn cut the shirt, exposing Amy's stiches and clammy skin. "Who the hell operated on her?" she asked and turned to the nurse. "She's in shock. I need to drop a line now."

"What are you doing?" Mika asked

She ignored him and inserted a triple lumen catheter into Amy's chest. "We need to monitor her cardiac, pulmonary, and renal function to find out what we're dealing with." She studied Amy's stitches, but her eyes moved to the dials. "Definite sepsis. Must be a secondary infection. What happened after she got shot?"

Mika told her about their flight and safe house.

She shook her head. "Are you trying to kill her?" She pointed to the antibiotics. "Those would not have helped her, not in those doses, not at this point."

"Can you get the fever under control?" Mika asked.

"The fever might help, actually. We'll start with a heavy dose of antibiotic and add others as we monitor her response. But it's going to be up to her." She picked up the towel from the nurse. "Now, everyone out, so we can work."

He was ready to protest, but Lambert put a hand on his sleeve as the nurse wiped the sweat from Amy's brow. Lambert stepped into the hallway. "Had a falling out, you say?"

"Didn't think you'd believe anything else."

"Didn't believe that either. Your bounty hunter routine needs work." She almost smiled. "There's been an intensive hunt for Chipps for three days. I'm impressed you made it this far."

He shrugged.

"Why not just ask for help?"

He snorted. "Seriously? How was I to trust you?"

"And you figured out you could after ten minutes?"

He looked at his feet, then into her eyes. "What now?"

"My word is good. You're free to go."

"Not a chance." He kept his eyes on Amy's unmoving form.

"Well, it appears Ms. Chipps is in no condition to travel, so we'll keep her here a while."

He nodded, gratitude and relief all rolled into one simple head motion.

CHAPTER 33
PARTNERSHIP

"Hope and fear cannot occupy the same space."
—MAYA ANGELOU

Amy's fever broke on the fourth day. He had promised Lambert he wouldn't attempt to break her out in exchange for staying in Amy's room. It had not gone well with Lambert's chief-of-staff, who still treated him like something stuck under her shoe, but he didn't mind. He hadn't come here for sympathy or to make friends.

He woke to Amy rattling the handcuffs dangling from the side of her bed frame. "This wasn't one of your best ideas."

He straightened up from the chair in which he had been curled sideways. Amy's eyes were open, quizzing him. The color was slowly returning to her face. "Actually, it was. I'm pretty impressed with myself."

The spark in her eyes was back. "How do you figure?"

"You're well enough to question my wisdom."

She grew serious. "How long was I out?"

"Three days in the cabin. Four here. They gave you pressors, four different antibiotics, and tons of fluid. That and the plasma finally did it."

"Why are we still here?"

"The commander didn't want to move you."

"Kuipers?"

"I don't think Lambert told her."

"There are so many sides now I don't even know if that's good or bad."

"It's good."

She gave a faint snort. He had missed that sound.

"What's our next move?"

The question washed over him like the first gasp of air after a long dive. He smiled at Amy thinking strategy, not survival or desperation. "Haven't figured it out yet."

She cocked her head. "You expect me to believe you didn't have a contingency for when I woke up?"

"Contingencies I have. Odds on them are hazy, though, so I can't pick our best play yet."

She closed her eyes, resting her head on her pillow. He got a second pillow and pushed it behind her head. She opened her eyes as he slid the pillow in. "I appreciate what you did, at the Sentinels, the Uregs, here. I really do." She reached for her water and took a sip, holding the cup with two hands. "I can get used to relying on your tactical sense."

Mika reached for the glass Amy had been squeezing hard and put it on the bedside table. "Would that be so bad?"

"Depends. We've been down that road before." She reached for the glass again, sipped it, and put it back. Her index finger moved back and forth between them. "You know how this partnership will work?"

He hadn't dared hope for anything, so he shook his head.

"When we're nicer to each other when one of us isn't dying."

He couldn't find the words to agree, her recent predicament still haunting him.

She laughed. "It's okay. You don't have to say anything."

He was still considering his reply when the door opened, and a guard pointed at him. "Colonel Lambert needs to see you."

"In a minute." His voice rose with irritation at the interruption. These were the first words they had exchanged in ages that didn't involve logistics, escape plans, or medical updates.

"She means now."

The more he argued with the guard, the less he would have to say to Amy. He accepted that it was already too late for that conversation. He turned to Amy. "You're right; we do need to be nicer. And that's a promise."

Because even Sierra, in all her bullheaded mistakes, had gotten one thing right.

He had been an idiot.

"May I call you Mika?" Lambert asked as the guard closed the door.

The office was larger than he had noticed in the dark. A round table with four metal chairs circling it stood behind the wooden chair he sat in. Past the table, a large screen monopolized the wall, hanging over a seven-foot console.

"Sure, Maria."

Lambert's lips pressed flat and then the edges moved up to a quarter smile. "I'm going to ask you a few questions now that I have your attention again."

Mika rubbed his middle finger.

"You mostly work for New Cal."

"Is that a question?"

She leaned forward, eyes drilling him.

"Yeah, mostly is right."

"Have you ever worked for Kern?"

Mika looked straight into Lambert's eyes. "No."

"Never?"

"Look, I do a lot of odd jobs. Could I have, through intermediaries, helped Kern? Sure, that's possible. But I did not directly work for Kern at any point."

"How about Marin?"

"Yeah, I did."

"Can you be more specific?"

"I'd rather not. Why are you asking me this?"

"So, in the last four days, you have not communicated with anyone outside this base."

Mika took a deep breath. "I have."

"After promising me specifically that you would not do anything to break Chipps out or jeopardize this base."

He ran his hand on the smooth, polished armrest. "I did neither of those things."

"You're telling me you had nothing to do with the Kern troops coming our way."

Mika's eyebrows shot up. "Come again?"

"You heard me."

"Look, I sent one very short, specific, prearranged, and extremely well-protected code to inform one person that we weren't in trouble." He smiled, "Beyond being detained, obviously."

"I want to believe you that you had nothing to do with it."

"What do I have to gain from a Kern attack on this place?"

"Chaos. A window of opportunity."

"And you think I can summon Kern troops with a message?"

Lambert frowned and pinched her chin between her thumb and index finger.

"The battalion up north is coming this way?" Mika asked, but Lambert didn't reply. "Look, I'm not asking for sensitive information. If a Kern battalion is on the move, just about anyone in the Uregs or Marin will know. They're not subtle."

She let go of her chin. "A third of the battalion that camped in the Uregs for the last year is moving toward Kern. Now that the civil war is over and Spindler is on the run, they've declared their allegiance to General Taggart."

"Taggart?" Mika didn't hide his surprise that a lower-ranked officer had risen to the top.

"Mitchell Taggart, second in command of the third army. He took over when General Langton was poisoned, blamed Spindler, and convinced the rest of the rebels to follow him."

"Only a third is moving?"

Lambert exhaled audibly. "The rest is still up north."

"You're not on their way though, are you?"

"We shouldn't be. But there are some interesting parties out there, with considerable resources. It seems we're less of an obstacle than those parties."

Mika played with his middle finger. "They'd rather antagonize a Marin base than Uregs compounds? That doesn't make sense."

"They're not Uregs compounds. One is a Kern battalion that has not declared for Taggart. The other is a rogue Marin unit. And the two are communicating."

"Why are you telling me this?"

"Because I don't think you're my enemy."

Was Eze the rogue Marin unit? Most likely, but why was Eze communicating with a Kern unit? "Just how close will this force get to us?"

"They've split into two, and one is headed straight for us."

He leaned back and stretched his legs out. "Any idea why?"

"My staff has been generating hypotheses, but I'm not convinced by any of them."

"Did you inform General Kuipers that you have Amy in custody?"

She pressed her lips again and chuckled, then shook her head.

"Four days after you find Amy, Kern decides to engage? Doesn't that sound strange?"

"It does, which is why I'm asking about your connection to Kern."

"Do you think you have Kern spies here?"

"It's possible, but I doubt it."

He leaned forward, putting his elbows on his knees. "How about Marin spies?"

"What do you mean?"

"I mean, a year ago, you were the chief of staff for the chief commander. Now you command a base of what—one hundred and eighty? Two hundred? In the middle of nowhere? You're clearly on Kuipers' shit list. Do you have informers here reporting to the general?"

"You don't hold back, do you?"

"Not when I'm trying to be useful."

"I was slow picking sides, so the general and I aren't on the best of terms."

"And it's possible General Kuipers has spies here who've informed her Amy is here."

"It is possible."

"So, you've really gone deeper into her shit list. Not only you didn't tell her you have Amy, but you've helped Amy."

"How did I help her?"

Mika shook his head. "Kuipers tried to have her arrested twice already. Just by admitting her to your hospital, you've helped."

"So Kuipers is sending a Kern contingent my way? That's a bit farfetched."

"She gets you and Amy out of the way. Maybe Kern gets a promise of noninterference from Marin forces for the retreating army. Not a bad deal for either side."

"That's not as bad as some others, but it's pure speculation, and I've heard enough speculation for one day."

"When will they get here?"

"Classified."

Mika stood up to leave when Lambert added, "Have an early dinner. Things might get bumpy after sunset."

CHAPTER 34

REUNION

"The point of power is always in the present moment."
—LOUISE L. HAY

The blaring sirens came first, wailing like angry furies. The uproar of aerial explosions followed as air defense systems and missiles collided. Finally, the *rak-rak-rak* of anti-aircraft guns reverberated through the air, announcing the Kern forces were on hand.

The rumble of a missile connecting with brick and mortar came three minutes later. Mika had packed all the medicine Amy would need into two coolers stuffed into a large duffel bag. Amy was dressed, ready to move.

He kissed her forehead. "I'll be right back."

He was ready to pick the lock on the door, but it gave way as he turned the handle. He stepped into the empty basement corridor bathed in the blue of the emergency lights. He followed the blinking lights up a flight to reach the exit toward the main road.

He pushed the door open and stepped out. Kern forces had breached the perimeter to the east. Fighting was fiercest a hundred yards away in the narrow strip between the barracks and the fence. Straight ahead, right past the buildings, Lambert was barking orders to Cox, her executive officer. In the distance, flames engulfed two barracks.

He ducked back around his building and down the ramp. The crates were gone. Two military ambulances sat by the loading docks, facing out. This was where he had brought Amy nearly a week or an eternity ago. He hopped into the first ambulance. The tida taped to the dash acted as a proximity key. He tapped the ignition, and the dashboard lights came alive. He jumped out and ran toward Amy, but a too-close-for-comfort explosion rattled the building.

He ran up to the main floor. Three Kern soldiers stood by the main entrance. From the breached perimeter in the distance, more came pouring in. The Marin contingent fought to keep the intruders at bay, but a Kern Humvee broke through.

It sped toward them, spraying bullets as it approached. Lambert and Cox engaged them. They hit the Humvee's tires, which buckled and toppled toward Lambert, sending her sprawling to the side of the building. The Kern soldiers by the door ran toward the commotion.

The aseptic medical scents urged him toward the ambulance and Amy who was ready and waiting for him. This was not his battle, but Lambert had been more than generous toward Amy. He considered what Amy would do. It took half a second.

He pushed the door open and ran toward the upturned Humvee. Gunfire erupted ahead, and Cox stumbled and fell. By the time Mika reached her, she was no longer moving. He grabbed her assault rifle and kept running. The Kern soldiers from the Humvee lay crumpled by the wall. The other three had pinned Lambert between the overturned Humvee and the building wall. She fired and took cover but had nowhere to go.

Lambert came around the Humvee to fire again, but took a bullet to the shoulder and stumbled back. Mika fired, hitting the two soldiers closest to him first, then the one about to reach Lambert. He ran toward Lambert, firing into each of the soldiers on the ground as he passed them. Lambert rested her back on the Humvee and slid down the frame. She took two deep breaths, exhaling audibly each time. Blood from her left shoulder reached her waist, staining her jacket.

He crouched in front of her, eyes on her shoulder. He spotted the exit wound on the back of her shoulder. "Okay?"

"Yeah," she grunted.

He extended his hand. She let her rifle hang from its strap and grabbed his forearm with her right hand. He pulled her to her feet. She put a hand on the Humvee and stayed bent, cradling her left arm and shoulder. She took slow, deliberate breaths.

He ran back into the infirmary. Amy sat on the foot of the bed as he burst in. He put the duffel bag on his shoulder and put one arm around Amy, half-supporting, half-carrying her toward the ambulance. He tossed the rifle on the driver's seat and placed the duffel bag in the back of the ambulance, stretching a rubber cord around it to keep it snug.

As he helped Amy into the passenger seat, Lambert came into the alley, left arm dangling, the assault rifle in her right hand. Mika stepped in front of Amy and faced Lambert empty-handed. Lambert lowered her gun and waved him away.

He jumped in and gunned it without a word. As he cleared the unguarded perimeter gate, two urban-combat transports buzzed them, speeding toward the battle in the back, guns blazing. In his side-view mirror, the Kern positions burst into flames. He hit a pothole and jumped, forcing his attention back to the road. His hold on the wheel tightened. The shelling had torn thin layers of asphalt like the road was a sardine can. They bounced in and out of holes the size of sheep.

He drove hard, putting miles between them and the base. After dropping the rear wheels to a foot-deep hole, the rattle of the rear axle intensified. Five minutes later, his tida chimed. He ignored it and pushed on. His tida came to life twenty seconds later.

"Slow down, will you? You're going to kill us all."

Amy's head swiveled to the tida still in his pants.

"Blue?" Mika asked.

"Yeah."

"Where are you?"

"You just passed me."

He slammed on the brakes and pulled to the side, his right tires dipping into the shallow ditch. He handed his rifle to Amy. "Can you handle this?" She took it without a word.

Mika stepped out and crouched by the ambulance's rear. The bent axle put so much pressure on the wheel that the boot barely held together. He hoped Blue wasn't on foot because Amy was in no shape to hike. He tapped his tida. "I can use some good news right about now."

"You're going to love me then." Thirty seconds later a Humvee appeared around the bend. "And I don't mean the Humvee."

Amy came out and stood behind him. The Humvee rolled to a stop thirty feet behind the ambulance and Eva jumped off, rushed past him, and hugged Amy. She took Amy's rifle and supported Amy to the Humvee, settling her into the back seat.

Mika opened the back of the ambulance and grabbed the duffel bag with the antibiotics. In under ten minutes, they had stripped all they needed from the ambulance and were back on the road. Blue had brought five of her rifles, six handguns, and two crates full of different caliber cartridges along with supplies that would feed the four of them for two weeks.

Mika took the wheel as they got back on the road, and Blue scouted for shelter. Eva sat in the back with Amy, speaking in hushed tones. As they drove, Amy's voice trailed with her words becoming more and more disconnected. She deteriorated fast, and fifty miles later she was sleeping again. "We need to set up camp," he said.

Blue straightened. "There's a farmhouse seven miles down the road."

He drove until he spotted a narrow opening in the tree line to his right, twenty yards past the top of a ten-foot hill. He pulled off the road and drove into the woods, stopping at a clearing after the first bend. He stepped out and walked to the road, followed by Eva. They wiped the tire marks away from the road with branches and tossed pine needles haphazardly.

"There's a truck following us," Blue said when they walked back to the Humvee.

"There's a what?" Mika glanced back. "Wait, how do you know that?"

"I've dropped sensors that link to my sniffers."

"Are you insane? That's like leaving breadcrumbs for them to come find us."

Blue turned beet red. Eva laughed, breaking the tension. "You can say 'thank you, Blue.'"

"What for?"

"For preventing you from getting jumped. They were likely on our trail from the get-go. Blue's sensors have nothing to do with them finding us. And she dropped the sensors on all the roads around that base for the last four days to help you."

Mika let his initial anger dissipate. "Thank you, Blue."

"How far are they?" Eva asked.

"They'll be here in eight minutes."

"I'm sorry," Mika said and handed a pistol to Blue. "Stay with Amy."

He walked to the road with Eva, and they took positions, one on either side of the road atop the hill. A hunter green Humvee with a stainless-steel roll cage appeared in the distance. It slowed down up the hill, drove past them, and stopped fifty yards later. Five soldiers stepped off, examining the tracks on the road. Four had their automatic rifles slung on their shoulders.

Within minutes, they started walking toward them. The recognition sent shudders down Mika's spine as the hostile lieutenant from the first night at the base led the pack.

"I know you're here," she called and put her gun in a holster on her back.

Eva didn't move. Mika pointed his rifle at the lieutenant but did not activate his scope's light. She stopped at the exact spot where Mika had veered off the road.

"We need to talk," she said.

Mika hit the light and a green dot appeared on her chest. "I recommend you hop back on your truck and drive away."

She stood on the road, unconcerned by the targeting laser. "Name's Jacqui Scall. Do you know why I almost shot you last week?"

Mika stepped to the road, a semi in each hand. "I've got a good idea."

"No, you don't."

Mika's grip on his rifles tightened.

"We're Special Forces. You can't scare us away. And you don't have to."

Eva took a step out of the bushes too, loosely holding a rifle.

"You know her?" he asked Eva. She shook her head.

Jacqui laughed. "You don't get it. I was about to shoot you last week because I thought you were betraying Chipps."

"Come again?"

"That's right. We've been looking for you, to protect the governor-chancellor."

"So, you're all deserting," he said. Then her words hit him. "Protect the what?"

Her expression soured. "No one is deserting. The head of our government was Yim. She's been illegally deposed, which means Vice-Chancellor Chipps is next in line."

"I'm not sure I should point this out, but you heard that New Cal seceded, right?"

"Because of the illegal seizure of power in Marin."

"So?"

"Chipps is still the lawful head of state as far as we're concerned."

"Will that mental gymnastics survive a direct order from Kuipers?"

"Do you really want a firefight?"

"No, but I'd like to understand what the fuck motivates you."

"As I said, we're Special Forces. We followed General Rose. We've been in the Uregs, teaming up with various parties, but we reached out to Colonel Lambert last month."

"What happened last month?"

"Are you on drugs? Kuipers seized power." She moved her right foot over the asphalt like she wanted to remove something from her shoe. "We've also coordinated with Colonel Eze over the last year. I'd anticipated a Marin unit coming to replace the leadership here, but the Kern attack was unexpected."

"Were you involved in the attack on the Pur—Kern base last year?"

Jacqui chuckled. "You can say Purie. I won't bite. Yes, we took the Purie base and neutralized the first missile, but they launched the second one with the bioweapon. Kuipers blamed Eze and Rose. Eze didn't agree and chose to stay in the Uregs."

"Were those Eze's forces flying in to help Lambert?"

Jacqui nodded. "Those Kern assholes can't fight unless they have overwhelming numbers. They turned tail and ran the moment Eze's forces arrived."

"How did you find us?"

"We never lost you. I'm guessing you're headed for the farmhouse over there?" She pointed in the direction of their Humvee. "A memo for next time. Driving fifty miles on a straight line and stopping isn't an escape strategy."

"Yeah, well, Amy isn't exactly in shape for more."

Her eyes grew wide. "Is she all right?"

"She will be if she could just fucking rest for a day without some asshole shooting at us."

"That's where we come in."

"I want to believe you, but I'm not letting you get anywhere near her with your guns."

"Are you shitting me?"

"If you're here to protect her, you'll want to stay. And the only way I'm letting you stay without a firefight is if I collect your guns."

She rolled her eyes but unholstered the pistol from her back, extending it from the barrel. Her eyes moved between Eva and him. "If this is all you got, you need all the help you can get."

He took her pistol, and she walked toward her team, barking orders.

Eva bit her lip and ambled toward Mika. "Not very useful as protection if they're unarmed."

"One thing at a time."

CHAPTER 35
HEALING

"Make peace with your past, so it doesn't spoil your present."
—REGINA BRETT

Mika split his attention three ways, foundering at each task. When he inspected their new digs, his mind insisted he was neglecting Amy. When he made sure Amy was comfortable, his mind chastised him for ignoring the five Special Forces soldiers he had let into their midst. And when he spied on the soldiers, he worried he hadn't secured the barn and farmhouse.

He stepped into the farmhouse to find a kitchen with a five-by-eight-foot wooden table to his left. A square living room with a sofa and broken reclining chair stood to his right. A narrow corridor hugged the living room's inner wall and led to two bedrooms and a tiny bathroom with a shower stall the diameter of a manhole cover.

Eva helped him install Amy in the first bedroom behind the living room and checked all the doors and windows. Mika then walked across the sixty-foot courtyard separating the house from the barn. The barn's door was open with Jacqui's crew moving their coolers, mats, and sleeping bags in. A ladder led to a loft, suspended across half the width of the barn. Below the loft, stalls with torn or decaying doors lined the back wall with feeding troughs heaped into two piles.

He spotted Jacqui behind the barn, on the narrow rotting porch. She bent down, a knife in hand, with Blue's horrified eyes glued to the quick knife strikes. As he approached, the carcass of a half-butchered ninety-pound doe on three large rocks came into view. Two flies buzzed about the doe's nose and filmy eyes.

"We shot it on the way over," Jacqui said. She emptied the guts into the shallow ditch she had dug to the side of the barn and worked the knife under the skin, slashing in quick movements.

A bullet tore into his shoulder as Jacqui's knife work had put him in a trance. The second bullet landed on the porch, inches from Jacqui's hand, spewing dust and splinters into the air. Mika put an arm around Blue, shuffle-ran on the porch, and dove into the barn, tossing Blue in. Jacqui plunged in right behind him.

"Blue, what happened to the sensors?"

Mika had been too lax with the watch because he had trusted Blue's sensors. He squeezed his jaw tight in anger for his stupidity. Blue was in shock, blinking, and taking quick shallow breaths.

"We fried those on the way," Jacqui said. "No offense, but it's a pretty shitty idea to drop sensors that can be traced."

Mika squeezed his eyes shut and reopened them as he approached the window. The rumble of two armored, double-cab pickup trucks filled the courtyard. One locked its front wheels and spun, stopping with its nose angled toward the farmhouse. The other stopped inches short of the first truck, pointed toward the barn.

Four assailants in fatigues and black flak jackets jumped from the first truck's bed and headed into the farmhouse. The two on the second truck stood in the bed and fired into the barn.

Everyone in the barn dove behind the troughs and stalls while bullets pinged around them. After the first barrage, Mika shuffled toward the door. "Bounty hunters."

Jacqui grimaced, still crouched behind the troughs. "You should have trusted me."

"Yeah," he smiled without parting his lips. "You did sneak in a couple of pistols, right?"

She shook her head. "I played by your rules."

He held out his handgun while pointing to her knife. "Trade?"

She stood up, took the handgun, and cocked it. "What about you?"

He gripped Jacqui's knife. "I'm going across as soon as—"

The staccato of assault rifles echoed from the house, followed by *pop-pop-pop*, a short silence, another round of staccato, then another pop, making it four.

"—that." He put a hand on the door. "Cover me?"

The two bounty hunters who had fired on them rushed into the farmhouse, leaving only the two drivers, who now crouched between the hoods of their trucks, rifles in hand, one facing them, the other eyeing the farmhouse.

Mika bolted before Jacqui replied.

Jacqui fired at the trucks. The man returned fire but was erratic. Two seconds later, Mika leaped over the truck, lunged for the bounty hunter, and sank the knife to the man's throat. He rounded the second truck's hood and ran toward the farmhouse.

Three bullets tore into his back, but the second bounty hunter stopped shooting as three pops from Jacqui's handgun replaced the assault rifle's racket. As more shots rang from ahead of him, he crashed through the farmhouse door, landing in front of a startled bounty hunter.

Mika plunged his knife into the bounty hunter's neck and sliced his throat and his gun strap in one continuous motion. He grabbed the rifle and fired into the bounty hunter by the bedroom door. He leaped over three more bodies to reach the bedroom. With the two he had killed, there should have been one more.

In the bedroom, Amy crawled from behind the bed toward a handgun with a trembling hand, face ashen from the effort. The place stank like a slaughterhouse.

Eva had collapsed on the floor between the bed and the wall to Mika's left, blood gushing from too many wounds to count. Her right hand was on the last bounty hunter's throat, her left hand on his gun-toting hand, but her holds were weakening. Mika grabbed the bounty hunter's collar and slammed his head into the wall, then fired in his face as he crashed on the floor.

Eva exhaled and let her head drop to the side. She blinked with half a nod.

Mika jumped back to help Amy stand up, but she slapped his arm away. "Help Eva."

He kneeled next to Eva as Jacqui rushed in. "Courtyard secure," she said, then held out a hand for Amy. "Are you okay, Chancellor?"

Amy nodded and let Jacqui pull her to her feet.

Mika waved at the bodies. "Check them. Do *not* assume they're dead."

Jacqui stepped away and returned four shots later. As she came around Mika, her eyes went wide at the sight of Eva on the floor, back resting against the wall. Eva's neck had stopped gushing blood, but the red wall and nightstand gave her state away.

Eva didn't need first aid, she needed calories. Mika ran to the kitchen and rifled through the cabinets. He found a half-full jar of brown sugar and rushed back to the bedroom. Jacqui knelt next to Eva, putting pressure on her neck.

He grabbed the water on Amy's nightstand, poured it into the sugar jar, and shook. The sugar didn't dissolve much, but he brought the thick brown liquid to Eva's lips. She took small sips, then gulps, dribbling some on her chin.

He jumped at Amy's fingers touching his shoulder. "I can do that."

He handed Amy the jar, grabbed the empty glass, and walked to the living room. He pulled the crate of guns that had belonged to Jacqui's team to the middle of the living room. "Here," he said. "Set up a perimeter and a full-on watch. And we'll need that deer."

Jacqui was right behind him. "I'll build a fire."

"I mean now. Just chop it into bite-sized pieces." He pushed Amy's empty glass into Jacqui's hand. "And don't waste the blood."

She raised an eyebrow, as though she needed more explanation. He reached for her forearm. "Look, just do it."

She reappeared a few minutes later with a bowl of meat and a pint of blood.

"We're going to need a lot more."

"How much more?"

"Most of it."

"That's a week's worth of meat," Jacqui protested.

He pointed to the bodies lying around the room. The bodies that Eva had dispatched even before he had made it in. "That's a week's worth of bounty hunters."

Jacqui headed out and returned minutes later with an eight-gallon pot filled with meat.

He had to force the first bites down Eva's throat. By the second pound, she was chewing. By the third, she sat up a little straighter.

Jacqui's team took the bodies behind the barn. Then two cleaned the farmhouse while two stood watch by the courtyard. Somewhere along the line, two five-gallon water bottles with dispensing valves appeared on the kitchen counter. The bounty hunters' trucks were tucked behind the barn, side by side, facing out. In two hours, the farmhouse had become an acceptable facsimile of an inhabited compound.

The wood stove appeared functional, but they cooked the venison on a fire in the courtyard. Dinner wasn't a social event. They got food in twos, eating out by the barn or courtyard in shifts. Amy ate a few pieces, and Eva inhaled another two pounds of meat. She lifted her eyes from her plate to spot Mika.

"What?" Eva asked.

"I don't think I've ever seen you eat before. You know, the chew-and-swallow kind."

She tossed him her fork. He caught it midair and deposited it on the heavy table that appeared even larger than it was with just Eva and Amy sitting side by side in the middle of it.

Mika poured a cup of coffee from the pot Jacqui had brewed and walked to find her in the courtyard, sitting on a folding chair by the fire, screen in hand.

"This was a real fuck-up."

Jacqui sipped her coffee but didn't reply.

"From now on, you're in charge of security." He sat down on an empty chair next to her. "I got distracted by Amy's condition and nearly got us all killed."

She gave him quick impatient nods. "One question?"

"Yeah?"

"How is Eva alive?"

"Because the idiots sent only four bounty hunters to take her on."

"No, seriously," she said. "Don't bullshit me, that wasn't bounty-hunter blood by the nightstand. That was Eva's. She must have lost what—three, four liters?"

"That's what the deer blood and venison were for."

"That's clear as mud."

"Didn't you run across anything like this with Eze?"

Her eyes went wide. "Hard-to-kill soldiers, yeah. But that meant they needed six bullets instead of two. Not this." She pointed to the farmhouse. "Whatever this is."

"Well, it's the same thing. Just better."

"And you? I didn't give you much cover. By the time I dropped the first guy, that second bounty hunter had hit you at least three times. I only got him because your immunity to bullets distracted him."

He smiled. "I'm not immune, but yeah, me too. It takes a bit more to bring me down."

"A bit?" She rolled her eyes. "Like Eva. Great."

He chuckled. "Nobody is quite like Eva."

She waved to the courtyard. "We're exposed here."

"What do you suggest?"

"Your hound is good. She dug into the screens in their truck. This crew was monitoring Lambert's communications. Apparently, they had set up an ambush to abduct Chipps during transport, but Lambert screwed up their plans by holding on to Chipps. When you came out in that ambulance, they put two and two together. There will be more. We need to move out."

"Not tonight," he said. "Both Amy and Eva need to rest."

"Fine, but we need to move out first thing in the morning."

She stood, picked up her screen, and walked to the farmhouse. Mika followed her. The kitchen was empty. He headed to the bedroom to find Amy asleep in a sitting position in the bed, a screen folded on her lap. He put the screen on her nightstand but didn't disturb her. He checked on Eva asleep in the next room before heading back to the kitchen. Jacqui sat at the table, making notes on her screen. He refilled his coffee and held the coffee pot for her. She nodded, so he refilled her cup.

"Look at Kern's movement. A third of the battalion is moving south. The rest is just parked north of everyone." She pointed to the Sentinels, "And these guys are doing all the things a Special Forces unit should do, except they're doing it all wrong."

He sipped his coffee. "Those are Sentinels."

"They're what?"

"Sentinels. Set up by Rendon to duplicate the hard-to-kill soldiers."

"Fuck! More like you?"

He chuckled. "The Sentinels' medics are amateurs. They're lucky to produce your can-take-six-shots-instead-of-two kind. Eva and I are the result of processes no one in their right mind should ever duplicate."

She blinked, unconvinced, but went back to the map. "If we leave at first light, we'll clear this ridge by—"

"No."

They both turned. Amy stood by the kitchen entrance, with her eyes focused on the screen. She swayed and took a step to stabilize herself.

He put his coffee on the table and stood up, ready to catch her if she stumbled. "No to what?"

"We're not running away."

"So far, we fought bounty hunters, but if we stay here, sooner or later, General Kuipers will find us. Chancellor, we cannot take on the Marin military."

"Stop calling me that."

His eyes moved from Amy to Jacqui, who stiffened, her left hand tightening into a fist.

"Either Chancellor Yim is restored, or we hold new elections when Marin is free again. But I am not the chancellor."

"Whatever you say," Jacqui said, relaxing her hand. "Governor?"

Amy put her palms at the edge of the table, steadying herself. "That'll do."

"As I was saying, Governor, we have optimal conditions to slip out without Marin or Kern forces noticing us."

Amy nodded with a glint in her eye, as though she agreed. "Then what?"

"We clear the Kern army."

"Then what?"

"Then," Jacqui hesitated, "we'll be in open territory outside of Marin surveillance."

"Then what?"

It must have dawned on Jacqui by now that she had plunged headfirst down the wrong path. She pushed her chair out and leaned back. "I don't follow, Governor."

"What is the point of supporting me if it won't lead to change in Marin or New Cal?"

"What do you propose?"

"We head to Cal City."

"Governor, we cannot protect you there." Jacqui turned to Mika, imploring for support.

Tactically, he agreed with Jacqui. But strategically, he grasped Amy's insight. Besides, Amy's tone implied this was not a debate. When he took too long to answer, Amy's eyes drilled into him, demanding that he not disappoint her again.

"We do what the Governor says."

Jacqui looked ready to protest, but Amy put up a hand.

"Everyone claims to be in charge. But does anyone provide a compelling vision? Not so much. The Kern generals in the Uregs don't know who to follow and who to fight. Marin generals don't know whether to ask for Yim to be restored or follow Kuipers. Lambert is in that camp. And the few who follow Kuipers don't do it out of any conviction. They just don't know what else to do."

"What do you propose?"

Amy smiled. "We give them a new vision. With a few allies, we can do it, and that'll give us more allies. But none of that happens if I'm not in Cal City."

"Very well, Governor," Jacqui said. "If you'll excuse me, I need to check on my team."

After Jacqui left, Amy walked to Eva's room, and Mika followed. Eva was in a deep slumber with her chest rising and falling silently, almost peaceful, with no tension on her eyes or cheeks. By morning, she would be her old self, ready to tackle whatever the world threw at them.

Amy headed back to the kitchen and sat at the long side of the table. She faced out, her elbows on the worn surface, palms connecting under her chin, and her hands cupping her face. He sat at the head of the table and reached out for her hand.

"You okay?"

She lifted her head. "Me?"

He nodded in awe of how much strength she projected on such unsteady legs.

"I'm the only one who sat out the whole thing." She leaned back on her chair. "I still feel like I'm carrying a fifty-pound backpack when I walk, but at least I can walk without the fear that my knees will buckle, or my head will explode."

"You just need time."

She drew a short breath. "I know you wanted to agree with Jacqui, and I appreciate that you didn't."

She got up, grabbed a plastic cup from the counter, filled it with water, and drank half of it. She refilled it and sat back down.

"You have to know I can't listen to her. She wants to minimize our risk by hiding away someplace no one will ever find us."

"In the short term, it's not the worst idea."

"It is. Because there is no long term if you do that."

"About that. You might want to stop arguing with Jacqui that you're not her boss. If she ever believes you, we're in real trouble."

Amy took a sip and shook her head. "I'm not the damn chancellor. If that's why she's here, she can leave now."

"I'd rather she didn't."

"They all want something. Jacqui wants me to be the chancellor so she can justify her actions. Cavana wants to crown me too, but for New Cal or a new, bigger state."

"That sounds appealing to you?"

"Eva wants to protect me but not like Jacqui. She'll go anywhere and take on anyone. But she'd be happier if we just went back to our old lives of dinners and wine and chats on the sofa."

She drained her cup so he took it to the counter and refilled it. He got himself one as well. He sat back down with his eyes on Amy's tight, serious face. She had told him what everyone around her wanted, except the one who mattered.

"What do you want?"

She flipped her hair behind her ear.

"I'm serious. What Jacqui, Eva, or Cavana want doesn't matter. The real question is, do you want to be chancellor or whatever they'll call it when all this shit is put back together?"

"You talk about what happens after we fix things like that's a given. It's far more likely this never gets fixed. So, I don't want to talk about what happens after anything. I want to talk about tomorrow. My first step is to get everyone to realize how deep the problem is."

"That's not an answer."

"It is. Because it's not about what I want. I've been moving up and up and up. I told Fontaine I'd have his job someday. Do you know what he replied? That I had to aim higher."

"You want to be the boss with a capital B?"

"I didn't set out on that path. Not growing up, not in the compounds. Not even when I moved to New Cal. But the closer I got to those at the top, the more I thought 'I can do better.'"

"You can, though to be fair, the bar is not very high."

She chuckled. "Yeah. But to do that, I'm going to need all the allies I can get. That's step two." She drew another breath. "Have you given any thought to our conversation in the infirmary?" He squinted and waited not sure what she meant. "Whether I can rely on you?"

"I don't have to give it any thought. If this is what you want, I'm behind you."

She nodded and sipped her water. "I need to give everyone something to believe in."

"Belief is good. But no one follows Kuipers because they believe in her. They follow her because she's in charge. If you want allies, you need to show them you can win."

"Exactly, and I can't do that if I'm hiding in the Uregs." She drained her cup and turned it upside down, tapping the bottom with her index finger. "I need you to do a few things for me."

"Anything."

"Find Lambert." She smiled. "Convince her I can win so she joins us."

"Oh boy. She's gonna love that."

"She will. How she treated us and how she hid my presence—that wasn't someone on the fence. She openly defied Kuipers. She already picked her side; she just needs to commit to it."

"What else?"

"What do you know about Eze, this rogue Marin Colonel?"

"Worked with Lori. Didn't come back after the biological attack. Most likely she was on team Lori. Either she didn't want to report to Kuipers, or Kuipers didn't want her back."

"Can we trust her?" she asked.

"To do what?" She cocked her head. "If you mean to back you, I really don't know. If you mean to not sell you out to Kuipers, then yeah, I think we can trust her."

She smiled. "This new Mika is very trusty."

He drained his water and smiled back. "I run with a better crowd."

She flipped her cup right side up and wiped the drops of water on the table with her sleeve. "How do I convince Eze to back me?"

He stacked his cup in Amy's. "From the little I saw, she's also already on your side. She just doesn't know it yet. So, show it to her."

"Once we know where we stand with Lambert and Eze, I want you to talk to Sierra."

He shook his head. "She's not joining you or New Cal, I can tell you that right now."

She put her hand up. "I know that. The naysayers are our third step. We need her to back down for a week or two. We also need her to release Cavana and his team."

"She's not likely to do either of those."

"Use whatever sway you have with her."

"Sway?" He raised his hand above his head. "I must be this high on her shit list."

"You shot her ticket to overhauling the Sentinels. The man who happened to be Kuipers' top adviser. And she barely made an attempt to hold you or find you."

"I'll do what I can."

"We'll also need a short-term win or two."

"What are those?"

She frowned but forced her lips to relax into a casual smile. "Still working on those."

"I'll round up your posse," he said but grimaced. "But I can't squeeze these trips into a single day, and I'm not comfortable leaving you here."

"Eva will be good as new tomorrow. And you seem to trust Jacqui."

He rubbed his middle finger with his thumb. "I wish I'd done that sooner."

"We trust her now. What happened yesterday doesn't matter. What happened an hour ago doesn't matter. All that matters is what happens next."

She reached out to his hand, stopping his flicking thumb, and frowned. "I really thought I was done dodging news from the field."

"Dodging news?"

"Yeah. When you used to disappear, I skipped the updates from the field to avoid bad news." She chuckled. "I know it's not rational. But bad news is final. As long as I didn't hear anything, you were fine, and I expected you back shortly."

"I will be careful, and I will be back."

She smiled. "You'd better."

CHAPTER 36
CENTER OF MASS

"When the whole world is silent, even one voice becomes powerful."

—MALALA YOUSAFZAI

In the two days since the bounty hunter attack, the farmhouse had morphed into a fortress. Four diesel generators puffed at the end of the courtyard. Sentinels loyal to Amy who had peeled off Sierra's command patrolled the perimeter. Lambert's officers buzzed around, barking orders to troops to shore up defenses, and Eze's forces camped in a semicircle around them. No bounty hunter with half a brain would get within fifty miles of the farmhouse and neither would any force short of a full battalion with air support.

Amy was the safest she had ever been and in the most danger. Because no one—not Kuipers, not Kern, and certainly no one in New Cal—could look at her and dismiss the threat she posed to their power, not anymore. By concentrating everyone who had irritated Kuipers into one spot, they had painted a bull's eye on themselves.

She got stronger every day. Glasses of water became lighter; each step propelled her farther; walks drained her less; headaches retreated to their normal fervor.

This morning she strolled the campsite with a single walking stick, a compromise that provided support while allowing her the use of one hand. She waved at Jacqui, who was in a heated discussion with Lambert's officers. Jacqui waved back, one of the few aware that Amy's walks were meant to be seen.

She reached the farmhouse kitchen and claimed the chair at the far end of the table and right in front of the counter and sink. A dark nine-inch ring marked a burn spot at the edge of the thick, solid maple top. It had appeared colossal on that first night as a dining table for a small farm. Today, as a conference table for a recruiting meeting, it looked puny, almost apologetic for not providing her with a grander setting to impress her guests.

She accepted a glass of water from Eva before moving on to coffee. It was a tricky balance to stay hydrated and caffeinated while not rushing to the bathroom too frequently and unsettling her guests. The secret calculus of politics did not make allowances for health problems, so the stronger she looked physically, the more convincing her arguments became. Her pulse picked up as the caffeine kicked in.

Eva poured her coffee in a pint glass, dropped in enough sugar to thicken it, and hopped on the counter to Amy's left and back. From her perch, she scanned the table, window, hallway, and front door. With her black zippered turtleneck, she became an extension of the slate countertop, disappearing into the background, though it took a special kind of stupid to forget she was in the room.

Mika had convinced both Lambert and Eze to listen to her offers. With her permission, Eze had also invited Ranford, who had been civil to her when she was detained at his base. That created a delicate problem. On one hand, the presence of a Kern commander forever clouded how everyone, from Lambert to Kuipers, viewed her. On the other, any Marin-Kern collaboration was too intriguing not to consider regardless of whether it came from two out-of-favor officers.

She sipped her coffee, forcing herself to swallow the odorless warm liquid. Her sense of smell was slow returning and without it, all her food and drink flavors had collapsed to a handful of tastes. This one hit all the bitter notes. She ran her fingers along the slight depression on the inner edge of the tabletop's burnt ring. Even with its scar, the table remained majestic, undaunted by what it had endured. It kept its position as the center of this kitchen without apology.

She tapped her fingers on the solid maple top.

We'll do just fine.

Mika's voice drifted in from the porch before he knocked and opened the door. He walked in and held the door for Lambert. "How's the shoulder?" he asked.

"Healing."

"Good to see you again, Colonel," Amy said as they came into view, Lambert's left shoulder in a sling.

Lambert walked around the table to reach her. "Governor. You look better."

"It's your fault," Mika said, drawing a proud smile from Lambert.

Amy hid her smile as Mika built rapport with self-deprecating banter that carried just enough honesty to disarm his audience. "Colonel. Mika informed me of your losses. I'm sorry."

Lambert pinched her chin. "I lost eighteen good soldiers, and I still don't know why they hit us." Lambert put her jacket on the back of a seat facing the window and sat down to Amy's left, leaving a chair between them. "Headquarters has been tight-lipped about everything leading to the assault and its aftermath, though I did receive a strongly worded rebuke from General Kuipers for not mentioning your presence."

"Just words?"

"There isn't a less important command she can assign me to. And that she can't afford to send her forces to spank me implies she's stretched pretty thin, doing what I'm not sure. Care to enlighten me?"

"I will, in just a few minutes. And if you're still here after you hear me out, I'm guessing your next rebuke from Kuipers will be stronger."

Lambert chuckled. "I don't think I can get any deeper into Kuipers' doghouse."

At another knock, Mika stepped to the door and opened it.

"You owe me a transport," said a deep, hoarse voice.

"It's still in one piece," Mika said. "Just out of fuel."

"Good, because you can't afford it." Eze stepped in. "Would have been easier to help you if you'd left the transponder working."

"Sorry about that," Mika said.

"How did you know the trackers were on?"

Mika grinned. "You gave me a transport. I'm charming, but not that charming."

Amy stood up and waved a formal greeting. "Colonel Eze."

"Good to finally meet you, Governor." Eze waved back. "I've heard so much about you." She waved a polite greeting to Lambert, who returned the wave.

Amy winced. "I hope to convince you to ignore that chatter."

"Oh, I hope not." Eze laughed as though a thunder trapped in her belly pushed its way out. "It made me want to meet you." She tapped her index finger to her lips. "Do you have a transport at your disposal?"

"Not at the moment, no."

"Then, by all means, use mine." She sat to Lambert's left at the end of the table and across from Amy. They exchanged pleasantries for a few minutes, and even while saying nothing, Amy became the center of the conversation. Lambert and Eze talked to her but not to each other.

Eze rose to a chime from her tida. "Are you still sure about my next guest, Governor?"

"I am." Amy turned to Lambert. "Colonel Eze has requested we invite another interested party. As she vouched strongly for him, I agreed."

"Him?" Lambert's eyes widened.

"Felix Ranford," Eze said. "Commander of nearly a thousand troops, and someone I have worked with for most of last year."

Lambert stood up, alarmed. "You invited a Kern commander?"

"Not exactly," Eze said and moved to the door seconds before the knock came.

Eva jumped off the counter and walked toward the door as Mika opened it. She stood in the entryway, arm on the wall, blocking the newcomer's path inside.

"Thank you, Eva," Amy said.

Eva took a step back, letting Ranford walk in. His cheeks were hollow, and the long sideburns made his face appear thinner than she remembered. He wore a long, dark coffee leather jacket with no insignia.

"Josie!" He reached for Eze who gave him a warm hug, both arms wrapped around his neck. He returned the embrace. As Amy studied the interaction, she spied Mika watching her watch them.

"Thank you for inviting me, Governor," Ranford said as he let go of Eze.

"Eze was very convincing, Colonel."

"Just the same, thank you for agreeing to it. Please call me Felix."

"Very well, Felix." Amy smiled. "So, you've finally become the military commander of a Uregs compound?"

"You were right the first time," Ranford said to her surprise. "It took me another few months to realize it." He took off his jacket and put it on the chair to Eze's left, his back to the window. "Governor, I'd like to apologize for last year."

Amy raised a hand. "You have nothing to apologize for. That was a different world."

He didn't hide the relaxed smile that broadcast his relief. Mika sat between Ranford and Amy. Eva retreated to her spot on the counter in the back. In a wordless exchange that lasted half a second, they had divvied up the room and dangers.

Amy leaned forward in her chair and put a strand of hair behind her ear. "Thank you all for agreeing to meet me. I think it's safe to say, not much out there is moving in the right direction. The Marin-Kern stalemate has produced two wars and a decade of setbacks." She summarized skirmishes, legal battles, and key decisions from the last year.

Lambert frowned. Eze remained expressionless as though Amy had been reading lunch options. Ranford nodded in agreement.

The irony that Ranford was the only one of the three she had shared a drink with wasn't lost on her. She tapped her tida, and a map floated over the table.

"I can keep going on what I think about the state of the world, but I'd rather we talked about what we know." She let her gaze move around the faces staring back at her. "I'm betting we have enough firsthand knowledge around this table to paint an accurate picture of the root causes of what's been going on for the last few years. I will start."

She pointed to the map, and New Cal turned cyan. "Cal City is hurting. General Kuipers is blockading the city. Food is running low, and panic has set in. Santa Cruz and Mountain View have sent supplies, but they cannot reach the city. Mayor Halsan has claimed power." She sighed. "Again."

She tapped, and the Sentinels' compound lit up in pink. "Cavana, my vice governor, is held by the Sentinels on Kuipers' orders. In isolation, all of these are surmountable problems. But together, they've brought Cal City to the brink of collapse."

"Sentinels?" Lambert asked.

Amy pointed to Mika, and he summarized the Purge's impact, how to activate it, and Sierra's efforts to create hard-to-kill soldiers. Amy rubbed her temples, letting Mika widen the circle of secrets a little more. As she listened to the Purge for the thousandth time, every word felt wrong again, beyond belief.

Lambert took it in. "I need to let that percolate for a minute, though from reactions around the table, I'm guessing I'm the only one who didn't know."

"General Rose told me... us," Eze said, pointing to Ranford, "during the last stages of last year's hostilities. Felix and I were tested before Rose let us take command in the Uregs. Both of us carry the Purge."

"How does Kuipers fit into this?" Lambert asked.

"Kuipers listens to a new group, one that's been exploiting the Purge's powers," Mika said. He summarized his last few months, his discovery of settlements, and Gibson's plans but did not mention Tulum.

Amy waved at Ranford, "Felix?"

"Just about everything I'm about to say is classified," Ranford said. "Taggart is in full control of Kern. His forces captured Spindler last week. He's keeping it quiet because it gives him an excuse to keep that battalion up north." He circled a region to their north and east, turning it red. "And yes, Taggart is a Purie."

"So, will they head back south now?"

Ranford shook his head. "No. They're up there to prevent Marin from claiming Mt. Shasta. They will not cede that facility to Marin."

"How do you fit in all of this?"

"Taggart knows I was the one who attacked the Purie bases last year. So, I've been neutral up to now, but that's about to change. I need to move away from this corridor," he said, moving his finger up and down in the eastern part of the map. "I need to dip below Tahoe and head west. He pointed to the area north of Morro Bay, turning it purple. "Somewhere here."

Lambert, whose eyes had scanned Eze as much as Ranford, said, "Why are you here?"

"I invited him." Eze made no attempt to hide her irritation.

"It's okay; it's a fair question," Ranford said. "I was the commander of the base Governor Chipps was brought into last year. I received conflicting orders, so I ignored them. Before I had to commit, General Rose attacked our base. We weren't equipped to handle her."

Eze smiled. "No one is."

"Anyway," Ranford said, "the conflict was short-lived, and General Rose made me an offer I couldn't refuse. Colonel Eze's forces joined mine, and as the general went back to Marin, we worked together to take out three Purie bases. So, I have a working relationship with Colonel Eze, as well as a passing acquaintance with Governor Chipps."

Lambert rubbed her chin. "Thank you. This explains a few things. Half the Marin military has been streaming north over the last week." She tapped to spread blue into a strip stretching north on the map. "The other half is turning Marin into an occupation zone. If you drove there now, you wouldn't recognize it. Troops patrol every street. Barricades block three-quarters of the roads and dozens of checkpoints choke the city. Citizens are being tested and need a biometric ID to move from zone to zone. I thought it was because of the bodies with Purge-like symptoms, but it's just as likely to be to see who has the Purge and who doesn't."

She let go of her chin. "No wonder Kuipers hasn't reacted to my actions. Even leaking information to the Kern battalion instead of sending troops to relieve me of my command now makes sense. She's spread so thin she can't spare the troops to arrest me."

Eze stood and waved at the map with a frown on her face. "So many colors, it looks like a four-year-old ate berries and puked on the map." She addressed Mika. "Do you have anything to drink?"

Mika shook his head. "I wish."

"Shit." She fixed her eyes on Amy. "Governor, I need a clarification."

"Yes?"

"In recent broadcasts, General Kuipers linked you to many disruptive organizations, but that's a dog whistle for saying you're a Purie. And to be fair, everything you've done is in opposition to Kuipers' aims."

Amy glanced at Eva who was stone still, her bent arms on the counter by her sides, one push away from somersaulting into someone's face.

Eze didn't back down. "And if your actions have nothing to do with Kuipers' fight against the Puries, why is Kuipers offering full amnesty to any out-of-favor officer who brings you to her?" Eze chuckled. "It's almost tempting."

"Only if you want to have a real short rest of your life."

They all turned to Eva, who hadn't spoken or moved from the counter since they had started. She hopped off the counter in one smooth motion, landed next to Amy, and held her arms by her side. "Amnesty is not useful if you're dead."

"That type of offer makes me far more likely to follow Governor Chipps than turn her in," Lambert said before Eze spoke.

"I'm guessing the offer doesn't apply to me," Ranford said, ratcheting the tension down.

Eze laughed in little coughs. "Hot damn, that was a bad joke." Her smile disappeared as she sat back on her chair. "Just for the record, and just so we're all on the same page, you're saying Kuipers is lying?"

"What are you asking?" Amy said.

Eze tapped her lip and faced Amy, ignoring everyone else. "Are you a Purie?"

"I do not carry the Purge virus."

Her response had no impact on Lambert who hadn't yet processed the implications that statement carried, but Eze's shoulders tightened.

"But beyond that," Amy added, "I refuse to accept our allegiances are biologically determined. Yes, some are pushing for that on both sides. The Puries, as you disparagingly call them, have shown they're willing to kill by the hundreds. And Kuipers, with her newfound friends, is cataloging the Purge status of every Marin citizen as we speak."

"With all due respect," Eze said, "biometric ID cards and attempted genocide aren't on the same playing field."

"Once you record every citizen's virus status and force them to carry ID cards, it's a short trip. Just listen to the words Kuipers is using. She started with Purge, contagion, safety, security, but now moved to dangerous, abomination, the agent of chaos, mortal enemy, and foreign interference. These are words selected to isolate populations, demonize her opponents, break down the rational thought process of her citizens, and get them to react in fear."

Eze turned to Lambert. "How about you? When did you hurt that shoulder?"

Before Lambert answered, Mika said, "Based on what I saw, I'd guess Lambert either is Purge-free or has never been shot or hurt before."

"I've been shot twice and broke my arm in two places," Lambert said.

"Then I'm pretty sure you don't carry the Purge," Mika said.

"Is that why you oppose Kuipers?" Eze asked.

Lambert pushed her chair back and rose. "Are you saying I'm working with the Kern force? The ones who attacked my base and killed eighteen of my soldiers?"

Ranford tapped two fingers on the table without producing a sound. Eze kept her gaze on Lambert but didn't reply.

"See what's happening?" Amy asked. "Civil rights are trampled in Marin, with forced blood tests and martial law. A city in New Cal is about to collapse into famine. A coup swept Kern. Two armies are jockeying for control of a facility up north that might spill into another shooting war. And here we are, fighting over which of us carries the damn Purge virus."

Amy flicked her hair behind her ear. "This is exactly what Kuipers wants. For us to fear each other because of our biology."

Lambert pinched her chin and sat back down.

"All I'm asking is for you to look at my actions over the last year," Amy said. "Tell me, how would carrying the Purge have made me a better or even a different leader?"

"What do you propose?" Eze asked.

"I need to reclaim Cal City. Now, I can do that on my own. But I can't defend it against Marin if Kuipers decides to take us down. I'm offering New Cal citizenship or asylum as you choose. Join me and we go to Cal City together. We show Kuipers, Kern, and all the Uregs that there is a new way to do business. That we are not defined by our gender or our virus status."

Eze interlaced her fingers. "And we put our forces under your command?"

"Yes. You will have a voice, but there has to be a chain of command."

"This is all a little too sudden for me," Eze said. "You offer a compelling cause, but I'm not ready to blindly jump into anything."

"Then do it with your eyes open," Lambert said. "I have limited firepower, particularly after last week's debacle. What I have to offer will not deter Kuipers, but it is yours."

"Thank you, Colonel, I appreciate your support." Amy turned to Ranford. "Felix?"

"I respect you, Governor. You have the right instincts and a compelling argument. But every time I commit to a new leader, bad things happen. I am willing to accompany you to Cal City. I am willing to keep your supply lines open. I am willing to defend you from aggression from the north and the south. But I am not ready to put my forces under your command. I'm sorry, Governor, but that's the best I can do right now."

Amy's heart sank. "Thank you, but I cannot accept your offer."

Lambert jumped in. "Governor, I can work with Colonel Ranford's conditions, at least to keep the supply lines open."

"I can't." Amy faced Ranford. "If you cover our back, I need to know I can rely on you. At some point, you will receive orders from someone. I don't much care who they are, but if it's not me, I can't have your army near me. You said you were headed west."

He nodded.

"You're welcome as far as fifty miles south of Santa Cruz, but no closer."

She turned to Eze. "This goes for you too. Fifty miles."

"If the offer is still good, I'd like to take that New Cal citizenship," Eze said. "And I expect all my officers and troops to receive the same deal."

Amy gripped her coffee mug tighter. "May I ask what changed your mind?"

Eze smiled. "I wondered how your actions would have been different over the last ten minutes if you carried the Purge." She raised both hands, palms up. "I came up with nothing."

After a few minutes of discussing logistics, Eze moved to the door. "I will inform my command staff." She put a hand on Ranford's shoulder. "Good to see you, Felix."

Ranford stood up. "You too."

They walked out—Eze first, then Ranford, and finally Lambert.

Amy drained her coffee. It had gone cold, another casualty of the evening. She stood and walked to the bedroom. The memories of the bounty hunter attack assaulted her, the mangled bodies piled on the floor, Eva bleeding in the corner. She would have liked another room, but this was the one she had, and this was the one she had to make do with. A lot like the assortment of officers and troops at her disposal.

She lay on top of the bed covers and closed her eyes for a second. She opened them at the thud of a glass of water hitting her bedside table. Mika stood by her side.

"I wouldn't mind a glass of wine right now," she said.

"We don't have any." He smiled, "And even if we did, you wouldn't get any for another three days. Doctor's orders."

"I've got my wits now, mostly. I've started paying attention, and I've been mulling over all that's been happening over the past weeks."

He dragged the chair with the low back and wooden armrests from the corner to her side. He sat down and leaned forward. "Anything interesting?" he smirked.

"Yeah, you. I've been going over your actions. How you convinced Sierra you were on her side and let Tulum become comfortable with you. How you came back into the Sentinel for me. Then as I got worse, how you hatched that plan with Lambert and backed her into a corner where she had to choose. It's a little disturbing how you operate."

"Disturbing?"

"Individually, each of those makes sense. Except for the Tulum part. But taken together, they scare me. There is a cold undercurrent, a detachment to what you do and how you do it. It almost reminds me of..." She stopped. "It reminds me of Lori."

"Is that a compliment?"

"It's not," she said. "It worries me that I can't figure out what drives you. You're moody, cold, charming, and indifferent. And when I think you don't have any interest in even talking to me, you break into the Sentinels to get me out and then run through a rain of bullets to help me."

He flicked his left thumb at his middle finger as though he was scratching it, as though he was spinning a ring that wasn't there.

"That business with Tulum wasn't right," she said. "It was cold, calculating, and if pushed to its limit, a scary place to be. I need you to stay connected to your humanity."

"I don't know what that means or how to tell what worries you."

"Then ask, and we'll talk through it."

He tapped the wooden armrest, moving his fingers like galloping horses. "Here's all I know. I relaxed for a second, got sloppy, and almost got you killed. I shouldn't have trusted Blue's sensors. I shouldn't have trusted Jacqui's team since I'd taken their guns away. I should have set up a perimeter the moment we stopped, not left it for later."

"You've been doing amazing. You can't heap more pressure on yourself."

"I have to, and it's not pressure. It's a way of life. Until last year, a mistake, a stray bullet meant I died. But now, it doesn't."

"So? You're accepting your new body."

"That can get you killed."

"You've done a damn fine job keeping me alive."

He folded his left leg and sat on it, with his left foot under his right thigh. "I need to tell you something. I talked to Sierra about it, and—"

She put her hand up, and he stopped. "If you tell me you slept with Sierra, I'll deck you. With the weakest right hook ever."

His neck recoiled back; his eyes widened. "What?"

"You should see the look on your face." She flashed a smile. "I'll take that as a no."

"It's about Lin." His face froze into a statue. "And yeah, we did have a thing."

It had been four months since the night he had left her house. What had she expected? And why did it bother her? A fling with Sierra would have created impossible-to-handle tensions. But one with a dead stranger? That was water under the bridge, and she had to accept it.

"When?" She wasn't even sure why it mattered because she couldn't be jealous of a ghost.

"A couple of weeks ago."

She let out the breath she had been holding in fear that he would say five months. She had to be fair. No, she didn't. "I'm not thrilled about it, but I can't blame you."

"I'm glad to hear you say that. But that's not the problem."

She frowned, and the pressure was building again in her chest. "What is the problem?"

He leaned closer to her and put his head on her thigh, avoiding her torso. She caressed his hair, letting her fingers get snared in his wispy hair.

"What is it, Mika?"

"I shot her," he whispered.

Her hand stopped moving.

"They had her locked in a concrete box with metal rods piercing her body. She was in pain and irradiated. I couldn't save her, and I couldn't leave her." He closed his eyes. "She made me promise. But it doesn't change anything. I pulled the trigger, and she's dead. I see her face every time I close my eyes."

She didn't trust herself to speak but let her trembling hand move through his hair again.

"She looked straight at me in that last moment, and she had to know I had her in my crosshairs. And she winked like it was okay. It wasn't. It wasn't okay."

His eyes glinted. If tears were forming, none came. She wondered whether he could even cry anymore or whether his tear ducts would just stop the flow of the unnecessary salty liquid. But tears didn't matter. What mattered was the raw pain frozen on his face.

She leaned forward and cradled his head. "I got you," she whispered. "I got you."

CHAPTER 37

BULLIES

"Never grow a wishbone, daughter, where your backbone ought to be."

—CLEMENTINE PADDLEFORD

The convoy stopped fifty yards from the first set of barricades on Highway 101 by the old airport. The collapsed ramps and wide asphalt created the perfect staging area for Marin's transports. Two dozen Marin soldiers stood behind heavy guns pointing south. A hundred yards past them, another battery of guns pointed north. Six provision trailers baked in the sun by the side of the highway, stuck there since Joy had sent them north from Santa Cruz three days ago.

The Cal City militia squirmed five miles to the north, not even acknowledged by Yallop, the Marin general in charge of the blockade. They hadn't gotten desperate enough to engage, which was good. They would be swept aside with a single brush of the Marin heavy transports.

The clean, orderly way in which the Marin soldiers moved around the blockade made Amy's blood boil. Her citizens were in a panic and starving fifteen miles north while the Marin troops were chatting, almost bored as though this were an unnecessary training exercise.

"General Yallop won't return our hails," her pilot said as they glided down at the center of the three-transport formation, approaching the blockade.

"I'll handle this, Governor," Eze said, and her transport broke formation and dove toward the staging area south of the command tent. As it hovered and landed into a dust storm, armed Marin troops surrounded it. Eze stepped off alone and stormed into the command tent. She stepped out four minutes later. "You're cleared to land, Governor."

Amy's transport landed behind the tent, past the air-conditioning units buzzing to provide comfort to the Marin officers while her citizens struggled without power. Before she stormed the tent, Yallop and Eze walked out of a back flap and stood by the shade of the tent's awning.

"With all due respect, Ms. Chipps—" Yallop started.

Eze cut her off. "Governor."

"Excuse me?"

"It's Governor Chipps," Eze corrected as Amy reached the tent's awning.

Yallop glared at Eze, nostrils flaring.

Amy pointed to the barricades. "You need to clear this road, now."

"I cannot do that. My orders are to prevent the shipment of illegal goods and block the movement of known enemies of the state."

Amy smiled. "You packed a lot of doublespeak into that sentence, General. We're not in Marin, so you have no jurisdiction here. What you've seized is food, and I'm not about to debate the legality of corn with you. As for enemies of the state, that depends on what enemy and what state."

"Nevertheless, I have orders."

"No, you have choices. You can step aside and let us pass or start a war."

"I cannot let you pass," Yallop repeated.

"Up till now, you've stopped civilians. I don't recommend testing the resolve of the New Cal military."

"New Cal militia, you mean?" Yallop sneered.

"I meant what I said." Assault transports rose up and hovered behind them.

Yallop's eyes moved to the transports. "Those are Marin."

"No, they are not," Eze said.

"You don't have to do this." Amy tapped her tida to authorize the first food transport to take off. It floated up, tipped forward, and passed over them, flying toward Cal City, flanked by two armed transports.

Yallop grasped the tip of her cap, moving it up and down and then rotating side to side. She let go of her cap and moved her gaze to the receding transports. Every second she stayed silent reduced the odds of a confrontation.

"Thank you, General. That was a good choice," Amy said, as the transport disappeared toward Cal City. "Now, the trucks."

Yallop stood and walked toward the barricades. The first truck in line nudged forward at five miles an hour and reached the blockade thirty seconds before two soldiers removed the spike strips from the roadway.

"That went better than I expected," said Mika, as they boarded their transport. He had stayed ten feet behind during the exchange. "I'll count that a definite win."

"We're not done yet," Amy said as they took off.

They were sandwiched between Eze's transport in front and Lambert's in the back. The flow of information that pinged back and forth from the field to the troops to the transports dizzied her.

Even the speed of the food trucks was monitored, assessed, and stored. Fontaine hadn't believed in investing in the military, claiming they would always be third-best by a mile. She now realized how wrong he had been. It wasn't the power that mattered but the statement it made about one's commitment to their cause. New Cal had lost out on organization and professionalism because it had never had a proper military. Till now.

Amy called Eze. "Colonel, under no circumstances are we to take out the defensive batteries along the shore."

"Governor, they can hurt us with those."

"I understand that. Get defensive flares ready, and if they engage, we withdraw. I am not going to declaw New Cal on our first approach."

The reply took longer than it should have, the first test of a direct order to her new military officer.

"Understood."

Amy had broadcast her identity and intentions since they had taken off. There should have been no confusion and no reason for a confrontation unless Halsan forced it. Before they came within range of the guns, her pilot said, "Incoming call from Commander Frank Cho."

"Good to hear from you, Frank."

"Governor, is that really you?" The militia leader's voice bubbled with relief.

"Yes, Frank it's me. And the approaching force is with us. Stand down."

"Done. Governor, it's good to see you."

"Thank you, Frank. Meet me in the Capitol and inform Mayor Halsan that I need to talk to him immediately."

"The mayor is gone. He left when word spread that you'd ended the blockade."

"Very well." She cut the connection.

When they landed, the reception committee consisted of Cho, three other militia leaders, and office staff. Then Ferg appeared at the Capitol's door, stepping down to hug her.

"Are you good?" Amy asked as she pulled away.

"It's you we worried about. There were so many rumors."

"I'm better," Amy said. "How is everyone holding up?"

Amy's frown deepened as Ferg summarized the situation. It was worse than she had feared. Electricity was out in half the city. So was the water. They had handled food shortages the first week, but hoarding had started in the second week. The militia had been called to stop looting twice already.

"And Halsan?"

Ferg shook her head. "He operated from his compound. We never saw him."

The mayor had tried to seize power twice, maneuvering himself to be seen as the legitimate governor. And he hadn't come to the Capitol when she and Cavana were out? When her return had been in doubt?

She turned to Mika, "Find him. I want to know what he's up to."

"Sure," Mika said as shouts rang from offices past the mezzanine.

"What now?" Amy asked. Ferg tapped a screen to display five Marin heavy transports floating over the bay. "Again?"

"I guess Kuipers decided to show a reaction after all," Mika said.

"Yes. But she knew I was on my way to Cal City before we ever got near the blockade and before we ever talked to General Yallop. She didn't stop me there. So why now?"

"Cal City won't survive another blockade," Ferg said.

"She wants you to know she's pissed," Mika said.

"She's not the only one who is pissed," Amy said as Eze and Lambert appeared in the corridor. Amy proceeded with the introductions but kept an eye on the hovering transports on the screen. "Frank, who is your best pilot, someone with nerves of steel?"

"I have aces with combat experience," Eze said when Cho hesitated.

"Thank you, Colonel, but for this, I need our militia." She turned to Cho. "Say, you need to squeeze through a tunnel two inches wider than the transport. Who would you pick?"

"Lieutenant Aleesha Woods. She's your pilot."

"Get an unarmed light transport ready and patch me to her."

"Unarmed?"

Amy narrowed her eyes. "That's what I said."

"Of course. If you'll excuse me," Cho said and walked out.

Amy leaned back in her chair. "This is all a game."

Eze tapped her lips. "She's testing you."

I know that.

When Fontaine sat in this chair, his decisions were not questioned. When he pushed them into a union, his wisdom was not questioned. Perhaps age would gain her that respect or at least immunize her to the ceaseless second-guessing she endured. But the reality was she was about the gamble with lives—others' lives.

Lieutenant Aleesha Woods appeared on her screen. "Governor."

Woods had a round face and almost no chin, a button nose, and thin lips. Her bright white eyes popped out inquisitively from her high cheeks. The cap she wore made her look eighteen.

Amy smiled. "I learned the difference between a bully and someone with real power when I was twelve. The closest well to the shack where I grew up was behind an abandoned depot. There was a narrow breezeway between the perimeter wall and the depot that cut ten minutes from our path to the well. But three bullies stood there morning and evening harassing passersby, extracting tolls they had no right to extract.

"I mostly took the long way to avoid them. But that one day, my buddy and I were tired and, without thinking, came back through the breezeway. We went through the routine, words moving to shoves. But we stood our ground and, in the end, we just walked past them. They only escalated the taunts and threats once we were well clear. Turns out, they wanted to intimidate and scare us into submission, but they didn't want to fight any more than we did."

"I got my nose broken by bullies."

"You have to be ready for that. Mostly though, the bullies are not."

"What can I do for you, Governor?"

"Lieutenant, I need you to face those transports, alone. Let them know you'll go toe to toe with them, but under no circumstances are you to engage them. Are we clear?"

Woods blinked. "Yes, Governor."

"Good luck, Lieutenant."

Amy muted the feed but kept the video from Woods' cockpit.

Eze leaned over Amy's shoulder. "Governor, may I make one suggestion?"

Amy's stomach muscles tightened. She respected Eze's expertise in military strategy and welcomed her advice, but she would have preferred a less public delivery. "Yes, Colonel?"

"We don't send a pilot out with 'good luck.'" Eze chuckled. "And there is no point wishing for clear skies in these parts. May I recommend, 'Good hunting,' or, 'Tailwinds'?"

Amy relaxed her jaw. "Thank you, Colonel, I'll keep that in mind," she said, though she hoped there would be no hunting of any kind, good or bad.

Woods was in the air six minutes later. Her external video feed played on Amy's screen. As Woods banked toward the bay, the five transports came into view, forming a V, growing to fill the screen like a threatening alien spaceship.

Woods slowed and then hovered as she reached the water edge. The display showed the lead Marin transport was two hundred fifty feet away.

"Closer," Amy called, and Woods inched forward. The distance displayed in green at the right of her screen dropped as the transports filled the entire screen. Woods stopped at one hundred feet.

"Do you see the Marin pilot in the lead transport?"

"No, only my reflection."

"Get closer."

"Governor, at this distance, our turbofans will interact and—"

"Closer," Amy said.

Woods edged forward and stopped at forty feet.

"Are they sweating?"

"Can't see that."

"Closer."

Woods halved the distance to the heavy transport that now filled her field of view. Woods paused "The pilot looks confused."

"I bet," Amy said. "Take off your helmet, Lieutenant."

A *clink* and *whoosh* exposed Woods' three-inch dreadlocks that had been crushed sideways by her helmet. Without warning, Woods' craft fluttered up and down but stabilized.

"Everything good, Lieutenant?"

"Yes. I got caught in their updraft. At this distance, our turbofan wash creates eddies our autopilots can't predict."

"Understood. Lieutenant, I need you to get closer."

"Governor, I'm at twenty feet."

"I see that, Lieutenant."

"How close do you want me to get?"

"Give them a gentle tap."

There was a five-second silence. "Repeat, Governor."

"Get close and tight and give them a tap. Do it gently; don't threaten them."

"You want me to collide with them without being threatening?'

"Exactly."

"Copy that." Woods inched forward.

The nose of the Marin transport grew till it darkened Amy's screen. The proximity alarm screeched with the distance dropping in green. At eight feet, the shadow of Woods' transport cut off the glare, and two pilots stared back. Neither flinched. They remained motionless and did not speak past the earlier warning to Woods to keep her distance.

Amy froze as the hand of the Marin pilot to the right moved toward a panel. Woods nudged forward, and their noses thumped at three miles per hour.

For five seconds, nothing happened.

Then the Marin transport pitched forward and so did Woods. Amy's stomach tightened, and for a sickening moment she feared they would fold up and get their turbofans tangled, but the Marin transport slid backward, nose still tilted forward twenty degrees.

In moving back, the transport crabbed to its port side, nearly colliding with the transport there. The second transport rose, breaking formation and pushing the transport to its port down.

"That was cool," Woods said.

In thirty seconds, the Marin transports were in formation again, but not as tight as they had been. "One more time."

Woods repeated the maneuver. This time, only the lead Marin transport moved back. On the third try, the lead transport rose up, preventing Woods from touching it. The backwash pitched Woods down, and the screen shifted to the onrushing ocean.

"Aleesha!" Amy yelled as the sea and sky spun around on the screen.

The bay grew toward them, fell away, and the Golden Gate Bridge appeared, stabilized, and receded. Then Woods yawed back toward the Marin transports, who were no longer in any type of formation. Woods moved against the lead transport again, stopping thirty feet in front.

"Another tap, Governor?"

"At your discretion," Amy said.

As Woods moved forward, the Marin transport backed up. Woods didn't stop till they reached the first tower of the Golden Gate Bridge.

"You can stop now," Amy called.

Woods moved another fifty feet before stopping.

"Well done, Lieutenant."

The Marin transports hovered over the bay, well away from Cal City's shore.

"You need to see this," Lambert said. She switched the top left of the screen to a feed from Crissy Field where the supply transports had set up the relief effort. Hundreds had left their stalls and turned toward the bay, cheering Woods on, shaking fists, and throwing sticks in the direction of the distant transports.

Ferg appeared on a third inset on the screen. "There is a call for you, Governor. General Kuipers is on the line."

Amy smiled at Lambert and Eze. "I guess we got her attention. May I have the room?"

Eze pulled the door shut behind her as she left with Lambert.

Amy took a sip of water in a futile attempt to wash her adrenaline down and calm her racing heart. Kuipers had tried to have her arrested and possibly killed more than once, yet Amy had to rise above that and present a professional face.

"It's never personal," Fontaine had said once when she had asked him how he handled all these people who didn't even hide their hatred for him. "Even when it is."

She had pointed out the inanity of that argument, but she got it now. The hatred was for the person's actions, words, status, and authority, not the person. The distinction was only a sliver, but it helped her frame the next few minutes as something other than a drudgery.

She even smiled. If she had generated that much reaction from Kuipers, she must have done something right. She hopped on her desk and tapped the screen across the room.

"Are you totally insane?" Kuipers hissed as she appeared on the screen, leaning forward. "Just what are you playing at trying to get that pilot killed?"

"We have a lot to talk about, General."

"Next time you pull a stunt like this, I will give the order to shoot."

"Let's agree to not have a next time."

Kuipers shook her head. "Yes, that would be good."

"Glad to hear that you'll remove the transports from the bay."

Kuipers chuckled, but her face went slack as she pulled away from the camera and settled into her seat. "Before we go any further, I want you to know I did not authorize anyone to fire at the Sentinels compound."

"I appreciate your apology. Let's move on."

"This said, I was perplexed with your disappearance. Then I saw your blood test result. How do you expect me to interpret your actions?"

"I left because I didn't trust you. Neither you nor Rendon gave me an indication that a rational conversation would have followed."

"And now, will you try to convince me that you're not pursuing the Purie agenda?"

"I will not try to convince you of anything. But I have no such agenda."

"Have you spoken to Mayor Halsan?"

"Not yet."

"He works with Kern and the Puries."

"You said this already, and I told you I'll deal with him."

"You are difficult to figure out." Kuipers pursed her lips. "I gave you the benefit of the doubt, but Halsan supports the Purie agenda. My forces will seize him and bring him to Marin."

"Seize him in Cal City? I don't think so. I will deal with Halsan."

"How do I know that? After all, you're also a Purie."

"Stop saying that. I do not have the Purge virus, and I cannot heal. I have never had any contact, nor do I share the agendas of the organization that infiltrated Marin and Kern. One is biology; the other is ideology. Stop mixing the two."

"I'd like to believe you. But I can't afford to trust you with this much at stake."

"At stake?"

"I'm going to assume you know about the abduction of infected personnel from the settlements. With such dangerous weapons in play, I can't gamble that you will do the right thing." Kuipers frowned. "Those weapons make Halsan too dangerous for me to step aside."

"This is all your fault, you know. Had you not chased me away and detained my vice governor in the Sentinels, Halsan would not have had the free reign to become a threat."

"Now, now. Halsan was a problem well before any of that."

"He was contained."

Kuipers leaned back, shrinking on Amy's screen. "How long have you known about the Sentinels?"

"A while."

"And you have not informed me?"

"As vice-chancellor, that was my prerogative."

"You informed Yim?" Amy did not reply. "By your admission, your actions were not in the best interest of Marin."

"Marin-New Cal, you mean?"

Kuipers chuckled. "Is this the best time to be pedantic?"

"I'm not being pedantic. I'm reminding you that you never understood the union."

"A union with an undefined purpose and no support on either side of the border and whose authors were assassinated before they even articulated why that union was necessary. That union? Come now, Amy, you never believed in the union either."

"That's a fair assessment."

"Let's build a better one. Come to Marin. Let's handle Halsan together. If you and I are on the same side, there will be no dissent."

The simplicity of the path Kuipers offered tempted her. But Eze and Lambert hadn't followed her to rejoin Marin. Or had they? Would they even welcome it? She had lectured Sierra on the difference between taking the easy path and the right path. The desolation of Cal City after a two-week blockade was enough to banish the thought. She bit the inside of her cheek, chiding herself for having considered this for even a second.

"My place is in Cal City, right here in the Capitol."

"I'm disappointed."

"But I agree, we need to work together. How about you recall the Marin troops enforcing the blockade of Cal City, release Cavana and all New Cal citizens held against their will at the Sentinels, and remove all Marin transports from New Cal airspace?"

Kuipers chuckled. "How is that working together? What do I get out of this?"

"A New California not controlled by your enemies."

"Excuse me if I don't fall out of my chair at your generosity. I have two battalions on alert. How about I send them to New California to contain the Purie threat and detain any leadership that gets in our way?"

"I don't recommend that."

"Why not?"

"One, you will not prevail, not with two battalions. Do an analysis of the troops within fifty miles of New California. You will need at least four battalions to overcome our defenses. And that will leave thousands dead on both sides. Two, that'll take all your resources away from your real prize up north. You'll leave Shasta to Kern."

Kuipers pursed her lips and gestured to someone off-screen. Her attention shifted away from the screen, and she nodded to what she heard. "I see." She returned her gaze to Amy. "So, you're trying to convince me you're not a Purie agent by threatening me with Kern forces right after the Puries won the Kern civil war. If you have a strategy here, I don't see it."

"When you analyze the allegiance of that Kern battalion, you will conclude they are not on the best terms with current Kern leadership, unlike the Kern force to your north. A stable New Cal under my leadership is in your best interests right now."

"I don't agree with your assessment, but I'll give you twenty-four hours to handle Halsan. That said, if you give asylum to any Marin offi—"

"I am not handing Lambert or Eze to you."

Kuipers forced a chuckle. "I am not concerned with a colonel exiled to an irrelevant outpost or one whose incompetence shamed her into going AWOL over a year ago. But you will not harbor any Marin officer or leader other than those two knuckleheads for a year—"

"I'll agree to that for the next month."

"One year. If you destabilize Marin by recruiting or by publicly talking about the virus, I will raze New California."

"I don't appreciate blanket threats, and I won't agree to vague conditions that trigger vaguer consequences."

Kuipers sighed again. "Let's be precise, then. You invoked Article 7. Reclaimed the Capitol. Faced-off against my transports over the bay. You're playing with symbols. So, if you harbor anyone who'll give you a symbolic win, I will destroy your Capitol. Symbol for symbol and no civilians suffer. Clear enough for you?"

Amy pushed strands of hair behind her ear. "That's not a bargain I'm willing to—"

"I'm not asking you, I'm telling you."

"Good day, General."

Amy cut the feed and put her elbows on her knees, cradling her head. Every victory carried seeds of defeat. She straightened and tapped her screen. "Ferg, can you send Mika up?"

"He left half an hour ago," Ferg said.

"Left? Where?"

"I don't know, Governor. He talked to Blue—that's the girl with purple hair. Something about a virus and a compound in the Uregs."

Amy cut the connection and closed her eyes. She wasn't mad at Mika. No, she was mad at herself for believing he had changed. "Unbelievable," she muttered.

"He's gone after Halsan."

Amy jumped at Eva's voice. Eva had become such a fixture in the back of every room that Amy forgot she was there. That was nothing but another defeat. One of her only friends erased and reduced to a forgotten role in the shadows. "What?"

"Halsan fled Cal City. Blue traced him to a compound south of here, and Mika believes he's got patients infected with the Purge variant. You did ask him to find Halsan, didn't you?"

Amy took a deep breath, letting it out slowly to cleanse her initial frustration.

"Cut him some slack," Eva said. "He's really trying."

Amy's tension gave way to a smile. Eva's protection now pulled double duty. She defended Amy against bodily harm and watched over her mental state. Which of the two required more talent was a debate for another time. "You're a gem, you know that?"

Eva bit her lower lip, almost becoming cuddly—as cuddly as a deadly bodyguard could be.

CHAPTER 38

RECOIL

"The most effective way to do it is to do it."
—AMELIA EARHART

Leaving Cal City had always filled Mika with glee, as though gravity tugged at him less outside of the Capitol's orbit. He had felt guilty at first, but he had enjoyed the freedom the Uregs provided too much to let it drag him down. Today, he felt neither guilt nor joy. All he wanted was to find what Halsan was up to fast and return to the Capitol and to Amy.

She was getting stronger by the day, extending her work hours, barking orders with a little more bite, and glaring at her audience with eyes penetrating deeper. If it weren't for the exhausted evenings when she collapsed and slept for twelve hours, it would have been easy to believe she was fully healed. But she was better, and that was all that mattered.

Jacqui sat on the passenger seat, her rifle propped against the spot where the dash met the door. She leaned on the door and faced back as they talked. Xin, one of Jacqui's Special Forces soldiers, drove their Humvee, nodding at the chit-chat but rarely contributing. Blue's bouncing in the seat next to him hadn't been Mika's idea, but she had made a simple point. They were going to need her skills when they faced whatever Halsan had cooked up for them. She had already shown her value by not falling for two feints by Halsan's transport.

He had first landed at a compound south of Cal City where three transports had taken off at six-minute intervals. Then he had stopped at another compound and left in a truck, with the transport flying toward the coast. Blue had not only identified Halsan's tida signature, but she had isolated the network pattern his comms generated. So even if his tida were left behind, she could spot him. Halsan had now reached an abandoned town forty miles to their southeast.

"Sentinel activity ahead," Blue said, eyes on her screen.

Jacqui reached into her jacket, pulled out her pistol, cocked it, and placed it on her lap. She took her rifle and put the strap around her neck, barrel pointing down, and sat straight, eyes scanning the road ahead.

"Do they know we're here?" Mika asked.

"Yes. One truck moved to an intercept vector," Blue said.

"Can we avoid them?"

Blue swiped at her screen with laser-focused eyes. "Not if we want to catch Halsan." She projected the map ahead of the windshield. The Sentinel vehicle was approaching an intersection ten miles ahead from the east. Any detour would delay them for more than an hour.

Jacqui pointed to where the road bent west, ahead of the intersection. "If we make it here before they do, we can make a stand."

He shook his head. "Can't afford a shoot-out. Broadcast who we are."

Jacqui gave him a sideways glance.

"It's either that or we're getting into a firefight we're unlikely to win," he said.

Sierra's transport landed in front of them twelve minutes later. The Sentinels truck had reached the intersection first and blocked the road. Xin stopped thirty yards short to avoid provoking the Sentinels. Jacqui and Xin stepped out, armed.

Sierra walked straight for them, trailed by six Sentinels armed with assault rifles. "What are you playing at this time?"

Mika stepped past Jacqui and Xin and stopped, feet shoulder-length apart. He had grabbed beers with four of the Sentinels though he hadn't been close to any of them. None of them made eye contact. "Trying to save your ass. Again."

"Not in the mood for games," Sierra said, her eyes hovering around Jacqui long enough to betray a shared past. Jacqui did not speak.

Mika pushed the soft dirt back with the balls of his feet, digging himself in. "Look, we're in a hurry, so either help us or let us pass."

"What do you want?"

He took three steps toward Sierra, and one of the Sentinels Mika didn't recognize stepped in front of her, gun aimed at Mika's chest. Sierra put her hand on the rifle and pushed it down. She followed him out of earshot.

"Halsan arrived at a spot forty miles ahead, carrying something he'd like to stay hidden. I need to get there before he moves again."

"Something?"

"It's likely he's got Purge-infected patients."

"And the most dangerous individuals in three states are so unprotected that you and these three," she said, pointing to his Humvee, "are going to take them on? Come on, you can make up a more plausible story."

"It's not a story." He pointed southeast. "They're thataway."

"I have reliable intelligence that Halsan is headed west, toward the coast."

"Your intelligence is wrong."

She gave him a fake smile. "Oh? You'd know that, wouldn't you?"

"Actually, I would." He pointed to the road again. "Halsan is that way."

"You know what my orders are?"

He shook his head.

"To arrest you." She tipped her head toward his Humvee. "And them. And Chipps."

"Not the best time for this."

"Convenient that you have such an important mission just when we intercept you."

"You didn't intercept us. We called you."

"A few minutes before we'd have intercepted you."

"Look, why the hell would I lie about Halsan transferring Purge-infected people?"

"You do know I can't believe a word you say."

"Why is that?"

"Seriously? Because you lied about Chipps being a Purie for the whole fucking year? Because you used false pretenses to be alone with Tulum and shot him? The one person who knew more about the Purge than anyone? How the fuck can I trust you on anything?"

"Just so we're on the same page, Amy is not with the Puries."

"How do you figure?"

"Nothing to figure. She's not with the Puries. Full stop."

"Is that why she destroyed the Sentinels?"

Mika shook his head. "You did that. You. The moment you accepted to follow Kuipers' orders, you killed the Sentinels."

"I have my orders," Sierra repeated.

"They're bad orders."

"I don't have time for games. If the Puries release a live version of the virus, thousands might die."

"Exactly. So, are you going to help us or what?"

Sierra put one hand on her hip. "You're just as unreasonable as ever."

Mika rubbed his middle finger with his thumb. "Asking you to join New Cal would be unreasonable. Asking you to help me take out a threat to both of us is a very reasonable thing to ask."

"I'm going to arrest you."

"Not a chance. Let it go, Sierra. You can't win this one."

She waved at her soldiers. "You don't think we can take you?"

He sized up the Sentinels behind Sierra, then those on the truck blocking the road. "Your odds are good."

"So why can't I win?"

"Outside chance, we prevail. You know Jacqui is good, and if you recall, I'm pretty hard to kill. More likely, we don't, but that means, all four of us are dead. And no matter how tough you talk right now, you won't consider that a win."

Sierra drew a sharp breath as if to speak but remained silent.

"Back in the Shed, you gave me some advice. I wasn't ready to hear you then, but you were right. I'd like to return the favor."

She broke into her first genuine smile. "You're going to tell me I'm an idiot?"

Mika smiled back, letting his lips part. "No. But you won't like it any better. You have to stop trying to become Lori."

Sierra's smile switched off, and her cheeks went slack. "You can't be her. No one can. Lori may have joined New Cal or blown up the Capitol or done any number of things that won't occur to either of us."

"We're done here," she said and took a step back.

Mika reached for her sleeve. "What I mean is, you don't have to come up with a crazy solution. You just have to do the simple thing. Let us go."

"Because you're right?"

"Because it doesn't cost you anything."

"You know where I'm headed? To New Cal to arrest Chipps."

"Eze and Lambert are there with over a thousand troops."

"You don't think I can sneak into the Capitol?"

Mika froze. "You're sneaking in to arrest her?" When she didn't answer, he closed his eyes and took a deep breath. "Don't do this."

"I have my orders," she said in a tired voice.

"You have Eva, me, and Amy on one side. Kuipers on the other. Just think this through before you do anything stupid."

"You want me to pick and choose which order I follow?"

"When your orders are that shitty, yeah, I do."

"Doesn't work that way."

"Just give it a few days."

"You think my orders will change?"

"They might."

"What happens when they don't?"

"Then we'll play that game with no winner. But we don't have to do it today."

She turned around and walked to her transport waving the Sentinels to follow her.

Mika hopped in the Humvee. Blue was still inside. "Call Eze and tell her to triple the security around the Capitol. Then tell Eva to not leave Amy's side for the next forty-eight hours. And tell her to shoot on sight if she spots Sierra."

Blue lifted her eyes like she wanted to read his mood. His concern must have been plastered on his face because she dropped her eyes and swiped the messages a split-second after they broke eye contact.

Jacqui and Xin stepped in, and Xin put the Humvee in gear. She edged forward, passing the transport and the Sentinels lined up ahead of them with guns ready but not pointing. No one fired, and she gunned it as soon as she swerved past the last truck in their way.

Forty-five minutes later and three miles before the compound, Jacqui asked, "What's the play here? Rendon had a point. We're not exactly a tactical team."

"We poke around and see what we find."

"Why are you so sure they have something?"

"Because Halsan isn't the kind to play nice. I thought he might try to hold on to power in New Cal, but he knew that was a losing move. Amy is too strong there. But why didn't he present Cal City to her and take credit for keeping it operational for two weeks?"

"That's it? We're here because Halsan didn't act like an asshole?"

"He disappeared right after we arrived. Why? What is more important than the prestige of being seen with Amy?"

Jacqui shook her head. "I guess we'll find out. But don't be too disappointed when it turns out he's here for a booty call."

They rolled into a one-street town that reminded him of his mission with Sierra a year earlier. That had been the day they had learned to trust each other, the trust that had stretched too far, if not to the breaking point—at least past the point it would ever return to its original shape.

The dwellings on the block were boarded up. A chicken-wire fence covered the gaps between sets of buildings. They drove around the corner, following the fence extending around, supported by eight-foot metal posts. Xin rolled to a stop by a wide gate on wheels, halfway through the side street.

"Disable all security cameras," he said to Blue, who was tapping at her screen.

A twenty-by-forty tent supported by a crisscrossing metal frame, reminiscent of a greenhouse, stood in the middle of the block in what must have been a parking lot for all the businesses lined up around the perimeter.

A guard appeared around the corner and walked toward them, pistol in hand. "This is private property." He had a dark blond mustache, reaching down around his mouth, but not connecting to the tuft of beard dangling from his chin.

Mike rolled his window down. "I have an urgent packet for Mayor Halsan."

"Who are you?" the guard asked.

"Drove from Cal City. He left these files," Mika nudged his eyes toward the greenhouse. "Medical data," he whispered.

"I'll have to call this in." The guard reached for the metal panel to the side of the gate.

Blue raised a thumb, meaning she had control of the security cameras. Jacqui stepped out of the Humvee as Mika pushed his door open.

"Stay in!" The guard took a step back, pistol moving from Jacqui to Mika. Jacqui's knife whooshed by, embedding itself to the guard's heart. He stumbled back, slammed onto the fence, and fell, spitting blood. Jacqui stepped around the Humvee and pulled the knife out, wiping it on the guard's pants as the guard twitched and stopped moving.

"Subtle," Mika said.

She reached in to hit the button to open the gate. "If you're right, we don't have time to be subtle."

He strapped his rifle to his back and walked the one hundred feet to the greenhouse with the Humvee in trail. He nudged the plastic sheet of the greenhouse open. It was a medical containment zone. There were three beds to his left and a long bench with medical supplies to his right. The first two beds were empty. The last one contained a woman who reminded him of Yasuo at the end. Her lips had split, her eyes were closed, a tube hung from her mouth, and three IVs were attached to her arm. The stink of the wet, sweat-soaked towels mixed with disinfectant turned the hot and muggy air oppressive.

He wiped his brow with the back of his hand. "Don't touch anything."

Jacqui gave him a quizzical look, one eyebrow up, screaming she wasn't going to touch a thing. Three steps in, Mika spotted drops of blood under the IV stands by the first empty bed.

"We're too late," Jacqui said, eyes on the bright red blood as well.

Mika stepped out and squeezed his eyes shut.

"One truck left four minutes ago with a stretcher in its bed," Blue said from the Humvee.

Jacqui moved toward the Humvee. "How do you know that?"

Blue pointed to her screen. "I have their security footage." She pointed to the two-story building in the far corner of the block, past the rubble, sporting a wraparound deck on the second floor. "The other stretcher went that way."

Mika turned to Jacqui. "Take the Humvee. Do not let that truck get away."

As Jacqui climbed in, Blue stepped off and pointed to the corner building again. "All their data are stored there. Second floor."

Xin and Jacqui sped away, and Mika ran to the building Blue had pointed to. From the parking lot side, double doors led to an open stairwell, going up around the well at the center of the building. Blue climbed the stairs and disappeared into what must have been the server room. After ensuring that the building was empty, Mika marched into the street. Three more blocks of rubble stretched ahead with the walls of demolished buildings sporadically breaking the sightline, as though creating a fake street for a movie set.

At an open field where the road dead-ended, two figures pulled a stretcher from a pickup truck. As Mika ran toward them, a Jeep pulled on the road. Mika dove behind a half wall, letting the Jeep pass. It screeched to a stop at the corner behind him, and two armed soldiers disappeared into the building Blue was in.

The truck with the stretcher carrying a dangerously contagious patient was two hundred yards ahead of him. Blue, head buried in a server farm, was fifty yards behind him. He ran back.

He climbed the corner post, clearing the railing and landing on the second-floor deck. As he glided around windows peeking in, shots rang out with bullets flying out of the fourth window. He shuffled to it to find Blue hiding behind an overturned table, hands on her head. Mika brought his finger to his lips, not that Blue was about to make a sound.

Mika slid his handgun toward Blue. She took it in two hands and put her back on the underside of the tabletop.

"Come out now, and I won't hurt you," a man yelled from below.

Mika unstrapped and laid his rifle on the deck. It was too unwieldy for close quarters, and its bolt-action, five-cartridge clip was a liability right now. He grabbed his knife and stepped into the room next to Blue's. A gun-toting arm appeared in the corridor, headed toward Blue. Mika pushed the barrel of the assault rifle up and jabbed with his knife. The man jumped back to avoid the blade.

Mika stabbed at the man's gut, connecting on the second try. The man's grip on the gun weakened, and Mika pulled the knife up, cutting as he went. The man's resistance whittled away, and Mika wrapped the gun's strap around his neck and dragged him down the corridor.

As Mika let go of the gun and slashed the man's throat, gunfire erupted from the stairwell. Mika stumbled back, hit by a flurry of bullets. A bald soldier stood on the middle section of the stairs firing in Mika's direction. Mika shoved the lifeless man away and tossed himself into Blue's room, landing on his back.

Blue stood from behind the desk, eyes wide, knuckles on the gun pointing to the ground.

Seconds later, Baldy appeared by the door. As he brought his rifle toward Mika, Blue fired two shots, both glancing off Baldy's rifle. Mika launched himself at the man. They flew out of the room, crashed through the railing, and tumbled onto the first floor.

Mika's right tibia snapped as they landed on hard tile. Next to him, Baldy lay with a broken neck. Mika pushed himself up, wincing at the pain from his elbow. He stood on his good leg and limped up toward Blue who stood by the railing, eyes open wide.

He tapped his chiming tida. "Got the truck," Jacqui said. "On our way back. We'll be there in ten."

"Good," he said and cradled his dislocated elbow. "Gotta go." He tapped the tida off and reached for Blue's hand, opening her fingers frozen on the handgun. She retracted her white knuckles into fists, keeping the same pressure she had kept on the gun.

It was inconceivable for Blue to miss Baldy. She had hit targets ten times smaller, ten times farther. And that both shots had clanged off the barrel meant she hadn't missed at all.

"You're okay?" he asked.

She nodded.

He stumbled into the room and stepped on the deck. A transport had landed next to the truck in the field. He grabbed his rifle and put his eye on the scope, finding the magnification to take the scene in. A soldier lowered the tailgate of the truck and pulled the stretcher halfway out. The cargo bay door of the transport was open. The pilot was talking to Halsan twenty feet away, both heads inclined forward, speaking under the whooshing of the rotors.

Mika brought the rifle down and wiped the blood from his nose on his sleeve. With his mangled elbow, there was no way for him to take out the pilot from this distance. Blue's concerned eyes moved from Mika's nose to his shaking elbow. "It's my fault you're hurt."

He extended the rifle. "I'll be fine in a few minutes. But we don't have a few minutes."

She didn't touch the rifle. "I've never shot anyone."

Mika let out a breath. He wanted to give her a hug and tell her it was all going to be fine. But they had minutes before that stretcher was loaded into that transport and disappeared. He flipped the eight-inch bipod open and went on his stomach, resting the rifle on the bipod. His right elbow was in full repair mode, with his arm twitching and shaking as he reached for the trigger. His finger trembled so hard he didn't get it near the trigger.

He straightened. "You're going to have to do this."

"I don't think I can."

"I'm really sorry, Blue."

She reached below the rifle and released the clip, slid out two cartridges, put them back in, and pushed the clip back into the slot under the rifle. She moved the bolt into place, went down on one knee, then leaned forward until her eye was on the scope. She rested her hand at the bottom of the trigger guard.

He took out field binoculars from his jacket pocket to spy the precise motion of three people, the first shouting instructions, the second balancing the stretcher on the tailgate, and the third going through the pre-flight check. It wasn't what they did that mattered but that they were flesh and bone, active and alive. And targets. Crosshairs reduced lives to targets.

He let go of the binoculars, letting them hang from his neck. "The pilot, Halsan, and the soldier," he said. "In that order. Even one hit will delay them. I don't suppose any of them are hard to kill, but you never know."

Her gun barrel moved in a precise pattern, three times: Pilot, Halsan, soldier. She rehearsed the shot order, with her right hand moving to the bolt handle in two-second intervals as she nudged the rifle from one target to the next. He waited for her to complete her pattern.

She exhaled and pulled away from the scope.

"Aim for the chest, not the head. Even if you miss, you hit something." She brought her eyes back to the scope, leaned forward, and exhaled again. "Forget the chest. Think of them as steel targets hanging from trees. You can hit those from a lot farther than this. I've seen you."

"Do you mind?" she said without taking her eye off the scope.

"Sorry."

Blue took a deep breath and let it out. Another breath.

He tightened his grip on the binoculars, but kept his eyes on Blue. Her fingers did not move, and neither did her chest. She was as still as a wispy leaf on a windless day.

He brought the binoculars to his eyes. The pilot stepped into the cockpit and reached for the panel. Mika was about to touch her shoulder when she spoke. "Steel target, huh?"

He lowered the binoculars.

She mumbled, "Not a pilot. Steel. Not a pilot. Let's see if it works that way." She took another breath and licked her upper lip.

She was motionless for fifteen seconds. He feared she had frozen again. The pop and flying shell told him she hadn't. Two more pops followed with two-second gaps between them. Her hands moved fast but rhythmically, pulling the bolt back to eject the cartridge and then forward. Three more seconds passed, and a fourth pop followed.

Blue let go of the rifle and lifted her head. "Turns out it does," she whispered.

He brought his binoculars to his eyes. Nothing moved. The pilot hung on the yoke. Halsan and the soldier lay crumpled by the transport.

"Missed the eye of the pilot the first time." There was no pride or anger in her words, just a dose of relief. And the disappointment of having done something she didn't approve of.

He put a hand on her shoulder, but she broke the connection and sat down. She leaned her head on the railing and closed her eyes.

"I'm sorry," he said, because he had nothing else to say. Telling her she had probably saved hundreds of lives was an abstract consolation. She had to find her way out of this and find a way to rationalize and live with it.

She didn't open her eyes. "I completed your other task."

Mika's eyes widened. He had asked her to find Lori, but she would not have waited to divulge that. He had also asked her to find Kevin because he most likely had helped Lori disappear.

"Kevin Jezek, yeah?" She swallowed and opened her eyes. "I found him. Or I should say, he found me."

CHAPTER 39

DAWN

"Things which do not grow and change are dead things."
—LOUISE ERDRICH

Amy lay on top of the covers on the left side of the double bed, her ankles crossed, her eyes closed. Her head rested on two pillows that barely provided support to her stiff neck. Her interlaced fingers rested on her stomach. Her back and shoulders hurt as though she had carried rocks all day, but she didn't have the strength to stretch. Instead, she took deep breaths, willing her tight shoulders to stop pulling on her neck.

Just reclaiming her house and her bed had improved her mood and outlook. She had lived in this bungalow since moving to New Cal. It wasn't just the familiarity but also the shared journey that soothed her mind and anchored her to the present.

Her door opened and closed, and footsteps followed. She didn't open her eyes. "Hello, Mika." She ran her right hand on the bedspread, her fingers catching a seam. She spread it out and tapped on the bed, inviting him to sit down.

"How did you know it was me?"

She smiled. "You're the only one Eva lets through without checking with me." She opened her eyes. He was leaning on her dresser with his hips flush with the top. She re-interlaced her fingers and kept them on her stomach.

He sat by the foot of the bed like a visitor. The bed creaked and the right side sank under his weight. "You're doing better."

She pushed herself up, leaning her back against the wall. "Whatever that means."

"It means you're stronger. And it means you keep everyone moving forward." His smile was open, his eyes warm. She kept her eyes on him. "You're scaring me. I love the way your eyes shine again, but they're quizzing me right now, and I'm trying to remember which antique vase I broke."

"You've been great over the last few weeks. And you've kept every promise. I'm really, really glad you're with me. But for me to open up, give more, and expect more, I need to understand what went wrong last time."

He clenched his teeth, his jaw pushing his cheeks out, but he didn't speak.

"I can't let you back in, not unless I understand why you left." She reached out to her side table and took the glass of water, draining about a third. "It was hard for me," she said, as she put the glass back down. "Harder than I've even admitted to myself. Not just because I'd started to rely on you, but because you disintegrated before my eyes, and I had no idea how to stop it."

"That was never on you. I was in a strange place, trying to grasp what was happening. I was just lashing out because I didn't understand."

"What do you understand now that you didn't understand then?"

He smiled. "That there is nothing to understand."

She shook her head. "You were getting better, and then you drifted away."

"I didn't know where I fit. How I fit."

He wasn't stonewalling. He was too good and too polished to be this awkward. This was a preamble. She smiled to encourage him.

"It wasn't any one thing. I was a stranger again. At the harbor, at Macky's. But I wasn't in a strange new town. I was where I'd always been, and I didn't belong anymore. I was an alien with no place to go.

And I didn't fit into your world. I—I didn't see what I brought to you. I saw how hard you worked. How much rebuilding meant to you. And how much you deserved to be happy." He lowered his eyes. "And how much you wanted a family. Children."

In all his arguments and meandering thoughts and word games, he had never rendered her speechless. Until now. She fought the urge to scream at him as her fury flushed her cheeks.

"You look like you're about to breathe fire."

"I'm so mad at you right now, I can't even—" she stopped and exclaimed "*Children?*"

His answer was barely audible. "I can never give you that."

"I'm so mad." She couldn't keep her voice from rising. "I can't believe this. All this time you pushed me away because of that?" She shook her head. "I don't even know what I want. What makes you think you know what I want?"

He didn't answer, which was good.

"I don't need you to protect me." She chuckled. "Okay, you can protect me from assholes with guns. But this? From myself? From you? I'm mad, mad, mad. I'm beyond mad."

"I'm sorry."

"You should be. What is wrong with you?"

He took a deep breath. "As I looked down the line, I couldn't see us."

"I didn't need you down the line. I needed you then and there."

He remained silent.

"If it was bothering you so much, why didn't you bring it up?"

"You talked about the sound of children playing in the street, about your buddy Justin and his kids, and how he was doing his part to save the world. Obviously, I can't do that part. I figured if we talked, you'd rationalize it and then regret it later."

"Did I mention I'm mad at you?"

"Yeah, you did."

She reached for his hand. He put his hand in hers. The tips of his fingers were cold. She held them in a tight squeeze. "You never, ever get to make a call like that for me ever again."

"Never, ever, got it. So, we're okay?"

"Stop being charming. I'm still mad," she said, but what she felt wasn't anger. Maybe a little relief and flickers of promise, but also caution.

She tossed her pillow at him, hitting him in the chest. She tossed the second one, and he swatted it away. It landed next to her hip on the bed. The silence stretched for twenty seconds. When she smiled, he stood and reached for the dresser, picking up a white cardboard box tied shut with a blue ribbon. It hadn't been there earlier, so he must have put it there while her eyes had been closed.

"You're not dying, and I'm not dying," he said.

"Are you about to be nice to me?"

He came around the bed and sat by her side, extending the box. "Happy birthday."

"My birthday was three weeks ago."

"You were busy."

The box floated up as she took it because it was much lighter than she expected. She rested it on her lap, untied the blue ribbon, and opened it. The white wrapping paper crinkled as she dug for the heather gray T-shirt. She lifted it up and smiled. A crimson '37 was emblazoned inside a circle on the front, with the words *A Classic Was Born* inscribed below the number, outside of the circle.

It was so thoughtful that he even remembered her year of birth, she teared up. "How did you find this?"

He shrugged while flashing a gap-toothed smile. "I have my ways."

She flipped the T-shirt. The Golden Gate was sketched in brushstrokes with the words *1937–2037* above and *Happy 100th* below it.

She extended her lips into a fake pout. "I thought it was about me."

"You're both classics."

Her smile broadened. It was so tempting to trust him again. A few sincere words were all it had taken for her to forgive him. Was she falling for his tricks again? In the end, there was only one way to find out, and that was to take a leap of faith.

"The hard work was finding one with thirty-seven instead of nineteen thirty-seven. You have no idea how much they love that nineteen nonsense, it—"

"Shush," she said, put the T-shirt on her lap and spread out her arms. He leaned forward and hugged her. She squeezed hard, holding on to him. He was solid as a rock, and she allowed the possibility that he might be her rock if she let him.

"My turn," she said as he let go of her shoulders. She reached over her nightstand and took an orange coin envelope. She turned the envelope down, dropping the ring into her left palm. She took it between thumb and index fingers and extended it to him. "I found it on the bedroom floor a few months ago."

He took his father's old ring between his thumb and index fingers and examined it. "Thank you." His left thumb went over the smooth knuckle of his middle finger. "Though I can't wear it anymore."

"I had it resized."

He brightened and tried to slide the ring on his middle finger. It was too small to get past the knuckle. He tried his ring finger and it slid into place. "Perfect," he said and gave the ring two quick spins.

Watching him spin the ring with his thumb, she almost forgot what they had endured.

He stood up. "I should let you rest."

"Stay." The word burst out, as though her lips feared being overruled by her brain.

"You sure?"

She nodded.

"I'll tell Eva to go home." He stepped toward the door, turning around with mock concern. "If I'm not back in a minute, call a medic."

She laughed not because he was funny but because he was familiar. "You're going to put a smile on her face," she said, surprised at the warmth of her voice.

CHAPTER 40
LEDGER BALANCE

"I've always been more interested in the future than the past."
—GRACE HOPPER

Amy's fragile truce with Kuipers had completed its first week, reopening trade routes among the four cities of New Cal under the watchful eyes of the Marin troops. Neutralizing Halsan and turning over the infected bodies had ratcheted down Kuipers' hostility. Cal City breathed again, though more like a sick patient than a healthy athlete, with the right resources getting to where they were supposed to go only after two false starts.

Kern had delineated the fortieth parallel as the boundary of a no-go zone and declared any Marin activity north of that an act of war. In a shocking display of common sense, Kuipers had not crossed that line, though that was more likely due to not having the resources to extract what she needed from the Shasta lab than any intent to abide by Kern's decree.

Mika was a new man, not merely on time to meetings, but early. He had been tense for days after the Halsan incident, spotting Sierra behind every rock. He was now his more normal self, moving from nonchalant to concerned at his own pace. In public he was the unflappable operator, lending a helping hand whenever needed. In private, he had let her see the caring side she had sampled last year but had not seen since.

She was oddly glad to discover how hard the ordeal with Lin had hit him. Not because he had nearly broken, but because it implied he *could* break. That meant there was a human spirit in there with needs and wants and, yes, with a heart that could only take so much.

The scale of the reclamation project in New Cal had convinced her the mayoral council was not a sufficiently strategic body. It was narrowly focused on the needs of the city-states. It had served Fontaine because he had never needed anyone's stamp of approval to push projects forward. But to implement her vision, she needed the public support a council provided. So she formed her body, the Governor's Advisory Council.

Eze was the military strategist; Lambert and Ranford were the Marin and Kern experts. Lambert had convinced her that even with his limited commitment, they needed Ranford. She had relented, not only for Ranford's strategic value but also for the council-building impact her listening to her advisors provided.

Cavana modulated the mood by tamping it down with logistics and lifting it up with his wit and reason. Joy spoke for the mayors, and Cho ensured the New Cal militia's perspective was represented. Eva, though not officially part of the council, was an always-there presence and offered her wisdom in private when Amy needed it.

Mika became a conflict of interest on two legs. She could not put him on the council without compromising her impartiality. But he knew more about the Purge and its variants than anyone there, so she had made a concession to practicality.

He wasn't an official member of the council, but he participated in any meeting where the Purge was discussed, which to date had been all of them. That he got along effortlessly with everyone on the council made this easier. She even welcomed his occasional tiffs with Cavana because they dispelled the narrative that she handled him with kid's gloves. She didn't ask Cavana whether he did it on purpose. Some things were better left alone.

Their presence in the Capitol conference room normalized the procedures, and the faint scent of freshly baked cookies moved the enormity of their task from desperate to manageable. She bit into a sugar cookie, happy to smell at all, and let the sweet, soft texture shield her for a few moments.

Believing that they were making progress was the first step. The positive energy peaked when Cavana rattled the repaired power lines, reestablished water pipeline, and improved energy output. It crashed when Joy flung out the grievances the cities claimed they had been subjected to. She would have dismissed them except that most were valid: the rebuild Cal City required had rerouted resources, shortchanging Mountain View, San Jose, and Santa Cruz.

Amy did her best to assuage Joy before Ranford summarized the disorganized, but still dangerous, Kern operations scattered all around them. As he got deeper into the details, she spotted wandering eyes, the same way they had wandered when Joy had spoken. They all wanted to help her, but they didn't yet trust each other enough to want to help each other.

Amy rose as Ranford finished. She stepped away from the conference table and stood by the window as the sun set behind a fifty-year-old oak tree. The light reflected off the leaves, forming dozens of beams, all different, yet all from the same source.

She turned to Lambert. "Maria, what's the latest on Marin?"

Lambert pushed her chair back and extended her feet. "I've been reaching out to my contacts in Marin for the last week. Only a handful even acknowledged my existence."

"Is it because of your…" Cavana paused. "Situation?"

Lambert gave him a sad half-smile. "These are people I've worked with, dined with, and drunk with for decades. They know who I am. No, it's because they're being watched. With so many high-profile arrests in the military, they're opting for caution, and I don't blame them."

"So, they are all going along with Kuipers?" Cavana asked.

"They are scared. They got hit from three sides. The bodies with Purge symptoms, the Kern ultimatum, and now the internal threat of quarantine and contagion. No one knows what's true anymore or whom to trust."

"That leaves Kuipers to do whatever she wants," Cavana said.

"Pretty much," Lambert agreed.

"And what is Kuipers doing?"

"She broke Marin's main districts into fifteen boroughs. Each has its own military official directly linked to her office. There is no movement among the boroughs."

As she wrapped up her Marin update, eyes turned to Frank Cho, who wiped the cookie crumbs from his fingers and leaned forward in his chair. He glanced at Eze, trying to hide his admiration. The professionalism she brought and the competence of her troops all showed him what his job should have been. Instead of shrinking, he accepted the challenge to emulate her to the best of his abilities. His reports became more thorough and precise, more like Eze's.

Amy nodded when Cho finished and turned to Eze.

Eze said, "Mika will summarize the latest on what we know about the virus. I just want to say that the settlements we uncovered in the southeast last year, after we dismantled the Puries bases on General Rose's orders, corroborate his findings. We observed six settlements, all destroyed and sterilized. One had about two thousand residents."

"That's more than in any we've observed," Mika said.

"All six settlements had bodies piled in pits. There was nothing remarkable about four of them. In the fifth, the bodies were short and thick." Eze glanced at Mika, who nodded. "That's consistent with the high G settlement Mika found, and he'll talk about that in a minute. But the settlement with the larger population has been giving me nightmares." She closed her eyes. "In that one, half the dead were children."

"Children?" Lambert and Cavana exclaimed at the same time.

"We'd just found out about Puries. I rationalized it as their killing non-Puries." Eze reached for her tida. "I have to warn you, these are pretty graphic." She swiped her tida. "Most of the children were toddlers or younger."

Amy didn't hear the rest. The charred bodies were revolting enough, but the tiny, ashen mangled ones made her stomach churn. Closing her eyes didn't chase the nightmare away.

"We found six settlements up north as well. We suspect in both cases, they were studying six different variants of the virus." Mika said. She was thankful for his words and for any attempt to move away from those images.

"There are more than the regular and radiation variants?" Cavana asked.

Mika nodded. "We found a virus that fights radiation damage, one that reduces oxygen need, one that increases bone density and lung capacity to handle high Gs, and one that protects against extreme pressures and temperatures."

He waited for questions, but no one spoke. "There is no reason to assume any of these four viruses increases fertility. So that's gotta be the fifth one, and we're still missing one."

"How do you know all this?" Cavana asked.

Mika spun his resized ring, propelling it with flicks of his thumb. "I observed the effect of two of the viruses firsthand. We also cloned a drive from Gibson's command center, so that's how we pieced the rest together. Some of the files were erased during the decryption process, so our information is spotty, but we know all Purge variants originated at the comet impact site in Tromso. They were transported to Shasta twenty-six years ago and never moved. For a year, they experimented with the variants. None of the viruses reacted with mice or monkeys. There wasn't even an immune response or antibody buildup in the mice. It's as though the virus just dissolved without a trace. In primates, mainly chimpanzees, there was a minor reaction, but the virus was quickly defeated. That gave the scientists the confidence to initiate live human experiments."

Cavana shook his head in disgust. "Unbelievable."

"Gets worse," Mika said. "The first dozen volunteers showed no response either. But then one got sick and died within days. They stopped all experiments and performed a full review. A few heads rolled. A month later, one of the volunteers who'd shown no reaction to the virus got a heavy dose of radiation in a lab accident. When she survived, mostly unscathed, they restarted the experiments to catalog the variants. Meanwhile, in a separate lab, on a separate floor, another team sequenced the viruses' genes. They isolated the common stem of all six viruses and also infected mice."

"The Purge," Cavana said.

Mika nodded. "Again, the mice showed no reaction. Neither did the chimpanzees. A few months later, a lab technician fell ill. The virus had jumped from the chimpanzee to the tech. They assumed the same three-day incubation and body fluid transmission of the six variants. They traced his steps back and isolated the lab and known contacts. But the Purge had gone airborne with an incubation period of up to three weeks. He wasn't patient zero."

Cavana shook his head. "It was bad enough to think an accidental virus had almost wiped us out. But you are saying we did this to ourselves."

"Appears so."

Amy raised her hand to stop the speculation and indignation. "What is this fascination with Shasta? What is Gibson going to find there that he doesn't already know?"

"Pure speculation here," Mika said. "Gibson probably thinks there are more clues on the viruses' origins. What I told you is what they pieced together. There's got to be more. What were the viruses for? Who made them? The answers are in Shasta." He bit into a cookie and smacked his lips with the satisfaction of someone who had earned his reward.

"And Kuipers?" Amy asked.

"I doubt that she cared about the origins of the virus. She's probably humoring Gibson to get her hands on an army of hard-to-kill soldiers," Lambert said.

"Kern wants them as weapons," Ranford said. "If they get their hands on these samples…" He shook his head.

"Exactly," Mika said after he finished chewing. "Halsan worked with Kern. They abducted two people with the radiation variant from the settlements up north."

Lambert waved at her screen, swiping documents. "Your report said you found three patients in the compound last week when you stopped Halsan from releasing the virus."

"I'm afraid Kern still has the infected subjects. I'm guessing the three we found aren't the ones who were abducted."

"Why do you say that?" Lambert asked.

"Because those two had survived the initial infection. They carried the virus but weren't sick. Most likely, Halsan's team—or Kern— infected many subjects just to yield those three severe cases. They were going to drop them off at hospitals in Cal City and Marin."

Lambert closed her eyes. "What would the impact have been?"

"At my last briefing, Tulum said the variants have about a four percent fatality rate," Amy said. "An outbreak will devastate Marin and cripple its economic and social base."

"The data we recovered implies a twenty percent hospitalization rate," Mika said.

Lambert pinched her chin. "Jeezus."

"Makes Kuipers' borough plan look less crazy doesn't it?" Ranford asked.

Amy picked the last few crumbs of her cookie and pitched them in her mouth. "I wish the news was better."

Cavana chuckled. "Basically, we have Kern and Marin at each other's throats, fighting over a virus no one knows much about with New Cal stuck in between. If you had slept for a year, you might think nothing changed."

"We've changed," Amy said. "But yes, I do wish our victories were less fleeting."

Lambert coughed twice, putting her fist in front of her mouth. "With all due respect Governor, two weeks ago you were dying in my infirmary, and I was operating with the assumption that the Purge was a natural catastrophe two decades in our past. I'd say building this alliance in Cal City, with an army, no less, and foiling an infection attempt while gaining significant intel on the origins of the virus variants counts as a solid win."

"You're not wrong," Amy said and took a deep breath. "When I asked you to join me, I told you I'd listen to each of you. I'm thankful that you trust me, I really am, but I also need you to trust each other. We need to get past who we were."

Her eyes found Ranford. "We aren't Kern." She turned to Lambert. "We aren't Marin." Her eyes moved to Eze, Mika, and then rested on the middle of the table. "We aren't the Uregs." She focused on Joy. "We aren't even New Cal—at least, not the New Cal of a month ago. Those statements are all true, but we can't define ourselves with what we aren't."

The sun had set, and a red glow filtered through the half-flipped blinds. She took the time to make eye contact with everyone around the room. Eze tapped her lips with her index finger. Lambert rubbed her chin, softening her hard glare. Cavana looked straight into her eyes and sank his fingers through his hair the moment her gaze moved to Ranford, who nodded. Joy moved his eyes to the screen. Cho smiled and averted his eyes.

She pointed to the horizon. "We lost another minute of daylight today. When we get it back six months from now it won't be progress. We need to move beyond reacting and beyond averting disaster. We need to articulate who we are, what we stand for, and what we'll fight for."

"If all Marin officers who cringe at Kuipers' actions supported Chipps, we'd push Kuipers out of office," Eze said and turned to Ranford. "You gave partial support to Governor Chipps, but you won't commit your forces, not fully. If all Kern officers who supported Spindler rallied around Chipps, you'd reclaim Kern as well."

Ranford chuckled. "Good luck getting Kern officers to follow Marin or New Cal leaders."

"You once did," Mika said, chewing his third cookie.

Ranford shook his head. "Let's leave ghosts out of this."

Amy pushed her chair back and stood, leaning forward to rest her fists on the table. She didn't want to end on a sour note, but she also didn't want to become a cheerleader. "You each have experience building something: a compound, an army, a rebellion. We gained valuable information over the last few weeks. Now, we need to figure out what to do with it."

She straightened and headed toward the door. "There are no shortcuts. Trust is built one action, one word at a time. We need to stop reacting and start planning a path forward. Work together, and I know we'll find a way."

She paused by the door and flicked her hair behind her ear. "I just hope it's soon enough."

CHAPTER 41

ROSY OUTLOOK

"Believe nothing you hear, and only one half that you see."
—EDGAR ALLAN POE

Amy woke to the rhythm of rain pelting the window and bouncing up from the windowsill. She glanced to her right only to find a solid wall because the window was to the left of the bed in her new digs on the third floor of the Capitol. Waking up at home some days and in the Capitol on others gave her whiplash for the first few seconds.

These quarters were a concession to her condition as she recovered from sepsis. If she didn't get ten hours of sleep, the day ran away from her with her mind and body unable to keep up with the demands of her job. She got eight hours spread across the night, but still needed an afternoon nap to get her fill. In the early days, she had tried to hide it but hadn't fooled anyone. Yawning and dozing off during critical meetings had a way of giving one away.

Cavana had arranged for two adjacent offices to be transformed into a suite by knocking out the middle two-thirds of the wall separating them. It gave her a sitting room with a round dining table and a glass corner desk, along with a bedroom to which she retreated most afternoons. And on nights when her exhaustion won out, she slept there. Partitioning the third-floor bathroom to create a private washroom in her new suite made it almost homey. Almost.

She pushed herself up on her elbows, swinging her feet to the side of the bed to sit up. She poured a glass of water from the metal pitcher on her nightstand and downed half of it. Her eyes wanted to remain closed, so she forced them wide, then squeezed them shut, and rubbed them with the heel of her hand. She drained the glass and put it back on the nightstand.

She twisted the cold metal crescent locks and pushed on the single-hung window frame. With the moisture, the old wooden frame had swelled, sticking hard enough that it didn't budge. She gave a final shove, and the panel edged up two inches. The whiff of the summer dust washed by the first rains tickled her nose.

A distant argument, muffled but not smothered by the walls, filtered through the corridor. She let go of the window and headed into the washroom. A face with dark bags below the eyes stared back from the mirror, reminding her that she didn't just feel tired, she looked it too. When she turned the faucet on, the water's metallic smell greeted her. Though the fixtures were new, the pipes were not, and the plumbers had not yet isolated where the smell originated. Most likely somewhere deep in the system, which meant that like most of her problems, this one was going to require getting used to rather than getting fixed. She splashed water on her face, turned the faucet off, and wiped herself with a hand towel.

The clamor from the corridor intensified with a male voice, most likely Cavana, asking someone to slow down. Amy opened her door to the hallway. Eva sat by the chair to the side of the door, the spot she never left when Amy napped. Across the hallway, the conference room door was ajar, letting the argument spill into the Capitol.

"What's going on?" Amy asked.

Eva's eyes moved from Amy's bare feet to the rumpled shirt hanging over her belt, a reminder Amy wasn't fully dressed. "It's best if you see for yourself."

Amy walked back in, tucking her shirt into her pants. With her door open, the distant voices became clearer. "There is no winning move if you play the game Kuipers wants you to play," a vaguely familiar voice said.

The words drilled into her, not because of what they implied about her leadership, but because the possibility of any new strategy gave her hope. And hope had been in short supply. There hadn't been any visitors planned for the afternoon, a break in the interminable procession of business leaders, old administrators, and concerned citizens. They all passed through, angling for favors with a precious few trying to contribute but not succeeding.

But why was a stranger speaking at the closed session of her advisory council?

"I'm guessing you want to wrestle control of Marin from Kuipers, head to Shasta to find answers, clean up the mess in Kern, and only then tell the public the truth about the Purge."

"That's about right," Lambert said.

"You're going about this in exactly the opposite order, mostly because you're missing the key point here."

"Which is what?" Ranford asked.

"The Marin or New Cal you want to save no longer exists. Those places are gone, and they're not coming back. You have to let them go if you want to move forward."

This was the sort of defeatist attitude Amy had fought all her life. She had said she wanted new ideas, but this one she didn't need. Her blood boiled as Eze and Lambert mumbled meek objections. She moved around the bed to grab the jacket that lay on the single chair next to her nightstand. A sudden rush of blood to the head made her stumble back, landing on the bed.

"Stop being cryptic," Cavana said. "What do you suggest we do?"

"I just told you. And it starts with the only weapon you have."

"And what's that?"

"The truth."

"That will tear up Marin."

"You can't win from within the system. You need to break the system."

Amy had to jump into the fray before this stranger did more damage. She stood, but the sudden motion worsened her dizziness. She reached for the nightstand to steady herself but only knocked the water glass down. It hit the tile floor and shattered.

Eva was by her side in two seconds, with one hand on Amy's waist for support, easing her back on the bed. "Don't move."

As Amy put on her socks and shoes, Eva picked up the pieces of glass from around her feet. She put them on the wooden frame of the chair, assembling the three large pieces to make sure nothing was missing. Once satisfied, she stood and offered Amy a hand.

Amy took the hand and let Eva pull her to her feet. Over the past weeks she had decided that accepting Eva's and sometimes Mika's help did not make her weak. It made her what she was: a recovering sepsis survivor. Eva reached for Amy's jacket and held it for her to wear.

"Thanks."

As she stepped into the corridor, two soldiers snapped to attention, startled as though Amy had interrupted their excited conversation. They turned serious as she walked past them, but couldn't suppress their giddiness.

"What exactly are you suggesting?" Cavana's voice boomed from the conference room's half-open door.

"Broadcast the Purge details to every Marin, Kern, and New Cal citizen. Flood every Uregs tower. Once that news explodes, Marin will be impossible to govern."

"That goes for us too."

The woman laughed. "You're not governing anything."

"Then what?"

"Then we infiltrate Kern and take it back from the Puries. My sources tell me Taggart's hold on Kern is weak."

"How weak?" Ranford asked.

"He has the true support of three of the nine generals with sizeable forces. Another four support him because he is the least objectionable candidate. If his duplicity with the Purge comes out, he'll lose that distinction and won't hold on to power."

"That is crazy," Cavana said.

The woman ignored him. "Then we move to Shasta and find out what secrets are still hidden there. Once that's sorted out, we clean up Marin."

Seconds of interminable silence exploded into the cacophony of six voices speaking at the same time. Amy put a hand on the conference room door to steady herself.

"Now, let's discuss the Kern offensive, shall we?" the woman asked, oblivious to the calamity she had unleashed.

"Have you gone completely mad?" Ranford asked.

The stranger's words sounded grand, but they weren't connected to their reality. Their troop numbers, supplies, and weapons suggested a different calculus. Any officer urging an assault on Kern would get laughed out of command. If she wasn't shot for stupidity. The woman wasn't crazy; she was criminally dangerous.

But as Amy cataloged how wrong this stranger was, the voice infiltrated her consciousness and sent ripples of recognition. It was higher pitched and more exuberant than she remembered, but the cadence was familiar. Amy pushed the door wide and stepped in with a quick, determined gait. The conversation stopped, and all heads turned to her, expecting—no, demanding—that she rescue them from this madwoman.

A map was projected above the wide conference table, a jigsaw puzzle of colors painting the state with migraine-inducing overlays of pie charts and tables displaying supplies, troops, and resources.

Lambert and Cavana stood to the left of the table while Eze and Ranford stood to the right. Mika sat away from the table, smiling at the speaker as though he had heard something witty. The stranger stood straight ahead, leaning forward, both palms on the table, her face distorted in the blue light and random shapes of the floating map separating them.

The straight blonde hair cascading around and hiding the thin blue face made Amy's heart sink. For a second, she had allowed herself to hope the stranger had been someone other than this young, tanned blonde in a tank top. Amy took a few more steps in, ready to call this stranger on the irresponsibility of divulging the truth without regard for its consequences, and on the recklessness of making promises that were going to get thousands killed.

The woman straightened as though she expected this reaction, as though power came naturally to her, as though the deference she received was a curse. In all her life, Amy had only known one person who had wielded power so effortlessly.

The woman waved her hand over the map, and the blue light cut off. She smiled as they made eye contact and reached back to massage her neck.

Amy cracked a half smile before her brow furrowed as Kuipers' threat exploded in her mind. She wasn't staring at *a* symbol but at *the* symbol of Marin military prowess.

Shit.

Amy had let the blonde hair distract her, the tanned arms sidetrack her, the youthful voice deceive her. Gone were the lines around the eyes, gone was the shoulder-length red hair, and gone was the tension that stretched the jaw taut. Though she looked at peace and ten years younger, no smile could hide the fire raging in those green eyes.

The excitement, the belief in the hallway, had been real because soldiers—or citizens, for that matter—didn't follow plans or ideas. They followed leaders who made them believe. The ideas that sounded irresponsible and suicidal coming from just about anyone else, now looked hopeful even promising.

Because they hadn't come from anyone.

They had come from Lori Rose.

KAGAN TUMER is a science fiction author and professor of robotics and AI. He attended seven schools in five cities in four countries, all before reaching high school and is steadily moving west, from Virginia to Texas to California to Oregon. Along the way, Kagan worked as a food server, registrar's office clerk, print shop copier, soccer referee, math tutor, and well logging engineer. He has a PhD in computer engineering and spent nine years at NASA working on multi-robot coordination. When not writing, he ponders AI ethics, teaches robotics, consults for TV/movie AI projects, and mentors future scientists.

ACKNOWLEDGEMENTS

Done with book two!
Just like my second half-marathon: from the outside, publishing my second book may look like more of the same, but to me, the process, difficulty, and accomplishment felt fundamentally different.

To those who asked, "Was it easier than the first book?," my answer is yes. And no. I mean, it was a little easier because I knew it could be done. But it was also harder because it was impossible for me to not compare my first drafts—which are never any good—to the published version of *Purged Souls* and worry that *Carved Genes* would disappoint my readers. I'm happy to say I no longer feel that way, but in the end, you'll be the judge of that.

Now, a whole other wrinkle this book faced stemmed from its topic. It's hard to ignore that my previous book, *Purged Souls*, which is set in the aftermath of a global pandemic, was released in the middle of a global pandemic. And that *Carved Genes*, where the threat of another contagion is wielded as a weapon, sat with my editor when the whole world went into lockdown. Upon reflection, I did modify a few details and removed a few descriptions that hit too close to home. Years ago, I decided to use a virus as a plot device—instead of say, AI or robots—so that my first novel wouldn't be weighed down by real-world entanglements. Yeah, that worked out like a charm.

I've received even more help for this book than the last one:

Chris Bombeck, a general surgeon with military experience, walked me through the ins and outs of field blood transfusions and helped me capture the language an emergency doctor might use when faced with a trauma patient. Thank you, and apologies for occasionally skipping a few steps and streamlining the medical descriptions.

Bob Paasch gave me a crash course on gun safety, took me to a gun range, and patiently walked me through how different rifles work. Thanks for adding that extra punch of realism to many scenes in this book.

Mick Haller first used "flowrate" to gauge alcohol consumption. Though I modified the concept, thanks for coining the term.

Colas Gauthier sketched the cover art that both tied this book to my first novel and looked fresh, and Claire Flint Last designed the cover to capture the evolving mood of the story. Thank you both for creating a punchy visual. Again.

My editors, Julia Houston and Catherine Rourke, made sure that you never saw my clunky wording and mistakes. Patricia Marshall, Kim Harper-Kennedy, Jamie Passaro, and the team at Luminare Press worked on this book in these strange times. Thank you for the continued education in publishing.

My awesome early readers—Liney Arnadottir, Kyle Niemeyer, Hazem Arafa, Guillaume Brat, Kait Wittig-Menguc, Ross Hatton, and Willem Visser—provided encouragement and critical advice that ranged from "Why is this character suddenly acting like an idiot?" to "Where do they get the gypsum for the Sheetrock?" Because they were thorough—and they were right—the characters are a little more consistent, and the walls are made of lath and plaster. Thank you for your invaluable feedback.

Over the last year, Irem added chief marketer to her contributions to my author career by sharing my book and reviews far and wide. Also, the opportunity she provided to observe what altruistic, confident, and empathetic leadership can accomplish certainly helped me with world building and character development. So, thanks for being there, and thanks for being you.

Made in the USA
Columbia, SC
25 October 2021